Praise for The Piano

What a fabulous read this was. ... . entangling the past and present with a nice twist. Happy Valley - Books Read

A real page turner in terms of story and plot. The gradual unravelling of ancestral secrets across four generations is skillfully executed. Chandani Lokuge author of 'My Van Gogh.'

It was easy to get lost in this well written multiple timeline novel. Dabble in the present day and take a step back in time with memorable characters, it's a guaranteed great read. Mrs B Book Reviews

Read the book in one day. I could not wait to see how the mystery unfolded. Goodreads

A wonderful story of a writer who is struck by a deep but fractured memory of her grandmother after hearing a stranger play a piano in a mall. I loved it. Amazon Books

Well written endearing characters and an unpredictable plot. Mel's Bookworm Reviews

The end wrapped up beautifully. I even shed a few tears when the whole mystery was revealed. Goodreads

As a fan of dual timeline novels this one hit the right notes. There is mystery and some romance and a well written compelling tale of families, traditions, and personal growth. Highly recommended. Author, Phillipa Nefri Clarke

The structure of the book was very well executed maintaining the suspense throughout. I was hooked until the end. Goodreads.

I'm waiting for the sequel. Goodreads

Praise for Making Up Amanda

I simply relished this story. A mesmerising and addictive read I couldn't put down. Suspense and surprise as the plot unfolded. What crime story is all about. Bianca Mal Amazon

Had me enthralled from the very beginning. I love an edge of your seat crime story, and this was one I couldn't put down. Sarah Amazon

A must read for crime thriller buffs. I could not put it down once I started reading. Highly recommended. Mephie Amazon

Refreshingly different setting ...a most satisfying read. Readinghighreviews

Great read. Kept me in suspense until the end. Lovereading Amazon

Fast paced and well written with its criminal construct delivered seamlessly. Happy Valley Amazon

A very engaging read. Emma Moon Goodreads

An intriguing story with great characters. Recommended. Ballaratti Amazon

Praise for One Night

This gripping crime novel pulled me in from page one! With layered twists, strong female leads, and a plot that keeps you guessing, One Night is a brilliant, suspenseful read that kept me guessing the whole way through. Highly recommended for fans of crime fiction, strong female leads, and intelligent storytelling. Reads on the Road

One Night is a well-grounded read for crime thriller buffs. Mel Hobbs

A detailed plot, twists and intrigue. Recommended. Brenda Telford

A great story that had me turning the pages. Highly recommended to any reader who loves a good crime story that will pull you in. I loved it and I do hope that there are more DS Bec Harpin stories to come. Helen Sibbrit

A tight crisp murder investigation undertaken by the formidable Detective Sergeant Bec Harpin unfolds with two dead bodies, many rabbit holes and a good friendship on the line. Cleverly plotted and set against a Melbourne backdrop, the lights of the city shine on this police procedural and crime infused narrative. Happy Valley BooksRead

Fans of great crime fiction will love this second Bec Harpin story. A clever plot with interwoven storylines sees the mystery unravel at a steady and satisfying pace. Highly recommended. Judith Kneebone – Librarian

Rozzi Bazzani is an award-winning author who has written scripts, libretti and songs for theatre including two stage musicals. She has been a regular contributor to the Arts pages of the highest circulation newspaper in Australia.

Before writing full time Rozzi worked as a 'session' singer in recording studios. She has performed live on stages across Australia and internationally and used her voice for both spoken and sung commercial work. She has backed some of Australia's best-known singers and supplied voices for anything from soap to sunglasses, face cream to dog food.

After returning to study and graduating from Melbourne University where she majored in Romance Languages, Linguistics and Fine Art, Rozzi's love of reading and history (her first job was in a public library) inspired her first book, 'Hector,' a fully researched biography of Australian TV mogul Hector Crawford which won the Victorian Royal Historical Society Publication Prize and was short-listed for the Ashurst Business Literature Prize.

Longing to write fiction, 'The Piano Woman' a mystery romance appeared in 2021, followed soon after by the first in a crime series 'Making Up Amanda,' featuring Detective Sergeant Rebecca Harpin, and 'One Night' the second book in that series.

Rozzi lives in Ballarat, Victoria, and with her husband and two big poodles is often seen walking the local tracks around Lake Wendouree considering the next plot twist for her newest book.

ROZZI BAZZANI

THE PIANO WOMAN

S & B Books

Level 1, 409 Keilor Road

NIddrie, Victoria, 3042

ISBN paperback 978-0-6456930-6-5

E book 978-0-6456930-7-2

How should we like it were stars to burn
with a passion for us we could not return?
If equal affection cannot be,
Let the more loving one be me.

W.H. Auden

Prologue

I wake up suddenly. It is dark and I am in a different bed. But it is the sound of unusual music that has roused me. Music has always affected me, but this time it's different.

I see myself sitting up. I am very young, barely five, but I watch as my face registers the crashing chords I hear.

I feel my feet touch the floor as I am drawn trance-like along a passage to a lit room, where the magical sounds seem to be coming from.

I peep around the slightly open door, still mesmerised by the music, and I see my grandmother at the piano. Her normally stern features are transformed as she plays. The power of the music and the expression on her face have transfixed me. Holding my breath, I stare at her in awe, the way I do looking up at the sky full of stars, overcome by the mystery of things I don't fully understand.

Suddenly she stops, and before I can escape back along the passage, I hear her calling out in that soft kitty-cat voice she saves for when we two are alone. 'Is that you, Maddi?'

Timidly, I edge forward from the dim passage, slightly fearful that I might be in trouble, and enter the room.

'Did the music wake you?'

I shake my head.

'Come,' she says, wiggling her fingers towards me, 'I want to show you something.'

Lifting me onto her lap, I feel the softness of her dress, and the firmness of her hand as she places my fingers onto the keys, gently pushing each one down one key at a time. She plays a few notes, and I imitate what she has done.

Then she has me play a few more. 'You just play those notes up and down.'

I do, and she plays an accompaniment with her other hand. I am playing up and down as she laughs and I feel her kiss the top of my head. But when I turn to smile back at her, I feel a bump in my back and the entire scene disappears. Gone.

Disconcertingly, I find I am back in the moment, and realise that it's a complete stranger sitting at a piano in a crowded shopping centre who has unearthed this long-forgotten memory.

The first indication that something 'more' was happening took place in January. I was in the city, head down and moving as fast as I could. A choking, northerly blowing filthy dust across the city had pinned my cotton shift tight against my legs, forcing me to take tiny little steps and walk like someone whose skirt was two sizes too small. How ridiculous I must have looked. Pushing back against a blast that would tow an ocean liner to sea, tight-chested, I held my breath and kept my eye fixed firmly on the open sideway ahead. It was usual for me to take this shortcut through the shopping mall, the one with the high glass roof, off Elizabeth street. On bad weather days like this, escaping inside was notionally like stumbling across an oasis in a burning desert. I glanced up at the red sign and quickly detoured left, away from the street.

Inside, the air was icy and cut sharply at the base of my throat. A sensation I imagined closer to swallowing knives than breathing cold air, but I didn't care. I gulped in large mouthfuls, happy to escape the ugly wind and heat. Once I was breathing normally again, I continued on through the arcade that linked directly to the heart of the mall, speeding along without stopping to gaze in any of the windows. Not one. I hadn't come here to shop, not today, anyway.

The food hall I entered was excessively bright and buzzing with life, and instantly, the familiar smell of deep frying clung to my sinuses. The pungent aroma of hot cooking oil was the same in all fast-food places, as far as I could tell. Every mecca for the busy and the hungry smelled identical to this. Just as well I wasn't feeling the slightest bit hungry, or I might have been tempted to line up for a box of hot chips in the little blue-and-white cartons I could see schoolkids happily devouring. A soft custard doughnut, or chips at the right time, on the right day really did hit the spot to make all things feel better. No matter what the health professionals say about only eating 'good' meals to stay healthy, so-called 'bad' food like hot chips can be happy making, and wasn't happiness good for your health?

My searching eye hooked onto another case in point, an elderly couple, octogenarians probably, a man and a woman, juicy hamburgers wrapped in serviettes cupped close to their mouths. Was it a late lunch or early dinner, perhaps? Either way, from how they were demolishing their meal, it could have been their last morsel of food in this life. The woman's eye, glowing with happiness, caught mine as I passed, and in that split second, I'd swear she couldn't have exuded more bliss if she'd tried. That had to mean something, surely. Right there and then, I made a resolution. After today's business was over, I would get myself some fast food and I would love every bite.

I hurried on away from temptation, towards the expanse of carpet on the far side. My motive for taking this route had been simply to exit onto the street beyond. It was the best I could think of, to avoid walking another block in those awful conditions. I glanced around, trying to decide which exit to use.

Yes, I could see that the grand piano was raised and in position where it always stood, over by the escalator. But, a small crowd lingering in the vicinity of the instrument unexpectedly caught my attention. What was that? Of course, I'd noticed the piano many times before. Usually, it loomed as a large somber lump draped in heavy canvas, with three glossy black legs below the only clue to its real identity. Actually, I'd often wondered why it was even there as I'd never seen anyone play it, or pay any special attention to it, at all. Ever. Not even at Christmas time.

I surveyed the scene, feeling oddly drawn to these people who'd randomly gathered with no obvious motive. What were they doing? As far as I could tell, none were balancing drinks or nursing food on cardboard plates, which ruled out a birthday celebration or an office party. Missing too were any touristy-looking maps, caps, or exaggerated posturing for selfies. I couldn't see their feet, but I felt sure none would be wearing those cushioned athletic shoes universally favoured by tourists. My feet veered right, but even as I approached, I was absently connecting my own curiosity with what happened to cats who stuck their noses over a fence where it didn't belong.

It occurred to me that I should stop now, too. Instead, I continued straight towards the piano group.

First, I wasn't sure if I was imagining it, so I couldn't help staring when a strange-looking woman crossed right in front of me. Rather rudely, actually, and if I hadn't slowed down, we would have collected each other. I stepped back to allow her to pass, but consciously observed her progress. From the way she walked, striding slowly through the crowd, her eyes fixed solely on the piano, she was giving a strong impression that she intended to play it. What if she was some old seventies punk rocker on a mission to trash the instrument and make a statement about her displeasure at the state of the world? Suddenly, I noticed the canvas cover had been dragged off, perhaps by someone in the crowd. My curiosity deepened. The piano was standing bare, open and performance ready. *Surely not.* The dark and heavy fabric of the woman's skirt had scraped along the floor as she swept past. I stared at the mane of long grey hair hanging down beyond her waist. No, this ragged creature looked more like a swamp witch from a children's fairy book, rather than someone who could actually play the piano. Maybe she was going to cast a spell on it?

I watched with some bewilderment as the crowd parted, assisting her progress to the raised podium. Had the gathering been expecting this woman?

'She moves from one to another, you know,' a woman standing next to me whispered, averting her eyes as if she and I were involved in some kind of conspiracy.

'One to another what?' I whispered back, matching her tone.

'She can just show up anywhere there is a piano. Bars, hotels, churches, anywhere …'

I turned to ask my informant more, only to find she'd moved off in search of a better view. I also edged nearer.

By now, a decent crowd had assembled under the glass dome. And the numbers continued to swell as afternoon shoppers and office workers, who like my whispering friend, seemed to know what to expect. Standing on tiptoe, I certainly didn't know what was going on. Yet, I couldn't move. The creature stepped up onto the podium. Perfectly still and silent, she sat studying the keyboard with a focus that was startlingly intense. Was she in one of those trance-like states you read about in yoga books? Fix your eyes on an object long enough, it'll strengthen the power of your mind?

Everyone around me was caught in the same tension, too; expectant necks craned, waiting for what was going to happen next. It felt like anything could. My questioning hit overdrive. What if she couldn't play? What if we had to wander off pretending to check our phones to hide our embarrassment, and hers? Yet, that just didn't seem possible, somehow. For now, the power of her attention on the piano had completely fixed ours onto her.

I checked my watch. Thirty minutes before I'd have to go. Luckily, I'd over-compensated the time it would take me to get to my appointment. I'd been disturbed enough by the request to 'come in for a chat', that I'd allowed more time than it would take to walk the two blocks from where I normally leave my car. The last thing I wanted to do was to rush in late and out of breath for a session I feared was going to entail a stern talking-to about why I wasn't meeting any deadlines.

The muzak that plays interminably in places like this went dead. The crowd hushed and more passers-by, curious to see what was going on, stopped and waited. I calculated there must be more than one hundred and fifty people now all squeezed together, peering up at the podium.

I was jostled forward, close enough now to notice tiny tears in the woman's clothing. I gasped, choking back a cough. How could I have missed it? The robe that flowed over the back of the piano stool was frayed and grubby, the lace-up boots resting on the pedals were shabby and worn, and the sole of the right boot, no longer attached to the toe of the shoe, hung loose. The thick mass of hair, probably once dark and lustrous, was matted and untended, tangles like birds' nests caught underneath the weight of long grey tresses. With her tall frame, boney fingers and striking hawkish profile, this woman had every look of someone who was sleeping rough.

I stared at her, sick in my stomach, ashamed that I hadn't realised at first glance the nature of her situation. My mind filled with unanswerable questions. Where did she sleep? Alleyways with strangers and constantly in danger? She had to be sixty years old, the age my mother would have been. What happened to bring her to this? Did she also have no family? I couldn't take my eyes off her.

A voice from behind called out, 'Play the Russian piece.'

Fascinated and horrified all at once, I watched her raise both hands high in the air. She held them that way for what felt like minutes, but in reality, must have only been a few seconds. Then suddenly, launching herself forward, she struck the keys with such force that I jumped at the commanding crash of sound. Her hands whirled up and down like a dervish, swooping over the keys, her profile harbouring a Mona Lisa–sort of secret smile, as if she knew something nobody else did. The rest of the world became silent as this mysterious stranger hypnotised me and her entire audience.

I recognised the music she was playing right away, even if I couldn't name it. I listened intently, allowing myself to be carried away by the sumptuous sound. This glorious melody twisting evocatively in my head was tormenting me. What was it? Why was it so familiar? Then it came, a sharp burst of painful memory that inserted itself in my heart like a small arrow. I'd heard this piece of music on a recording my mother used to spin repeatedly. She loved it, she said, because it was a piece her mother used to play.

A shiver ran down my spine, and I felt uneasy, unsure if it was the memory of the music or if I was missing my mother. Or something else. In any case, I couldn't move even if I'd wanted to. A tear slid silently down my cheek. Music affected me that way, sometimes. I brushed it away with the back of my hand.

Then without warning, I found myself captured so completely by this stranger's energy, I was transported back in time. It was no longer the homeless woman on the podium who was playing, but my own grandmother, and I wasn't standing alone in a crowded shopping mall, I was basking in the solace of familiar sounds and the warmth of her love filling me with happiness. Swept away by an irresistible force of emotion, I was completely enveloped by the melody and the love of someone I'd hardly known. I seemed to be floating. How long? I didn't know, but I stayed like that until my reverie was cut short by a sharp shove in the back. Someone pushing from behind knocked me so hard, I almost lost my footing.

'Hey,' a voice nearby said, 'what happened to excuse me.'

I was shaken, yet when I came back to reality, with both feet firmly on the ground again, it was with the feeling of my grandmother Abbey's hands still on mine, and her kiss burning the top of my head.

Scalding tears welled.

How could I have forgotten such a moment?

Had I forgotten?

The whole thing seemed crazy because I'd never known enough about my extended family to forget.

My mother, Marianne, an actor, and single for all of my childhood, never wanted to talk about her past. In fact, she would clam up at the slightest hint of detailed questions. I didn't know what she was afraid of. Our life wasn't always easy, yes, I understood that. What I didn't understand was why, whenever I asked about her life, simple things like what it was that had made her want to become an actor in the first place, she never wanted to engage. But I was her daughter, for heaven's sake. We got along. And weren't actors all meant to be natural talkers? Marianne's actor friends were positively garrulous. It was one of the things I loved dearly about them, how their profession made them that way. Or was it the other way around? Anyway, I'd always found uncomfortable silences in the company of actors a rarity. In fact, it was hard to get a word in edgeways mostly amidst the hurly-burly of joke telling, self-promotion and politics. Not my mother, though, at least not when she was talking to me. Curiously, she was even reticent to reveal much about her own mother as well. To this day, I didn't know the reason for that.

The best she did whenever I asked was to repeat the same stories, almost by rote, it seemed to me. Her mother, Abigail, was an orphan, with no known brothers or sisters. She played the piano, she'd been married and produced two children, my mother and her brother, Uncle Gerry. Marianne's father, my grandfather (whom I gathered my mother loved dearly from the fond expression that came over her face whenever she mentioned his name), had been much older than my grandmother, and had died long before I came along.

So, there was nothing from my mother, no fragments of memory that might explain the woman I'd just seen teaching me to play the piano. All I'd ever had to draw on really were pictures of the dour face she adopted in photos, or I could fiddle with tiny scraps of memorabilia that had survived my mother's travels. But I had nothing like the books stuffed with memories and experiences most people had tucked away in their cupboards. That's what made this experience so strange. Where did it come from?

After Marianne's death, and the tragic circumstances surrounding her accident, there'd been plenty of times I was desperately in need of comforting memories to hang on to. Now, with my grandmother's touch and her playing resonating inside me, my mind clung to her.

The street woman crouched low over the keyboard, and with the tips of her fingers she made a sound so tender and soft it reinforced the emotions I was feeling. I dabbed at my eyes to stem more tears.

When applause for the woman on the podium broke out, I joined in.

An unusual mixture of feelings accompanied me as I rode the escalator down to street level. Guilt that I hadn't found where to leave money for the ragged old woman who had gifted what she had to the lunchtime crowd. But mostly, I was puzzled by a strange sense that my grandmother Abigail was still with me.

PART ONE

Maddison

Melbourne 2016

I lived a good forty minutes away from the city, so there was plenty of time to replay the scenes of the day in my mind. Luckily, my appointment wasn't as bad as I'd feared: a gentle talking-to about the value of deadlines, and a few laughs about my state of mind. No direct questions about *Love Under Summer Rain*, my as-yet-unfinished manuscript, which was a relief, considering how far away I was from actually meeting any deadline. And thankfully, no in-depth questions, either about why I appeared to have lost my touch for romantic tales. The sort where the female lead, after some adventure eventually snares the hero, an attractive guy, who is bad in the beginning but turns out alright in the end. Just as well nobody asked, because I had no answers. Or none that I wanted to reveal, anyway. The state I was in wasn't a simple equation. Something deeper was going on. I needed to find what the paralysis was, and fix it. That much I knew, even if I didn't know exactly how to go about it.

Turning off the freeway onto the road home, I was aware how deeply I'd been affected by this out-of-the-blue recollection of my grandmother. It had sunk in deeply and refused to budge. How I wanted someone to tell. The picture had been so clear. No one had ever mentioned to me that my grandmother played like a fiery concert pianist. A few charity fundraisers, I was told. Accompanying tepid old-time sing-alongs and lacklustre community halls, is what I'd imagined from my mother's sketchy descriptions. Now, all of that was changed after my flash of memory. There was nothing tame about the woman I'd remembered. She was all energy and passion, and I could still feel it surrounding me.

It struck me as odd that Abigail had been an orphan, because I was as good as one myself. Was this a fate that befell all families, a cycle of patterns invisibly at work, handed down from one generation to the next like a family heirloom? At one point, my grandmother had no one. Now I too had lost everyone. No mother, no uncle, no grandparents, alone since the age of eighteen. I couldn't say with absolute certainty that I'd lost my father, but given I'd never known who he was, it made no difference.

An overwhelming frustration at my mother's refusal to tell me more about our family returned, as it always did when I thought about it.

I heard her exploding when I pushed too far, 'For goodness sake, Maddison, what's past is past, there is absolutely nothing to be gained from this. When your grandmother is an orphan, there is no family history, there's just us.'

Actually, when Marianne spoke of her mother, she always made her sound like a bit of a cold fish.

'Abigail,' (she always used her mother's first name, too) 'wasn't a homebody, she could be distant sometimes.' Then she'd put her arm around my shoulder and say, 'Not like us.'

These words were spoken without bitterness, but I would see the set of her jaw and know that the subject was closed.

Uncle Gerry once said, taking pity on me and my rapid-fire questions about family, 'Her life was always off limits, Maddison. We didn't talk about things like that with our mother,' he explained. 'I thought later it might have been because she was an older mother, you know … While all our friends' mothers were hitching up their skirts and throwing away their bras, our mother was serious. I thought she might have been embarrassed by that. You know, not being "with" the times in that way.'

Naturally, his comments sent me off on another flurry of questions but he closed me down. 'She was gentle and kind but removed, Maddi. That was our mother. You know, you only have one. You take what you get and make the most of it.'

I still remembered the resigned smile he gave me after saying that.

Then, without any warning, there was no one left to ask. I was alone in the world, and the only evidence of my grandmother's existence was a marriage certificate from the Public Records Office stating, 'Abigail Browne (nee Rooney), parents unknown'.

Winding my way up the mountain road, the whole experience seemed increasingly bizarre the more I reflected on it. I'd read about recovered memories, people who unexpectedly 'remembered' events, but they were mostly proven to be false. Is that what this was? Was I 'losing it'?

By the time I pulled up outside the general store, I'd calmed down, but was still mulling over how little I actually knew about my family, and how frustrating it was that there was nothing in the world I could do to rectify it. Slowing down with my destination in view, I was also still trying to shake a number of possible scenarios for the poor street woman, and what her story might be.

On the drive home I'd bestowed on her a name. It was all I could do, so as not to think of her as a 'street person'. Katya seemed like a character the Brothers Grimm might have invented – 'Katya the Woodland Witch', had a ring to it. Yes, I endorsed it wholeheartedly; I repeated it and spoke the name out loud in the car, hoping it might help to keep her safe.

I always checked for mail whenever I passed the general store as I didn't have a box at home, a deliberate choice on my part. Because soon after moving here, I realised how handy this place was to visit regularly. Most of life's daily necessities could be gathered under this rusty tin roof; mail, milk, wine, coffee, groceries and fresh muffins every day. The historic wooden building with the friendly country-style verandah was convenient, but I soon discovered it was also the backbone of this mountain-side community. On foggy winter mornings when visibility on the mountain was low, and the temperature was so cold it needled your nose, I loved to linger inside, taking time over coffee and striking up a conversation with whoever happened to be around before heading back home again. I'd met quite a few of my fellow mountain dwellers this way.

Surprisingly, the weather was also an aspect of life here that suited me well. I hadn't known this before, but mountains, mist and snow were some of my favourite things. How often did you hear people attributing climate as a way of clarifying 'who' they were. Someone would say, 'I'm a hot weather person,' 'I'm a beach person,' or 'I'm a tropics person.' Well, I knew now that I was definitely a cold-weather person. Whatever that meant.

Today, the place was quiet. I scooped out a pile of envelopes from my box, returned to the car and threw them down onto the passenger seat. Probably all bills. Who wrote letters anymore? I pushed the radio onto FM nonstop music to force my mind away from obsessing over the scenes of my grandmother, and worrying about Katya.

Once I was home and the events of the day began to recede, I made some tea and started to casually leaf through the mail. The first envelope I opened was a note from the local book club, an enthusiastic note from Julie, the club secretary, who confirmed that I was to be their next monthly speaker. This was courtesy of the club's tireless publicity organisers, who also happened to be my next-door neighbours. This engagement promised to be fun, and I was going to enjoy talking to the group. I marked the date in my phone diary, and put in a reminder for the day before, to prepare.

The last envelope was heavier than the others; the paper was parchment thick. My eye caught the English post mark right away. My first thought was that this letter had been delivered to the wrong box. But no. It was definitely addressed to me. I checked the sender, and a firm of solicitors in Kent had printed their address next to some sort of fancy seal. I turned it over, back and forth. What could an English law firm possibly want from me, given I had never been to Kent in my entire life? I slipped the envelope knife under the flap and slid it open.

As I began to read my legs folded. I sank onto the nearest chair and read the contents again. This time quite slowly, telling myself there must be some mistake. After what had happened today, how could this possibly be real? My grandmother, Abigail, had a family in England, and someone over there knew about me? It was ridiculous. I got up and splashed water on my face to make sure I wasn't dreaming. If this was my mind playing tricks, I needed it to stop.

Returning to the letter, the feel of it in my hand again produced a sudden urge to examine the few physical links I had to my grandmother. If I touched the treasured photos and souvenirs handed down to me from Marianne, it might inspire some insight about what was going on. I jumped up and literally jogged into the next room.

My heart beat strongly as I slid the drawer open, but seeing the weathered little book of anonymous poems lying exactly where I'd left it, next to a small black box of trinkets, I breathed a sigh of relief. How comforting it was to see the old, worn book, and wonder how many times a word here or there between those dog-eared covers had inspired hope or love in someone, or maybe even changed somebody's life. I picked up the tiny volume, flicked randomly through, pausing to glance at one or two of the verses and wishing I could know which of them had been Abigail's favourite. I set it down by the letter. Next, I opened the box, picked out my favourite piece, a fine little silver necklace with a clover charm, and hung it around my neck.

Sometimes I talked aloud when I was looking for an answer to something that was bothering me. More often than not, speaking the nature of the problem aloud returned an answer immediately. Not always, of course. But after the day I'd had, it was worth a try.

'Who were you, Abigail?' I asked the air, as if my grandmother were seated at the piano right in front of me. 'How did you come to be in Melbourne in the first place?' This time silence was my only response. I looked back at the solicitor's letter from England, and thought about the memory of Abigail that had surfaced in the shopping mall. How were these things related? How could I be inheriting a piano from a female relative I knew nothing of?

Later, I decided, it had to be a moment of stars aligning; Katya triggering my memory of Abigail's piano playing, and leading somehow to the solicitor's letter. There had to be something cosmic going on. Crossing paths with the homeless woman had to be a sign of things to come. After all, it was the vision of her, and the music she was playing, that had spurred the hidden memory of my grandmother.

The clarity of hindsight made it clear that Abigail appeared before me because there were things I had to figure out in my life. It made no sense, of course. And only later could I find a way to understand it.

At the time, though, I remembered I sat curled up in my favourite chair in my mountain home, mulling over what it all actually meant, and what, if anything, I could do about it.

Maddison

Mt Macedon

We think that you, Maddison Browne, are the great-granddaughter, the last surviving female relative, of Lady Rose Hampton of Hebden Estate in Kent, and as such are the rightful heir to a part of her estate. We wish to inform you that it was her express wish that the last extant female in her line should inherit her piano. I wish to add that until recently we had no knowledge that this 'broken arm' of the Hampton line existed.

Lady Rose has been dead for many years, and as the solicitor to her estate it sorrows me greatly to tell you that it has taken me, and my father before me, decades of searching to find you, which means that it is only now that I am able to finally carry out this, her last wish. The piano itself would be considered an antique but is in perfectly good playing order, although it may require a little attention by the time it reaches your shores.

If you are able please provide a copy of your birth certificate or a passport with the appropriate information, that is sufficient to fulfil our requirements to arrange immediate expedition.

If for some reason this matter is of no interest to you, we will quite understand. But I will require a letter, formally stating that you have decided to relinquish the gift. Should this situation come to pass, be assured that we will be able to make suitable alternative arrangements for the piano. So, this need be of no concern to you.

I hope this news will bring you great pleasure, and in the meantime, I await your reply.

I was just through the front door, shopping bags in one hand and keys in the other, when I heard the phone start to ring.

Slinging the bag of groceries on top of the kitchen bench, I reached over, checked the number and picked up.

'Hi, Amy,' I said. 'Great minds, I was going to call you later.' I flopped down onto the closest bench stool. 'Got a minute?' I was churned up and still weighing how best to handle the situation. I hadn't spoken to a soul about the letter, or the piano. Not yet.

'Sure,' she said, 'what is it?'

Amy's immediate reaction to my brief summary made me laugh and relax a little. 'So, you're a toff?' she said.

'I guess I am, but it has thrown everything I thought I knew about my family out of the window. My grandmother wasn't an orphan. And not only do I have relatives, but I'm inheriting Lady Rose's grand piano. Can you believe it?'

Amy's voice reflected the disbelief I felt. 'You didn't know anything about it before this?'

'No, nothing.'

'Didn't your mother say anything at all about her family?'

My mind was actually still reeling from the shock of the lawyer's letter.

'Not a lot, no, she didn't, it wasn't her thing,' I said. Even to my own ears, this sounded unlikely, so I kept my voice light, as if there was nothing unusual about it. 'A maternal great-grandmother. After all the secrecy and years of "what's past is past", now it all crumbles with one letter. The only thing I knew for sure,' I said, speaking too fast to get it off my chest, 'was that my grandmother Abigail was an orphan. The weird thing is that on the day the letter arrived, I had this moment when a crystal-clear memory of her playing the piano jumped into my mind.'

'Before the letter arrived?' said Amy, sounding ever more incredulous.

'Yes.'

'Oh, Maddi, that's given me goosebumps. So you knew her, the orphan?'

'No,' I said, 'I didn't know her. Not really. She died when I was quite young, so I haven't ever really had any conscious memories of her until the other day. I've got a couple of photos that Mum kept on her dresser. And a few other bits and pieces, that's all.'

'A memory from nowhere and now a family from nowhere. That's weird to me.'

As usual, Amy had got to the heart of my situation, which was why we had been friends for so long.

'I don't know about any actual family,' I said, as if to reassure her it wasn't so weird. 'Just having found out that Abigail was the daughter of some aristocratic woman who died years ago doesn't automatically give me a family.'

'Who knows what happened for no one to ever talk about it?' said Amy, which sent a shimmy of recognition down my spine. Once more Amy had asked the very same question I'd been asking myself. And I didn't have an answer.

I thought about how my grandmother looked in her photos. I'd inherited her fair skin and longish nose, and according to my mother, I'd also inherited her stubborn streak.

'Will this all be in your next book, Lady Maddison?' Amy's smile came through the line.

'Maybe, I hope so.' The problem was that I didn't actually know what the story was. 'I'd have to find out a lot more before I could use it,' I said, thinking aloud. 'The solicitor referred to me as a "broken arm" of the family. That could mean anything, couldn't it?'

'Will you go over there after you finish your current book?' Amy asked.

'I'm not sure, I haven't decided.'

The thought of my unfinished manuscript brought me back to earth with a solid thud. I was so behind and feeling like there was no deadline in creation I could meet. Especially now, when I was so preoccupied with Lady Rose and her piano that without weighing my own responsibilities, I was considering running off to Kent to find out more. Not that I was about to admit that to Amy. Maybe I should change the name of my latest manuscript to *Avoidance* – that would probably be more appropriate, given my thoughts about travelling.

'You are so lucky, Maddi.' Amy sounded a little frustrated suddenly. 'Finish a book then take off to England to track your new family, while your book rides up the bestseller lists. Ha,' she sighed. 'Listen, I've gotta go. Kids to pick up. I'm so jealous. Can't wait to hear what happens next.' And she was gone.

I sat for a second considering what Amy had said. My situation didn't feel like anything to be jealous of right now. But she was correct about one thing. My early books had sold well and past success meant that I'd been able to buy this mountain-side cottage, my special place. Whenever I remembered that it filled me with renewed hope that I could do it again. If I focused only on that, I might forget that at the moment, I was in a huge hole.

The intention behind this 'tree change' had been simple: it was meant to be my new start, my sanctuary, where I could recover from the heartbreak that had driven me out of the suburbs in the first place. The problem was, things hadn't worked out the way I'd hoped. My once-reliable imagination wasn't flowing like it used to. My work had slowed to the extent that I'd already had to polish up two old stories from the bottom drawer to meet deadlines. The well appeared to have run dry. Was it that the first flush of success had worn off? I didn't feel burnt out in that way. Or maybe it really was that in a Maddison Browne romance, the woman always got her man, while in the real world I never managed the happy ending.

Long ago in my secret heart, I decided that the reason I wrote about characters who were winners in love was precisely because it never happened to me. True love for me had been as elusive as catching a glimpse of the lyrebird that supposedly lived in the mountain forest behind my house. I was always looking out, sighting traces, but never actually found the real thing. No amount of craving or longing for love made it happen. I could spin stories on the page for my characters, happily 'fixing' up their lives, but I seemed incapable of finding anything close to that in my own. My ex, with all his 'forevers', was now playing happy families with a new 'soulmate'.

The mere thought of him was enough to start my stomach churning. It was over. Of course it was. I chose to end it myself. But why did I still yearn for the time when I thought he was as crazy for me as I was for him? Now, I longed only for the day when I could hear his name without my pulse reacting.

Tall and slim, with a lovely shock of hair that fell appealingly onto his forehead, Andrew could have played the romantic lead in any of my books.

Unfortunately, I did use him in one of my stories. Only a little bit, but enough to be recognised, apparently. I never imagined from the way he laughed and teased about my 'romance' books that he would ever actually pick one up and read it. I was surprised when he announced that he had, and I saw from the way he looked at me, part wounded deer, part angry Martian, that there was trouble ahead. Anxiety wrapped tightly around my heart, the way I imagined an anaconda would, twisting and squeezing me half to death, and my fear was soon realised.

After more than a year together, it was that moment that turned out to be the start of our unwinding; our irreconcilable differences. He wasn't comfortable with my occupation, he said, and he didn't want to be making cameo appearances in my books for the rest of time. He'd be a laughing stock amongst his friends. And he could never relax with me now, never knowing when something he said or did might end up in the pages of a book. I thought he was being childish and ridiculous, but no matter how I tried to make light of it with throwaway comments like, 'I thought you'd be pleased to know I saw you as the dashing-hero type,' he would have none of it.

Things became so uncomfortable so quickly that I gave up trying to justify my actions, even though for a while I blamed myself for not thinking it through.

However, soon after we met, I remembered suspecting that he was not comfortable being attached to one woman, but given it was early in our relationship, I passed it off as me being paranoid. I told myself that he was acting the same way I'd seen other handsome men behave around women, flirty, but nothing really to worry about. It was way too late when I discovered that my instinct about his behaviour had been stunningly accurate. The minute he met someone new, out would come the smouldering look (the one I'd found so charming), the casual touch on the arm, and the twinkling smile, until the object of his attention (including me) was ready to eat dust from his hand. Amy said she even thought he was coming on to her, once. Most of his victims (not Amy thank goodness) responded to his attention by flirting right back.

'What is his problem?' my friend Lucinda asked when it was all over.

'An insatiable need to have his sex appeal confirmed at every turn,' I said. 'That's his problem. And don't ask me what it means.'

Of course, I could see it now. But back then, I was so infatuated I couldn't. Or rather, I just didn't want him to be the womaniser he clearly was.

I was still haunted by how a successful woman like me could have fallen for him; unreliable, untruthful, and in the end, untrustworthy. Why not William, the barrister, who seemed genuinely hurt when I refused his proposal. He was kind, and a pillar of propriety; I'd never have had to deal with messages from secret girlfriends with him. Why not Lucca, the bistro owner, for heaven's sake; I would never have to cook again, he said, unless I chose to. He 'wished to make it clear' that he didn't want to cramp my style if cooking was 'my thing', which made me laugh. How sweet. However, it dawned pretty early that to survive a proper relationship, I would need to talk about more than food, and read more than rising prices of matured meat and organic greens. So, the question remained. How could I have fallen for an advertising salesman? Anyone who could talk the ear off a pot night and day wasn't obviously my 'type'. I didn't see it coming. In fact, relationships had been off my radar when I first encountered Andrew at a friend's party. But once he started to spin his charm, I was hooked.

'I've been waiting for you all my life,' he cooed in my ear. And I believed him. I cringed now at my own gullibility.

The first time I discovered he'd been running communications with a number of his old girlfriends throughout our entire relationship, I was upset. Really upset. He laughed it off, saying things like, 'That noodle head, you must be joking,' to allay my concerns. And for a while, it worked. The crazy thing was, I actually didn't mind him having women friends. On the contrary, I thought it rather civilised of him, as long as they were 'just friends'.

But on this particular day, his phone had been lying on the kitchen bench when I heard it beep. I was chopping onions to make his favourite chicken meal. I didn't really mean to lean over and look. My eyes just sort of went there. That was when I saw the message with the heart. I grabbed the phone and scrolled down.

You were hot today, lover boy.

I almost threw up right there over his dinner.

He denied it was 'anything', of course, 'just a friend and a bit of fun with words'. I should understand.

I cried bitter tears for weeks, trying to make up my mind what to do, especially when he didn't come home some nights. But when you discover that someone doesn't love you as much as you love them, there are only two choices. You either put up with it and stay, or you leave.

I could have forgiven him, I supposed, completely love afflicted as I was, but I knew that would have meant stepping into (heaven forbid) a pseudo-mothering role. Me always forgiving, never knowing when the same thing might happen again. I'd read about women like that.

My powers of forgiveness were hopefully intact when I ended it with him. I wouldn't like to think I'd become bitter, but one thing I definitely knew about myself, deep down in my private love heart, I would not be a victim and I absolutely would not be a mother-type to a lover. What self-respecting character in any of my books would put up with that? I wasn't ashamed to admit that I drew on them for inspiration. My women appreciated men, but they were not pushovers. They would not put up with just anything a man dished up, even if they loved that man. Which was what must have given me the courage I needed to leave. But to this day, I wasn't exactly sure where that strength came from, much less how I survived the pain that stabbed my heart a million times a day.

For me, the price of extracting myself from him, and the disintegration of my own 'happily ever after' story, was the way it affected my writing. Well, 'affected' was an understatement. The breakup impacted so negatively, it blocked my previously unstoppable ability to write. No matter how much I told myself to 'get a grip', and 'stop allowing him to do this', nothing was going right.

'Are you okay, Maddison?' was a frequent question these days from those who knew me; everyone seemed to think there was something wrong. Maybe they were right.

My current book wasn't working, I had no love interest to hold me here, and an intriguing letter from a very formal-sounding lawyer had just shattered everything I believed about my own family background. I had nothing to lose. Why not fly to England? Why not allow my inquisitive nature to run free?

I wanted to know more about this mystery piano, and why it was so important to Lady Rose Hampton that I inherit it. But more, I was curious to discover how Lady Rose's lawyer could find me, but not her own daughter, my grandmother, Abbey. Surely, these solicitors would not have bothered to spend decades trying to carry out this lady's wishes just to place a piano? To find the rightful owner of an ancient castle, or a large dowry even, perhaps, but a piano? It didn't make sense.

The more I thought about it, the more a trip to Kent seemed the only thing for me to do. Family secrets were the staple of romance writers, and now, out of the blue, I had one of my own. Had Abigail been given up for adoption? Was she a baby this Lady Rose didn't want? Maybe Abigail didn't know that she had a family at all?

I checked the lawyer's letter for an email address.

John

Kent, eight weeks earlier

'My piano is to go to my last extant female descendant …' At last those words would haunt him no more. It was done. Well, almost.

John sighed deeply and removed his glasses. It was ridiculous in this day and age to feel so compulsive about doing the right thing, but he couldn't help it. John understood his responsibilities better than most given the law was his business. The Lady Rose matter, together with twenty-five years in the chair as principal of the firm, had taken its toll.

Recently, John observed strands of newly popped silver at his temples during his morning ablutions, and he'd attributed their sudden appearance to the years of service.

His firm, Nettlewood and Son, had handled Hebden Estate's business as far back as his grandfather's day. Over the years, there had been the odd hiccup, of course, but who in the legal world didn't have a few of those? Their family business had always managed to triumph over adversity, surmounting any difficulties without so much as a whiff of scandal or public blemish. John was proud of that. The office he presided over had been located on the first floor of the most historic building in the village for a very long time. The Nettlewoods' small contribution to history had been as 'Trusted Advisers'. Three generations privy to all the issues faced by the reigning Earl of Hebden, and overseeing affairs of the manor.

John was aware that some saw him as conservative, stodgy even, because yes, he did still wear a tie, but he didn't let this view bother him unduly. He was comforted by the knowledge that this was not the sum of him (how could it be?). John had always done the right thing, or at least he'd always tried to.

Now, at last, in a fashion befitting the example of his forebears, he could dot the final 'i' and cross the last 't'. The never-to-be-closed-until-it's-done file had been completed. The estate would soon be sealed finally. And with it, his own niggling guilt would be put to rest.

Lady Rose Hampton's last will and testament had been specific. The piano had to remain in her family on the female line. Had she not realised what an undertaking this would be? Probably, that question never even crossed her mind. The problem for his firm was that Lady Hampton had died some time ago. John knew the exact date by heart. And as there had been no one to claim the instrument, his father, David Nettlewood, as executor, had finally packed off the piano into secure storage, leaving that one final piece of business unfinished.

John could easily have left it, too, let the detail of an old will, and an even older piano, slip into oblivion, or sell it, as his wife had suggested once. Who except he would know, or even care? And, since the sale of Hebden Manor, no one could accuse him of chasing fees since there were simply none to be had.

The manor house and grounds had been sold off, sadly. What had once been a grand estate, the jewel of their county, had been purchased by an educational institution and now operated as a school, which had no need for his special counsel. None of the traditional estate pursuits were carried on there anymore, either. Small armies of girls in blue uniforms had taken the place of hunting parties of lords and ladies. Lines of buses queuing along the tree-lined driveway, choking the air with smoky diesel emissions, had replaced fancy cars delivering famous faces to the manor, for one of the Hamptons' infamous parties. Alas, the new world had completely overtaken the old as far as he could see, and John knew his continued search for the rightful heir appeared all the more feckless in light of this change.

It amazed him that no one had ever enquired about the piano. The school hadn't even noticed when it didn't show up in the sale inventory. After John's father stepped down, leaving the running of the firm to him, he too had left the piano tucked away in storage. Still, for years, on his own time and at his own expense, John had persisted, doing whatever he could to find the rightful owner.

Heaven only knew why, his father, while he was alive, had not been remotely interested in the piano. Whenever John had broached the subject, his reaction was always the same.

'You work it out, I can't think about that now,' he'd say and wave him away.

Janet, his wife, had lost patience long ago. 'Honestly, John, you are just being absurd now. Can you please just leave this piano business alone once and for all? I don't know what you hope to gain, and these people won't thank you for it. Why can't you let it rest? You've gone above and beyond the line of duty.'

Her reaction had made him stop and think about it. Were his efforts just about doing the right thing? Or were they also to do with stories told to him by his grandfather, about 'the Australian' and the glamorous parties she used to throw?

As far back as John could recall, his memory of Grandfather Llewellyn, founder of their firm, was of him sitting comfortably in his easy chair, legs and hands crippled with arthritis, talking misty-eyed about the past.

'Have I told you that I met Noel Coward several times at the manor?' he would repeat, sitting up taller, the way he did when telling stories about his life. 'Almost family to them he was, just like we were.'

Despite his features collapsing with age, John could still picture remnants of the handsome man his grandfather must have been.

'A most charming and delightful man was Coward, wicked wit and quick as lightning. Not afraid to ask a few favours for himself, though, or for any of his writer friends, either.'

John, with his eye on the future, recalled asking naively, 'What sort of favours?'

'You'll will find out soon enough, lad when you take your seat with the firm,' his grandfather said, eyes twinkling with mischief as he patted John's arm. 'Arty types, you know the sort, mostly flying by the seat of their pants. Always looking for a spot of advice "on the house" about their professional matters.'

John's imagination as a young man had been fired up by these grand stories. Once or twice, he'd even contemplated that the 1930s might have been a better time to be living than now. Only later did it register that his grandfather had chosen never to mention the Great Depression, the food lines, the strikes, or catastrophic unemployment caused by the economic downturn. Instead, Llewellyn had preferred to gild the lily and remember only the good parts, saying things like, 'Those of us who lived through two world wars, laddie, knew what mattered in life.'

One thing John had come to understand from these stories was that his grandfather's generation could certainly throw a party, and they most certainly did know how to make the best of things, no matter how dire the circumstances. However, it was also true to say that the hardships of wartime had fuelled a brief and bewitching period where loosening social boundaries was commonplace.

'Chorus girls and officers, too, you know, all regular attendees at Hebden parties, a real mix it was – marvellous, never a great deal to eat, mind, sandwiches and gin mostly,' Llewellyn would ramble on wistfully. 'Oh, but the singing, dancing, the fun … party all night long to forget the rest.'

Unfortunately for John, all the glamour associated with Hebden Manor was over by the time he'd taken the reins. He was part of the new modern do-everything-yourself Britain. Dull by comparison.

'You should have joined Scotland Yard, John, instead of becoming a lawyer,' his wife had grumbled whenever she found him pursuing some new lead on a possible heir for the piano.

Sometimes John even thought that Janet was right. Maybe he should have become a policeman. For amidst the run-of-the-mill cases he handled every day, death probates and divorce, discovering any new clue about a possible heir too often was the most thrilling part of his day. Which actually meant that John hadn't minded at all scouring the outreaches of the Hampton family tree, squeezing his detective work in between his scheduled meetings.

One day, after a promising lead fizzled into yet another dead end, it dawned on him that he knew more about the Hamptons than just about anything else. Yet frustratingly, he was no closer to finding an heir for the piano than the first day his search began. Lately, to keep the peace, he'd even stopped mentioning his efforts to Janet. He'd even begun to question if there was no heir to be found, after all.

Perhaps as a result of this thought, or for other reasons he could not fully explain to himself, John had made a sudden and unlikely decision. He'd picked up the phone and arranged to have Lady Rose's piano unpacked and delivered to the sitting room of his own home.

His daughter, Crystal, had been struggling with mood swings from a young age, until one of her teachers had recommended piano lessons.

He and Janet had never considered this as a strategy. 'Could it help?' his wife had asked. 'Yes,' they'd decided it could and embraced the idea. Right away, Crystal's moods began to slowly improve. It seemed that learning to play a musical instrument had helped her somehow. (John wasn't sure how this worked, except to acknowledge that sometimes the world did move in mysterious ways, beyond legal precedents.) As an added bonus, they'd been informed that their daughter also showed some promise.

Soon enough, Crystal began to beg for a piano of her own. And although John could easily have afforded to buy one, he'd pictured Lady Hampton's piano lying in storage, beautiful and covered with invisible imprints of all the famous hands that had touched and played it. And something just came over him. That piano with magic in its DNA was one degree of separation from the grand days and glamour of a bygone era that he could only dream of. He would be helping his daughter. What harm could there be if …?

'Oh, Daddy it's so … beautiful,' Crystal exclaimed when it arrived, throwing her arms around his waist and hugging him. 'I'm going to learn to play Chopin.' His daughter's eyes brimmed with happiness as she watched the walnut grand piano, creamy keys, ornate legs and lattice music stand being gently moved into their sitting room.

'It is quite grand and lovely,' his wife conceded, appeased at last. 'It looks rather good in here, don't you think, John?'

John had instantly regretted his impulsive decision. Although, the glowing expression on his daughter's face and Janet's contentment had made his actions seem worth it. But each time he saw the piano by the window in their sitting room, John was seized by a sharp pang of guilt for taking something that was not rightfully his.

He worried that his actions marked him as a part of that malaise of modern times, where just because you want something, you think it is your God-given right to take it. John had spoken eloquently and often on this topic over the family dinner table. 'If everyone concerned themselves more with their own endeavours, and doing things properly, we'd all be better off ...' He worried now. Had he joined the Age of Envy? Had he become one of those who coveted the experiences and possessions of others? No, he was honourable and useful, and just trying to help his daughter. But was it that? The piano being in his home, on no authority other than his own, suddenly made John feel a bit like a thief. Watching Crystal's face, her eyes shining with joy as she sat down to tinker over the keys, and Janet fussing with a cloth, he knew that he had created a situation from which there was no easy way out. That moment of decision, he feared, would shape what was to come.

He had done the wrong thing. He would give the piano back, of course. Yet, the question still burned in his head. Was it so wrong for Crystal to have it here to use while he continued his search for the rightful owner? She needn't know the piano wasn't theirs. After everything his family had done for the Hampton Estate, wouldn't even Lady Hampton herself think that the piano was better to be here, being played and loved, instead of rotting in some massive metal storage place over an hour's drive away?

And so the piano had remained in their home, Crystal had excelled at her lessons and learned to play Chopin, and the greatest miracle of all, her mood swings seemed to vanish altogether. More than once John had found himself wondering if there truly was a magical element in the piano that had helped his daughter through a difficult period of her young life. Logically this could not be the case, yet sometimes, he found himself gazing upon the piano with emotions that bordered on affection.

John's relief at seeing Crystal dedicating herself to practising the piano meant that for a while, he put his search for the real owner to the back of his mind. In fact, Crystal's demeanour and her rapid progress meant that he no longer worried much about whom the piano really belonged to at all.

Their circle of friends simply assumed that he had forked out a small fortune to buy his daughter an antique instrument. And when Crystal played, as she often did after a dinner party for family friends, Bunty, David or one of the Peaks would lean across and smile.

'Nice to have deep enough pockets to buy something special, eh, John?'

When the piano sat idle after Crystal went to university to complete her Public Relations studies, John had tormented himself about whether he should continue his search. Janet certainly wasn't interested. She thought of it as theirs now, and whenever she heard Crystal was coming home, she would begin to lovingly polish the piano in readiness for their daughter's arrival.

This was how the business of finding the piano's true owner just slipped into that little corner of forgetfulness, where all things unreconciled lived and breathed.

And there it would have remained, had it not been for the day when Crystal came home with an Australian in tow. James Carlyle arrived without warning. He was taller than the average lad around these parts, and a few years older than Crystal's normal crowd. His daughter introduced him as 'a friend' who was hiking in the area and whom she'd talked into giving her a lift home. But from her smile and the way she was gazing up at him, he'd made an impression on their daughter far greater than the term 'friend' would suggest. John and Janet exchanged glances. An Australian? Was it possible? While he and Janet afforded the newcomer the same cordial welcome that was given freely to all of Crystal's boyfriends, John hoped this was just an infatuation that wouldn't last. After an initial moment of panic, he saw his wife's face relax as she came to a similar conclusion.

Crystal's happiness had long been the unifying glue between them. Indeed, it was paramount to their own wellbeing. Crystal's earlier bouts of depression had scarred them both quite badly. Was it their fault that she'd suffered this malaise? Had they as parents done something wrong? As their eyes met now, the tacit agreement between John and his wife was to wait and see what happened.

'James is in law, too, Daddy. Fast-tracked through a firm in Brisbane before coming over here, weren't you, James?' Crystal batted her eyes and spoke a little too admiringly of this new friend for her father's taste.

'So, what brings you to London, then, just a break is it?' John's words sounded more formal than he'd intended.

The Australian seemed not to notice. 'Yes and no. I paused my professional life to take up further study here. I'm finishing a Master of Laws at the London School of Economics.'

'Isn't that amazing, Daddy?' said Crystal, her eyes swimming with admiration.

John admitted that it was impressive – it was an institution held in high regard – but he began to worry that maybe Crystal and James already knew each other rather better than they'd first indicated. These feelings escalated when James noticed the piano in the sitting room and said casually, 'Come on, Crys, are you going to let me hear you play?'

John almost interrupted to suggest that this Australian use his daughter's proper name, but desisted, seeing that James's smile was so genuine.

'I've not heard her play yet,' he remarked, casting his eyes in both John and Janet's direction. His gaze was so forthright that John forced himself to relax a little.

On first impression, he found James hard to dislike, and glancing across at Janet, he could see that she appeared quite taken with him, too.

Wait and see, he counselled himself, as he settled back to listen to what this strapping lawyer from the antipodes was telling them about his own family's connection to music.

'My mother, especially,' he said proudly. 'She teaches piano at the Conservatorium in Brisbane.'

'I'd better be good, then, if I'm to make an impression,' Crystal said, before she launched into a piece John had heard her play many times before.

The performance came to an end, and while they were all still applauding enthusiastically, James leaned across to John and whispered, 'Looks like a beautiful nineteenth-century job. You must have been lucky to pick up an instrument like that.'

John tensed. It was the directness of the question that startled him first. He wasn't used to being spoken to in such a forthright manner. He'd heard that Australians could be quite unnerving with their straightforward approach, asking things directly that might take an Englishman a month to get to. But it was the significance of the question that rattled him the most. So far, John had managed perfectly well to avoid any detailed queries about the piano. Now, after only five minutes under his roof, this Australian had him on the back foot, exposing the very issue that for a long period of time had been quietly eating away at John. The very matter he should have settled long ago.

'Yes, I was,' he whispered back. 'But it's a long story.'

Crystal played another favourite, and when their second round of clapping died down, James, with the speed of a prize-winning pigeon, got right back to the topic.

'You were magnificent, Crys, but your dad was saying that this beautiful piano has a bit of a story attached to it, isn't that right, sir? I'm always fascinated by tales like this, where old instruments come from and how they survive.'

Janet, who by now was serving tea on the dining table, almost dropped the pot and appeared to freeze in her actions, waiting for her husband to respond. He saw her fearful glance.

Crystal responded easily. 'Oh, I s'pose every old piece of furniture has a secret history. Daddy picked this up a long while ago, I'm not sure from where. We've never talked about it.'

All eyes turned to him.

John cleared his throat and leaned forward to pick up the cup of tea Janet had placed before him. He poured the milk, popped in two cubes of sugar and stirred in slow circles, biding his time like a barrister in the Old Bailey. His cheeks felt warm. His daughter had brought home a smart young man of the law to meet her family, and in their first conversation he discovered that her father was not who she'd said he was, and learned that John had been less than scrupulous in his dealings with a client of longstanding association. A client who, in addition to everything else, was a lord of the realm. The discretion required to deal with decades of estate business was one thing John personally had clung to over time, as lawyers and their services had become increasingly devalued in the public's mind. For that reason alone, he most definitely did not want to be the one to sully his family's rock-solid name and reputation with what might look like tawdry theft.

'Well, as a matter of fact,' he said tentatively, clearing his throat for the second time. 'It is a very interesting story ...'

His daughter was staring innocently at him as if she was expecting some playful surprise. 'The thing is ...' he began slowly, 'James, you see, the piano doesn't actually belong to us at all.'

'Whatever do you mean, Daddy?' Crystal exploded. 'I've played this piano since I was a child.'

Crystal was exaggerating, of course. But before he could correct her, his wife came to his aid.

'It is on loan, darling,' Janet said, 'aren't you lucky to have had the exclusive use of the Hebden Manor piano for all these years.'

'What? It belongs to the estate?' Crystal put her hands on the instrument. 'This is my own special piano bought for me by my parents.' Her eyes were filled with confusion, darting between the three of them and searching their faces for an answer.

'Yes, well we did get it for you, darling,' Janet offered again, 'and we have it here. It's yours until we can find the rightful owner. Isn't that so, John.'

'Storing it … here … while I track the beneficiary …' John trailed off.

Crystal's face flushed as she searched for a handkerchief in her pocket. 'Storing it?' she repeated. 'But it's my piano, I love this piano …'

From the expression on the Australian's face, it was clear he was mortified. 'Look, I'm awfully sorry, I didn't mean to open a can of worms here.'

John himself was deeply embarrassed. He should have clarified ownership of the piano in a more concrete fashion years ago. 'Can of worms' was rather too much of the truth.

John felt a surge of panic. Crystal was looking strangely at him. He had probably lost the respect of his daughter over what had been, on his part, an act of sentimentality, which in the sudden glare of attention appeared impossible to fathom. He had stupidly embarrassed his daughter, his wife, his firm and himself, and for what? He should have bought Crystal a new piano.

'Anyone else for tea?' Janet battled on bravely.

'I think the occasion merits something a little stronger, don't you?'

'I'll have tea thanks, Mummy.' Crystal flicked her eyes away from her father quite deliberately.

'Brandy anyone?'

'I'll join you in a brandy, sir,' said James, gallantly moving to John's side near the fireplace.

John watched his daughter talking intensely to her mother. His heart filled with panic. If this was the reaction to revealing who owned the piano, then that most painful secret passed on to him by his father on his deathbed, in light of this, would most definitely have to remain his alone, for the rest of time.

'It's funny how these things happen, you know,' he ventured quietly to James. 'I think I've been in this business too long.'

'I'm not sure I understand.'

'What I mean, I suppose, is that sometimes, even with the best of intentions, our best is not good enough. The fact of the matter is that I should have dealt with this outstanding bit of estate business long ago, and not left it for my daughter to find out in this manner.'

'I do most sincerely apologise for my ...'

John brushed the apology away with a wave of his hand. One part of him wanted to talk about it, the other part of him was shamed. 'It might be for the best if I tell you how it was,' he said, noticing from the corner of one eye his wife's arm reaching around Crystal's shoulders.

'Over here,' he gestured to James to move to the window, ensuring their conversation was out of hearing.

John embarked upon the story, recounting key points about Lady Hampton's wish for her piano to go to her last-in-line female. How he, and his father before him (the part about his father trying wasn't strictly true) had tried for years to locate the heir to the piano without making any headway whatsoever. He even offered some detail of his own explorations. Enough, he hoped, to demonstrate that he'd always tried to do the right thing.

The younger man's gaze remained focused on John throughout as he listened.

'There is a strange coincidence for me to be telling you this story, James. Lady Hampton was not English, you know. She came from Australia, from a little town called Beechworth. Do you know it?' And without waiting for a yes or a no, he ploughed on. 'It appears that from the time she married the earl, what marked Lady Rose out from one born to the role so to speak, was her unique capacity for organisation and hard work. Her charming manner also drew many admirers to her side, including Crystal's great-grandfather.'

'You mean the Lady Hampton who owned this piano was Australian?' From the twinkle in his eye, James appeared to find this amusing. 'I hope she didn't put her foot in it like I just did the first day she met the family.'

'Our firm,' John continued, a flush of red creeping from his cheeks to his ears, grateful for the chance to finally unburden himself about the piano, 'has had a long connection to the Hebden Estate. Although the manor itself is a school now, Lady Hampton's last wish was left to my firm to carry out, and it is to my regret that neither I nor my father before me have managed to do so.'

The younger lawyer was regarding him with sympathy, but with a gaze so steady that John found it more than a little disconcerting.

'I can't tell you how heavily it weighs,' he said, suddenly speaking more openly than he normally would. 'Although it may not appear ...' he paused, and took a sip of brandy, gesturing to the piano with his left arm.

'I mean, from outward appearances, it wouldn't seem obvious that my not finding the real owner bothered me very much at all, but I can assure you that from the day I first read Lady Hampton's will, it has been my goal to locate the proper owner.'

'As I'm sure it would be after such a long and distinguished association.' James smiled disarmingly.

John carried on, offering only scant detail about the difficult times that faced the Hampton family between the two world wars, which he said had made his task even harder. He explained unnecessarily how, after numerous and lengthy investigations, he'd discovered Lady Hampton's sister was a spinster who'd pre-deceased her, leaving no children.

'In the end, you know I probably brought the piano home for lack of knowing what else to do.'

'Do you think you have considered every option to find the heir?' James asked, his face deadly serious.

'Whatever do you mean?' John snapped, uncertain that he'd heard correctly.

'The reason I ask is not to be impertinent, sir, but to suggest that I may be able to help with your enquiries with … a fresh approach.'

'Please don't call me sir, John will do.'

'Um … John, if I could perhaps see some of the documentation? You never know, there may be some alternative avenues I can explore.'

John heard himself mumbling something incoherent. Once again, this young man had completely caught him off guard. Probably, he should have felt slighted by the inference that he, an experienced practitioner of long standing and solid reputation, had not been sufficiently thorough. John wavered. He would happily accept the offer of help to get him out of the mess he was in. Although he didn't believe for one second anything would come of it, it might help to make amends with Crystal.

'That's very good of you, James,' he said. 'I am tempted to agree. But I don't wish to be dumping my matters into your lap. This may have already caused some issues between you and Crystal.'

'I'm pleased to offer any assistance. But I think perhaps you misunderstand my relationship with your daughter, John. She and

I, well, we met through mutual friends. We did go out to dinner, and please don't get me wrong, I think she is a great girl, but we're just not each other's cup of tea in that way. We're just friends.' James paused, searching for the right words. 'She seemed a little up and down over the last weeks, and I was worried about her. So, given I was coming this way, I thought I might bring her home to see if that helped.'

'She can be a little moody,' John said lightly, covering his concern about what James had implied about Crystal's mental state. Was his daughter not well again? Would she be even more hurt and offended when she discovered that he had entered into an arrangement with James without first consulting her? His mouth felt a little dry. He was taking another risk. Before he could change his mind, James spoke.

'I can't promise anything, but I'd like to give it a try, especially after putting my foot in it so categorically.' The Australian extended his hand to seal the deal.

John took a deep breath, trying to calm himself. 'Very well, James, agreed. Now, shall we join Janet and Crystal? They will be wondering what on earth we are talking about,' he added, feeling no relief at all from his sense of foreboding.

Maddison

Mt Macedon

The prospect of uncovering who my grandmother was could be a Pandora's box. But once I'd made the decision to travel and booked the ticket, I couldn't help feeling stirred by what I might discover. So far, it didn't seem likely that Abigail's family had been so destitute they'd been forced to give her up. Not if her mother was Lady Rose Hampton. To me, it seemed likely that despite bad times in Europe from two world wars, the Hamptons had remained a family of 'means'. And although the odds of untangling this mystery were slim, I couldn't help feeling deep in my bones that there was more to this than an heirloom piano.

Yet, sitting at home listening to light rain falling on the roof, and going from staring at my grandmother's photo to the solicitor's letter, a familiar terror descended. What if the story really wasn't a happy one? What if there was some darkness in my family that had been hidden for very good reasons? What if my mother and Uncle Gerry had known about it all along, and spent their lives protecting me from it?

That was the problem with a vivid imagination, it could take over. And in the weeks after the letter arrived, mine took me to some very dark places. Normally peaceful sleep had been interrupted by nightmares of terrible things happening to Abigail, and to this unknown Lady Rose. Day times were better. I could focus on stories based on wartime England, foundling babies and even the accidental swapping of children in hospital. But night-times brought family accidents and crimes, and leaving baby Abigail as an orphan.

Actually, it was only after the lawyer's second letter arrived that my resolve to travel to Kent became resolute. Up until that point, while niggling doubts remained, I might have rescinded my plans and convinced myself it would be better to struggle on, finish the work at hand, complete my *Summer Rain* manuscript and be done with it. But the dismissive nature of his reply raised my hackles.

I had informed him that I would be coming over and would bring my documents. I was keen to find out more, I told him, as Hebden Manor and my connection to it was a complete mystery. His response, when it came, was rather terse. There was no real need for any 'in person' visit, he said, because there was 'very little he would be able to share regarding my connection to the family, beyond the piano, and his duty to Lady Rose'. This reluctance, or evasiveness (which was how it seemed to me), caused me to dig my heels in.

Who was he to tell me there was 'no purpose to be served' by my presence? Yes, he could just 'ship it', of course he could, but inheriting this piano meant more to me than that. I wanted to know what happened to my 'orphan' grandmother. And her family. My family. Who was I, for heaven's sake? The answer to this question mattered very much to me. Even if it meant nothing to the rather pompous English lawyer.

I read and re-read every word of his original letter. But when I dragged my *Oxford Dictionary* off the shelf to double-check the meaning of 'extant', as in 'last extant female', the words contained within it took on a new depth of mystery.

'Extant' meant that I was alive at the time Lady Rose died. I blinked hard and may have even stopped breathing for a moment. Then I repeated the words out loud: 'You mean there was a time that my great-grandmother, grandmother, mother and I were all on the earth at the same time?' The concept was overwhelming. And it was grasping what it meant that really changed things for me. After that, there'd been no going back.

Abigail was not, and could not have been, an orphan. Obviously, if her mother was still alive thirty-three years ago. Had she known this, too? Did my mother know? The questions were coming thick and fast.

What happened for my grandmother to arrive here and claim orphan status, for my mother and Uncle Gerry to believe it, while all the time, her mother, this Lady Rose, was living an aristocratic life in England?

I looked down at the photo of Abigail I was nursing, and although any sort of logic dictated that I had to be making it up, I could swear there was a little more warmth in her eyes than I had seen before.

'What is this mystery about you that comes to me in the guise of a piano?' I whispered, half expecting her to reply.

I wasn't sure the email I sent to the lawyer was the most well written I'd ever sent, but I was pretty sure even a staid solicitor in Kent would have realised that it was pointless to object to my visit.

Three days later

'Here she is,' Amy chirped when I arrived. 'You're late. We thought you weren't coming.'

'Sorry, caught in traffic.' I threw my bag down, happy to sink into the chair and catch my breath.

Once more I was in the city where I'd arranged a farewell lunch before my departure. Things were happening so fast my mind was starting to spin as last-minute preparations mounted. Being late was not my favourite thing, not even with friends, but when I'd set out early this morning in search of one last piece of intelligence about my grandmother, it took longer than I'd anticipated.

Last night, leafing through Abigail's little book of anonymous poems, I'd noticed for the first time a faded, almost indecipherable stamp, the sort that libraries used to mark their ownership of books, down the bottom of the back cover: 'Property of the Melbourne Orphan Asylum.' The what-if question had jumped instantly to mind.

My internet search uncovered that, *'The Melbourne Orphan Asylum, founded in 1853, was the first organisation established by women in Victoria, for the welfare of children, three to sixteen years old, regardless of pedigree, parents, creed or country.'*

A shiver careered down my spine, as page after page of information about the hard work these dedicated women had undertaken flicked onto my screen. Acknowledging how they'd joined forces to care for and help children and young people left without parents so long ago, made me feel tight in the chest and brought tears to my eyes. How could I have not known about that?

Further searching had produced one other amazing fact. The Melbourne Orphan Asylum still existed. It wasn't called that anymore, but the building remained standing.

Clearly, any attempt to develop a hypothesis about how my grandmother got to Australia meant that this establishment had to be my first port of call.

The double-storey Gothic red brick building, located in the posh bayside suburb of Brighton, had been re-badged and was now dedicated to 'family welfare'. Surely, they would have kept records? With everything else I'd ever known about my family up in the air, I figured it was worth a try. I wasn't hopeful exactly, but I simply couldn't leave without first going to check the place out for myself.

I sat in my car outside the historic building with a list of questions multiplying every minute. What was my grandmother's connection to this organisation? How was it she'd had a copy of an Orphan Asylum book amongst her things? Was it possible that she, the daughter of an English aristocrat, once had been cared for herself inside these severe-looking walls? When would that have been? And why had no one ever mentioned anything of it to me?

'We don't call them orphanages any more, you know.'

'Yes, I know, sorry.'

It was cool and dank inside, with little natural light, and walls in need of a good coat of paint. I could only hope it hadn't been like this when the children were here. Family Services was certainly in need of some renovation.

'Abigail Browne, you say? Never heard of her.'

'It was a while ago,' I said, staring at the young woman as she skimmed some kind of list she'd brought up on her screen.

'When was it?'

'Any time between nineteen thirty-six and nineteen eighty,' I said.

'Wait here.' She got up, opened the door behind reception and bellowed, 'Helen.'

A stooped, frail woman walking with the aid of a stick appeared.

'Miss ...'

'Browne.'

'Yes, Miss Browne is enquiring about someone.'

'Abigail Browne,' I said, projecting my voice.

The frail one peered into my eyes. 'And you are?'

'Her granddaughter. I was hoping you might be able to help me.'

My arrival at the usual trendy café in Little Bourke Street was greeted by distracted smiles and limp waves of welcome. My friends kept talking about their husbands, wardrobes, children's schools, and the topic I'd interrupted; how Jackie, the young woman from their Pilates class, the one with the gorgeous body and large breasts, was openly having an affair with the manager of the local gymnasium. They agreed that not only was she too young for him, but he was married so it just wasn't right. They wondered too if they should boycott the establishment by joining another fitness club as a kind of protest.

'Come on, Maddi, you're meant to be the wise one. What do you think?' All eyes turned to me.

'It's difficult to understand people who are hellbent on flagrantly flouting social contracts,' I said, settling into my chair. 'But is that enough to change gyms?'

Nobody spoke; however, an exchange of looks meant the question was being thoughtfully considered.

Probably it wasn't, I decided. This was another of those unwanted questions of modern social philosophy. As none of us knew the wife in question, and except for a kind of pity for the young woman whom we also knew nothing about, it seemed a pointless exercise given our response would have no bearing on their behaviour or the outcome. Besides, I thought, if every indiscretion by someone we met in our lives caused us to change direction, there would be nowhere left in the world to settle.

Before I could voice any of this, Amy cut in with, 'I think we should let that guy know what we think of him.'

'It's not my problem,' said Beth, 'I can't think what she sees in him, anyway.'

'I've got an idea what that might be,' Lucinda said, to groans of laughter around the table.

While their exchange of opinions continued, I tried to put the picture of Helen and the 'Orphan Asylum' aside, to quietly wonder who it was better to be? The woman doing the cheating, or the one being cheated on? Was that young woman really happy to be the third cog in this man's life? She had to know he was married; everyone else did. Not all women wanted the same things out of their relationships, which caused me to wonder if I should explore this in a new story. Probably. After my own first-hand experience, it should be a cinch to write about a cad and a heartbroken lover. Thinking about how much fun I could have with the new love interest, I felt my evil sister rising to the task.

'I think we should wait and see what happens,' Beth announced, which thankfully stopped my mind from delving any further for now. My friends decided unanimously that they would not act impetuously.

'I agree with Beth,' Lucinda seconded, 'it's not really our business. She'll tire of him, or his wife will find out. Why should we have to change gyms just because of them? The location is so convenient, it's at least an extra ten-minute drive to get to the next nearest.'

'Let's just hope it stops before his wife finds out about it,' said Amy as if she'd read my thoughts.

'What a nightmare,' said Beth.

And with that pronouncement, the topic lost oxygen and the conversation swung back to ordering lunch, and my trip.

'What are you actually hoping to find over there?' Lucinda asked in her usual forthright manner that was sometimes a little brusque.

'Nothing new,' I said. 'It's just that with this piano I'm about to inherit, I know my grandmother could not have been an orphan. So, I'm just trying to find out what the truth really is.'

'Why would you bother? I mean, it's all a long time ago. And do you even play the piano?' Amy finished, with all the confidence of someone who knew every skerrick of detail about her own family history. A few years ago, she'd conducted extended genealogy searches, 'Just for the sake of the kids,' she'd said, but since then, had never missed an opportunity to mention how this profession or that was 'in the family'. It definitely seemed to have given her a confidence boost. Was that what I was looking for? I couldn't put my finger on why it was important to me. I guess it was just the knowing. But even if I found something interesting, it was unlikely it would change my life, really. Not in any substantial way.

The elderly woman at the old orphanage had explained earnestly that she was a volunteer, and my request might take a while to fulfil.

'I'm only two days a week now, you see,' she said weakly.

I thanked her, thinking that if anyone could find the information I was looking for, she could.

Sometimes, watching the TV news show armies of people rolling up their sleeves to offer their precious time for a cause, I wondered if it was volunteers that kept our country ticking. What would happen if one day they decided not to bother? Chaos, probably.

I was longing to ask this volunteer if my grandmother's connection to the orphanage was related to her having resided there as an inmate herself. But I held that in for now; time would tell.

'I do have some recollection of her piano playing, though,' she said, squinting up at me. 'It was lovely, and she was extremely good. I'll look to see what I can find, but I can't promise anything.'

'Of course.' *Don't push her*, I thought, hoping that Helen would say more.

'When this organisation amalgamated, things went haywire,' she said with a frown. 'The shredding truck was here for weeks. Not much more than the names of the orphans themselves remaining, I'm afraid. And even that's not all digitised. Even now.' Her face looked as if she'd eaten a sour onion. 'I'll do the best I can,' she said. 'It's not every day a granddaughter comes searching.'

I thanked her again and left my phone number, email and postal address, just in case. She smiled fleetingly as we shook hands. I walked out of there with a huge knot in my throat. Talking to someone who actually remembered my grandmother playing the piano came as a shock. But one thing I knew for certain, by the time Helen finished her search, if Abigail had ever lived there, I'd know about it.

It was warm under the oversized black umbrella. The coffee was good and strong, and the atmosphere between us convivial.

'I suppose a romance writer is always on the lookout for a good story,' Amy offered, glancing across at me to see if I appreciated her insight.

I reciprocated with a smile to show her I did. 'Yes, it was a long time ago. And you're right, I don't really play the piano. But that means I'm even more interested in finding out what happened.'

'But what's the point?' Lucinda persisted.

'She's going over there to find all her toffy relatives, of course, why do you think,' Amy said, hinting of jealousy.

I couldn't actually answer Lucinda's question. I couldn't articulate what I hoped to find even to myself. I just knew that since the letter about inheriting the piano had arrived, I was beset with a deep longing to know more about my extended family, and where I came from. I wanted to find out what happened to my grandmother. I didn't expect my friends to understand. With an itinerant actor for a mother and no father to talk about, my story was different to all of theirs, with their generations of life-long extended family. I literally had no one. And no story to explain why.

I felt their eyes on me. 'You just better look out, if I'm related to royalty … after the insults all these years. Off with their heads!' I said, wagging my finger at each of them, which made them laugh louder.

'Can I come too?' said Bethany. 'That would give Jack something to think about. I think it's so romantic, Maddi.'

I smiled. *Was it?*

'Go girl,' Lucinda added.

'I guess it is really, isn't it? You're all welcome to come with me, but you wouldn't leave Jack and your boys to fend for themselves for five minutes,' I said to Beth.

It was no secret that Bethany, who had exchanged a high-powered advertising-agency executive position to raise two sons, struggled with the domestic side of life as a stay-at-home mum. She missed her job, but believed that children needed their mothers at home. More power to her, I always thought, that she'd actually carried it out.

'Let me think for a minute.' Beth grinned. 'Of course not. How could I?'

'Boo,' said Lucinda. 'Just when we thought something interesting was going to happen.'

'You'll be free as a bird,' said Amy, 'I wouldn't mind some of that.'

'Careful what you wish for,' Beth chimed. 'Remember the gym guy; he obviously had too much time on his hands, and look what happened there.'

'Oh, thanks for that.' She looked away.

We all knew that early on, Amy's marriage had been through some rough patches. It was all fixed now, she said. But sometimes, it seemed that in her mind, those days had not entirely gone away.

Beth turned to me. 'How long will you be gone?'

'Not sure. I'll meet the solicitor and take it from there.' I wasn't able to give any precise details of when I would be back, or much detail of anything else, either. The travel situation was up in the air, something I was excited about. A change of scenery might be the right medicine to get my writing going again, instead of worrying about my 'situation' or the mystery of love. *Utterly ridiculous trying to fathom the chemistry of that*, I told myself, trying to find some other point of interest to add, but finding none.

With everyone still thinking about what Beth had said, the vacuum created a small lull in conversation, so Amy bounced right back onto her favourite topic.

'To even more pressing matters,' she nudged me in the ribs, 'I might have someone else to introduce you to when you get back, Maddi,' which made the rest of the table giggle. 'He's a nice, handsome type who'd make a good daddy. That is, unless you surprise us and come back with a Prince Charming of your own.'

'Have you ever thought I might be unmatchable?' I said, dearly wishing she would stop feeling personally responsible for my dating habits.

'Only in your own mind. You're a romance writer, remember? You just haven't met anyone as wonderful as your leading men.'

'You're probably right about that,' I conceded with a laugh. 'Maybe I might be destined to remain a quaint old spinster churning out love stories, hugely successful, with no man in her life to annoy her. And no children to keep her from her work.' I smirked cheekily. 'Ever considered that?'

The truth was, I wasn't at all sure my life path was ever going be the same as theirs. My life started on the outside just the way solicitor Nettlewood described it, as a 'broken arm', and as far as I could tell, it was still orbiting on the same trajectory. After the young life I'd had, I wasn't convinced I was cut out for a regular family life like theirs, anyway. Actually, I was pretty certain that I wasn't.

'Daytimes are okay, then, but how will you fill your nights?' Lucinda sparked, which sent us all into gales of laughter.

'I can't wait to hear about the skeletons you find in your family closet,' Amy cut in, which thankfully steered the conversation away. 'And you know we're expecting the biggest of big parties to show off this piano when it arrives.'

'Yes, a piano party, you must, Maddison,' they chorused, including Amy, who had already made her point.

After a quick raising of coffee cups, good wishes for the trip, and me committing to an extravagant piano-themed party on my return, it was time to leave.

'Don't forget to think of us back home slaving away while you're gallivanting around England,' said Amy, having the last word.

I was still wondering if I shouldn't join the shopping expedition when I heard Beth calling out behind me, 'Hang on, Maddi, I'll walk the first block with you, I'm going your way for a bit.'

As we were walking, Beth casually linked her arm through mine.

'Have you packed yet?'

'No, that's why I can't stay in town now. I've still got a few things to do.'

'Oh, don't worry, I'd choose preparing for London over shopping any day, too. How exciting, not knowing what you'll find over there. Have you ever thought it might change your life?'

'It has already, if that's what you mean.'

'Stuff like this, so unexpected, like when I met Jack, can take you by storm.'

'In some ways, that might not be a bad thing,' I said. 'Hopefully, something might happen that will stop Amy trying to match me up with every single man she's ever met in her life.'

Beth laughed. 'She's just being Amy. She wants to help.'

'I know, she's convinced that I'm not going to find Prince Charming on my own, but …'

'But with help like that, huh?'

'Exactly.' And this time we both laughed.

Dodging our way along the footpath, Beth suddenly blurted out what was bothering her.

'Would you think I'm a terrible mother if I told you I was going back to work? I've had an offer of part-time work from my old agency.' She squeezed my arm.

'What does Jack think?'

'He says he's okay with it.'

I could see from the little frown on her face that she'd just needed to tell someone to get it off her chest.

'Is it wrong of me to say that I miss the company of adults, Maddison?'

I listened as we made our way along, dashing to catch the green lights, both puffing from the exertion while she explained that she had child care lined up and the scheduling all in hand and how the extra income would be helpful. I told her I thought it was a terrific idea.

'Thanks, I can always talk to you, Maddi. Now, I'm going to leave you here, I'm going that way.'

'You'll probably be a director of the company by the time I get back.' I grinned at her, thinking that she just might be.

'In my dreams. Now you have the best time, okay?' She reached out and hugged me with both arms. 'And don't get into any trouble.'

'Yes, Mother.'

Horrified, she held me at arm's length. 'Oh my God, do you see?'

'No, see what?'

'That's what happens. You start ordering little children around, next thing you're doing it to adults.' Beth was standing perilously close to the edge of the kerb. 'That's what motherhood can do to you, see, that's why I have to get back to work.'

I was mortified at the effect of my words on her. 'Beth, don't worry,' I said, pulling her back onto the footpath. 'I was only kidding, it's all good.'

'I love my boys, don't get me wrong, but …'

'I know. I'm not.'

'Are you sure?'

'Yes, I'm certain.'

She was staring into my eyes.

'Beth, it was meant to be a joke.'

'Okay, then.' Her face creased into her lovely smile. 'I'll let you know how it goes.'

'Please do. Listen, I was going to ask you for a favour, but I've left my run a bit late.'

'What?'

'Just a couple of phone calls … I thought you might know the best way …'

'Anything you need, you know that. Send me the details and what you want me to do. Gotta go.' And with that, the lights changed and she took off across the intersection.

I waited until the sight of Bethany's blonde bob bouncing up and down disappeared from sight as she turned into one of the laneways further up the hill. Her reaction to what I'd said was an indicator that maybe she was finding it even more difficult to stay at home than she had ever anticipated. Her boys were lucky to have a mother like Beth, the way she thought about everything. As I headed towards my car, I thought, *If I were a mother, I would want to be just like her.* After all, I never had any great examples of mothering in my life.

John

Cobham, three weeks earlier

Crystal had spoken nothing of it to him, so John thought that she may have let the matter go. At least he hoped she had. He even dared to assume that the piano issue and the Australian had left his daughter's head entirely.

The weeks passed, and each time Crystal came home, she was by herself. On these occasions, the atmosphere in the house was agreeable. No mention of James, although John had noticed that Crystal wasn't playing 'her' piano so much at the moment.

When he raised this observation to his wife in the privacy of their bedroom, Janet sighed wistfully, and her response was enough to prevent another word on the subject from escaping his lips.

'Oh, John, why would you think?' She frowned. 'Sometimes you can be so lacking in sensitivity.'

So, he asked her about the flowers she was cultivating instead, red tulips if his memory served him right, as this topic had never failed to bring a lovely smile to her face.

* * *

It was on the tail end of one of Crystal's solo visits that John, Janet and Crystal were strolling back through the village after a delightful lunch in a small café that overlooked the river, when Crystal made her announcement. 'Did I mention that James will be calling by later? He's promised to drive me to university.'

John tried to cover his surprise. 'Oh, it'll be nice to see him again.'

From his daughter's beaming face, she was extremely pleased.

Janet said nothing.

When he arrived, James appeared relaxed. 'Sorry I'm late,' he said apologetically. 'Had to drop off a mate and it was further than I thought.'

Kitted out in hiking gear, he definitely looked the part of a sporting type. Janet flashed John a look that said, *Can you believe it*, when she heard James offer to remove his boots at the door.

Crystal led James inside, taking him by the arm, his wife made tea, and they all sat talking politely about where he and his friends had been walking. The mood was informal and John noticed that Janet appeared to relax more, too, when it became obvious that their daughter was not remotely interested in pursuing any hiking expeditions herself.

'Really, I can't see the interest in it at all, James, sleeping in tents being eaten by mosquitoes.' She turned her nose up. 'I can think of better ways to spend my time.'

James laughed good-humouredly, not making any attempt to persuade her otherwise. But the moment he'd seen an opportunity, he'd drawn John away for a quiet aside.

'I think I've found your piano heir.'

A sharp stab of dread hit John in the solar plexus. He caught his breath. 'Oh?' He stared mutely at the younger man, wishing for the ten-thousandth time that he had never let this matter out of his own hands.

'I think you'll find my research interesting. Do you have some time to go over it?'

Luckily, at that moment, Janet, announced that she and Crystal were going to inspect her tulips blooming in the glasshouse at the bottom of the garden.

Without a further word, James took his cue, and by the time he returned with the file from his car, John was on tenterhooks, waiting anxiously in his favourite upright chair.

'So, you really think you've found the heir?' He waved his arm, gesturing for James to sit.

'I do,' said James, quietly placing himself opposite, oblivious to John's intense stare. 'I've put a detailed file note in there. It explains all of my discoveries. I'm sure you'll find the research is watertight.'

'Where did you say she is?'

'She lives outside Melbourne in Australia. That was the key. Her name and address are both in there. You should be able to take it from here.'

'Thank you,' John responded weakly.

James leaned forward and held the file aloft for a second before finally handing it over. 'Pleased I could be of assistance.'

John gripped the file with both hands, tense with anticipation for what he was about to read. Had the Hampton heir, after so long, really been found?

He smiled amicably. 'It's taken you no time at all to do what I couldn't achieve after years of endeavour. I must confess to being more than a little curious to see what you have found, and also to know how you managed to do it.'

James responded with a transparency John could only admire. 'To be honest, it wasn't all my own work. I recruited a few mates to the case. The results do raise a few questions, though. Perhaps another day, when the time is right?'

John stiffened as one of his leg muscles twitched. 'It goes without saying, James, that this information is … how shall I say?'

'Highly confidential? Of course.'

John was beginning to feel like a piece of putty in this young man's hands.

'Now,' said James, 'if you have no objection, I'll leave you to take a look. I need to get back to London. I've put my number in there, too, in case you'd like me to clarify anything.'

'Yes of course. I must say thank you again, James,' said John, hugging the precious information hard against his chest and praying desperately that no ticking bomb lay within its covers.

As soon as he and Janet waved Crystal and James off, John locked himself into his study and wasted no time devouring the contents. By the time he finished processing all the possible ramifications of what James had uncovered, there was only one thing he knew for certain: the path ahead would have to be traversed very carefully indeed. Wasn't this what he'd wanted for so long, to find the rightful heir, he asked himself? *Yes, but not like this.*

The village was mostly still asleep the next morning when John unlocked his office. His secretary arrived sometime later, and was more than a little surprised to see him at his computer so early.

'What on earth are you doing?' she asked.

'I'm typing a letter,' John responded. 'How much is a stamp to Australia?'

Maddison

Mt Macedon

'Is there something wrong, Maddison?' my agent's concern was real.

How could I answer that? I could have said, everything and nothing.

'Do you have the time to travel?' she persisted.

Her question turned my face an even darker shade of crimson. *Thank goodness she is thousands of kilometres away*, I thought, doodling onto the notepad next to the phone.

I couldn't tell her that my mojo had come to a screaming halt and that I was going away hoping to recover some of it. The worst thing was that her questions made me realise again that I might be running away, rather than simply putting my head down and getting on with it.

Her decorous manner usually soothed any anxieties, but this time her words set my teeth on edge. 'Are you sure there's nothing else?'

'No, nothing at all,' I said guiltily.

Normally, I didn't lie bald-faced to people. 'I'm trying something new that's all, and things are taking a little longer than I anticipated.'

I hated lying, even when it was 'a little white lie', the sort that people used socially all the time for self-protection in situations too awkward for truth telling. This was one of those. No matter how strong a person's desire for transparency was, however, sometimes the truth simply didn't work. I wasn't betraying a best friend's trust here, or withholding information that might help to solve a crime. It was a little fib to the one person who needed to believe in my abilities to complete work. On this occasion, it was my professional survival at stake. How could I have told the whole truth, and nothing but?

I was trying something new, that much was true, and it was going to take longer because I was going to England. But more than that, I actually didn't know what was going to happen, or how things would pan out. So, it wasn't possible to divulge any more than I already had.

As if sensing something was amiss, she responded tartly, 'Okay. Just try to pull yourself together before it's too late.' As an afterthought she added, 'And while you're over there, it might be useful to contact a publicist. Appearances and publicity can only help, you know. Make the most of it.'

I heard the line go dead. My legs were shaking.

I was still mulling the conversation over, when I heard footsteps on the verandah. I glanced at the time – three-thirty pm. I heard the familiar voice.

'Yoo-hoo it's only me.'

Quickly folding the solicitor's letter, I slipped it back into the drawer, where all my personal details lived. One dark night after I'd first moved in, it occurred to me that the information contained in this slender drawer was an actual summation of my life thus far. It had been a sobering thought, and remained so. I made for the door, more than pleased to leave that line of thinking.

Ruth, my cheery-faced neighbour, smiled a greeting. 'Oh, you are in, dear, I thought so, I told Joan that I hadn't seen you go out again.'

On her head, I noticed a colourful crochet affair that fitted tightly around the crown of her head like a skullcap. Something she must have picked up at a fundraiser, I thought, because for sure the sixties hippie movement would have passed her by completely. I smiled to myself. If she could read my thoughts, she'd be horrified.

'Hello, Ruth,' I said warmly.

Soon after moving into this house, I realised that the widowed sisters next door were more reliable than a security service. All I'd been able to glean of their status was that one husband had run off, another had died young, and a third sister lived overseas, which had left them to depend on each other.

'Would you like to join us for afternoon tea? Joan's made one of her strawberry sponge cakes.'

From the first day I met them, their concern for my wellbeing had been touching. The sisters were heartening to have around and I had grown very fond of them. Since the original house-warming party, slowly but surely, they had become a major part of my mountain-side network, such as it was. Up here, I had nothing like the spread of acquaintances and people I knew in the city, so their friendly faces meant the world to me. The sisters didn't know it, but they had saved me from many a miserable night eating alone thinking about things I shouldn't, which was why I was sorry to have to ask them to change the speaking engagement they had taken upon themselves to organise on my behalf. Here was an opportunity to break the news gently.

'Sounds irresistible,' I said.

'Haven't disturbed you, have we, dear?' Ruth peered up at me. I smiled inwardly; why did people say that when they knew that they just had?

'No, not at all,' I said, pulling the door closed. There, another social lie. 'Never too busy to eat cake, Ruth.' This part was true.

These were the rituals we went through every time one of them arrived at my door with no prior arrangement. There would be enquiries about whether they had interrupted my work, and I would respond that they hadn't. This was part of my social contract with them. The words slipped easily off my tongue and I appreciated their civility in at least asking. Even if the polite enquiry didn't change the interruption itself.

At my old city place, someone could be thumping on the door at any time of the day or night, with no concern about disturbing me or my working routine. One of the best or worst things (depending on your viewpoint) about an inner-city address was that there was always someone who needed a chat or a glass of wine, or a comfort break, or all three, and you being close at hand seemed to come easily to mind as a desirable destination. Most of the time, I hadn't minded, except for early mornings when I let the phone ring off the hook and left the door unanswered. That was my precious uninterruptable space, when it was just me and the page. At least that's how it was then, when I had something to put on that page.

I hurried after Ruth, who was already marching off down the path.

'Come along, then,' she commanded.

The solid step of the rotund silver-haired figure ahead of me with the splash of colour on her head, made me smile. I imagined generations of schoolchildren trained to obey Ruth's instructions. She made me feel like one of them.

'What's wrong with your skin,' said Ruth, unlatching the picket-fence gate.

'Too much chocolate,' I mumbled, thinking she must have X-ray vision as well to see my skin blemishes under the thick makeup I'd plastered on.

'Well, you know what they say about that, don't you?'

'No, I don't.' I held my breath, expecting her to start on about chocolate being a substitute for no discernible love-life.

Thankfully, Ruth was so taken up opening the door and returning the key to its secret spot on a hook inside the door, that she completely forgot what she was going to say about eating too much chocolate.

Once the key was in place, Ruth stepped quickly through the door.

'Maddison's skin has broken out,' she announced. A delicious smell of baking hovered in the air, and Ruth's sister Joan had prepared the table that overlooked the garden with a lace cloth and rose-patterned teacups and saucers.

'Beautiful,' I said to the older of the two. 'Fit for a queen.'

'What did you say, dear?' Joan gave the cushions a last-minute plumping. As usual, her bluish curls, lacquered and rendered immobile, gave her that 'ready for any sort of occasion at a moment's notice' look.

'This looks beautiful,' I repeated, speaking directly to her face. I always forgot that Joan was slightly hard of hearing. On this occasion that was a positive, because it meant she'd not heard her sister's comment about my skin.

Joan smiled, and her eyes shone with pleasure. 'Let's see how it tastes first before we start praising,' she responded, speaking in the austere self-deprecating style of her Scottish ancestors, as if to hide her delight.

Joan had always been a proud housewife, which made her particularly sensitive to her domestic achievements, unlike her sister. I liked her. She was kind and comforting in the way a cup of hot chocolate could be on a freezing cold day. I took a pastie from the tray she offered and put the whole thing into my mouth, chewing the crispy pastry and succulent vegetable filling with relish.

'Thank you, Joan, this is yummy,' I said, with my mouth too full.

Ruth had a sharp tongue and spoke rather too directly for my liking, a legacy, I thought, of her teaching years. I appreciated her, too, because she was feisty and inquisitive, even if I couldn't find answers once she got on a roll with questions about my personal situation.

'How is it that you are a romance writer, but you never seem to have any romance yourself?'

I'd heard that question a thousand times, but it smarted nevertheless. Naturally, they knew nothing about my motivation for moving out here, and I would never be able to confide in them my reasons for doing so. Sometimes a bit of mystery was good even in your own life.

'Ah, it was all before we met, I'm afraid,' had been my most effective response. I would tell them that after my mother died, I suffered unrequited love for a barrister while working as a secretary in his chambers, and I would see their eyes soften with sympathy. I'd suggested it was that experience that had got me writing romance novels in the first place, instead of murderous crime. Then one day, probably in a moment of misery that I couldn't clearly recall now, I just slipped into writing a love story and that had been it, my start.

'Sit down now,' commanded Ruth, as if I were a child in need of discipline.

The first day I told them what I did, not knowing that they were staunch members of the local book club, I will never forget.

'Oh, you're a writer,' they exclaimed in unison and exchanged knowing looks. Sometimes they were like twins. 'And would we know any of your books?'

Joan had been delighted to discover, after I named my top-selling titles, that she had actually read two of them, and by the next time we caught up, Ruth had read them.

The thought of living next door to an author had appealed to them right away, and the three of us getting to know each other had only encouraged them to freely express their views on new authors and their opinions on other old favourites, as well; Joan loved Coileen McCulloch and Nora Roberts. Ruth, with her passion for crime, loved to read Agatha Christie; she confessed proudly one day that she had read 'every word Agatha had written three times over'.

'Cut Maddison a big slice,' said Ruth as her sister plunged a knife into the velvety sponge, 'I think she's looking too thin.'

'I hope you're not on another of those ridiculous diets, Maddison?'

'No, no I'm not.' I sank into the cushioned seat on 'my' chair where I always sat, forking some sponge cake into my mouth.

Ruth sat, cleared her throat, and beamed eyes that were thrumming with interest directly into mine.

It wasn't hard to recognise my signal. Taking another quick mouthful of cake and a sip of tea, I swallowed hard and put down my fork. *Never mind telling them about the trip*, I thought, the moment had passed. *Fill them in later.*

'If you've no new handsome love in your life to report to us, then what are we working on at the moment?' Ruth asked, moving her head quizzically, reminiscent of a tiny yellow finch common to this area and known for its striking colour. Joan leaned forward, delicately balancing her side plate on one hand.

I swallowed again, looking wistfully at the remainder of my cake, but at the same time adrenaline had caused my energy to rise and extinguished any desire for food.

Since knowing the sisters, I had rediscovered my old talent for making up stories on the spot. The unpredictability of this sort of game playing, never knowing what would leap to mind, had been quite addictive when I was a kid mucking around with my mother's actor friends. It had become so again; unconsciously ignited one night, after the sisters and I had drained all other topics of conversation. Trying to escape cross-examination about my latest writing, and avoiding any reveal of the true state of my desperation, I'd simply begun making up a story for them.

Their wide-eyed reaction to my make-believe had been enough for the actor in me, the daughter of Marianne, to take it through to the end. Now, this game had become an integral part of our company, my part to play for the sisters, quid pro quo for a regular supply of cakes, company and a ferocious PR team.

Sometimes, of course, I wished they would leave the subject of my work alone, but truthfully, I loved the challenge; it was helping to keep me on my toes. It might not have been visible in my writing at the moment, but sooner or later I figured it had to translate to the page.

'So, this time,' I said slowly, playing for a fraction of time, 'I'm changing direction slightly for me. This story, I think, will be set completely in the past ...'

I didn't know why I said that, probably to do with the letter from England, and whom I dreamed I might be going to meet there.

'Oooh,' the sisters cooed, 'do tell.'

'The heroine will come from the old country,' I said decisively, and saw Joan's lips twitch with pleasure.

This was enough for me to launch off on a flight of fancy, drawing on things I'd no doubt absorbed watching TV dramas and read in books. I wove a tale about a lord of the manor, and a woman from 'below stairs', embellishing a love story set in nineteenth-century England, imagining the world of the piano I was about to inherit, while they sat sipping their tea, listening intently.

Once my characters' journeys had been resolved, some happily, some not, the bad guy given his come-uppance, the wicked woman her just deserts, the heroine (naturally) intact, the sisters broke into applause. My face, warm from the flow of energy, was tingling. I lowered my head and took a mock bow.

'You are better than an old-time radio drama, Maddison, do you know that?' said Ruth, who normally needed to be drawn out to show enthusiasm.

'You are,' her sister echoed, warmly patting my hand. 'Very good, thank you, dear Maddison, that was most satisfying.'

Joan poured the tea, and we proceeded to drink the pot dry. I allowed their praise to nurture me, but as we chattered on, I could feel the excitement of my trip welling up. I ate a lot more cake, then gently broke the news that I was going away.

But even as I spoke, I realised my brain was off onto a new story. This time, one much closer to home, about my own family.

John

London, three days later

If she must come then he would do all in his power to get it over and done with as quickly as possible.

John arrived early at the Moorgate area of the city, umbrella under one arm and a small briefcase in the other. Was there nothing James couldn't do, he wondered, pushing through the doors of Legal and General into the vast modern foyer that was bristling with activity. When James told him that a friend of his had arranged for them to use one of their meeting rooms to settle the Lady Rose business, John had felt a sharp little pang of envy. Once he'd had a book of 'contacts' he could rely on, too, for favours.

'Should impress the life out of her,' said James, in his sometimes awkward but hard-to-dislike manner.

It was still a strange thing how he'd become involved in Hebden's business. John could only put it down to one of those serendipitous moments that defy explanation. At this time of his life, John was finding more inexplicable occurrences cropping up than he was comfortable with. 'Go with the flow,' was an expression his wife had shared with him after a meditation class. 'Try to relax,' she said, rubbing his shoulders. John was doing the best he could, but as far as he could tell, it wasn't going well. He had too much on his mind.

The Australian reminded him of the kind of go-to chap he'd rather hoped he might have been once, at a similar age. But in the end, country life and his family firm's connection to Hebden over several decades had appealed to him more. Also, at the time it would not have been prudent to make such a move, as he had just met Janet, who was a local girl. John still had some city connections, but London was a far cry from his life now. He gazed upwards through vaulted glass so high it seemed to touch the sky. The Australian girl shouldn't have any trouble finding this building right in the heart of Liverpool Street.

He'd chosen to walk the ten minutes from the underground rather than take a cab, using the time to run over the details in his mind for the hundredth time, double-checking with each step that he'd remembered everything and covered all the contingencies. Not that there was any doubt that this Maddison Browne was Lady Rose's great-granddaughter.

James's research made the whole situation clear. Far too clear, leaving John no option but to bring this whole matter to an end, rapidly and forever. He could not, and would not, allow the Hebden family situation to blow out any more than it already had. From his own professional experience, too many family estates wound up like the fiery awakening of a greedy, insatiable dragon. This was the risk he needed to eliminate. Of course, if in the process he managed to wrestle out some personal information about Lady Rose's other descendants, for his own interest, well and good. But she should take the piano and go.

It was clear to him now that Rose's clever daughter, Abigail, had never wanted to be found. She had changed her surname to Rooney, her mother's maiden name, the minute she landed in Australia. And but for the thoroughness of James's team searching all death notices on several continents, not just for the name of Hampton, but for Lady Rose's maiden name as well, this remaining female descendant would never have come to light.

Throughout his own searches, which appeared lightweight by comparison to the Australian's team, John had only ever expected to find a relative so far removed that they barely qualified. Not for one second did he consider the possibility of a great-granddaughter. He thought he knew the story inside out, but he'd never expected to find that she had reinvented herself on the other side of the world. And he'd been startled to discover that her one grandchild, this woman Maddison, had been born a matter of months before her ladyship passed away.

No matter how he tried to mask his reaction, John had been utterly shocked to learn the truth. He had come to believe that there was no more 'female extant', that Crystal would never have to relinquish Rose's piano.

But once James revealed that he'd uncovered an heiress, once the real birth name and place had been established, and the 'broken arm' of the Hampton family revealed as 'alive', for John, there was no feeling of relief. Only an extremely uncomfortable feeling that the revelation raised more questions than it answered. On top of the tightly held family secrets when he took over running the firm from his father, now he had to deal with Abigail's Australian family. Not to mention the question of his own daughter's disappointment.

James, dressed in sharp pinstripes, was coming towards him, waving a pass key. 'The fifth floor,' he called. From his expression, he expected to find John out of his comfort zone in the city, which was true to some extent, but it wasn't the whole story. John wasn't entirely without resources. In fact, he had managed to secure a table at one of the most infamous dining rooms frequented by the legal fraternity, where tall tales of courtroom vi ctories provided the main fare, and which for him, was infinitely more interesting than the plates of solid fare they served up, notwithstanding the fine French and Australian wines drunk as an accompaniment. It would be a nice surprise for the lad, to thank him for his efforts. John planned to stay overnight himself after the dinner. He would not head home until morning, when he should be feeling calm, with all piano business properly taken care of, and the whole matter packed in an archive box, forever.

Again, he thought how impressive it was that James had managed to bring such resources to bear to help him. Not that Crystal said much to him about it. John knew she was not one bit pleased that the piano was not hers. She'd cried when she heard that it would be shipped south and that the rightful heir had been found.

Janet also was miserable. 'Crystal loves it. And I do too. Does it really have to go?' she pleaded.

'I'm afraid it does,' John said, wishing he could say otherwise. 'We'll get her another.'

'That's not the only point, John,' his wife said, 'Crystal feels unhappy because we lied to her. And she feels this piano has been special for her. Couldn't we just find another old piano and ship that off, instead?'

'Help me with this, Janet, please. Tell Crystal that the piano definitely has to go to the rightful owner, and she will have a new one to replace it.'

'If you hadn't been so —'

John could see where this was heading and gently cut in. 'What do you say we visit London together like we used to, once this is over?'

'You mean get a life again?' Janet said, and almost laughed.

His wife had been in an unusual emotional state of late, and the reason for it was obvious enough. Crystal was still talking incessantly about James, and the more she did, the more Janet became irritable. She blamed him for the fact that they were in danger of losing their daughter to a man, about whom they knew virtually nothing, and whose family lived on the other side of the world.

Although James had told John once that he and Crystal were not together, he knew very well that circumstances could change on a turn. What if Crystal decided she wanted to go to Australia, what then? James didn't appear to be someone who'd be willing to settle in a village and take over a family business, from his sharp turnout today. John's heart felt heavy. Hadn't he been the one to say, 'let her fly'? Now the danger was, as Janet had shouted at him the other night, their daughter might fly away altogether.

'Would you like to go up first? Room five-o-one, give yourself a minute to settle. I'll wait here and bring her up if you like?'

James was at his most charming and was doing all he could to be helpful, but John still felt mildly irritated. If this Australian hadn't asked about the piano in the first place, he wouldn't be in this situation. 'I might just do that if you don't mind,' was John's easy response, and the truth of it was he did need a moment to prepare himself.

'Please, the lifts are right there.' James gestured.

John saw an entire wall of flickering lights.

'I'll be up as soon as she gets here.' James grinned. 'I've put my name and number at reception. I'm looking forward to seeing if our romance writer looks anything like the photo on her website.'

Again, John found himself wrong-footed by the younger man. Why hadn't he taken the time to look her up himself? Scowling, he responded, 'Yes, and James, can we just do this as quickly and efficiently as possible, I just want it over with.'

James smiled and handed him a security pass key. 'Yes, sir.'

As he walked over to the lifts, John found his thoughts wandering. Perhaps these two Australians, Maddison Browne and James Carlyle, would fancy each other on sight. And wouldn't that solve a number of his problems? They could even fly back home together. John allowed himself a wry smile as the doors whooshed closed and ferried him swiftly upwards.

John

London, eleven–thirty am

The pair seemed to be sharing a joke as they came through the door.

'John, this is Maddison Browne,' said James, making the introductions with some sense of pride. This was, after all, his own work. 'Maddison, this is John Nettlewood, the solicitor whose family firm has administered the affairs of the Hampton family for generations.'

John, already on his feet, offered a greeting and extended his hand. 'Maddison, delighted to meet you. How was your journey, not too exhausting, I hope?'

'It was a long trip, but comfortable, thank you.'

'Please, take a seat.'

She sat, and James took his place next to her, directly across from John.

She was not at all what he was expecting. He hadn't known what to anticipate, really. But as she had firmly insisted on travelling, despite all of his efforts to dissuade her, he'd perhaps imagined a more bullish style of woman. Someone more accustomed to barging into the affairs of others on some flimsy pretence, clearly out for all they can get. Certainly, he had not counted on this tall, fair-haired woman with a straight nose, and a tannish complexion standing before him. From her photos, Lady Rose had been more of a traditional Irish beauty, with flashing dark eyes and a rounded face. This girl must follow the Hampton side, as her grandmother Abigail did, all blondes and gingers.

'James tells me he can catch up on all kinds of work in the time it takes to fly from London to Brisbane, isn't that right, James?'

'Yes, too true,' James responded promptly, 'we are a nation of travellers.'

'We have to be,' said Maddison, extending a smile that included both of them. 'Australia is a long way from everywhere.'

'Yes, indeed it is, and it's a very long way to come for a piano,' said John, trying to be convivial. 'Do you play?' he ventured, thinking this might explain her insistence on coming to England.

'Not that anyone would like to hear, anyway,' she responded with a laugh. Her voice was warm and smooth, and her accent not as twangy as James's. She was looking at him appraisingly, which made John feel a little uncomfortable.

'I've told Maddison how it has taken a good many people a great deal of trouble to track her down,' James said disarmingly. 'Now she can't wait to discover how we did it, and how she fits into the picture.'

'It's true that I couldn't have been more surprised when I received your letter, John. I imagine you'll be wanting to see this.' She pulled out her passport and pushed it towards him.

'Thank you.' John flicked a few pages, making a show of scrutinising the contents. 'This all appears to be in order.' Then for something more to say he added, 'I see your profession … author. James tells me you write romance books, how interesting.'

He was thinking he should tell her that Lady Rose had tried her hand at a novel once, too, but decided to save this juicy piece for later. If, and only if, the time and circumstances were right. The departure lounge of the airport, for instance, or somewhere similar. Being too friendly at this point was not an option. Then again, if a little snippet here and there would encourage her to tell him about her Australian family, there was no harm in that. She could go back to her life, and he could at last close the estate business once and for all.

'Yes, it can be. But my trip here feels like the real mystery at the moment.' She was smiling into John's eyes, making him even more uncomfortable. 'Hopefully, you can provide the ending for me.'

'I'm not sure I can give you much more information than I've given you already ...' John's heart flickered in panic. 'Well, let's get down to it, shall we,' he said, shuffling his documents, trying to maintain an untroubled expression on his face, when he was feeling anything but calm.

'I've ordered tea,' said James, 'it should be along shortly. Can I take your coat?'

'Thank you, it's lovely and warm in here.'

John noticed her eyes flash at James. He saw James reciprocate as he took her coat to hang it. Were all Australians charming like these two? John only hoped she wouldn't draw James out to say too much.

She spoke first.

'I should explain, John, that my grandmother told everyone she was an orphan, with no living relatives. So, I'm rather curious to hear what you have to tell me.'

'Little wonder you were surprised to hear from us, then.' John noticed James was having difficulty taking his eyes off Maddison.

'Surprise is one word for it,' she laughed, 'bomb shell is more like it. Was Abigail swapped at birth or something, or is that just the romance writer in me?'

When she laughed, John noticed how lovely she was. The tiny dimples in both cheeks and snowy-white teeth made him almost forget his nerves. James seemed struck dumb.

Interpreting his silence as no comment, she continued. 'Let me ask you this. I'm intrigued to know how you found me, and who is

Rose Hampton really? Why do you suppose I haven't heard of her until now?'

She was talking sweetly, but John's sense of unease was rising. Who would come in firing off a whole lot of questions without first hearing his prepared summation?

'Alright, Maddison,' said John, using her name and injecting some authority to his tone. 'Let me see if I can fill in some of the scant detail I know for you.'

He launched off with a brief summary of his family and their professional involvement with Hebden Estate and the Hampton family. But the more he spoke, John could hear that slightly self-deprecating manner he saved for tricky situations starting to creep in.

She sat quietly watching, until he'd finished.

'Do you have any questions?'

'Not so far,' she replied evenly.

'James, would you like to take it from here?'

Handing over to James enabled John to sit back and observe her for a moment, and gather his thoughts. The girl had unnerved him asking all of her questions.

James picked up the sequence of events, but when he got to the part about Abigail's runaway romance and her apparent death in childbirth, John saw her face change.

He interjected quickly, 'But let us tell Maddison more about Lady Rose and the piano, James. Surely that's more relevant here?'

'So, there was a child?' Maddison raised her palm. 'One moment, John, I'm quite interested to hear about my grandmother and this child you mention, James.' She reached over and dragged her bag across. John watched her extract what appeared to be a small black-and-white photograph. 'This is my grandmother, Abigail Browne, with her children, my mother and my uncle.' She pushed it across the table to him.

'Thank you.' John couldn't help himself and picked up the photo. Staring at it, he sensed where she was heading, and it was not a good place.

'What's most interesting to me,' he heard Maddison say to James, 'is what happened to my grandmother's baby? Was that my mother? The time sequence doesn't seem right. Do I have another uncle or aunt?'

Suddenly, noticing his scrutiny and before James had a chance to respond, she asked, 'Any resemblance to the rest of the Hampton family, John?'

John felt under siege; he had seen the family resemblance the moment she entered the room. But her questioning was incessant. Were all romance writers like this? Barbara Cartland was the only one he'd ever heard of (he vaguely remembered a woman swathed in pink and makeup as thick as house paint), but she was a Dame. Surely, she would not be so direct, or persistent.

'I think Abigail followed her father in looks,' John responded, restraining the impulse to say more. His eyes again flicked down to the picture of Abigail's face. How serious she seemed.

Thankfully, James returned to the conversation with a convincing response to her question about the child. 'The child apparently died at birth, I'm afraid. Unfortunately, we couldn't find a record for the death. Mind you, record keeping from those days was often sketchy.'

'Fascinating,' said Maddison, her eyes moving back and forth between the two of them.

John thought he would have to buy champagne for James later, so grateful was he to hear him talk so persuasively.

'And given it was John whose family has managed the Hamptons' affairs for so many years,' James added, 'he has no record of any baby, and was never asked to explore the matter.'

Her face was solemn. John hoped she was convinced.

Then, as if offering proof of his argument, James produced a facsimile copy of Maddison's grandmother's death certificate.

John scrutinised her more deeply.

He'd seen it right away, of course, the pendant around her neck on a fine silver chain. Unmistakable. The Hampton family symbol, similar to a clover leaf, was everywhere at the manor house, even carved into the wooden trimmings. Now, here it was set in silver and hanging so prettily on Maddison's green floral dress. That very same pendant once would have hung around Rose's neck, and then her daughter, Abigail's. A dark premonition came over him as he studied her. No matter what John had hoped for, his feeling now was that Maddison Browne was not going to let the family secrets rest.

A tea lady carrying a tray rattling with cups, saucers and biscuits pushed her way into their meeting room. John was thankful for the interruption as it allowed them to sip tea and chat for a moment about things other than the reason for their meeting.

'Would you like to see what the piano looks like?' John asked, finally placing his teacup down. He reached for the photograph he'd taken himself before he left home.

'It's beautiful,' she murmured with her eyes glued to the image.

John watched her trace the shape of the piano with her finger. She was an attractive woman, the way she sat straight up and moved her hands so gracefully. The sound of her voice was as warm and clear as a chime. Certainly, his first impression was that Rose's great-granddaughter was as impressive as his memory of Rose herself, not someone to mess with. Abigail too had been called 'strong-minded' by his grandfather, who said he knew her well.

'Would my grandmother have played this piano as a child?' Maddison asked him, with a wistful smile and more than a hint of sadness in her eyes.

John nodded while she studied the photo.

'I didn't know her well. Not enough to consciously remember too much, anyway. She died before I was old enough. But to the best of my knowledge …' her voice trailed off.

John noticed an odd expression pass across her face, and seized the moment to steer the conversation. 'Could I also show you this one?' He produced a different photo from his folder. 'Lady Rose, your great-grandmother, at her piano, which of course is now your piano,' he said.

She took the photo to inspect it more closely. 'Well, it's easy to see from this that I don't have the family face.' She crinkled her nose. 'We couldn't be more different, really.' Her eyes searched his, but John looked away, fearing she might read his mind, or that he might be coaxed to say the wrong thing if he allowed himself to gaze too deeply into those sea-blue eyes.

'As I said earlier, your grandmother, Abigail, took after the Hampton line in her looks. Rose was of Irish descent, with dark hair,' he said, using a matter-of-fact tone.

'Pity those genes haven't come down the line to me, isn't it?' she said, with quiet amusement in her eyes.

'You mentioned you don't play, but you never know, down the track you may consider taking some lessons,' said John, aware he was trying to draw out her real reason for coming. If it wasn't for having a piano to play, then why?

'You are about the fourth person to say that to me lately, John. I did play a little when I was young, so perhaps I should think about it again.'

'Alright, now, given that everything's in order, might I propose what I think would be the best way to tackle things from here? I should arrange, I think, express expedition of the piano, while you perhaps enjoy a few days of holiday in London.' John used every single facial muscle to squeeze out what he hoped was a friendly smile.

'Thanks, but what I'd really like …' her eyes fluttered, 'is to see the piano with my own eyes first. Is that possible?'

'Yes, I'm sure that can be arranged,' said James, quick as a flash, then, glancing at John added, 'it's not too far away, actually, just down in Cobham.'

John's mind was racing forward to breaking this news at home. He hadn't imagined for one second that she would ask to see the actual instrument before he shipped it off.

'Excellent, I hope that it won't be too difficult for you to organise. If it's in storage, which I imagine it is, there are cranes and equipment these days.'

James was silent, but he'd started flicking his pen, which annoyed John even further.

Click, clickety-click.

'I'd like to see it for myself,' she said, 'because it might be too fragile to move.'

Click, clickety-click.

'It may be, depending on the condition, best to leave it here.' Her eyes moved between them. 'I mean, I wouldn't want to wreck a historic instrument. I think it might be best to get someone to look over it to check it's still playable.'

'Of course,' said James, placing the pen down to John's internal relief.

'I wouldn't want it to disintegrate on the journey. What do you think, John? When you last saw it, was it in a good enough condition to withstand the journey in a shipping container all the way to Melbourne?'

'Yes, perfectly playable, the last time I saw it. I'm sure, with the right packaging … But by all means, call in an expert. Get a second opinion. I certainly wouldn't want you to be suing me for damages.'

Seeing the look of panic on James's face, John made a quick decision. 'You see, Maddison, the reason I can make a statement like that with such confidence is, the last time I saw your piano ... was actually this very morning.'

Her smile showed concern. 'I hope it didn't take you too far out of your way.'

James was following the conversation like a spectator sport, his eyes moving back and forth, from one to the other.

'No, not at all. Actually, the piano is currently located in the drawing room of my home.'

Her back straightened. 'You moved the piano into your own home?' She stared disbelievingly. 'Just so I could see it?'

'Well, probably above the call of duty, isn't it? But as I wasn't sure if I would ever be able to track you down, rather than risk any careless handling in commercial storage, I kept this beautiful instrument in my own drawing room to protect it, until the rightful owner, you, could be found.'

'And is your home close to Hebden Manor?'

'Yes, it is, in Cobham, not far. But Hebden Manor has, as you will know, become a boarding school.'

'Yes ... well, I don't know what to say, except thank you. For keeping it safe all this time. I can see my great-grandmother was a good judge of character entrusting her affairs to your family, John.'

John couldn't risk looking at James. But if he had dared, he would have seen admiration for the way he had just successfully manoeuvred around a tricky and potentially dangerous situation.

Satisfied that he had settled something at least, John clapped his hands together. 'Very well, all that remains now is to organise a suitable day. Perhaps afternoon tea at my home? I will have to check a few details first, of course. James, you might like to join us.'

James agreed with a quick nod.

'After that I'll get some experts in to check it over for you, then we can make the final arrangements for shipping.'

'Perfect,' said Maddison, with a smile so lovely that John forgot she'd almost tripped him up. He began gathering his papers, keen to bring the meeting to a close as quickly as possible before he got into any more hot water.

'If you don't mind, before we finish up.'

'Something else?' John cleared his throat. 'Yes of course, please go ahead.'

'I'm sorry to be digging into this,' Maddison said, 'but I find it hard to grasp how the daughter of an aristocratic family could just go missing for the rest of her life without the family looking for her.'

A moment of intense anguish took hold of him. After all these years, for the first time John wished he had never taken over the family firm and become the key holder to the vault of secrets. More than that, he wished he had never kept what he knew from his wife. Unless he could make this situation go away, or resolve it in some way, he could find himself in such deep water he might drown.

'Unfortunately,' he said, 'that is all well before my time.'

'I understand, but she came from a prominent, wealthy family, yet she told everyone in Australia that she was an orphan. Until you contacted me, that was one of the few stable facts of my life.' She flicked her palms to the ceiling. 'Now my imagination is running wild with possibilities of what could have forced her to cut herself off so completely.' Setting eyes firmly on him, she added, 'Your family knows more about the Hamptons than anyone, John. What do you think happened?'

John heard himself saying firmly, 'I agree, it does seem unusual. But just because our firm handled the family's legal matters doesn't mean we would, of necessity, have known about internal family matters.

Upstairs, downstairs, I'm afraid. All I can say is that the accepted story was that Lady Abigail died in childbirth.'

'But wouldn't your firm have been called in to act on something as serious as the Hamptons' daughter dying or the possible adoption of her baby that may have survived?'

'A perfectly reasonable point, but sadly, it all seemed to have happened around the time my grandfather was starting his practice in Cobham, and it would seem that we were not, how can I put it, "in the loop", on those particular matters.'

He saw doubt written all over her face. He hadn't convinced her.

His intention had been to keep the conversation running along about the piano. Tell her about famous names who had played her magnificent instrument, enchant her with a few tales. That kind of approach always worked for him whenever some matter he didn't wish to discuss came up. He was skilled at it. Create a decoy, use some delightful story, and in his experience, most people would run off down the path, happy to chase moonbeams.

Maddison went on. 'Something serious must have happened in that family for her parents to declare their daughter dead, don't you think, John? Luckily for me, of course, or perhaps I wouldn't exist, but I am absolutely fascinated to know what it was.'

Desperation seized him. 'Yes, Maddison, but I'm not sure we can help you with that. "Ours is to reason, not to wonder",' he trotted out, cringing inwardly at his desecration of Lord Tennyson's famous line, 'Theirs not to reason why, theirs but to do and die.' If she kept up this approach to inheriting the piano, it was exactly what might happen to him. John couldn't risk looking at James.

Also weighing heavily on his mind was why she hadn't asked about any other property or monies due to her. Surely, as the great-granddaughter to an old English estate she must have considered that she might be entitled to more than the piano? But the question hadn't come. At least not yet.

The relief John felt when Maddison excused herself was palpable.

'I can't think of too many who wouldn't have asked about further inheritance,' James said softly, leaning over the table. 'If I'd just found out that I was descended directly from an English earl's family, I think it'd be one of the first things I'd ask.'

John feared James was reading his mind. 'Yes, I know what you mean.' He nodded. In his long career, he'd not seen many cases where it wasn't the first question posed by family members.

Maddison Browne had a number of successful books to her name, according to James's research. Perhaps that meant she was quite well set up and had no big need for money. But for him, that still wasn't reason enough. Even the wealthiest of his clients would have asked. *Especially the wealthy*, he thought.

'She said she came to find out about the missing parts of her grandmother's life. Maybe she's telling us the truth?' suggested James.

'Maybe that is all there is to it,' said John without conviction. 'My guess, though,' he spoke quickly, catching sight of Maddison through the glass petition heading back towards them, 'is that when she manages to put some more pieces together, she'll be back to us with that specific question.'

Maddison

London, next day

After a wakeful night, I decided that fresh air and getting out of the hotel was best to walk off the jet lag and clarify my thoughts.

There'd been a heavy downpour overnight, and I noticed through my window that light rain was still falling. I took the stairs down to street level and stepped out. The smell of wet diesel, thick air and the deafening noise of a large city roaring in my ears was an assault to the senses for one accustomed to hearing birdsong first thing. But, energised by the change of scene, I took a deep breath, pushed up my umbrella and set off.

I hadn't made it far, just two blocks along, when I found myself standing outside one of those music mega stores. I stopped and stepped up to the window. It was like Christmas inside, all bright and intriguing. Walls lined with guitars of all types and makes, glossy pianos shimmered under hot spotlights, and contours of golden brass glinting gold dangled tantalisingly from the ceiling. A rise constructed in the middle of the floor led upwards like a stairway to heaven guided my eye to a gaggle of drumkits and percussion at the summit that looked like a huge, unusually decorated wedding cake. I felt the pull of this festive scene drawing me in, and not just because it looked so magical, but because it had given me an idea.

I spent a half-hour in the store until I found the stairs up to somewhere quieter, and eventually located what I was looking for.

I was feeling quite pleased when I finally took to the streets again, with my new purchase securely tucked in my bag.

The meeting with John Nettlewood had ended abruptly yesterday, and still I was none the wiser about my grandmother. At best all I had was a flimsy concession. Only at the last minute had he promised to do what he could to help, while at the same time he'd cautioned, 'I wouldn't be too hopeful, Maddison, it was all a very long time ago.'

Replaying some of his reactions this morning had left me with a feeling that he was holding out. I sensed strongly that he knew more but didn't want to share it with me. Yet I couldn't seem to come up with any reason why he would not want to tell me. It was my family, after all.

His face had drained to ghostly when I said, 'My main purpose for coming here is to find the truth about my grandmother and how she ended up in Melbourne.'

His reaction surprised me because it wasn't as if I hadn't made that clear in my earlier emails.

James hadn't been comfortable, either when I said, 'Knowing what happened to Abigail, might help me come to terms with a few things.'

'Fill in some gaps?' he'd queried.

'Exactly.' I'd looked into his eyes before adding, 'And those gaps are getting bigger every day. It wasn't only the piano I came for,' I repeated, 'but for the right we all have to know where we're from. I want to know who my family is.'

'With the best will, Maddison,' James had said, 'I'm not sure we can help with your grandmother's story … and if I may say, who isn't left with unanswerable questions about their parents or even their grandparents for that matter?'

He was right in one way, I supposed. But my cheeks had been flaming with frustration when I suggested I might visit Hebden Manor to at least see where my grandmother was born.

At this point, John had begun stuffing all the paperwork into his satchel with urgency.

'Visit the manor, yes of course you must. Forgive me, I should have suggested it sooner. It was, and still is, a magnificent building.'

I still couldn't come up with anything reasonable to explain his unusual reactions. It was straightforward enough, surely. Once he'd had proof of my identity, it should have been a relief for him to close his last Hebden Manor file, after all this time.

With the noise of cars swishing by on wet roads in my ears, I recapped one incident with amusement. John's tortuous enquiry about my books.

'Do you think I would enjoy them?' he'd asked in the lift on the way out.

I giggled to myself now, and huddled further under my umbrella.

'Probably not; they are classed as romantic fiction,' I'd said, 'which doesn't strike me as your preferred genre. But the women in your family may like them.' I'd left it at that and watched him try to work out if I'd just gently insulted him.

James's amused expression and raised eyebrows showed that he at least possessed a sense of humour.

I had hoped that one of them was going to suggest we get a drink at the Globe or one of those other cosy little pubs I'd seen in the area. But buttoned-up John couldn't wait to get away, and James, his attractive sidekick, was not far behind.

I'd fought the urge to turn back as we walked off in our different directions. But once I was sure they couldn't see me, I did sneak a glimpse. With light rain softly bathing the streets, I'd felt a little empty and unsure of what to do next as I watched their progress along the wet grey footpath. Two figures barely distinguishable from all the others in dark clothes huddled under umbrellas, until a black cab pulled alongside, they got in and disappeared into the traffic.

Since then, I'd been thinking about James and wondering if I would get an opportunity to find out who he was.

Back at the hotel, all thawed out and warm, my mind returned to different scenarios of my own to possibly explain my grandmother's actions. Did she run away from England? Who or what was she fleeing from? Why did Rose never try to find Abigail? Didn't she even care about her only daughter? And if so, why not?

As different theories circled in my head like a recording on high rotation, niggling in the pit of my stomach were thoughts of one person, the one I believed to be absolutely key to the situation. John Nettlewood. I may not have understood the full extent of his involvement yet, and getting him to reveal the truth was not going to be easy. But meeting him yesterday had only strengthened my resolve to get to the bottom of this mystery.

Maddison

London, one week later

Having to talk about my books with publicists was stimulating. So much, that some of my old self seemed to return with each conversation. Steadily and incrementally, the way small amounts of air filled a balloon, allowing it to lift off and float freely away, the me who could write, charm and match it in company, was there. The energy of the city itself, together with a growing urgency to find my grandmother's story and untangle these newfound family threads, seemed to have woken me up.

I'd been out lunching with different people, and spent a couple of days with a lovely man called Peter, who ran a small chain of independent bookshops. It was fun walking the streets, checking on his competitor's stock and prices and trading stories over a bite to eat. He was charming. Plus, the way he looked at me made me feel desirable again, which after my recent track record with romance, was just what I needed. He told me that his business partner sister, Katie, a brunette I met briefly, loved my books. It was refreshing to talk with someone who could understand what a writer actually did.

The last of my 'dates with mates' arranged by Amy had left me with a fear that there would never be anyone to 'get' me, or heaven forbid, love me in the way I wanted to be loved.

Her husband had a friend, Amy said. 'He works in IT. His name is Victor.'

As it turned out, Victor of the too-much aftershave had been an overconfident, insensitive clod whose company made me panic that I may never even try to date again. I should have run for cover when I heard the first words he uttered on my front doorstep.

'You are the first romance writer I've met, and you're not at all what I was expecting.'

'Really? What were you expecting?'

'You're tall for starters.'

Please. It was unbearable. He hadn't read a book since high school. We had uncomfortable conversation all night long, with me floundering like a fish out of water, while he appeared to think there was nothing wrong. It even made me wonder if Amy was playing a trick and any minute she would call to say it was all a set-up.

At least Peter of the bookshops just asked me why I chose to write romance, and when I said I had just started and couldn't stop, he laughed out loud. I thought from the way he kissed me goodnight he might have been hoping for more, and maybe if James hadn't sent a text message asking me to call, I might have succumbed to the bookseller's charms and agreed to meet him again.

Hearing James on the end of the phone evoked a strange mix of reactions. Surprise, apprehension, and an unexpected quickening of my heartbeat.

'Maddison, thanks for calling back. Are you still in London? We've been waiting to hear from you.'

'Of course I'm still in London. Where did you think I'd be? On the first flight back to Australia?'

'No, I didn't pick you as a person who would cut and run. Perhaps scouring the countryside of Kent for long-lost relatives …'

'If I hadn't had so much to do. But as of now, that's exactly my plan.' I thought he was right on track with his guess.

For a minute, I felt James might be going to ask me out on a date. Instead, his voice went straight to business.

'Excellent. John is wanting to settle the matter of the piano, so the sooner we can arrange for you to see it the better, and perhaps I can point you to some interesting places to start your research.'

'Thanks, later this week would be great, if that's suitable? I have a couple of things left to do here in London.'

'I'm sure that'll be fine.' He paused. 'There was something else.'

'Yes?'

His tone altered. 'I was wondering … if you had time to join me for coffee tomorrow morning? Is that possible?'

I was right. 'Oh, yes, I'd like that,' I said.

'Good. I'll text an address. If all else fails, we can exchange Aussie yarns.'

'I have a few that will curl your hair,' I said.

I heard him chuckle quietly, then answer, 'and I thought I'd have to eat my bread crusts for that.'

'Seriously though, I might have a suggestion on your search for ancestors. And I'd love to hear what you've been up to in London.' His voice sounded genuine.

'Fine with me,' I said. 'I'm more than a little curious to know about the Hamptons.'

'Lady Rose and the earl,' I heard his playful upper-class accent, 'the Lady Abigail and her mysterious disappearance,' his accent reverted, 'it all sounds a bit Miss Marple, doesn't it?'

I laughed with him. 'Yes, it does a bit.' A picture of Ruth and Joan flashed into my mind. They both loved Jane Marple.

I hung up, and found myself after a minute or two still smiling. I had no way of knowing what this call meant, if anything at all. He was probably just following up for John, but I had a feeling it was going to be interesting to meet James Carlyle alone.

On the table next to the phone, a 'Literary Guide to Kent' brochure that I'd grabbed off a counter on one of my bookstore visits caught my eye again. I'd leafed through it several times already and calculated that with all the towns and villages situated so close together, it wasn't going to be difficult to find my way around. In fact, I could hardly wait to get started.

The notion that I really did belong to an aristocratic family from the southern coast of England was finally sinking in. I figured James, too, after all that research to find me, had to know more about the Hampton family than what I'd heard so far. And without the former estate solicitor to shut him down, I rated my chances of extracting fresh information as pretty good. It was a long while since anyone had made my heart beat faster. So, there was no harm chatting with him over coffee. No harm at all.

He was sitting at a small table in the corner, and stood up as I approached. He hadn't slicked his hair, so there were strands of it sticking up like he'd just gone three rounds with a mini-cyclone.

'I hardly recognised you for a minute,' I said, slightly flustered as I stood before him. He was relaxed in jeans that defined his hips, and an open-necked shirt. Not as young as I'd first thought, either. He extended his free hand to shake mine.

'The old "bag of fruit" is a bit of a disguise.' He laughed easily. 'Can I get you one of these?' He pointed to what looked like the crumbs of a chocolate muffin, and sat down.

'Thanks, but I've sworn off them,' I said, 'A strong coffee would be great, though.'

'Not very well mannered of me to start before you arrived, was it? Forgive me. I was starving.' He grinned disarmingly. 'I don't know about you, but when I'm studying hard I get hungry. Late nights, early mornings in front of a screen. You'd know about that.'

'Long hours in front of a screen, absolutely. But I didn't realise you were still studying.'

'Last weeks of a Master of Laws.' He looked straight into my eyes. 'I've been up to my neck writing papers, trying to not ask for an extension on every topic. That's why I haven't been in touch before now.'

'Well, I certainly know about deadlines, they're tough, but I'm sure you'll get there.'

'I wish I had your confidence,' he responded, 'but at least this is the end of it.'

'Is that relief I hear?'

'I s'pose so, yes. It's why I left a perfectly good firm in Brisbane.'

'I promise I won't keep you for long, then.'

'Trust me, you are a very welcome distraction.' He consulted the menu. 'Now, would you like eggs or cake with your coffee?'

A waitress appeared at the table. I wasn't hungry, but I scanned the menu and ordered something (a bit healthy), acutely aware that his eyes were on me. The atmosphere between us was laidback, yet tension was humming through the air like an expectant audience waiting for the curtain to rise. The waitress departed, her ponytail swinging from left to right. Watching her stride off, I was visited by a memory of my own hair at a similar age, long and caught back like that, same colour, similar jaunty step and feeling of freedom. The memory of it made me smile inwardly, although I had no inclination to return to that age.

His first question startled me. 'Okay, I've read the website version, but what's the real Maddison Browne story?'

'My story,' I repeated stupidly, which even to me sounded pathetic. Where was the author on a publicity tour when you needed her?

'Yes, you don't expect me to believe just that, do you?'

'Yes,' I said. 'Why not, it's pretty close.'

'What about the part about working in legal chambers?'

'Yes, that part is completely true.'

'Go on,' he said.

I wasn't usually forthcoming about my private life, but I heard myself telling him how, in fact, I had started writing romance fiction at the same time I was employed as a typist in a barrister's chambers. 'I'd wanted to write crime,' I said, 'but my stories always came out as romance.'

James seemed highly amused by this. 'I've met more than a few barristers here and back in Brisbane, and I can't think of one who'd inspire anyone to think of romance.'

'Yes, I know what you mean.' I grinned. 'I must have had a different reaction … Anyway, I kept my writing life apart from my working life back then.'

'You appear to have come out unscathed,' he said, his eyes still smiling.

We were suddenly chatting happily, and by the time food and coffee arrived, he was telling me how he was a Queenslander and going home soon for his mother's sixtieth birthday party. 'We're a pretty average lot. My father is a marine engineer. That's a fancy title for someone who fixes boat engines. My big sister, Zoe, runs a homewares shop in Sydney, and I'm here trying to finish this Master of Laws.'

I watched as he comfortably devoured avocado and poached eggs on toast, and washed the whole lot down with a strong coffee. I forked in a few mouthfuls of a sweet apple strudel with cream (healthy enough) just to be sociable.

'You won't need to eat for a week after that.'

'Wouldn't bet on it.' He sat back, carefully placing his cutlery on the plate. 'Have you thought about how long you're planning to stay over here?'

I answered as best I could. 'Not sure, a few weeks maybe. That's the thing about my job, I can do it anywhere.'

'I guess you can,' he said. 'Not stuck in an office all day. I'm envious.'

'Maybe. Sometimes I think the regular hours in an office would be great. I guess that's a grass-is-greener argument isn't it? Anyway, I haven't locked in a firm return date. Sometimes research takes longer than you think.'

'Oh, you're researching a new book?'

'I'm always researching a new book,' I said, thinking he wouldn't know what I meant.

'How about you? Aside from going back for your mum's birthday, are you staying in Brisbane?' Even to my ears this sounded like a getting-to-know-you conversation.

He shrugged. 'Not sure. I actually came here to have a crack at the big pond of Europe, you know?' His eyes lifted to see if I understood. 'Or rather, I should say I came here to try to land a job in one of the big internationals, which when you come from the wrong side of the tracks ...'

I must have looked surprised, because he added, 'No line of blue blood in my family tree like yours.'

'Not anything I knew about, either, until a couple of weeks ago,' I said. 'But surely blood doesn't count anymore. Isn't it talent over connections?'

'I wouldn't be too sure about that in the stodgy world of law. No denying you need a tidy score of marks, but at the high end, contacts can make all the difference. If it comes down to a choice between some chap who's socially connected and me …'

'You want it badly, then?'

'Well, I'm giving it my best shot, let's say, but, and this will sound contradictory, a big part of me misses home. So, maybe not badly enough.'

'You look pretty comfortable from where I'm sitting,' I said.

'Appearances can be deceiving.'

'Yes, but what do you miss exactly?' I asked, genuinely curious.

He paused. 'The bush, actually.' His eyes were casually delving into mine to see if I understood.

'I get that, I live on a mountain.'

'Yes, so you do.'

It felt strange to hear him acknowledge where I lived. *Don't be silly*, I told myself, *of course, he knows that. He's the one who found you hidden in piles of public records.*

He kept talking, oblivious to my whirling emotions, and I thought how pleasant his voice was. James had acquired a slight English accent for sure, but he'd hadn't lost all of his antipodean twang with the distorted and nasal vowels so familiar to my ear.

'I'm a serious hiker, you know, and even with this beautiful countryside,' he waved his arm in a circle, as if to encompass the entire scope of England and the surrounding countries, 'no matter how beautiful it is, I do get homesick for our own scrubby old bushland. Some days, I'd do anything to hear a magpie carolling. Crazy, isn't it?'

Our eyes met briefly.

'Now, what else can I tell you?'

I wasn't sure what he meant exactly. 'You mentioned some advice on where to start to find my family history?'

'So I did.' His forehead creased in thought, as if trying to remember what he'd said. 'If I were you, I'd start in a town called Strood.' He paused, scanning my face for some recognition. 'Have you heard of it?'

'No, never.'

'That's where you'll find a place called the Medway Archive. They're specialists in this sort of family history. It's not far from Cobham, so given you are going down to see the piano anyway ...' His eyes had a disconcerting habit of catching mine. 'I'm sure you'll find plenty to interest you there.'

'Can anyone just show up and request to see any relevant documents?' I asked, aware that all this eye gazing was having an effect on my concentration.

'Not sure, but you aren't just anyone, are you? In that area, a Hampton is a Hampton.'

Of course, he was right. I was a Hampton even if I had only just discovered it myself. But still, the same jolt of recognition surprised me every time I registered fully that I had an English family connection.

'A call beforehand never hurts,' he added. 'I mean, it might give someone time to prepare for you. Same goes for the piano.'

'I can't wait to get started,' I said enthusiastically. 'Especially now I know where to begin looking.'

'I could ask if Crystal is available to show you around if you like? She has more local knowledge than I do,' said James.

'Sorry, who is Crystal?'

'Oh, Crystal Nettlewood is a friend.' He smiled bashfully. 'She's John's daughter, that's how I came to meet him. We met at university a little while ago.'

His face flushed, and I didn't know if it was the eggs, the sugar burn, or something else.

'That's how I could help him find you in the first place,' he said.

My own face felt warm. *He has a girlfriend, you idiot.*

'I see.'

'What do you see?'

'I had a feeling there was more between you and John than a purely professional relationship.'

His face changed. 'It's not what you think,' he said quickly.

But I was off and running. 'I was going to ask you about John, but that won't be appropriate anymore,' I said a little too sharply.

'Ask away,' he said. 'What would you like to know?'

'No, it's fine, thanks. I'm glad you could help John track me down,' I said, covering my initial reaction.

'So am I,' he said.

We exchanged smiles and silence reigned for an awkward moment. 'Well, this has been lovely, James. Now I must let you get back to your studies.' I gathered my bag to leave.

'There is just one more thing before you go,' said James. 'And this is a bit of a heads-up to get you started.'

I paused, my radar on full alert. *Let me guess. Crystal isn't really your girlfriend?* But I kept that to myself and waited to hear what he had to say.

'I don't think we mentioned the other day that your great-grandmother, Rose, was Australian.'

'Was she?' I was shocked at the change of topic and the new piece of intelligence about the Hamptons. 'You didn't say where she was from earlier. You just said she was a piano teacher.'

'Yes, she was that, too,' said James. 'But she came from a country town called Beechworth, in Victoria. Do you know it?'

I was suddenly annoyed at the way James and his cohort, Nettlewood, were doling out facts to me in dribs and drabs, rather than giving me all the information up front.

I nodded. 'Yes, I've probably driven through there sometime.' My voice sounded frosty now, but I didn't care. 'I can see the sooner I get to this magical place of family records, the better.'

I remembered that I hadn't paid my bill and dived into my bag.

He waved me away. 'No, this is on me, my pleasure.'

'Alright, thank you, and for the archive address, too.' I was as polite as I could be.

'I'd like to hear more about your writing next time,' he said warmly as I rose to my feet.

I could see he was trying to recapture the easy banter of earlier, but my defences were on high alert. Another fake romance was exactly what I didn't need in my life.

He got to his feet and offered me a handshake. 'Can I tell John that you'll call about the piano?'

'Yes of course,' I said, proffering my fingertips. 'You can tell John what you like. But I did say I'd be in touch just as soon as I finished my appointments here.'

I could hear my girlfriends saying, 'Maddi, are you in a mood or what?'

'See you later, then?' he said, trying to catch my eye again.

I nodded and slung my bag over my shoulder. I walked through the door onto the footpath, feeling cross at myself. I could still feel his eyes on my back.

John

Cobham, Kent

'She's coming here? To our home? And you want me to throw a tea party for her?' Janet spoke sharply, and turned to face him.

John touched her arm, gently. 'Yes, I know it's not convenient, darling, but I'm sure it will be fine.'

'Not convenient,' she gasped.

'We have to do something for her, you know that.'

'Yes, but how did it become entertaining her in our own living room?'

'I just didn't expect she would want to see the piano before I ship it off, that's all. I thought the photograph would do. I couldn't lie when she asked me directly where the piano was. Not in front of James …' He trailed off, sounding lame even to his own ears. The truth was that Maddison's request had caught him completely off guard, and he didn't want to admit that. And the part about not wanting to lie in front of James was true.

'Obviously, not to James or her you couldn't, a member of the hallowed Hampton family,' came his wife's stinging reply, 'yet you've been perfectly happy to lie to me for years. And don't talk to me about James, I don't care what he thinks.'

'You know very well it's not like that,' he said softly.

'What is it like, then?' she said, frowning. 'This business of Rose Hampton and her wretched piano has gone far enough, John. It started out as some mad frolic of yours and now it's become utterly ludicrous. Our daughter might go to live on the other side of the world and we'll be lucky to ever see her again. All because you couldn't leave it alone.' He watched the rims of her eyes become red and hoped she wasn't going to cry.

John couldn't bring himself to restate that James and Crystal meeting had nothing whatsoever to do with him, and even if James should be the one to stop Crystal's revolving door of boyfriends, where they settled, or if they would ever raise a family, was at this stage all conjecture. His daughter hadn't managed to stay interested in any of her young men for very long. John seriously doubted James was going to be the one to change that. For goodness sake, James had practically told him that he and Crystal were just friends. But in the face of his wife's growing anger, he kept his own counsel. Experience had taught him that silence was the best way to handle Janet when she was in this fragile mood.

The next evening, motoring home after an appointment in a nearby village, John was still mulling over his wife's reaction to the whole situation and his forthcoming meeting with Maddison. His mind was working overtime on how to handle his wife, and how to deal with this inquisitive Australian woman whose lively intelligence had impressed and frightened him in equal measures.

No sign of her yet. Not a peep. After meeting her in London, he'd expected to hear right away about when she planned to visit. Where was she? Maybe he should get James to contact her. Maybe she'd changed her mind and gone back to Australia. Maybe he should insist that he just ship off the piano and be done with it. John almost laughed at the desperation of his own thoughts. He knew she wasn't going to change her mind. Just as he knew he wouldn't, if their positions were reversed.

Maddison had told them that her grandmother had devoted herself to the welfare of orphans. Knowing the reason for her disappearance was one thing, but to learn that Abigail had lived on the other side of the world and dedicated a large part of her life to children without parents was a very sad thought. It didn't take much divining for him to understand that alone in a faraway place with a new name and a new life, she must have felt terribly lonely. She would have identified with those children who'd been lost or abandoned by their parents. How brave she was. Especially as, at the time Abigail had sailed for Australia, she would have been about the same age as Crystal was now. Starting a new life without a soul in the world to ask for help. The mere thought of it pained his heart.

Beyond contacting the current Rose's elderly surviving son, Gerard (the earl), to inform him that a great-niece had arrived in England, John had been waiting, and worrying. Since the sale of the manor, Abigail's only brother, as sole heir to the proceeds of the Hebden Estate, had become a wealthy man in real terms. Living what could only be described as 'the good life' in the Bahamas, he visited London only for bits of business or when required to fulfil his obligations as a member of the House of Lords. Until now, he'd been oblivious to John's search for the right owner of his mother's piano. With the arrival of an heir who had some entitlement to the whole estate, Gerard would certainly not thank John for his zealotry.

John imagined Gerard exploding: 'What the devil have you done, man?'

He had no answer for the earl (or anyone else for that matter, except himself and who would understand that?). Unfortunately, Maddison showing up in their lives after all this time wasn't great news for anyone. What would he do if she decided to take legal action over the estate? What if, beneath that lovely smile, lay a calculating minx? John shuddered.

Gerard had loved the change of country and lifestyle, and it agreed with him. He wouldn't want that interrupted. The last time John had caught up with him, Gerard had been sun-tanned and walking without a cane, in his nineties. John remembered thinking, if that was what a life of warm-water swimming and sunshine could do for someone in advanced years, maybe he and Janet should consider a move to the Bahamas. Immediately.

An intense feeling of looming disaster settled on him as he motored across the flat countryside. Sometimes, driving alone in his car gave him too much time to think. To relieve his tensions, John listened to music. Remembering this, he leaned forward to switch on the radio. But, hearing 'Phantom of the Opera' roaring through the speakers, he slammed it off, impatiently.

There were enough phantoms in his own family, already. He settled back, preferring instead the reliable purr of his Rover.

The landscape with its grey canopy of cloud was comfortingly familiar to him. 'The conservation zone' of Cobham, John knew like the back of his hand. To behold the rural feet of old-world Cobham, the ancient heart of the town where Granite and York stone houses had stood for centuries, always warmed his heart. No big neoclassical mansions here, no celebrity residents with personalised number plates, no flashy foreign cars of the sort found parked in driveways of newly constructed, outlying estates, either. John had seen his beloved Cobham described as 'The Beverly Hills of Britain' in a newspaper, recently. And recalling that, he drove on for the remainder of the journey staring desultorily out of the car window.

Usually, John loved this drive. For the small amount of time it took to motor from his office to home, past solid homes forged in previous centuries, he could pretend not much had changed.

But of course, it had. And it wasn't just the boats of all sizes arriving from faraway places, packed with people wanting to resettle in this part of the world. That was nothing new. Not really. It was John's own personal circumstances that changed irreversibly, on the day he'd become privy to secrets buried in the family files of Nettlewood and Son. He'd been forced to confront undeniable truths about his family. And this had been his burden to bear, ever since.

Most of the reason he'd kept Janet from knowing the truth was that he loved his wife. He hadn't wanted her to feel as betrayed as he did. Although, if he were really truthful, what worried him most was a fear that his wife might think less of him if she ever came to know the whole story. She might not believe in him anymore. And anything that diminished him in her eyes was too unbearable for John to contemplate.

He turned into the familiar cobbled driveway, and the first thing he noticed was that Janet's car was not parked in the usual spot.

John let himself into the house, steeling himself for whatever mood Janet might be in today. She had been unusually preoccupied lately.

This past week, whenever he entered the room, he'd found her on the phone to Crystal or measuring for new furniture. Yesterday, she'd been in a frenzy of spring cleaning, and it wasn't even spring. This morning he even thought he had heard her humming under the shower. It wasn't normal. But then, what was normal behaviour? John wasn't sure he knew anymore.

As far as he was concerned, the sooner Maddison Browne and her piano disappeared from his life the better. One minute he and his family had been coasting along, reasonably well off, middle rung, well thought of, with a certain amount of clout as a result of their dealings with the manor. Next, ever since Maddison Browne arrived, John had felt the security of his world threatened. It was hard for him to acknowledge that he'd brought it all on himself. His own ridiculous obsession with doing the right thing and a wretched piano that wasn't his. If he'd only left it alone.

Moving through the house calling out his wife's name, John felt anxious. When he heard no answer, his anxiety lifted further. Passing from room to room he continued calling out, until finally, he entered the kitchen. There, propped against the teapot in the middle of the kitchen bench, was a letter addressed to him, written in his wife's neat hand. John almost choked when he tore it open. The first line began with *Dear John*. Was she leaving him?

He read on. Thank God, no. She had decided to go up to London for a few days to spend some time with old friends. While she was there, she intended to see Crystal. What old friends? It wasn't as if Janet hadn't seen their daughter recently. Why make a special trip? Unlike some people who complained that once their children leave home, they hardly saw them, he and Janet had been blessed that Crystal returned home at every opportunity. When Janet's note went on to make a list of mundane tasks for him to undertake, it felt more like their normal life, and John was finally able to breathe a sigh of relief.

A casserole in the fridge that he need only, 'place in the oven for forty-five minutes'. His wife had become as methodical as he was. But why was she so concerned about his dinner rather than confiding in him what was really bothering her?

I'll call later, if I can, closer to bed time, she wrote, with an x for a kiss.

When the phone rang, John was brushing his teeth, and in his dash to pick up, he tripped accidentally on his slippers, parked half under the bedside table. He stumbled sideways and fell awkwardly onto the bed.

He pushed the phone to his ear, and from this odd angle heard his wife's voice.

'Are you alright, John?'

Shifting himself to a more comfortable position, he glanced across at the clock – ten forty-five pm. 'Yes, I am, how about you?' At this hour, Janet would normally be in bed reading or sound asleep. But her voice, he noticed, sounded wide awake. 'Where are you?'

'At the moment, I am bunked in with Crystal in a nice hotel, and I'm so glad I came.' Her voice sounded calm, happy even.

'Good. And how is our daughter?'

'Crystal is wonderful, and John, she agrees with me.'

John stopped himself from raising his voice, although he easily could have. Instead, he said evenly, 'And what is Crystal so agreeable about? Janet, I do wish you had mentioned to me that you were planning to go up to London, I was worried.'

'Oh, didn't I tell you? I thought I did. It wasn't a family secret.' She giggled down the phone, making him wonder if she had drunk an extra glass of wine with dinner.

John let the comment pass. He had no choice.

'I've been out and about meeting up with some of Crystal's friends and their mothers, and it's been a most wonderful day,' she offered contentedly. 'You know, John I think you and I should make an effort to get up here more often. Crystal has been having a lovely time, too. She's met some nice new people I'm thinking of inviting down to stay. What do you say we make this Easter really special?'

'That will be fine, but who are these people, Janet?'

'Oh, just friends of Crystal's.'

'Alright,' John acquiesced, knowing it would be quite some time before he would be let off the hook.

'How long will you be staying, then? Can I expect you back tomorrow?'

'It won't be tomorrow, but you'll be alright there for another night or two, won't you.' Her tone brooked no disagreement. 'Any news yet on your tea party?'

'No,' he said, deeply wishing he could say something that would bring her home.

'Try to let me know when you find out, won't you. I'd better go. Goodnight, John.'

She had already hung up before it dawned that he hadn't heard what it was that Crystal and her mother had agreed upon. He realised too that Janet had not once mentioned James's name amongst her plans.

Lately, every time Janet mentioned Crystal, she made some disparaging comment about James in the same breath. This omission caused him to wonder. Surely, his wife would have informed him if James and Crystal had fallen out? Janet had become obsessed with the possibility of their only child moving to the other side of the world. No, he ruled it out. She would not be able to stop herself telling him something like that. In any case, more than likely James would be studying his heart out. And Crystal ought to be doing the same, instead of running all over town with her mother. Sometimes, he thought, trying not to think badly of his wife, Janet showed a callous disregard for their daughter's career path.

Again, John turned his attention to James. When he'd asked the Australian about his ancestry, James had laughed. 'Cumberland, I believe it was. I'd like to think I'm part Nordic invader, part Scottish warrior, and part English gentleman, but whichever it is, someone in my family was sent down or decided to risk the journey to Australia. So, the simple answer is, I don't know.'

John recalled someone told him once, James probably, that it was quite the thing nowadays in Australia to be derived from free-settler stock. A feather in the cap, apparently, to have 'clean' ancestors, someone not sent down for theft, murder or other crimes. Aside from Abigail, who'd had her own reasons for departing English shores, great numbers of his countrymen and women had embarked upon that treacherous sea journey of their own free will. So, from where he sat, stuck in his time-managed chair, handling the minutia of human lives, there were times when a pioneering life of adventure looked almost appealing. Especially as many of those entrepreneurs had achieved wealth and influence for their trouble. Not many people could claim that nowadays. He certainly couldn't. John didn't have a modicum of influence in his own home, much less in some far-flung country like Australia.

John had a special fascination for history, even if today, as far as he could tell, no one else seemed interested in what happened five minutes ago. Yet, reading about past events always got him thinking about the 'bigger picture'. It helped him to keep some perspective, to understand the values that made us who we were. He believed that lives were shaped by history. Especially his, for better or worse.

John climbed into bed wondering what Janet was doing in London, and just how he would deal with the two-headed problem of Maddison and Lord Hampton. Would he be able to find a way to tie the many loose ends together with one large bow, and come out of it with his family name and self-respect intact?

Maddison

Gravesend, Sunday

I was scouring local maps of the area when my phone rang. I didn't know whom I was expecting, but the hesitant-sounding voice came as a surprise.

'Maddison? It's John Nettlewood ... the solicitor,' he added, as if I mightn't remember him. 'I was wondering ... where are you now?'

When I told him I was staying in Gravesend, he seemed even more uncomfortable.

'Oh, so close ... I'm sorry, but um ... my wife has had to go to London, you see,' his said. 'It was unexpected ... I'm afraid it'll not be this week but the Saturday after. If you could come over and see the piano then? Say mid-morning?'

'I'm in no rush, John, I have a lot to follow up,' I said.

'Good, of course, of course. You know that the instrument is just waiting for your inspection. Once you give me the go-ahead, I'll have all the arrangements for shipping underway.'

'Yes, thank you.' I had a picture of myself sliding under the piano doing an 'inspection' like some kind of mechanic.

'So, we are agreed, then, you'll come Saturday week?'

'Yes, that's fine.' I took his address, thinking, *What is his problem? Why does he always make me feel like something's wrong?* and put the phone down. Actually, I was relieved, the piano could wait for a couple more weeks, really. I wanted to see Hebden Manor first, and then to the archive.

From the first moment I arrived in Gravesend, taking to the cobblestone streets in drizzling rain, down through the historic port and on to the south bank of the River Thames, I felt the disappointing part of my life pulling away to the outer reaches. Memories that not so long ago had been crystal clear in their sadness, were becoming as distant as grainy old film. Under this dismal grey sky, not far from the actual location of Hebden Manor, I had a real sense that the future might not be written in weighty stone. That here, something could conceivably happen that was capricious and effortless. And I liked that.

Even choosing where to stay had been hassle free. Tourists in Gravesend were spoiled for choice. At first, I'd been hugely tempted to take a room in the grand hotel located on the edge of the river where the King of England once slept, but I changed my mind at the last minute. *Too formal*, I thought, *it won't do*. Yet, the minute I laid eyes on the quaint little B & B, painted white, sloping slate roof, and run by an elderly couple, I took it right away. The instant I stepped through the front door and felt how warm and cosy it was, with the faint aroma of toast in the air, I thought, *I can work here* and signed up.

Husband George had closely supervised my check-in, while his wife, Edith, had absolutely insisted on taking me up to my room.

'Jus' follow me, lassie.' Watching her heave herself slowly up the stairs, gripping the bannisters for support, I feared for her safety. What if she put a foot wrong? But she made it, and was incredibly cheery as she showed me where I could make my own breakfast, pointing out cups hanging on small brass hooks in a brightly painted little kitchenette that was utterly charming.

I answered her questions as best I could. 'I'm not sure exactly how long I'll be staying, is that alright?'

'Quite alright, luv, jus' let us know.'

Listening to her footsteps (and trying hard not to) slowly clumping their way back down, I unpacked my things, set up my notepad and laptop on the table in the corner, and checked the view. It was only a small window, but seeing the water so close was quite lovely. Next, from a stack of tourist brochures piled on the benchtop, I chose a hire company and booked myself a car.

It was well past midday, but I couldn't wait a moment longer.

As I was leaving, Edith popped her head around the door closest to the entrance. 'Goin' out already, are yer?'

I must have looked as startled as I felt.

'Oh, I didn't mean to frighten you, luv.' She patted my arm.

'It's fine,' I said, trying to smile reassuringly. 'I'm just going to pick up a car.' I pulled out the brochure and pointed to a blue Astra.

She nodded approvingly. 'Should we be expecting yer back soon, then?'

'I'm not sure.'

'If it's not too late, you'd be most welcome to share a bowl of soup here wi' George and me.'

'That's very kind, but I'll probably just grab something while I'm out, thanks. I just need to get my bearings first, you know, arriving in a new place and all.'

'Oh, I quite understand,' said Edith, nodding. 'Not that I've been to any new places in a long while mind, but if I did, I'd be wanting to get my bearings, too. Have you got your key?'

I held it up.

'Alright, then, luv, see you later.'

Walking away, I had the strangest feeling that I might have met Edith before, but probably it was only that she reminded me strongly of my neighbours at home. Edith was especially like Ruth, checking on me as if I were ten years old. I smiled thinking of them. I'd already sent two postcards, one from London, and the other from the station here when I arrived. I reminded myself to snap a few photos as well. One of the last things Joan had asked me was to, 'Take a few shots of those lovely English rivers.'

With my little blue hire car scooting along narrow wet roads, my reflexes were alert. Particularly, when I was almost forced off the road by a Range Rover with dark-tinted windows that tooted at me as it flew past, well over the speed limit. Although I was accustomed to treacherous driving conditions at home, it probably wasn't the most sensible decision to come out in a strange car in wet weather. But since James had deepened the mystery about my new family with revelations that my great-grandmother had been Australian, I simply couldn't wait to see the place she had left. On the internet Hebden Manor looked impressive.

After almost thirty minutes of squinting at road signs, and windscreen wipers slapping back and forth, I slowed. Finally, a sign looming through the mist said, 'Welcome to Hebden Women's College' with a large arrow pointing to the right. Beyond, way through the mist, was a huge, ominous-looking shape that seemed to dominate the horizon.

'Hebden Manor,' I murmured.

The enormous wrought-iron gates were securely closed, so there was no possibility to simply drive in. I wound down my window in order to see more clearly. Just inside the grounds, a gatehouse (security, I presumed) appeared to be unmanned. The manor beyond was set amongst acres of fenced grounds, linked by a long driveway and lined with huge old trees that rose out of the fog and disappeared into the distance. A knot of emotion hit my stomach. This had to be a mistake. The thought that my grandmother had been born here, that this grand palace was part of my family story, was quite overwhelming. I got out of the car and breathed in. Freezing, thick air bit at my lungs while heavy rain belted down on my head.

I stood staring through the rain and fog, getting completely drenched, until the cold weight of my dripping clothes forced me to clamber back into the car. Shivering, I turned the engine back on and waited for a blast of hot air to dry my face and warm my hands.

As I sat on the other side of the world to my real life, effectively an outsider from all of this, it dawned on me that what had happened was more remarkable than any story I could ever make up. A person I didn't know existed had left me a piano that had brought me to this historic manor house, where generations of my own flesh and blood had lived and died. It was hard to grasp. I was connected to a world that I'd known nothing about.

My grandmother had been raised in this air, and in the young impressionable years of her life, her feet had trodden this earth. A mass of different emotions rushed around inside me, and I didn't know how to react. My limbs felt stiff and not just from the cold; I must have been in some state of shock.

Comprehending the scale of Hebden Manor had only intensified the most vexing question of all: what happened to Abigail here that caused her to run off and invent a completely new life for herself? I stared out through the rain, searching for answers.

As the daughter of an earl, Abigail would have had suitors, high social standing, and a sophisticated life of privilege. Why would she give all that up in exchange for what she became, an anonymous woman playing the piano in suburban halls to raise money for orphans? Or if her decision to leave was as a result of some sort of misdemeanour, John Nettlewood would surely have known about it. He'd seemed quite genuine when he said that until recently, he hadn't known about Abigail living the rest of her life in Australia.

For the romantic in me, it left one answer. Love could be the only reason she would flee England and leave her family and friends forever. What else could make a beautiful young woman want to change her life so completely and with such conviction? If not the hot fire of passion, it had to be love unrequited or love forbidden. With rain water dripping from my hair onto my shoulders, my clothes soaking wet, I made a silent promise to the grandmother I barely knew. I would get to the bottom of her story.

You don't have to worry, Abigail. Whatever I find I won't judge you. I'm curious and fascinated by you. And a little sad. You and I, maybe what we share is that we both suffer too much for love.

I was blasted out of my reverie by a large bus blaring its fog horn and flashing headlights in my rear-vision mirror. I started the engine, and by the time I edged forward to allow it past, the school gates had swung open and a row of other buses had joined the first. All were roaring along the driveway to where I imagined the school entrance was.

With my motor still idling, I watched the stream of tail-lights wind their way through the trees, disappearing in the mist, then reappearing, until finally coming to a halt. A continuous bell, loud enough to be heard miles away, sounded, cutting through the thick fog like a saw. School was out. Pressing my forehead against the car window for a last glimpse of Hebden Manor, ghostly and watery in the distance, there was so much emotion tugging at my heart. My feelings of joy for having found Abigail's past were balanced by a deep sorrow for what could never be; people I would never know, experiences I would never have, family connections I would never feel.

I wondered what Marianne would say if she could see me sitting here like this? My poor mother. I was sure she knew nothing about Hebden Manor. A sob rose up from somewhere deep, wrenching my body. I covered my face with both hands and fell forward to rest my forehead on the dashboard. My nose was running and my cheeks were wet with tears when another bus honked. I sat up, wiped my face and turned the car around for the drive back to Gravesend.

I parked on the street outside and scampered through the rain, keeping my head down as I dodged a booby trap of puddles that seemed to be lying in wait on the path leading to the door. I turned the lock over quietly and waited for a moment. I didn't want the smell of fried food wafting up from the parcel under my arm to draw Edith and George out of their nook. I was in no state to answer any of their questions. I felt like a shipwreck and looked like one, too. Thankfully, the television was playing so loudly that I managed to climb the stairs without disturbing them.

After drying myself off and pulling on some fresh clothes, I made a cup of tea, then sat down to unwrap my dinner. Hot and salty fish and chips, my number-one comfort food. Relishing the blessed familiarity of the fried food, I ate the heavenly fare, my spirits lifting (as I knew they would) with every bite. I was reminded suddenly of my mother. I picked up a chip and raised it in poignant salute. How often had we shared a wrapper of fish and chips sitting on the bench in front of the pier in Port Melbourne? Poor Marianne. 'If you could just see me now,' I said aloud.

The thought that I was close to finding out what I felt certain she had never known, returned me to the present. I licked my fingers and sipped my tea, then began to mull over all that I'd found so far.

In London, in that huge music shop, I'd finally found my way to the classical department and hummed a fragment of melody to a seriously thin young man in a tight-fitting purple shirt, hoping for a clue.

'It's a piece for piano, Russian maybe, do you know what it could be?' I'd asked, and hummed those few notes that came out more like a cough than a melody. 'I'm sorry, these are the only ones I know for sure.'

Incredibly, this pasty-faced youth, who looked barely old enough to have left school, said without looking up, 'Too easy. Rachmaninov's "Rhapsody on a Theme of Paganini, 19th Variation". Who do you want playing it? We have a least a dozen or more performances.'

I didn't answer because I didn't know.

When he finally lifted his head to look his customer in the face, he spoke to me like I was some forgotten species from the dark ages. *Who on earth wouldn't know that* was what the tone of his voice inferred. I must have appeared crestfallen or something, or maybe he just took pity on me, this poor creature from outer space who didn't have a name for such famous music on the tip of her tongue. Next thing, he'd proceeded to outline a brief life history of the composer, and offered advice on which selection he would make. I followed his suggestion (why wouldn't I? He seemed to know what he was talking about!) and purchased a CD copy played by a large Russian woman called Lisitsa and downloaded her performance onto my phone, too, so that I could listen at any time. Like right now.

Scrunching the food packaging, I stood up and placed it in the bin. I wiped my hands clean and grabbed my phone. Flicking quickly onto iTunes, I hit 'play', then sat completely still and listened through to the end.

I pushed 'repeat'. Comfortably recovered, with salt lightly burning my lips, and wriggling warm toes in cashmere socks I'd summoned the foresight to pack, I opened my laptop and started making notes, with the classical music playing not too softly in my ears. I began tapping into my thoughts about the events of recent weeks, and once I did that, some sort of catharsis seemed to take place. Unlike my frozen brain of a few weeks ago, once I'd started, I found I couldn't stop. *Maybe I'm not done for, after all*, I thought. *What is this new story?* I tapped on, receiving characters, settings and conversations from words that flowed through my fingers, long into the night, the way they used to. I was still typing, sipping yet another mug of milky tea, with a full treatment plan in front of me, when the first light appeared, faintly visible through the high window above my bed.

Part Two

Maddison

Gravesend, next day

The only sounds I could hear in the little kitchenette where I was eating a bowl of cereal for breakfast, were faint strains of a radio playing downstairs. I presumed it had to be coming from George and Edith's own rooms, since the rest of the place was quiet.

Thankfully, the Cosy Cottage was true to its name. It was lovely here. Water heaters along the walls of my room throwing out a fierce warmth had dried the clothes I'd draped all over them. I'd always loved the smell of ironing and clean washing. I couldn't think of anything more relaxing and homely. In fact, the atmosphere in my room was so snug, I was tempted not to go out at all. But, with so much to explore, not even this cushy warmth was enough to prevent me from visiting the archive. I was searching for what I had begun to think of as Abigail's secret.

Now that I'd seen where she grew up, I had to know what happened to her. I was accustomed to thinking about fictional characters, and knowing that whenever I wanted to, I could change their actions and alter situations. But this was different. All I could do here was find the truth.

After a lifetime of knowing nothing of my family, to Hebden and a countess for a great-grandmother and an earl for a great-grandfather, it seemed curious, exciting and ridiculously funny, all at the same time. I was alive with anticipation for what the day might bring.

'Your light was burning late last night, lass,' said George, just as I was about to open the front door. 'Anything we can help yer with, don't hesitate to ask now, will yer, lass.'

The car I'd chosen was fitted with satellite navigation, but more directions could only help. George's manner was so genuine, the slow drawl, the way his lips moved upwards when he smiled, it couldn't hurt. So I said, 'You wouldn't happen to know the easiest way to get to Strood, would you?'

'Strood?' he exclaimed, 'why it's only a hop, step and jump from here. You take the first right at the bottom of the street, then follow the signs for the A2. It'll take yer only about fifteen minutes from there.'

I could see he was dying to ask why I was going to Strood, but he didn't. Well, not directly anyway.

'It's a lovely place is Strood, down there on the River Medway.'

'Is it? I'm looking forward to seeing it, thanks, George.' I paused, trying to think of something else to say, but nothing came that wouldn't entail a long conversation, so as warmly as I could, I said, 'Okay, thanks again for the directions, I'll get going.'

'Righto, luv, what time can we expect yer back?'

'This evening some time, I think.'

'Take care now on those wet roads, won't yer?'

I pulled up the hood of my parka and edged out of the door into the weather.

The brightness of my mood couldn't be dampened by the freezing temperature, nor the blanket of dark clouds dumping waves of sleety rain over the car as I set off. I hadn't felt so upbeat in ages. I was a little strung out from lack of sleep, but my energy was running like a dam about to burst the floodgates. Confident in my surroundings, I decided to follow George's directions and followed the road signs to Rochester.

A few streets from the turn-off, I noticed a building similar to my B & B, only this one was called the Good Shepherd. What first got my attention was a group huddled outside like a clutch of abominable snowmen, all layered up in mismatched coats and hats, crouched under umbrellas and squatting in a ragged queue against the wall. The sign under the name said, 'Homeless shelter, all welcome.'

It was so unexpected that my kneejerk reaction caused the car to swerve slightly. I didn't know why seeing homelessness over here should come as a shock, when it was the same at home. Why would there not be similar concerns here? It was a sharp reminder of an uncomfortable truth about the world we lived in. Around the globe, there were people prepared to leave their country of birth, and face dangerous sea journeys, to escape wars and persecution to find a better place to live. The law of averages alone meant that things could not go right for everyone. How could they?

Inevitably, Katya came to mind. No word from my friend Bethany meant she'd probably had no luck finding the mysterious woman in Melbourne. I had begun to think of her now as a messenger of everything that had happened to me, from the day she appeared in the shopping centre. Katya was my own good-luck omen. I was hopeful that Beth might be able to track her down in my absence. If not, I would leave no stone unturned when I got back.

Twenty minutes later, I was driving down the main street of Strood when a car backed out not far from my destination. I thanked my lucky stars, and swung in to park.

I got out and dashed across the road, trying to avoid cars from splashing icy sludge onto my boots, then set off briskly towards the towering stone façade of the old library that was home to the genealogy archive.

James's suggestion about this place had saved me a lot of valuable time, but I was in no doubt that I would have found it myself eventually. Still, I wondered why he'd gone out of his way to give me the name and address. Was it some kind of two-timer date bait? *Forget about him*, I told myself, and pushed all else aside to focus on the building in front.

Taking the stairs, once through the main entrance doors, warm air hit my face like a change of climate. I unzipped my parka and approached the information desk. This was going to be a test. To introduce myself as a direct descendant of the Hamptons of Hebden Manor for the very first time.

At first, the archivist, a middle-aged woman with dyed black hair and thick lenses, appeared unwilling to accept my status. From the way she peered at me, when I asked to see all original documents for the Hampton family, she was clearly sceptical.

Having seen for myself the imposing scale of Hebden, and having digested an internet precis of the Hamptons' role in centuries of tradition, it did feel improper for me to say the words out loud. The look of disbelief on her face when I stated my business heightened my awkwardness threefold.

But, while she was making up her mind about me, I observed her. Had her sight always been poor, I wondered, before she took on this line of work? Often, the professions people chose for themselves, as against the ones they should choose, didn't tally. I found it funny sometimes. The fitness instructor who was never good at sport, the accountant who struggled with maths and couldn't add without a calculator. This woman, as an archivist, would have to be wrestling daily with fading ink on old documents, worn-out newspaper prints, cursive styles in old letters and old photos. Poor sight, I imagined, would make her job a nightmare, that was unless she loved it more than anything. I realised my inner writer was doing its thing, making up her backstory without any evidence at all. I chastised myself. It was a bad habit of mine.

'If you'll forgive me,' she interrupted, 'sorry, your name again was?' Her softly spoken voice was in direct contrast to the severity of her appearance.

As calmly as I could, I said, 'Maddison, Maddison Browne.'

'I am sorry,' her eyes flicked quickly past my left hand, and observing no ring, she addressed me accordingly, 'Miss Browne, but much of the archive is still private and, as we don't know you, you understand, we would need some authority to expose those private family documents to you.'

'That's alright, Stella.

Reaching into my bag, I extracted the lawyer's original letter, and my passport, and placed them slowly and carefully on the table for her inspection.

'I should have called ahead of time,' I said, 'but …'

She wasn't listening. Without making any comment, she had taken each item from me and was slowly examining them. I saw her double-check my face to the passport photo. For a second, I panicked. It was an old shot, my hair was a different colour, and why had I pulled that face? But after she had carefully inspected both, she smiled for the first time, revealing two dimples that gave her face a warmth not evident before.

'Most unexpected … remarkable in fact,' she said, staring at me like someone who could hardly believe what her eyes were telling her. But she recovered herself enough to say politely, as she handed my documents back, 'I am delighted to meet you, Maddison.'

Did she bow slightly? I thought. *Good heavens.* I smiled to hide my own discomfort at her reaction, which in the blink of an eye had gone from Stasi officer to reacting the way a fan of the royals might.

'I have always had special interest in Hebden Manor,' she whispered confidentially. 'But I've never actually met a member of the family.' She blushed. 'Please, if you'd like to come this way we can get started.'

I didn't need to say another word. Without further ado, Stella was off, guiding me in her sensible flats, talking to me over her shoulder now like a fellow conspirator she had known for years.

'You know, the assumption has always been that the Hamptons' daughter, Abigail,' I nodded, 'died in childbirth, but if Mr Nettlewood found you, then she can't have died, can she? Oh, this is most interesting.'

'Like I said, I'm here to try to find out what happened. And of course, I'd like to know more about Lady Rose, too.'

'Oh, there's plenty of reading about Lady Rose,' she said. 'Like all good women of her day, she kept diaries.'

'Sounds promising,' I said, trying to contain my excitement at hearing this.

'No one could sneeze in the manor house without it being noted by someone in the general household records. I'm taking you directly to their designated space, where all the originals are kept,' said Stella, heading for a flight of stairs that led downwards. 'We have scanned part of it for safety's sake, but not all yet, so you can look at electronic copies for some things, rather than handle the original documents.'

'No problem,' I said, feeling butterflies in my stomach the way a sprinter might at the start of an important race. Was that exhilaration I was feeling for what I might find? Or was it foreboding? Both probably, swishing around together.

'There'll be plenty to interest you,' she said knowingly.

'And is this,' I said, 'I mean here, in your establishment, would you say are you holding everything to do with the estate under this roof?'

'To the best of our knowledge, yes. But we can't be sure. There may be other material, letters, that we don't have. For instance, we have nothing about Abigail after the time she was said to have died. She just isn't mentioned after that date. I've always wondered why we didn't have a death certificate for her.'

'Yes,' I said. 'That is unusual.'

'But now we know.' She nodded her head. 'So, that's one mystery solved. And actually, there was another enquiry about that recently, but we never heard any more about it. That wasn't you, too, was it?'

'No, no it wasn't,' I said, without mentioning that I probably did know who it was. James or one of his offsiders would have been asking that very question.

'Sometimes we get random enquiries for no good reason,' Stella said. 'So, to respond to your question, other than those few stand-out matters, we have pretty much all there was when the manor house was sold.'

I observed during the course of our conversation that the more Stella spoke about archives, the more animated she became. 'You enjoy your job, then, Stella?'

Her step slowed and she turned to me. 'It shows, does it?'

· I smiled in answer.

She picked up the pace again, but kept talking. 'I think it's so important to record what we've done, and where we've been on this planet, don't you? But then, I would say that wouldn't I?' She laughed in a self-deprecating way. 'Sometimes I think we are all a bit bonkers. What about you? Were you always interested in history before this came up?' She waved her arm around in the air.

'Yes,' I said, 'but not enough to become an archivist.'

She laughed again. 'No, it's not a job for everyone, just the special few. Nearly there.' Stella rattled the keys in her hand.

We walked the last few steps in silence. I was taking in the quiet, serious feeling of the space, thinking how there had to be more personal histories, accounts of lives and events from this region stored here, than I could even imagine. And a part of me was feeling pretty proud that my newly discovered family was more than a small part of this rich resource.

'Okay, here we are, are you ready?'

I nodded, and Stella unlocked a heavy door and swung it open. Surprisingly, it didn't have that stale smell that often prevailed where old books and papers were stored in one place. Floor-to-ceiling containers and air vents in the ceiling had given the room a clinical feel, more like a laboratory.

'There is rather a lot, as you can see.' Stella made a gesture with her arm that encompassed the whole room. 'We'll be delighted to offer you all the help we can.'

'Thank you.' I glanced around, wondering where on earth to start. Stella took the initiative and pulled out a box from the bottom rack.

Her action was spontaneous. 'Up here,' she said, pointing, 'is the record of successions, the number of countesses, baronesses, dukes, barons and viscounts and social machinations brought to bear on the title, Earl of Hebden. They are all here, dating back to before fifteen eighty. You'd have a field day should you decide to browse here, at your leisure of course, but I can guarantee you a juicy read.'

The shelves of worn leather volumes with faded gold-leaf titles on their spines, the kind only found in very old libraries or archives like this, didn't look 'juicy' at all.

'You'll find this is the best place to start,' said Stella authoritatively. 'Your great- grandmother, Rose, wrote down some of her thoughts as a young woman, and it's a fascinating record of her early life in Melbourne. That is where you said you're from, isn't it?'

'Yes.'

'Then you'll find it more than interesting.'

'Thank you,' I breathed in, full of anticipation. Was I finally going to find longed-for answers to my family questions? Things I'd wondered about all my life?

'See what you make of it,' Stella said matter-of-factly, 'and any other help I can give you, just ask. I must insist you use these, though.' She handed me a pair of cotton gloves and a magnifying glass. 'Don't touch anything without wearing them, please. And I'm sure I don't have to tell you, no use of a pen on anything. Alright? I'll leave you now.' And with a final 'Enjoy,' she turned on her heel and left the room.

It was so deathly quiet down here I could hear my own breathing as I drew the soft cotton gloves over my fingers. Reaching into the folder Stella had set out for me to read first, my insides were positively vibrating. Here was my great-grandmother. The woman who'd been imagining me prior to her death, bequeathing to me her precious piano. Well, not me exactly, but by leaving it to the last living female in her line, she was ensuring that one day someone might find me. Now, here I was. For one who loved words as I did, opening Rose's own diaries filled me with the most indescribable and exquisite pleasure; my fingers were tingling as I delicately turned to the first page. It was the beginning of what could only be an unpredictable journey of discovery to understand what happened in this family and to find who I really was.

Rose

East Melbourne, Australia, 1907

I was giving Tommy, the youngest of the Robinson children, his daily piano lesson when I heard footsteps in the passage. A face I didn't recognise popped around the door and startled us with, 'Boo!'

Tommy stopped, screamed out, wriggled off the piano stool and bolted straight into the waiting man's arms.

'Did you bring it?' he cried, his little voice wild with delight.

'I did, and what's more, it's being set up in the library right now so we can get stuck into it,' the man replied, then turned to me. 'It's a new board game, "The Man in the Moon". Tommy has been waiting to see it, haven't you, Tommy?' He tousled the boy's hair. Tommy wriggled and squirmed, but his eyes were shining. He was very excited.

The first thing I noticed about our visitor was his thick moustache and his posh English way of speaking.

'You must excuse my rudeness please. Let me introduce myself, Will Hampton,' he said, sticking his hand out. It seemed so natural for me to reciprocate, even though I knew it was not my place to shake hands with family guests. He bowed, holding the tips of my fingers in his hand. 'And you are?'

'I'm Rose, Rose Rooney, the music teacher,' I said, feeling my face flush pink.

'Yes of course you are. I'm sorry to barge in on you like this, Miss Rooney, but when Tommy's mother said he was in here I couldn't resist.'

He smiled, gazing right into my eyes, and I felt my previous annoyance at having Tommy's lesson interrupted melt right away. My legs were shaking a little as I took my hand back.

'Not at all,' I murmured, lowering my eyes, 'anyone who makes Tommy smile like that is always welcome in my classroom.'

I recognised the name immediately. How could I not? Standing before me, and making my heart skip a beat, was the younger brother of an English earl. William Hampton had finally come to visit. There had been talk of little else these past weeks. I hadn't even known really what an earl was until it was explained to me by the children, and I'd opened the large encyclopedia in the library to find out more. It was just that no one had mentioned how friendly he would be, and no one had said anything about how playful the twinkle in his eye would be. Or how I would feel when he looked at me.

This particular house guest's arrival in Melbourne had been so anticipated by the Robinsons it was if the King of England himself were going to pay a visit. The children had nagged their parents endlessly, 'How many sleeps till Uncle Will arrives?' He wasn't their real uncle at all, of course, but from what I had gleaned from snippets of conversation overheard at dinner, William Hampton was a businessman who had been raised to the status of 'uncle' after a long and productive association with the head of the house, John Robinson. His family ran a large country estate somewhere in England with a huge manor house on it and had been visiting Melbourne regularly since the Great Exhibition of 1880, which the Robinsons described as a time, 'when the whole world was here in one place'. Will Hampton and John Robinson had had a number of successful dealings over the years since then. The Robinsons themselves were wealthy graziers who ran large holdings of sheep on their big country property in East Gippsland, too. If only Lady Caroline could drag herself away from her endless round of city engagements, a trip to the country estate had been planned, with a date set for the autumn. I had been counting the weeks, placing a cross next to the date of every one that passed.

'I don't know who's going to enjoy playing this game more, me or Tommy,' the smiling visitor said, patting Tommy's head again while carefully keeping his eyes directed towards mine. 'Come on, Tommy, won't you invite Miss Rooney to watch you play?'

'You bet,' said Tommy. 'Will you, Rose, will you come? I promise to practise my scales even harder if you watch me beat Uncle Will.'

I knelt down, placed my hands on his shoulders and spoke gently. 'Tommy, I would love to see you play, but you know very well that I must prepare your lessons.' But as these words passed my lips, a fervent wish that I could say 'yes' ran through me.

What would Lady Caroline say if I were to accept such an invitation from a house guest? I could just imagine the uproar. Not only was it beyond my station, but such behaviour would be tantamount to a sacking offence. I may have been raised in a country town, but I knew from my own father's position as magistrate for the community, that some relationships were out of bounds. Also, I was fully cognizant of how important it was for my mother to receive whatever money I could earn. Widowed early with two children to raise, the amount went straight to her. Mother had moved heaven and earth for me to get this job. It was my responsibility to carry it out as best I could, and to do that meant maintaining a certain distance from guests, even charming, friendly ones.

I was grateful that my life as part of the Robinson family had already taught me a lot. I had changed since coming here. Back home, even as the daughter of a magistrate, there would be no possibility of meeting an English gentleman and being spoken to so nicely. Like an equal. I swallowed the lump in my throat, remembering how Father had died so unexpectedly, as I kissed Tommy on the cheek. 'Now you run along and I'll see you before bedtime and you can tell me about it.'

Tommy pouted. 'Very well, I'll just have to beat him all by myself.'

'You will.' I laughed, but when I raised my eyes, I was looking straight into the visitor's, whose gaze caused my heart to flutter so wildly I feared I might not even be able to stand.

As if sensing this, the visitor reached down and helped me to my feet. 'Thank you,' I murmured, removing my hand from his and straightening my skirt, trying not to look at him. 'Perhaps, Tommy you might like to play one of your best pieces for your uncle some other time.'

'Yes, yes, I will, but can we go now, please?' Tommy grabbed the visitor's hand and tugged at it to draw him away.

'Very well, let's get on with it, then shall we, and may the best man win,' said the visitor, then added with a mischievous smile over his shoulder to me, 'I hope to see you later, Miss Rooney.'

'See you later, Rose,' chimed Tommy.

I stood grounded to the spot, listening to Tommy's excited chatter all the way down the passage, noticing how my own heart was beating very fast. When it was quiet once more I sat down at the piano and gathered myself to prepare the next week's lessons.

Little more than a half an hour later another interruption broke into my concentration, only this time it was Lady Caroline herself.

'Rose my dear, may I have a word?'

The lady of the house bustled in, and the first thing I noticed was her dress, ankle length, cut in the latest flattering style, a most glorious green-and-black silk that perfectly complemented her olive complexion. I admired how Lady Caroline always took great care with her appearance. I knew for a fact, because Lady Caroline had told me herself, that she'd made several appointments with her city dressmakers to prepare for the earl's brother's visit. *This must be one of her new outfits*, I thought admiringly. How lovely she looked. It was hard for anyone not to feel plain in the presence of Lady Caroline. I touched my hair awkwardly, feeling gawky in my simple tunic with its long white apron and special pocket that I used for carrying pencils and rubbers. Technically I was the music teacher, but in the absence of a proper tutor for several months, I had also taken on quite a lot of reading and writing lessons with the children, which was why Lady Caroline had been so kind to me. 'Rose,' she had said, 'I see that English was your best subject at school, so I don't see why you couldn't teach the children yourself?'

I had been hugely flattered to take on the role without formal training and I had done so with great delight, given that reading books and writing were what I regarded as my guilty pleasures. And I'd felt so proud. For not only had I managed to increase my earnings, but I could read almost anytime I liked, because like my piano playing, it had become my livelihood. Mother had always said I would be more valuable than any other because I knew about English and Music. And now, since I had been able to explain things to Tommy and his sister, Sarah, I often thought how right my mother had been. It made me feel very grown up.

From her demeanour and how she held her head tilted slightly to one side, I saw right away that Lady Caroline was going to ask something out of the ordinary. 'My darling son has sent me on an errand, Rose,' she said with a sigh. 'So, I've come to ask a favour of you.'

'Of course.' I lowered my eyes, wondering what on earth it could be.

'Good.' She clapped her hands in delight. 'More than anything Tommy says he would love you to see him playing this new game Will has brought from Europe, "The Man in the Moon" or something. I'm sure I haven't a clue what it's about. I know this is your own time, Rose, but seeing as John and I are due out at any moment, and Will has declined any invitation to join us, I wondered if you might go along to the library to watch them play? Could you do that for me?'

My first reaction was shock, then trepidation. Would spending time in Will's presence be too much for my beating heart to manage? *Don't be ridiculous*, I scolded myself. He was likely just being gallant. He probably wouldn't even remember my name.

'Yes of course, Ma'am,' I murmured.

'Rose, my dear, thank you.' Lady Caroline patted my arm. 'What is it about men that they must always have a woman to watch even their smallest endeavours?'

There was nothing I could say to that. The only men I knew were my father, who wasn't like that, and my uncle, whom I knew absolutely nothing about.

Lady Caroline, beaming that special smile when she was pleased with her own words, confirmed the arrangements. 'I will see to it that a light supper is served in the library. Dear God what is the world coming to, dining in the library. Thank you again, my dearest Rose.'

Then taking several steps towards the door before turning back to Rose she said, 'You do know that I would love to stay back. But I was rather looking forward to this little cocktail party ...' Her bottom lip trembled slightly, like she wanted forgiveness for something, from someone.

Shortly after arriving here, I came to realise that the lady of the house loved nothing more than dressing up to attend parties, especially gatherings held in the grand homes of her social set, who, from what I could glean, all lived in mansions with ballrooms of their own. Far from judging her, I thought I would feel the same way if I were as lovely as Lady Caroline and had such a wardrobe of fine dresses. Her husband was so often away on business, Lady Caroline had to feel lonely sometimes, which I imagined was the main reason she constantly went out. It seemed to me that she wasn't comfortable spending too much time with her children. I thought it might be because she couldn't show them how to play the piano or teach them how to read books for themselves. That was my job. Whenever I thought about it, my heart melted with a special softness for Lady Caroline, whom I almost felt sorry for at times. It seemed to me that even with all of her beauty and finery, her society friends, her significant household and her children, Lady Caroline couldn't seem to find a place in her life to settle. Not even in the large and glorious home made from hewn sandstone constructed specially for her in the best part of town.

Shortly afterwards, I heard the *clip-clop* of the Robinsons' horse and carriage pulling out, and a voice calling to shut the gates. Then, silence. I waited for a couple of minutes, excitement welling up until it formed a knot in my chest, and I could wait no longer. Taking a deep breath, I straightened my skirt, patted it down twice with both hands until it was smooth, then set off for the library. Lady Caroline leaving me alone in the company of a male guest was quite out of the ordinary. I knew that my own mother would never approve of any such arrangement. She was a stickler for all social customs, especially domestic protocol about house guests and staff and how the two should never mix. Ever. But how could I have refused? What could I have done? I wondered what the answer to this conundrum might be, as the sound of my footsteps click-clacking along the parquetry floor mirrored the beating of my own heart. I crossed through the main sitting room, down the long passageway and turned left without encountering any other household staff I might have to explain my mission to, coming to a halt only when I found the library door closed.

I hesitated just long enough to hear muffled giggles emanating from the other side, and when I imagined Tommy and the visitor leaning over their board game having fun, the warmth that flowed through me on hearing their happy voices made me smile. What was I waiting for? Lady Caroline had specifically asked me to do this. Throwing caution to the wind, I raised my hand and knocked three times.

'Come in.'

Maddison

Strood, three hours later

The diaries so far, without doubt, were romantic. Reading about the attraction between William and my great-grandmother written in her own hand, for me, was nothing short of thrilling. Rose herself had a way with words, too. Each line made me feel like I was peeping through a window of time, a beguiling glimpse of a world long ago. Rose the music teacher and William the grand aristocrat falling in love against the odds, in Melbourne, was fantastic. No mistaking the eternal laws of love and attraction there. The spark between them had been ignited at first glance, and I couldn't wait to see how they managed to end up together.

Gently cradling the next volume in the palm of my hand like a freshly hatched bird, I was easily able to picture the sort of young woman she was. Especially poignant was the entry she'd written one month after taking up her position as a music teacher with the Robinsons. Alone and separated from her own family for the first time, her words were lucid, and I was impressed by how self-possessed she sounded for one so young.

I was terrified when Mama told me I had to come here, but now I find that life is not lost after all. I am happy. The house is big, and the Robinsons are very kind. I have my own room. It's small with a bed, a wardrobe and a small dressing table, and oh joy, it has a mirror. Call me vain to be pleased about this, but it is so much easier to do my hair being able to see what I am doing. Oh, and my room has a small window from which I can look out over gardens opposite, to huge canopies of trees and large expanses of undulating green lawn. Life here is so completely different to what I have known, that I can find no real way of describing it other than to say, the world seems somehow 'bigger'.

Amidst specks of stains, faded ink and a youthful cursive script, through her writing the spirit of Rose came to life and I could see a young woman struggling to make sense of her world. It was incredible to be living and breathing her words.

I am pleased that I can help Mama after our terrible ordeal with our dear daddy dying so suddenly. A police magistrate is not a popular occupation. I think that must be what killed him. I will never forget the look on his face when people threw stones at our door after he committed a man to trial for murder. And later, when the man was sentenced to hang, how awful it was, the way people would shout abuse at him whenever we left the house.

The more I read, it seemed to me that Rose's escape to city life with the Robinsons had been like a dress rehearsal for her life as the wife of an English earl.

Lady Caroline loaned me something to wear for another afternoon where I must play the piano. I felt like a real lady in her red silk dress. She is so kind to me, she says that seeing her children happy in my company and hearing them play the simple tunes I teach them fills her with joy. Still, I worry about Mama and my sister and how they will cope. I am expecting any day to hear that Tilly has been sent to work with another family. How I wish she would come to Melbourne, too. But as sisters, we are not alike. Tilly is a different character to me. She was always more comfortable with the rigours of country life than I ever was, so maybe I should stop wishing her here, for she might not fit in as easily as I have.

A part of me experienced the emotions of Rose's journey as if they were my own, while another part of me could barely wait for Rose to marry and for my grandmother's story to begin. I badly wanted to know what happened to her.

The first reference I found of Abigail was not in Rose's diaries, but within the household records; a hand-written entry in a large cursive script, in a sturdy black volume, most likely scribbled by the head butler.

The household today at four-thirty am, welcomes the arrival of a baby girl for our newlyweds. Abigail will be her name. We are all overjoyed, and before dinner preparations, we cheerfully raised a glass to the health and happiness of our newly arrived little one.

Oh, I thought, *the 'orphan' has arrived.*

The warmth of their words filled me with joy and sadness. No one in that household, the cooks, the maids or butlers, would have imagined in a wild dream, that Abigail's life would have turned out the way it did. My fingers trembled lightly as I turned the pages. Would my mother or I be different people if we had known about all this? But there was no answer for that question.

Still, I was nothing short of captivated by their world, busily jotting down notes for my own purposes, lifting words and situations I might use for my latest writing. The time passed so quickly, I barely noticed the clock ticking.

I was about to call it a day, when Rose mentioned in another of her diaries that she was pregnant.

'Oh, my goodness,' I said aloud and I sat bolt upright.

The way she described the expression on her beloved William's face seeing his son and heir for the first time was poetic.

It's as if his eyes will melt. We have been blessed with a son. An heir at last. His name will be Gerard. This precious beautiful baby boy with rosy cheeks is smiling up at me like he already knows me.

I took a deep breath and held it in. No one, not James or the solicitor, had mentioned to me that Abigail had siblings, although it was perfectly reasonable that she should have a brother or sister. There was nothing about the children at all, actually on the poorly maintained Hebden Estate website. He was younger than my grandmother, but most likely dead now, too. While a brother had no direct connection to Rose's desire for her piano to follow the female line, still I found it odd that no one had mentioned him to me.

Gathering the diaries to put them away for the day, my fingers fumbled and one slender volume slipped from my hand. Horrified, I watched it land with a sharp slap on the floor. Fearing it might be damaged, I leaned down quickly to pick it up. I turned it over to check the condition (how would I explain a broken spine to Stella), but as I did so, an envelope slipped out from between the pages. I gathered that up, too, expecting it to be a bookmark. But I was completely nonplussed to discover it was a letter, and the address on it said, '*My Mother*'. The seal had been broken and the flap was open. I reached in and pulled out one fine sheet of paper, and unfolded it. There was no address, only a date, July 1936. My eyes flew to the signature at the bottom – '*Abbey*'.

I breathed out strongly, my heartbeat racing. I was just about to delve into this private letter from my grandmother to her mother, when I heard footsteps. I was so engrossed I hadn't noticed Stella's approach until she was almost through the door.

'How did you go?' she asked, appearing larger than life in the doorway. I got such a fright I almost jumped out of my skin.

Some instinct I couldn't account for in that moment, made me shove the letter unceremoniously out of sight. My heart was thumping as I resumed my seat. I knew it was the wrong thing to do, but somehow, it felt like I was meant to read this letter, that it was for my eyes only. I didn't know what it was, or if Stella had ever seen it. Although I doubted that she would have read it, given the manner in which I'd come across it. *What were the chances of that?* I wondered. *Slim*, I decided. And what if the letter contained a dark secret, something deeply personal from Abigail to her mother? Shouldn't I keep that private? Shouldn't I protect my grandmother?

'I love her candour,' I said brightly, feeling truly ghastly. Stella was being so nice and I had hidden a letter in my pocket that technically didn't belong to me.

'Yes, Lady Rose certainly has a way with words. Mind you, I love reading any diary, even if the writing isn't as engaging as Lady Hampton's.'

'Have you looked through all of them?' I asked.

'No, just dipped in here and there,' she said. 'Couldn't hope to read every single line in here.' Stella spoke absently as she busily searched, running her finger along a line of folders on the second shelf. 'I don't think I'd be spoiling anything by telling you. Later in life she tried her hand, as a few upper-class ladies did at that time, at writing novels.'

'What?' I gasped. 'You mean Rose?'

'Yes, she wrote just the one, and it was never published.'

'Oh, I had no idea,' I said.

'A little surprising, though, isn't it? It's not like she had nothing else to do. She'd a large household to run. Still I s'pose it was quite the thing there for a while, wasn't it, Edwardian ladies trying to be the next Jane Austen. Or maybe some even fancied themselves as the next Elinor Glyn after her novel *Three Weeks* sold so well.'

'You are full of surprises, Stella,' I said, genuinely impressed with her knowledge.

'She wasn't one to shy away from telling a saucy tale of romantic love,' she continued matter-of-factly. 'And all inspired by her own scandalous affairs with British aristocrats, one of whom was nearly twenty years her junior,' she finished breathlessly, puffing from the exertion of lifting the folders down. 'There you are.' She stared me squarely in the eye. 'That'll keep you out of mischief getting through that lot.'

'Do you have it here?' I asked.

She raised her eyebrows. 'What, *Three Weeks*?'

'No, Rose's novel.'

'Oh, it should be here somewhere. I can dig it out for you sometime, if you'd really like to see it.'

'Yes, I would like that, only when you can, of course.'

'No worries, I'll get to it soon, won't be till after next week, though, if that's alright?'

'That would be terrific, thank you,' I said, my face burning.

I knew I'd turned the colour of a dark red apple. But thankfully, Stella was too busy to notice. Excitement at what I'd uncovered so far was lifting me up. Not only had I found two generations of women from my family tree, but I'd discovered that one of them had tried to become a novelist. And I had a letter, one that might provide a clue into their mother–daughter relationship. Did they argue? Is that why Rose kept it?

'It's a part of my job that I never tire of,' said Stella, with her ample back facing me, 'reading the diaries and letters of those departed. I find you hear voices from the past much better that way. I get a feeling for the times through their original words rather than some novelised version. Oh, but don't mind me,' she puffed, triumphantly dumping another stack of folders down in front of me. 'I'm not much of a fiction reader, anyway.'

'From what you said, it sounds like you know all about Elinor Glyn.'

'I'm aware of some historical facts that's all,' she responded, her face free of any readable expression. So, I couldn't tell whether she had read Glyn's racy novel or not, although I kind of hoped she had. 'Here we are, then, we can leave these here for tomorrow.' She turned to me quickly. 'I presume you will be coming back?'

'Wild horses couldn't keep me away,' was the best I could manage. Although hearing myself use the hackneyed phrase, I realised this was one time in my life that it was absolutely true.

'Good,' she said, nodding her approval, 'we can leave these out, then. That way you can get started immediately. I'll leave a note for one of the others to escort you down. I have a seminar first thing, but I will be in later.' She glanced at her watch. 'I'm afraid we are closing up now.'

'Yes, sorry,' I said, checking my watch. 'Goodness, how time flies …' I'd been tempted earlier to mention my romance titles to this passionate archivist, but this was not the time. *And my stories might be too tame for her, anyway*, I thought, smiling to myself.

'Are you right to go?' she said, standing by the door, keys in hand. 'I don't mean to rush you, but …'

'Yes,' I said, pulling the gloves off quickly. 'It's been a most interesting few hours.' I got to my feet and stood still. 'I'm afraid there's much more to take in than I anticipated.'

'Are you finding what you want?' she asked like she sensed something was not right.

'Oh yes, thank you,' I said.

As we climbed our way back up the stairs, she chatted happily about a local history talk she was giving later that evening.

'You're an authority on other local history, too?'

'Not exactly,' Stella said, looking pleased at my question. 'It's just that all of the menfolk on my father's side have been watermen. My father worked the tugboats, youngest captain on record,' she said proudly. 'Always happy to talk about that.'

I thought how wrong my first impression of Stella had been. She wasn't harsh at all, she was funny and thorough. No rings on her fingers, which made me wonder, did she share her life with someone? Hopefully, she did. I knew only too well the ins and outs of a solitary life.

'Thank you again, you've been most helpful,' I said, shouldering my way into my jacket. The talk sounded interesting, but with the stolen letter screaming to be read I had to decline. 'See you tomorrow, and best of luck with your presentation.'

'Maddison,' I heard her call after me.

I stopped and turned. 'Yes?' My heart was thumping, the letter burning a hole in my pocket. Did Stella know it was there, did she see me pop it away?

'You would be most welcome to attend the seminar, if you'd like to know a bit more about our local history …'

I toyed with asking her if she knew anything of my grandmother's brother, but decided against it.

'Unfortunately, I've made plans for this evening, Stella, but thank you just the same.'

I walked out of the archive, ran down the stairs, and resisted the urge to keep running. With icy-cold air stinging my face, I decided to head for a place near to my car. I remembered it from earlier. It wasn't far.

Inside the Wild Rose Tea House, the room was almost full and the temperature was warm. Soft pink-and-white walls covered with framed sketches of roses made for an inviting atmosphere. The smell of cinnamon in the air, the hum of chatter, and the chinking of teacups brought Ruth and Joan to mind. How they would love this.

I took a seat in the corner, aware of how fast my heart was beating, and pulled out Abbey's letter. When I looked up there was a young woman with the richest scarlet hair I'd ever seen standing next to the table looking down at me. She began to recite a long list of tea varieties, then asked me which one I preferred. I saw her eyes fall to the old letter in my hand. I panicked. *You are really an archivist working a second job, and you know this letter doesn't belong with me.*

'I think I'll go for the rosehip,' I said brightly.

'Good choice for this weather,' she responded casually, before sauntering back to the counter.

I unfolded the letter carefully, and started to read.

Maddison

The Waldorf Hotel, London, April 1936

Mother,

My eyes are dry, I haven't a single tear left to shed. I can't tell you how deeply it pains me to write these words. My mind is overflowing with questions, trying ever to comprehend your actions, and fearful that I never shall.

Were you trying to break my heart, lying to me, manipulating people behind my back? These are not the ways of a loving mother, unless being the great Lady Rose is the only thing that has ever really mattered to you.

I am uncertain what the world holds for me now. I can find no peace to sleep. I toss and turn, and feel as an orphan child surely must, alone and bereft. My grief knows no end, for those I have lost, and for what might have been.

I ask myself how I may ever find it in my heart to forgive you.

I hope I shall.

But at the time of this writing, I have found no answer.

Abbey

Hands trembling, I carefully refolded the letter and placed the envelope back in my bag. I certainly needed the cup of tea when it arrived to calm myself down. I sat quietly sipping. Here was hard evidence of a huge breakdown in their relationship. Brief and tortured, Abigail's letter had been written in the same year she arrived in Australia. What had happened to cause her such terrible pain and vehement anger against her mother? Rose had tucked this angry letter away within the pages of one of her diaries, to keep forever. Was it their last communication?

A hot shiver of recognition ran through me as the letter seemed to transmit its own memories. This had to be about a love affair somewhere, somehow, it just had to be.

Allowing my mind to drift, I pictured my grandmother sitting alone in a hotel room. A younger, prettier Abigail, rather than the older serious-faced woman I knew from my photos. I saw her in a grand room sitting by the window, dabbing her eyes, allowing the hanky to drop from her hand onto the credenza, where it lands next to her handbag and a half-drunk cup of tea. Her cheeks are flushed deep pink, and her eyes are puffy. She hasn't slept. There's a small tote, held fast with a thick leather strap and large buckle, on the floor by her side. She is well dressed. A soft pink silk shirt, beautiful tones with skirt of brown plaid. A matching jacket, tucked and buttoned, highlights her tiny waistline. Only her hair, light brown and softly curling, is dishevelled. The messy hair gives her a forlorn and lonely air, like a desperate lover who has been waiting too long. With a sudden but decisive movement she picks up the pen, straightens the page, then begins furiously penning a letter …

Was that how it happened?

More confused than ever, I wondered why my grandmother had never revealed to her Australian family that she'd come to Melbourne as a result of some dreadful family row. Had she never wanted to return? Not even once? What happened that was so damnable that she'd cut herself off completely like that? Wouldn't she have wanted us to know she was the daughter of English aristocracy? Wouldn't she have missed her mother when my mother and Uncle Gerry were born?

Whatever her reason for running away, she was clearly laying the blame at her mother's feet. Prickling with impatience, I shifted in my chair. All I wanted was to rush straight back to the archive and keep searching, but I knew I couldn't. The best I could manage was an early start tomorrow.

The unexpected appearance of this letter was a gift. But as I emptied my teacup, thinking about Abbey in that hotel room by herself, I also decided there must be some reason for John's silence on the subject of Abigail's brother. My instinct said James Carlyle would probably know what happened to Gerard, and that I should contact him to find out. But my cautionary brain said no. Before I asked anyone else, I should make my own investigation. That way I would know exactly where I stood.

Sometimes in my life, when something negative happened, like now, worrying about the secrets I strongly sensed were being withheld from me about the Hamptons, another event would roll in to hike up the tension. On the drive back to my lodging, I passed the Good Shepherd, and again my thoughts switched to Katya. And in that instant, incredibly, my phone beeped and I saw it was a message from Bethany. Marvelling at the coincidence, I pulled over and scrolled down to read it.

How's it going over there, Maddi? Met the queen yet?

Was it some kind of telepathy? It would be nice to think so.

The woman you saw playing in the street stays occasionally at a hostel for the homeless and mentally ill, she texted. *I went there. No sign. Privacy a hinderance. Manager can't talk about residents. But did get him to confirm a woman answering your description comes in. Sometimes. Long hair. Known to play piano. Sounds like her, getting closer! I'll keep looking. On the home front, working three days, 'mummy hours'. So far so good.*

I was pleased for Beth that her chosen circumstance was working out, but news on the Katya front was not so good. My thoughts wandered back to her. Had she been born in Australia, or had she arrived from somewhere else more recently? It was sad to have it confirmed that she was homeless. This, while I was in the middle of discoveries at the other end of the scale. There was nothing I could do for Katya at the moment. No matter how much I might want to.

So, I sent back: *Hi Beth, thank you so much for your efforts, appreciate lots, please don't worry anymore, I'll work it out when I get back. Apart from freezing cold, all good here. Having an 'interesting' time, no, make that VERY interesting. No queen yet! Happy your plan is working out. Love to all. Maddison xxx*

Edith and George called out a greeting as I made my way inside.

'Had a good day, luv?'

I paused at the foot of the stairs. 'Thank you, yes. The rain has eased off.'

'It has,' their voices synchronised as one.

I could see they were keen to chat, but I didn't feel up to questions about how I was spending my time. Tomorrow, perhaps.

'I'm going to turn in early, if you don't mind.'

'No worries, luv, g'night, then.'

They were so nice and friendly I felt guilty about not wanting to talk, but with my emotions in turmoil, I just couldn't. In truth, I was afraid I would say too much.

Back in my room, I quickly retrieved Abbey's letter and read it over several times. Holding the crispy, thin paper in my hand, I wondered if Abigail really had been alone at the time she wrote it. Or had there been someone there with her, in that hotel room? It was hurting my head trying to reconcile the serious face of the grandmother I knew, with the heartbreak behind what she wrote to her mother. Had Abigail really held all of that hurt inside for the rest of her life, and never forgiven her mother? It didn't seem possible that she could have lived the life she had, if that were the case.

I decided to run a bath. More than once a good soaking in hot water and bubbles had revealed plot points to me in the past. It might again. Maybe, I should try to find if the brother was alive and he could tell me more. *See what the archive turns up tomorrow and take it from there*, I decided, before my toes hit the water.

In bed, warm and comfortable, sunk back into the soft down pillows, inviting sleep and trying not to think about Rose, Gerard or Abigail, I heard my phone beep a message. I lay perfectly still, telling myself to ignore it, but knowing I wouldn't.

I swung my legs over and stood up, cursing my brain's inability to stop me. Listening to a voice message from James Carlyle, my pulse skipped a beat. *Damn it.* He was calling, he said, with the address for Saturday's morning tea. *'How's it going down there. Need any help?'*

Not from you I don't.

But then, I thought better of my reaction, and texted back: *Did you know my grandmother had a brother?*

The phone vibrated instantly in my hand. I picked up.

With no introduction, he said, 'I remember something about a brother.'

'Do you know if he's still alive, or where I could get in touch with him?'

'Hey, I thought the Spanish Inquisition was over?' He laughed, and the sound of his voice soothed my anger.

'You did ask if I needed help,' I said.

'Yes, but my research was all about the piano and finding a female descendant, remember? Have you spoken to John about this?'

'I haven't, given he doesn't appear to want to share any family information with me.'

There was a beat of silence. 'Leave it with me,' he said.

I smiled to myself, feeling pleased that I'd taken the call, after all.

'There is something else.'

'Yes?'

'If I find out about the brother, I think you should agree to come out with me. I think that's a fair trade. Besides, I have something to show you.'

'Really, and what is that?'

'A surprise,' he said.

'Look, James, I don't have time for surprises, I'm right in the middle of ...'

'You'll have time for this,' he said, 'I promise. And it won't take long. How about tomorrow first thing. You'll have plenty of time to get back to the archive.'

Again, my brain let me down when I heard myself agreeing to meet him and feeling pleased about it, despite Crystal Nettlewood.

'But aren't you in London?' I said.

'Not for you to worry,' he said. 'You Just let me know where you are, and I'll be past at nine am to collect you. Deal? You won't be sorry.'

'I don't know what I'm agreeing to, but alright nine it is,' and I gave him the address.

'Trust me,' he said, before he disconnected.

Trust me. The last time I heard those words, it had ended badly.

Maddison

Gravesend, next day

James was leaning against the car, overcoat collar up, blue beanie pulled over his ears. I saw him right away, and hurried to where he'd parked a few doors along the street.

'Now it's my turn to be taking you away from your research,' he said, and opened the door. 'Watch your step, it's pretty low, I borrowed this from a friend.'

'I hope I fit,' I said, folding myself in awkwardly into the worn leather seat of the old MG.

He slammed the door closed and dashed around the rear of the car, before getting in. 'It's not as fast as it looks,' he said.

'Did you drive this all the way from London?' I said, hearing how incredulous I sounded.

He laughed. 'Slow, draughty and uncomfortable. What more could you ask? I promised to show you around, remember?'

'Yes, but you didn't have to …'

'Yes, I did,' he said, rubbing his gloved hands together. 'I have no entrée to Hebden Girls to offer, so I had to find something …'

I saw the curtains move on the front window of the cottage and smiled to myself. *Just like home.*

'Did I say something funny?' said James, as he started the engine.

'No, I was just thinking how the owners,' I indicated the B & B, 'Edith and George, they remind me of neighbours at home, always keeping an eye on my movements.'

'Stickybeaks, you mean,' said James, turning to look up at the front window of the house.

'Maybe I think they're just interested and neighbourly.'

'Well, in my part of the world we call them stickybeaks.'

'Harsh,' I said.

'Alright, probably, doesn't mean they're not okay,' he said, 'just stickybeaks.'

James wasted no time, and as soon as we were underway, he said, 'So, how's the archive going?'

I glanced sideways. 'Lady Rose kept a diary, did you know that?'

'Yes, I did hear something about that.'

'I must say, they're absolutely fascinating. I can't tell you how much I appreciate your suggestion to research there. It's quite an experience to read her own words.'

I couldn't go into the range of emotion I was feeling about it. And I certainly wasn't going to tell him about Abigail's letter, which was in my bag to return. My mind had been on fire all night with the revelation of my grandmother's distress. Until I could find what drove her away from here, I could not rest. Lucinda's words came back to me, 'What does it matter it's all so long ago.' That was true, but it was so important for me to find out. Whatever happened I needed to know.

'That's good, then,' he said, hands firmly on the wheel, eyes straight ahead. 'I'm glad it helped. I'd like to say I knew what would happen when I offered my assistance to John,' he glanced quickly at me, 'but I didn't.'

His words left an opening for me to ask how that came about, but before I could think of how to phrase it, he continued.

'Maybe when you're done in Strood we can meet up again and I can tell you all about the search for Maddison, and how I found you.'

'Sounds like a romance novel,' I quipped, genuinely curious to find out how he did find me.

He smiled disarmingly. 'Maybe it is.'

Rattling along in his friend's old car, I was wondering about that last exchange, when he surprised me again.

'Is it too early in the day to ask a personal question?' He glanced quickly at me then back to the road.

'Probably,' I responded lightly to cover the tension I suddenly felt. 'Can't promise I'll answer.'

'Good, but first, I have to make a confession.'

'A confession and then a personal question? You're moving faster than your car.' He seemed nervous and didn't laugh at my line.

'Before coming down here, I picked out a few Maddison Browne titles from a local bookshop.'

I felt blood surging to my face. The memory of Andrew (the cad's) confession when he said he'd read my books flew uncomfortably to mind. Had James really just said he'd taken the time to search out my books? What next? 'I thought you said you were up to your ears in textbooks,' I said as nonchalantly as I could.

'I should be, but I wanted to understand what you do,' he said, 'but you know, flicking through to the end each time, I noticed something.'

I twisted my shoulders to face him, hoping my cheeks weren't as bright red as I felt they were. 'And what was that?'

'That in your books the heroine always gets her man.'

I laughed, relief billowing through my body. 'Why yes, of course she does. That's what's meant to happen,' I said. 'It's a romance. What did you expect?'

'Okay,' he said, 'so that's what happens in your books. But what about in real life? Is there a hero waiting for you?'

I was dumbstruck by the directness of his question, so my initial reaction was quite defensive. I thought, *What business is that of yours?* Yet, I heard myself respond spontaneously, while instigating some heavy-duty self-protection. 'You could say there is someone, yes.' *Another white lie*, I thought. *Lucky I'm not Pinocchio. Why did I not just say there was no one waiting for me anywhere?* I wondered. *Why did I not say that I was footloose and fancy-free? Because*, I concluded, *you didn't want him to think you were an easy mark.*

'I'm getting a picture here,' James said, in a good-natured way. 'Workaholic, protective stickybeak neighbours, aristocratic writer, heroic boyfriend in tow ...' He had me smiling again in spite of myself.

'Something like that,' I said lightly. 'Your turn. I notice you have a rucksack in the back there. Are you running away from your studies, perhaps?'

'I could be,' he said with a laugh. 'But I think I mentioned last time, I'm a pretty keen hiker. Some friends and I have been walking the coastal pathways these past weeks. It helps to keep my mind clear.'

I was struggling to picture Crystal in walking boots and a backpack.

'There's a great walk from Gravesend right along the water if you're interested,' he said.

The car turned a sharp right before I had time to respond. 'Here we are,' he announced, 'Anchor Cove, my secret destination.' He pulled the car in behind a charming sandstone church that stood just behind heavy wooden buttresses, protecting it from the sea.

'What is this, an ancient port?'

'It is,' said James. 'Only it's still working.' He jumped out, then came around to help me out of the car.

A blast of wind caught my hair. 'I love a sea port,' I said, breathing in the salty air. I looked around already captivated by the atmosphere.

'The Thames.' He pointed up and down the river. 'This used to be the first point of entry for shipping.'

'What an amazing place.' The sound of choppy seas smashing against the buttresses caused a water-works of foam to leap high in the air like a display of fireworks.

'This dock was the embarkation point for Brits sailing out to Australia and New Zealand, and the disembarkation for immigrants coming in,' said James, not waiting for me to react.

I grasped suddenly why he had brought me here. 'You mean …'

'Yes.' He nodded. 'This is a place where lives have been changed irrevocably. Right here, where we are standing.'

A chill raced up my spine.

'Oh my goodness,' I said, as full comprehension of what James was saying sank in. 'You mean this would be where Abigail left for Australia. This exact point.' The back of my throat tightened.

'Yes,' he said, 'and Rose landed with her luggage here, too, when she sailed from Australia to start her new life with William as wife to the Earl of Hebden.' James tapped the ground with his foot.

'It must have been so romantic and terrifying, and wild all at the same time …' I said, staring out to sea, then across to a chapel where whispered prayers for passengers ready to embark would have been given, or joyful thanksgiving received for those who'd survived the epic sea journey.

I was overwhelmed picturing my female forebears' paths crossing here. How fearless they were. The wind tugged ferociously at my hair, carrying on its breath the wailing siren of a ship's horn further up the estuary.

I stood completely still, lost for words. Whipped by the wind, my eyes were focused across the water as I listened to the pounding of the sea.

James said, 'It's still a place where new arrivals without papers try to dock with small vessels.'

I turned to him. 'Really? How dangerous.'

'Yes, I suppose once a place like Anchor Cove has a history of accepting and despatching travellers, then nothing in the universe can stop it.'

Neither of us spoke as we got back into the car, nor for most of the drive to my lodgings. I broke the silence as the Cosy Cottage came into view.

'How did you find it?'

'Like I said, we've been down this way walking a bit, so I asked a few questions, plus I saw a photo in the local paper.'

'Since you found me in the mists of history, James, do you feel a responsibility to help now in all things, is that it?' I was uncertain about where this was going and why he would put himself out like that for me.

I had to admit James was attractive, but with Crystal lurking in the background and my fragile trust, this was not something to be caught up in. *Forget about it*, I thought. *Thank him for this and move on.*

James brought the car to a stop, and smiled. 'There you are back in plenty of time, as promised.'

'Will you return to London now?' I asked, still trying to figure out his motivation.

'No, I'm planning to catch up with some hiking mates who are staying at the Leather Bottle Inn. I have someone to see about a professional matter, too,' he added, not elaborating on what the 'matter' might be. *Was it something to do with Crystal?* I wondered.

I untangled my legs and got out. Then, extending my hand towards him, I said, 'That was special, James, really special, thank you.'

He took my hand. 'I'll be in touch,' he said. 'And by the way, I think we got off on the wrong foot at breakfast the other day. But that's for another time.'

I watched him drive off, then dashed inside. Climbing the stairs, my thoughts ranged between imaginings of my grandmother waiting to sail to Australia, Rose's arrival from Melbourne to marry her beloved William, Abigail's horrible letter to her mother, and James. What did get off on the wrong foot mean? And why was that for another day? *What does he want?* No way was I about to get involved with someone who was already tied up, no matter how appealing or helpful he was.

I decided to follow my own advice, leave all thoughts of James aside, and get back to the archive. 'You have a story to write and a promise to fulfil,' I said aloud. 'You can't allow yourself to be sidetracked now.'

It was no surprise that Stella had done as she'd promised and left a note of introduction for me. No sooner did I offer my name at the enquiries counter than I was ushered downstairs.

My first action was to return Abigail's letter to her mother's diary. I'd already photographed it with my phone, and now I placed it carefully between the pages of diary two, closed the covers, and with a great sigh of relief, put it back. Who might be the next person to see it, I wondered? Was I the last? Yes, I probably was.

My strongest hunch from what I'd gleaned so far, the most likely circumstance that drove my grandmother away from her home here to Australia was a failed love affair. Someone her mother didn't approve

of, most likely. Judging from Abigail's letter, and the words she'd used –
'behind my back' – her mother may have intervened and put a stop to it.

Marianne had never done anything like that in my life (thankfully),
but I remembered Amy's mother being quite against her first choice
of partner. And in the end, Amy had left that relationship and married
someone she and her mother had been happy with.

I picked up Rose's diary to immerse myself again, aware of a
tension in my chest, for what lay buried in its pages.

Rose

Hebden Manor, 1936

Music was playing softly on the radio. I lay there waiting with only the sound of it for company, longing for the lagging hours of darkness to transform into translucent early-morning light. One moment was like one hour. Endless as eternity. Would I ever grow accustomed to Will being confined to his rooms?

And was that Anna Neagle and Jack Buchanan singing their famous duet, 'There's Always Tomorrow?' I leaned across to the wooden box and turned up the volume. 'Stand up and Sing' had been a smash hit for them on the West End.

I lay propped up with pillows, listening but feeling restless. My eyes filled uncontrollably with tears. The mere thought of a better tomorrow was enough to bring my emotions bubbling to the surface.

I threw back the covers, set my bare feet down on the floor and crossed the room. Staring through the wide picture window that framed the horizon perfectly, I gathered myself, holding back tears and breathing deeply. I couldn't fall apart. Not now. Now, more than ever, I had to stand tall and strong.

The view of Hebden grounds from my window still took my breath away. The first time I saw it, Will was holding my hand tightly, while I, relying on all my powers of self-control, was trying not to faint with fear. That day, I'd drawn on Lady Robinson, acting the way I'd seen her behave to retain her composure at difficult times;

straight back, still hands, and a smile fixed on her face. That was how she sailed through any demanding situation. I confess, on my first day here, meeting Will's family for the first time, I copied her, wishing only that my performance be as convincing as hers. I desperately wanted Will to feel proud of me when he introduced me to his father, the earl, and his mother, Lady Margaret. They were as good as royalty to me. And who was I? Just a policeman's daughter from the colonies.

I had married 'up'. That was what Lady Robinson said when she heard about Will and me. She said that she feared I would find myself out of my depth in the role awaiting me, but she would wish me well, nonetheless. But as she embraced me, the final thing she whispered in my ear as I walked out the door was, 'Rose, remember you are always welcome, any time, to return to us.'

She expected me to fail. The effect of this, and the words of other doomsday naysayers, people who professed their 'concern' for me on the one hand, while predicting my fall from grace with the other, citing my lack of social standing, my 'unsuitable' religion and more as reasons why I should go away quietly and let the earl marry a person who was 'right' for him, meant that by the time I arrived here, I was rigid with fear. And for a long time afterwards, these words rang in my ears. I feared I would never be good enough.

After all, the best anyone imagined for me growing up in Australia was that I might become a nanny or marry a farmer. If I were more ambitious, I might open a little grocery store locally where I was known. Patronage would be regular from people thinking it would be a good thing to buy their supplies from 'the copper's daughter'. But I loved music and reading books. I'd never been able to imagine myself as one of those farmer's wives with brown arms and weathered faces. Strong women who could birth a lamb, or ride a horse like a man. I'd prayed that there would be a different sort of life for me. And my every prayer was answered the day I met Will.

Since our wedding, the happiest years of my life had been spent here at Hebden. Foolishly, I'd even thought this enchanted life would never end. Lovingly, I allowed my eyes to roam, tracing the outline of the magnificent landscape, drawn by canopies of faithful oaks that kept watch over acres of beautiful manicured garden. This picture was so familiar to me now, that it had all but obliterated childhood memories of dusty paddocks and the Australian countryside.

The song on the radio ended abruptly. Often in my darkest hours since Will's car accident, I've wondered if fortune hadn't smiled too fondly on me. Was I being punished for having had too much happiness? His stroke afterwards, and the consequence of it, had changed our lives forever.

Rubbing my lips together slowly, I thought about the last time he'd kissed me, and wondered if he ever would again. I stood there until a gunshot sounded outside, reminding me that it was later than I thought. The game keepers were already out, it was time to bathe and prepare for the day.

I slipped a cardigan over my silk shirt, adjusted the collar and checked my skirt was in place. I smoothed the pleats, swivelled my shoulders and caught the reflection of a woman I barely recognised.

Delicate skin, barely a line, only a few flecks of grey amongst neatly rolled hair to indicate the passing years. But the eyes, once described as a 'triumph of intrigue and beauty', shone no more, 'like black onyx brimming with life'. Instead, a brooding pool of darkness lingered behind their lustrous colour these days. Too much had happened. The figure, slightly fuller, no longer the slender hourglass it had once been, was still a fine specimen of womankind.

With that, Fletcher bustled into the room carrying my jacket over one arm.

'Any news of Lady Abigail yet, Milady?'

I smiled fondly at the woman who'd been tending to my needs since I first arrived as a new bride, twenty-five years earlier. From the start, her kindly manner and steady personality had calmed me. It was Fletcher who had gently offered little pieces of advice to help me understand the protocols of what was expected. Especially when William's older brother, Granville, died suddenly and William had to take on the role of earl. I'd been thrown in at the deep end, as lady of the manor. Fletcher had come to my rescue. She'd been my rock of Gibraltar through the hard war years, and the downturn that followed. And still was, to this day.

'No doubt she will let us know where she is when she is good and ready.' I tried to sound untroubled, tucking away a stray wisp of hair.

'I think it's high time she got in touch instead of causing us all such worry, what with everything.'

'I can only agree,' I said, still fiddling with my hair.

'Would you like me to help you with that?' she asked, moving towards my dresser.

'Thank you, Fletcher, I do try to be modern, but I'm afraid I can never get my hair to stay in place the way you can.'

'I still say, it's all this talk about women doing what they want that's influencing her. All those young women rushing around forgetting their place, it can't be a good thing,' she mumbled, picking up a hairbrush and deftly winding stray hairs into the rolls that framed my face.

'I'm not sure I can agree with you completely on that score, dear Fletcher, nothing wrong with the suffragettes' cause. My daughter, however, should know better, that's all. She's been brought up to be aware of her responsibilities.' I heard the sharpness in my voice and regretted instantly using that tone to one so dear to me.

Fletcher, unflappable as ever, responded normally, as if she hadn't heard anything wrong. 'Is there nothing that can be done? Surely his lordship knows a lot of important people up in London.'

'Yes, he does, and I fear that might just be part of the problem,' I said, choosing not to elaborate. There was enough gossip downstairs as it was regarding our daughter's absence. A mysterious suitor? Just yesterday passing along the upper passageway, I overheard whispers speculating that it was either a European count or an American movie star.

Choosing my words carefully I said, 'If Abigail has decided to make herself uncontactable, short of setting a detective on her tail, I don't see what more we can do. Except wait.'

'And hope,' she finished, patting my hair. 'There you are, Madam, all done.'

'Yes, and hope,' I repeated in a small voice, as she left the room. 'Thank you, Fletcher.'

It was a mistake to allow Abigail to go to London, I know that now, but when Abigail pleaded with me, I had seen myself imploring my own mother to sanction marriage to the man I loved. My own bid had failed, and I had never reconciled with my mother, not even when I heard of my sister's death. So, no matter how I tried, I simply couldn't find it within me to deny our only daughter. Despite every single bone in my body telling me that I should.

At first, I blamed Will for allowing our daughter to stay on in London after her coming-out party.

'They are a fine bunch. They'll look after her,' he'd maintained of his old family friends.

But things had turned out rather differently. From what I found out from Abigail herself, she'd been treated to theatre visits, music-hall entertainments and even introduced to the sordid scene of new jazz dance clubs.

Her head had been completely turned by people whose idea of what it meant to be a guardian were totally different from my own, and Will's, too, for that matter. In the short time she was away, Abigail had acquired a taste for the sort of life that was not only unsuitable for her, but completely inappropriate for her role as the daughter of an earl. She had come home begging for her freedom, saying that she wanted to be an American-style pianist-actress, of all things. My daughter was a gifted piano player. I had spent many hours sitting by her side, teaching her myself, I clearly saw her abilities. I thought it was understood that showbusiness was not a path for an aristocratic young lady.

But the manor was no match for the bright lights of London, particularly at this restless time. Not that it was dull at Hebden. Not by any stretch. Will was a generous host, even if demands on him from his parliamentary friends had diminished in recent times due to his precarious health. Abigail had played at the manor for actors, playwrights, friends and political guests from London, and always to great acclaim. In this, she had overtaken the level of my own playing and excelled beyond all of my wildest expectations. Why wasn't that enough for her?

'You've got a star there, Rose,' was a common refrain amongst our friends. Our daughter had been presented to the Prince of Wales, for goodness sake. Abigail could not possibly have considered that her life here would be boring, lacklustre or even that restrictive. But yes, it was not the life of a screen siren, which appeared to be lacking in boundaries of any kind, and to me, was hardly a proper way for any young woman to live. Despite that, her freedoms at Hebden would have been considerable.

'But, Mummy, I want to be independent of you and Daddy. I want to know what emancipation feels like, and I want to stand on my own two feet. Anyway, it's the new way of things. You can't stop it, no one can.'

When she explained to me what she actually wanted to do (and it didn't involve the recital halls of classical music), pleading with me, 'I can earn my own money playing in marvellous clubs, I can, I know a few people now, please let me try,' it wasn't that I didn't believe her. It was just that a mother's instinct said there must be more to it. I could easily acknowledge how the glamour of a life in showbusiness might seduce a young woman to run off, even a daughter whose upbringing had been far from cloistered. But I sensed immediately that the problem lay elsewhere.

After her return from London, she'd talked too much about one particular friend of her father's. Will's group were a mixed and lively bunch, but in Abbey's own words, this particular person had either instigated, or had been present at, all of the theatrical outings that she was so enamoured of.

I was shocked the first time I heard her say his name out loud, given the man in question had, on a visit to the manor not so long ago, supposedly on government business, and despite having a wife back in London, made serious overtures to me. Was it possible he was now pursuing our daughter?

I'd not mentioned the incident to anyone, certainly not to Will, but hearing that man's name on my daughter's lips made me blush with embarrassment. Not so much for the proposal itself, but rather for my reaction to it. One moment of weakness, deep in the night, lying alone in my cold bed, I'd actually seriously considered taking him as a lover.

For the truth was that this man of letters with his smooth-talking, easy manner, was charming and attentive; he knew how to make a woman feel desirable. *Was that so wrong?*

'Given Will's *condition*,' the suitor had whispered gently in my ear, pulling me aside and gazing deeply into my eyes, 'it makes perfect sense that a woman as lovely as you should not be lonely. I am the perfect choice, don't you see? A colleague of your husband, married, reasonably well off, no threat whatsoever in any way.'

I had been tempted by his proposition, and I almost fell under his spell, the warmth and energy of his body dancing close to mine, audacious and exciting, as he'd begged me to come to his room after the guests left. Under my own roof, for goodness sake.

The next morning, although I didn't act on his pleading or my own reaction to it, I almost wept with remorse seeing Will's broad smile, his eyes shining at the sight of me carrying his breakfast tray myself.

I became suspicious when I asked Abigail how it was that someone so much older than her friends, a married man at that, had been socialising with their group? She snapped at me, 'And what's wrong with knowing your way around the city?' Which did nothing to console me. In fact, it had the opposite effect and made me fear the worst. How she steadfastly refused to speak a word of sense about the future, rejecting point blank suitable offers of marriage from two lovely young men, constantly demanding that she be allowed to live on her own terms, made me wonder how I could have raised a daughter so headstrong and unwilling to listen to reason. Will laughed heartily when I posed that question to him.

'Oh, dearest Rose, do you really not see that our beautiful daughter is strong-spirited just like her mother? Not just anyone could have done what you did. What we did,' he added, 'can't you see that?'

Although there may have been more than a grain of truth in Will's comments, my growing terror was that Abigail had been seduced by the same man who very nearly had his way with me; a charming rogue, entirely unsuitable for her.

In trying once more to get to the truth of my daughter's situation, I confronted her, and a most dreadful argument ensued. One that I shall never forget. I only wish I could erase from my memory the bitter taunts she hurled at me.

'You married the man you wanted, why won't you allow me to do the same? Are you jealous that I might find my own happiness?'

'Marriage?' I said. 'Marriage? You think he will marry you?'

It shames me to recall how I responded. The look of complete anguish on her face when I said, 'He won't leave his wife for a … distraction.' It was not my proudest moment.

'Are you saying that's what I am, a mere distraction?'

Now, I see that my daughter was right. I rode roughshod over her. Too taken with my position and my duties to William and his family. It had never been (heaven forbid) my intention to hurt her, but in loving her so, I had not given due consideration to her life. I'd taught her to play the piano yes, but now, I understood that was not enough. I was too harsh with her. Why did I behave that way when I wanted what was best for her?

Next morning, when Abigail didn't appear at breakfast, the household assumed that she had simply overslept or was sulking in her room. How with all of my heart I wished that were so. If only I could turn back the clock and reverse the cross words that had passed between us. For the terrible truth was that, on that night, Abigail fled her home and her family, completely. Not a soul downstairs saw or heard her leave, or if they did no one ever admitted to it. Now two weeks have passed without a word from her. Fletcher sent out search parties around the village in the hope that someone might have seen something, but to no avail.

I even suggested to Will tactfully that he might send word to London, to the friend of his I considered responsible for our daughter's erratic behaviour. At the very least, he might have some clue where she was. Will discounted my theory, but to please me he made the call, only to discover the man in question had been going about his business normally, and claimed to know nothing of Abigail.

'You see, Rose,' Will said. 'I'm not sure why you think he would know anything. He's a fine lawyer and is well thought of in his government work. Matter of fact, he had a quiet word with me the last time he was here with us, said he was thinking about setting up a business down this way. Asked me what I thought.'

'What did you say?'

'I said I thought it was a good idea. That I for one would be most pleased to have a respected lawyer close by to handle our business. And I was certain that others would feel the same way. It'd save us having always to go up to London every time we need legal advice, Rose.'

I knew that Will's life would be easier if he never had to leave home again. He hated the contraption of a chair he had to be wheeled around in. He hated being fussed over by others. But when I said that I thought there would be plenty of others to assist with our affairs, he snapped at me. 'Rose, leave that to me. You will need good help locally if anything should happen ...'

'I'm sorry, my darling, of course you're right.' I kissed his cheek to stop the words I didn't want to ever hear him speak. Will looked up and stared directly into my eyes.

My heart thumped with guilt. *What could he see? That I almost said yes?*

'Said he won't always be flavour of the month in London, and his wife is fretting for a quieter life, can't be all that bad.'

'No, it can't.' I stroked his head, consoling him while in my deepest heart, forgetting about myself, I sensed that something had gone seriously wrong for our daughter.

If William could become one of the frightening numbers of road casualties – a quarter of a million people injured or killed in road accidents this past year according to *The Listener* – what of Abigail? A headstrong young woman like her, roaming the streets without proper supervision. She was at risk of becoming a statistic of another kind. The best I could hope was that our daughter was hiding somewhere with friends who would not betray her. But I couldn't get the terror out of my mind. I resolved that if there were no word or clue forthcoming by the end of this day, I would have to go and look for her myself.

Lightheaded all of a sudden, I excused myself and returned to my rooms. There, I placed my hand on the dresser to steady myself. Heaven knows it was hard for anyone to believe in the future, between the slump, the strikes, the wretched business of Edward and Wallis making headlines every day, and talk of another war when the last was barely over. It was hard to see any silver lining. Now our own daughter was missing. I couldn't remember ever in my life feeling so low.

I considered bringing Gerard back from boarding school. No. He was too impressionable. I didn't want him learning to rebel like his sister. Instead, I sat down and wrote him a note suggesting that he remain in boarding school this holiday break.

It felt awful to put him off. 'Be a "summer boy", darling, just this once, for your mother. Do you mind?'

He wouldn't understand. He would have looked at me with those doe eyes of his, nodding his head in agreement, but hating what I'd asked of him. Gerard loved coming home to the manor during school breaks. But Will and I had been of one mind about this. Gerard must be kept in the dark about his sister's disappearance, for now.

Abigail's absence was taking a hard toll on her father. I'd heard him making other discreet enquiries amongst his London circles, asking for anyone who might have knowledge of her whereabouts. I witnessed him weakened by despair each day, head bowed sitting near the telephone, lying to his friends when his efforts proved fruitless.

'Very well, thanks again, old chum, just keep in your mind if you see or hear something, anything. Just let me know, would you, even if you think it's nothing? No, no trouble at all, she's a bit headstrong, that's all.'

And the only way I'd found to save myself from going completely mad was to be completely engrossed in every manor activity, while planning how I could find Abigail.

A rustle and soft footsteps, and Fletcher was back. 'Can I get you some tea, Madam?'

'No, thank you, Fletcher. I'll be down in a little while, then we can go.'

Keeping up appearances, as best I could, Fletcher and I would soon head down to the fair held in the village hall behind the church. A good turnout was expected. The manor played its part by providing eggs from estate hens and fresh vegetables from the patch. Church committee members would have been up baking all night to prepare. The proceeds were to be distributed amongst families with no bread winner, and those with family members battling injuries from the Great War.

I wanted to attend, yet a part of me did not, but of course I would, I was dutybound.

'I've got the baskets all prepared, Madam, so you've no need to worry.'

I waited for Fletcher's footsteps to recede into the distance before opening the drawer of my dresser. Reaching in, I pulled out the small cardboard packet. Popping two white tablets from the box, I placed them on my tongue. Quickly removing the doily covering my glass, I took a sip of water and swallowed hard. I shivered as the bitter aftertaste caught in my mouth. Whatever did I do before this little miracle for headaches?

William had purchased shares in the Aspro company when it moved from Australia to England in search of investment. His eyes had lit up as he'd told me about an industrious Australian called Alfred Nicholas, who'd found a way to manufacture acetylsalicylic acid, or aspirin, by converting the powder into a tablet form.

It involved, he said, 'developing a special dry granulation process so that salicylic acid would not be released. Brilliant. Just the kind of product I would have invested in sooner if only I'd known about it.'

Luckily, William was a great futurist, and a canny investor, too. Had he not been so, the manor might have succumbed like some other estates who'd found themselves in financial trouble when the economy turned bad.

Over the years, he had often mentioned Hebden's investments in Australian industry. William had maintained his interest in the country of my birth, even though we'd never returned after our marriage. No words had passed between us to explain this. Just a silent understanding that the cruel tongues and bigotry at the time of our betrothal had created a shadow we both preferred to leave in the past. I didn't care. Hebden was my home now.

I took another sip of water and allowed my eyelids to close. If I sat perfectly still, the constant pounding in my head would subside. After one minute I stood and put on my jacket.

Later that night, the clock chimed eight pm, and still with no word from anyone about Abigail, I made my decision. I was going to take charge of the situation. I'd packed a small tote myself, in readiness. I would go to London to employ the services of a private detective. I didn't know exactly how to carry off such a transaction, but I would find out. I would break the news of my plan to Fletcher tomorrow and leave immediately after that.

William had forbidden me to go. When I suggested that we might contact a detective agency and directed him to an advertisement I'd found in the Sunday papers, he was horrified. And not just for the scandal.

'If I, with all of my connections, cannot find our daughter, how could a complete stranger unless …?'

When he discovered I had journeyed without his consent, he would be furious. But short of making a public announcement, William had virtually admitted he was bereft of ideas what to try next. Something had to be done. If he could not, then I must try. The compulsion driving me to find our daughter was too powerful. My need to know where she was would overwhelm me completely if I did nothing. Was this really all my fault, was the question that was haunting me? What if something unimaginably terrible had happened to her? I could not carry on a moment longer, pretending, participating in community charities, showing no obvious concern. Finding my daughter, holding her in my arms and telling her that we only want her safe, was all that mattered to me now.

William leaving 'unless' hanging in the air, and all of the unspoken implications contained in that one hesitant word, was the final straw that had driven my decision to defy him. Since our conversation earlier this morning, and all through the community fair, my restless mind had been formulating a plan.

The more I thought about the details, the more trepidation crept into my heart. Especially when I was forced to confront one cold, hard fact.

Many years had passed since I'd done anything on my own. Crossing my fingers would not be enough this time, nor would simply believing I could do it. Finding Abigail would be my brave new world.

After nine-thirty pm, I was still up and highly agitated, with every nerve in my body jangling. So preoccupied was I with my plan, that I didn't even hear the light tapping at my door until it became loud and persistent enough to catch my ear. I glanced at the clock. Senior staff would be retired already for the evening. I opened the door to Fletcher's assistant, a dainty young girl called Mary.

'I'm sorry to disturb you, Milady, but I thought it best,' the young woman stammered, extending a silver plate in my direction.

'Mary, whatever is it that brings you to my door at this hour?'

Without wasting a second, she explained how a person unknown had knocked on the kitchen door and asked that this letter be delivered to the lady of the manor with utmost urgency. The young girl's face was flushing as she spoke, as she was fearful that she might have done, or said, the wrong thing.

'Thank you, Mary, you were right to bring it to me.' I smiled encouragingly and picked up the envelope. I turned it over. No stamp, no indication whom it might be from. But blazing through every fibre of my being was hope, luminous and clear. Here it was, the moment we had been waiting for. Abigail was making contact. At last.

I closed the door and steadied myself. My fingers were shaking as I tore the envelope open. I was thinking how any minute I would have to dash to Will and wake him up with the splendid news that Abigail had returned. I even thought our daughter might be waiting outside, shivering in the shadows, waiting to be brought through the front entrance. If so, I would rush out, take her in my arms. I would tell her that it was wrong of me to interfere. I would tell her how much I loved her, and how her life was all before her. I would promise never again to presume that I knew what was best for her.

It was only when I saw it was not Abbey's hand that my heart started to constrict. Whose writing was this? My eyes raced greedily to read the name signed at the bottom. When the identity of the writer registered and I read the words he'd written, I felt my whole body stiffen. Breathing heavily, I drew on what was left of my strength and screamed out, pelting the note into the air, staring as it seesawed down to settle on the floor. I ran to the window and peered out into the darkness, hoping to see what, I don't know. My stomach was threatening to expel all of its contents. I held my arms tightly by my side, clenching and unclenching my fingers. I wouldn't be travelling to London tomorrow. My journey was going to be much closer to home.

Maddison

Strood

I was spellbound, but the diary had run out. I flicked hurriedly to the end, only to find that the last few pages were all blank. Right at the point of revealing the most critical piece of the puzzle, the words stopped. I rifled through the boxes looking for the next diary to follow the story on, to no avail. I was close, but as things stood, I now had more unanswered questions than I started with. I'd been left with the worst kind of cliff hanger. Who was Rose going secretly to meet? Where had Abigail run off to?

One thing struck me: if my grandmother had ever read these diaries and understood the depth of her mother's contrition, she might not have been able to cut her off so completely. On the other hand, it would have been devastating for her to read that the mysterious friend of her father's she seemed to have been involved with, had also attempted to seduce her own mother. So, there was no way of knowing, or predicting, what might have happened differently.

A whole new understanding was dawning on me, how unresolved arguments between parents and children especially, if left unforgiven, fester, multiply and flow on down the generations on a tide of ignorance, wreaking havoc on the innocent. I had only to consider my own family's relationship, Rose and my grandmother, to acknowledge that.

What did it take really to forgive someone? Understanding of another's position, a softening of the heart, or was it love pure and simple? Plenty of times, my mother had said things to me that I didn't like, and plenty of times she'd made promises she hadn't kept. I might have huffed for a while, but I always forgave her. In light of what I was reading here, that at least was pleasing to me.

I was packing up slowly, a cloud of nostalgia and sadness for what could never be hovering over my head, when Stella arrived. Observing me from the doorway, she said, 'Not finding what you're looking for today?'

I gaped at her. I was hungry, tired, sad, and overwhelmed by the documents and boxes I'd just trawled through with no solution in sight.

'Who was the last person to see this material before it came here?' I asked, indicating the documents piled up on every surface. 'Would it have been lawyers for the estate?'

'Yes, delivery to us would have been sanctioned by the lawyers,' she said, unperturbed by my brusque tone. 'We are very particular about ownership.'

'So, Nettlewood and Son?'

'Yes. I believe they handled all the manor's affairs for a very long time. That being so, they most probably would have been the last people to access this material before it came to us.'

She paused, regarding me, then looked around at the mess. 'Didn't you say it was one of the Nettlewoods who found you in Australia?'

'That's right.'

A soft whirring from a vent in the ceiling sounded.

'Maybe someone there can shed more light on it for you.'

'Thanks, Stella. And don't worry, I'll straighten this up before I leave.'

'No need. We'll take care of it.'

I grabbed a takeaway sandwich and returned to my lodgings, intent on getting back to my own writing for the rest of the day, but on the way, my brain travelling fast made a snap decision on what my next step was going to be.

By the time I'd trawled through numerous numbers and relevant phone extensions for the House of Lords, answered mostly by recorded voices telling me to state my business and number, I was feeling so frustrated and trying not to blow my top that when a real person bid me good afternoon and asked the purpose of my call, I almost missed it.

'Yes, I'm looking for Gerard Hampton, the Earl of Hebden, I wonder if you could tell me how to contact him?'

'And you are?'

'A writer from Australia.'

I heard the phone click, then ring out again before a tired voice said, 'House of Lords media enquiries.'

My free hand formed a fist. I was finally being connected to someone who should be able to answer my question.

'Yes, good afternoon, can you help, I am trying to contact Gerard Hampton the Earl of Hebden. I wonder if you could give me a point of contact. Someone has recommended that I speak to him.'

'About a trade matter, is it?' said the voice, absently.

'Yes, yes, it is, or rather an interview about a trade matter.' This was a long shot, I was flying blind here, but what the heck, if it gave me what I wanted. They were only words on the telephone. I couldn't be arrested for that.

'Who do you work for?'

'An independent Australian publication.'

'Are you staying in London?' the voice enquired.

'No, I'm down in Cobham staying with friends.'

'Very well, just a minute.' While I waited, I tapped my second finger on the bedside table, wondering what she could be looking up.

'Are you there?' the voice said, at last. 'Sorry to keep you waiting.'

'Yes, I'm here.'

'I just had to check the earl's whereabouts. I thought he might be in London at the moment, he does come across sometimes.'

He is still alive. I had to control myself to not yell that out at the top of my voice. But I couldn't help punching the air. George and Edith were right. When I'd asked what happened to the earl, George had said he was certain the current earl was still around. He just wasn't living in Cobham anymore. 'Somewhere overseas, I think.' His wife had agreed.

'If he's not in London, where could I contact him?'

'Can you hold for a minute?' I held my breath.

'Are you still there?'

'Yes.'

'I'm told that he is at home. So, probably your best would be to liaise directly with him. Lord Hampton has plenty of support staff.'

'What do you suggest?' I asked as diplomatically as I could, trying not to sound desperate.

'If I were in your shoes I'd jump on a plane and fly straight over to the Bahamas, but as you'd need to speak to him first to arrange that, I should just give you his direct number. It's not easy when our people live abroad. Could you give me your phone number and passport number, too, please, so I can to place your details with this enquiry.'

With my spare hand rifling around in my handbag to retrieve my passport, I said my name out loud and spelled the 'e' on the end of 'Browne', hoping she wasn't going to ask for any more credentials. I smiled inwardly at the thought of her looking me up after I put the phone down, only to discover I was a romance writer, not a journalist on assignment.

I repeated the long number back, with its Bahamas prefix, thanked her, and put the phone down.

My legs folded as I fell onto the bed, and I lay for several minutes breathing hard. But with a huge smile plastered on my face.

Outside my little window, I could see the afternoon drawing to a close, and it was raining again. After the rush of excitement from finding that my great-uncle was still alive, and disbelief that I had a phone number for him, it was hard to settle. I counselled myself to calm down, and as soon as I stopped my brain yelling out, *Abbey, I've found your brother, and he's alive*, I did.

I grabbed my phone and pushed 'play', letting Rachmaninov set the mood. As strains of his Variations filled the air, I lay down on my bed, pushed two pillows together to prop up my laptop, and started typing. This particular piece of music seemed to do the trick to unlock my brain. My latest writing was going well. The story was flying along, and I was well into the first draft. Whatever had caused my return to speedy writing, I was loving the feeling of being back on my game. Although, I was still hedging bets with two possible options about how the ending would go.

Barely settled, I heard footsteps clumping up the stairs, followed by a polite tap on my door.

'Sorry to disturb you, luv. But there's that man waitin' outside,' Edith hissed loudly, as if there was somebody other than me to hear her. 'In that old car of 'is. I think you should invite him in, don't you?'

I swung the door open.

'Sorry, luv, but it's dreadful out there.'

'Edith, sorry, who's where?'

'Down on the street, luv. That young man you've been steppin' out with, in that old car.'

'James, do you mean?' She could only mean him, given she'd not seen me with anyone else.

'I don't know 'is name, luv, I just know the MG that's all. And this is for you, too, came this morning.' She dug an aerogram from her pocket, and handed it to me. And before I'd turned it over, she volunteered, 'Ruth and Joan.'

It took a second to register. I stared at her.

'Friends of yours?' she asked.

'Yes, neighbours from home,' I said.

'Isn't that nice now. Who'd o' thought? Real-life neighbours writin' actual letters to one another,' Edith said, her voice seething with questions.

James could be right about stickybeaks, I thought a little unkindly as I gathered my coat to go downstairs.

The other night, when I was having trouble sleeping, I ended up chatting with Edith and George until quite late, and they had given me some new leads to pursue. And George's comment about the earl living overseas had just paid off. *Do not be grumpy.* Of course, I'd had to reveal that I was a writer working on a story about a grand manor, to explain why I was asking them so many questions about Hebden.

'You mean you're a writer having one o' those "undercover" experiences, luv?' George beamed guilelessly at me.

I almost laughed out loud. 'Yes, you could say that, George.'

'I knew it had a' be something like that, wi' all your comings and goings.'

'Oh, I do love to read a nice romance myself,' Edith sighed. 'Did you hear that, George? We've got our own writer staying here, just like back in the day up at the Leather Bottle Inn.'

No amount of me saying that I wasn't anything like Charles Dickens made the slightest bit of difference to them. Edith and George rambled on about the manor at Hebden, reminiscing about all the local families they'd known who worked there. I was only wishing I had a pen and pad to write down some of the names they mentioned, so my memory didn't have to work hard to recall everything they were saying. But I'd thought that if I started to write down what they were saying, it might frighten them.

'Yer know there were a few scandals up there, too, apparently?' said Edith.

George cut his wife off, as if he knew where she was heading. 'Now, Edith don't you be repeating tales. If they're not facts, then what it amounts to is gossip, and yer know what I think about gossip.'

His wife looked slightly affronted, but pursing her lips continued, 'Just sayin', George, there's no need to get on your high horse. I just thought Maddison might be interested to know, that's all …' she looked at me dolefully, 'for her story.'

I smiled at her. Actually, I was relieved that George had diverted the conversation. I feared it was only a matter of time before Edith started asking me more personal questions that I didn't want to answer.

Before she did, I'd thanked them and begged my leave.

Now, I was aware she was waiting for me to move. 'Thanks, Edith, I'll run on ahead if you don't mind.'

'Of course not, luv, you go right on.'

I bolted down the stairs and stood at the front door for a minute.

She was right, there was a car, engine running, lights on, and inside I could see it was James.

I pulled my hood up and dashed out over to the driver's side, crossing in front of the headlights.

'Hi, what are you doing here?' I kept my voice upbeat, thinking, *What on earth does he want?*

'Hello again, twice in one day, not bad, eh? I was wondering whether it was better to call, text, or just knock on the door.'

'Now the stickybeak has decided for you.' I leaned over and peered in. 'Would you like to come inside?' I said. There was a stream of water trickling down the inside roof of his car.

'No, I won't, thanks all the same.'

'Is there something wrong?'

'Do you want to hop in for a minute. You're getting wet.'

'Will it take long?'

'Depends,' he said, sounding annoyingly cheerful.

'Alright.' I ran around and clambered in. 'It's not much better in here,' I said, as a drip of water landed squarely on the end of my nose. I wiped it off with the back of my sleeve.

'I thought you'd have returned to London by now. Very brave, you and Crystal out walking in this weather,' I said, still rubbing my nose.

'I found the number you were looking for.' He produced a piece of paper and handed it to me.

I saw the name Lord Gerard Hampton, and a string of numbers. 'It's in the Caribbean,' he said. 'And don't tell anyone it was me who gave it to you.'

'Okay, I won't, but surely you didn't come just for that.'

'I did. But now I really do have to go, job interview, or else I'd invite you up to the pub for a drink.' His face was serious. 'Wrong end of the stick again if you think Crystal would be out walking in any weather. More Pilates studio for her, I think. Not anything I go for.'

Crystal or Pilates? I wondered, but said casually, 'That's terrific. Hope the interview goes well.' I flipped the door open. 'Thanks very much for this.'

'Are you going to call him?' he asked.

'Yes, probably, I'll work it out,' I said.

'I'm sure you will. Apparently, he's ninety-five years old and still with it, amazing! And by the way, that coastal walk offer still stands. Unless you prefer Pilates, too.'

I got out, leaned over and said, 'Thanks again,' without responding to the rest.

How could I tell him that I already had the number?

I watched him drive off until the tail-lights disappeared. James had a way of always leaving me off guard. *Wrong end of the stick...again.* He was almost as frustrating as my search for answers about Abigail. At the same time, I couldn't deny that he'd returned in the pouring rain to deliver the number, without knowing that I'd already found it myself.

Perplexed, I wandered to my room and tore open the letter from home. It was a chatty note from the sisters about how Chips, their dog, was missing me, and how without our long walks he was getting quite pudgy. The 'veggie' garden was producing a bumper 'best in years' crop, Ruth penned, in her tidy, even script. And 'Joan has made a tomato relish to die for, which if you aren't going to be away for too much longer, you will surely get to taste.' The mountain community was happy, she wrote because, 'volunteer numbers for the Fire Brigade this year have reached pleasingly high levels. The book club is awaiting your return,' she said, and finished by saying how much they missed me. I missed them, too. Ruth's lovely words from home were just what I needed to get back to work.

At midnight, I stopped typing, pleased with the story so far, although I was still mulling over how to skew a few different scenes. The interruption and seeing James again, had made me restless.

The time difference between Cobham and the Bahamas was five hours, I'd double- and triple-checked already. It would be cocktail hour there about now. Should I call? What would I say? It wasn't so simple to just ring a ninety-five-year-old out of the blue and introduce yourself as a long-lost relative. What if he was frail with a bad heart? The shock might kill him. What if he was in a nursing home with dementia, and a nurse answered the phone and said he couldn't speak. How sad would I be at having got so close? James had said he was still 'with it'. I picked up the phone. But what if he wasn't? I felt my resolve wavering. It would be too sad. I put the phone down again.

John

Cobham

For no good reason other than he couldn't sleep, John had come into the office earlier than usual. The place was quiet when he let himself in. With no phones ringing and no one around to ask questions, he saw a chance to catch up on the backlog.

Moving about slowly, he switched on his computer, made a pot of percolated coffee and ruminated on his actions. He'd thought it only proper after meeting Maddison in London, to write formally to the earl in an attempt to clarify how unearthing this new relative had come about. He'd explained how his endeavours to track the heir to his mother's piano was the final bit of closure for his firm's handling of the sale of Hebden. Now, he regretted his own inability to keep things to himself. Why had he felt the need to tell Gerard at all? Why couldn't he be anything other than a stickler for accuracy? *Because it was clear*, he thought, casting his practised eye over his computer screen, *that this trait had come back to bite him, again.*

It was hard to miss, large as life in his inbox. A note from Gerard, thanking him for all his efforts, but attached to this was a file addressed to Maddison and a request that John forward it to her. He could hardly believe it. Unable to stop himself, ignoring privacy, John clicked on the Maddison file and opened it.

It might just be the lack of sleep, his disrupted routine with Janet away and having to get his own breakfast, but right now nothing was making sense to John, particularly the earl's reaction to the news that he had a new relative.

To my dearest great-niece, Maddison,

How delighted I was to learn recently from my solicitor, John Nettlewood, that in his search to place my mother's piano, he found not only a living female relative, but my darling sister's granddaughter. I will never be able to thank him enough for this startling and delightful gift.

You see, I lost my sister, Abigail, a very long time ago without ever really knowing what happened to her. And it has been an utter joy for me to learn that she did not die young as I have always believed. I cannot express the profound happiness it brings me now, to know that she made a life for herself in Australia. We have much to talk about, you and I. I want to hear everything about Abbey, her children, Marianne and Gerard. I have many questions for you about yourself, too. John tells me you are a writer of romance fiction. This came as an even greater surprise because my mother, Rose, tried her hand at penning romance stories, too. I would wager you didn't know that. How she would have loved to meet you.

I can barely contain myself, but I'm afraid I must wait a while for us to meet. You see, due to a silly topple down some wretched stairs, I am presently indisposed. Nothing to worry about, I am told, missed my footing that's all. Not sure when the medicos will tell me I'm fit to travel.

So, you see, dear Maddison, as much as I would rush with full haste to meet you, I am unable to get away just now. Yet nothing would please me more than to welcome my sister's granddaughter into my home. So, if you would like to stay in the village for a bit, which I imagine you will, since you will be discovering a whole new world there, then please use my home at your leisure. I have asked John to ensure that it's opened up and ready for you. It's not the grand manor, you understand, but you will be comfortable in the gatehouse at Hebden. And if you happen to still be about in a little while, well it will be a great pleasure to meet you then. It takes a while for an old man like myself to get travelling these days, but please know that I shall come to you as soon as my body permits. I suppose, if all else should fail, you might consider coming to me on your way home. It's the strangest thing, but I have always wanted to visit Australia.

With much anticipation and love, your Uncle Gem (Gerry).

The tone of Gerard's letter to his unknown great-niece was sickening. Good grief, he'd even referred to himself as 'Gem', a nickname bestowed on him when he was a boy. As far as John was aware, even Gerard's colleagues referred to him as Gerry. Only the earl's absolute inner circle called him 'Gem'.

But what amazed him most, was that Gerard didn't appear to be too upset with him at all for having brought this unwanted complication upon them. On the contrary, the earl sounded positively chuffed. And it didn't seem to matter to him that he had not known of any offspring's existence, nor was he vaguely worried that Maddison had arrived on the scene from nowhere. Well, not exactly nowhere, but Australia had certainly not been on his radar when he'd been searching for the heir to the piano.

Did the man not consider that this great-niece might challenge the life that he had grown accustomed to? The luxurious tropical lifestyle that so obviously suited him? One that John had even felt mildly jealous of? The old aristocrat wasn't stupid, for heaven's sake. But did he not see the danger?

John remembered how devilishly hard the sale of the manor had been. Gerard's only involvement then had been to sign where he'd been told to. It was John who had personally guided Gerard step by step, unwinding centuries of tradition. The earl had never really had to worry much about family and estate issues, which possibly explained his lack of caution. He'd ascended to the title and joined the Lords as a young man following the death of his father. His mother, Rose, had run the estate, and John's family law firm had done the rest.

Maddison was Gerard's blood relative. That much was true; it was documented, and on the record. John had even seen the Hebden symbol on the delicate chain around her neck. But as far as he was concerned, she was still a stranger.

The way this situation was unfolding, John's terrors welled again. What would happen if Maddison and Gerard met face to face?

Uncertain of what to do next, he took a sip of coffee. It tasted bitter. He placed the cup down. A quick walk to stretch his legs before staff arrived might resolve the question on his mind. Would he pass Gerard's invitation on to Maddison? Or would he deviate from a lifetime of doing whatever the Hamptons asked of him?

Two days passed and still John had not lifted a finger to contact Maddison. After a busy morning, he was irritable and considering what he might do for lunch, when his private line lit up.

'Daddy, it's me. Do you want the good news or the bad news first?'

'You know I hate these games, Crystal. Can you just tell me what it is you have to say.' John had been immersed in a vexatious family settlement for the past two hours. Janet was still in London, and he'd been scraping together whatever he could find to eat at home. After dealing with clients sobbing, and arguing all morning, his patience was at an end.

'Is your mother there with you?' he asked, unable to prevent the sharpness in his voice.

'She is, but I have something to tell you, Daddy.'

He heard his daughter start to sniffle and felt his heart soften.

'I hope you're not going to be angry with me.'

'Go on,' said John, thinking he hoped so, too.

'I'm ringing to let you know that James and I have broken up.'

For an instant, John wondered if this information was the good news or the bad news. He hesitated, unsure what he was meant to say, given James had told him directly that he and Crystal were not actually 'involved'.

'I don't know what to say, darling. I'm sorry, what happened?'

'He does nothing but study, work, work and study.' His daughter sounded defiant. 'And it's not what I want.'

'I can see that,' he said, almost tenderly.

'I don't want to be with a workaholic, whose job is more important than me.'

Sometimes John thought that he and Janet had been too protective of their daughter. That they had given in too easily to her demands, fearful of 'those' moods returning to darken her beautiful face.

'I want to be with someone who has time for fun, Daddy. I can't tell you how many parties I've had to go to by myself.'

'That's not really the end of the world, is it, darling,' murmured John.

'Not the end of the world? He told me that we "weren't compatible",' Crystal shouted the words. 'He said he thought it best if we both went our own ways. Not compatible.' She gulped back a sob.

John heard his daughter's confusion. In the past, she must have always been the one to close down her romances. She would recover, he felt sure. Crystal had never been short of suitors. A part of him felt sorry for his daughter, but any disappointment on his part was soon offset by delight.

'So, no Australian holidays?' he asked, knowing he was on safe ground.

'Of course not, Daddy. Actually, I'm not even sure what I ever saw in him, really. He's such a nerd.'

How easily the epithet might be applied to your own father, John thought, as he caught Janet's voice quietly urging Crystal in the background.

'Well, that's the bad news, Daddy, do you want to hear the good news?'

'I do, of course I do,' said John, steeling himself, just in case.

'I'm dating a stock broker. His father is an MP.'

'I see.' He sighed with relief. Janet's fingerprints were all over this.

His daughter continued. 'Jonathan Evans, he's from a really good London family. Mummy has met his aunts and says they are a most lovely bunch.'

Before he could make any further comment, John heard his wife's voice come on the line, warm and conciliatory, quietly triumphant.

'It's me, darling, sorry to be away so long. I'll be back in plenty of time for the piano woman.'

John didn't like the way Janet had taken to referring to Maddison Browne as 'the piano woman', when she didn't even play the instrument. If there was anyone entitled to be called that amongst the Hamptons, from all he knew, it was Abigail. His grandfather had told him once that Abigail played so well that she could have filled the Royal Albert Hall by herself, and remembering this made John feel worse for all that had happened. More so because there was not one single thing he could do about it.

'Oh, and could you speak to James please, John darling?' Janet's voice in his ear brought him back to his own reality.

'And what would you like me to say?'

'Oh, I don't care, but tell him how much we enjoyed his company, thank him and tell him we are sorry for the trouble.'

'But that's not the truth, is it, Janet?'

'Not the whole truth, but then what is the whole truth?' Her laughter tinkled down the phone line. 'It actually wasn't a relationship at all,' she whispered. 'I think it was all in our daughter's mind.' Her voice went back to normal. 'Anyway, I think you're going to love this new chap. And,' she added quickly, 'just so you know, after this emotional upset, Crystal has deferred two of her subjects this semester.'

Who said matchmaking was a thing of the past, John thought, shaking his head as he put down the phone. His daughter was a grown woman, free to make her own choices, but apparently that was not the whole truth, either.

His immediate problem, however, was Saturday morning's tea party. John feared he wouldn't cope dealing with the piano, the situation, Janet, Maddison and Crystal, all together in the same room, at the same time. He'd been relying on the Australian's communication skills to help him. James around women was like watching Fred Astaire dance, effortless.

'Annie,' he called out to his secretary, trying not to sound crabby.

'Can I have the stamp,' she asked with an apologetic smile, as she placed the envelope down in front of him. John knew her young son was an avid collector.

He glanced down at the letter marked EXPRESS and felt his day get even worse. The Bahamas postmark meant this could only be from one person.

Gerard had already signalled by email that he wanted to make changes to his will in light of Maddison Browne having come into his life. John glanced apprehensively at the brightly coloured postmark. This would be his new set of instructions. With no children, no partner anymore, and no male heir to the Hampton title, John could not even guess what Gerard's intentions might be.

One thing he knew for certain. The Earl of Hebden title would die out with Gerard's passing. Unless the British Government acted with haste to amend laws, hundreds of years old, that prohibited females from inheriting a family title. Although this was highly improbable in John's view, even without such intervention, the Hebden peerage was rapidly and literally approaching the end of the line. Otherwise, had the law not been so constructed, an Australian romance writer could have been in the running to take it on.

'Would that be such a bad thing?' had been Janet's question to him one night when the topic had popped up in their conversation over a glass of wine. 'A woman taking the reins? It's going to happen one day, John, so you'd better get used to the idea.'

Suddenly he felt tired, and rather than face the contents of Gerard's envelope, John grabbed his briefcase and stuffed the letter in the front pocket to read later.

In Gerard's note to Maddison, he had signalled his desire to meet her in person. Would she still be here when Gerard's doctors gave him the all clear to travel? John vehemently hoped not.

Show her the instrument, expedite it out of his life forever, and wave her goodbye. That was still his best plan. Face the music about women in the peerage later, and all in good time.

Maddison

Cobham

I drew up outside her house at eleven am on the dot, and double-checked the number to make sure I was in the right place. It was a plain house in a dreary street of identical, ugly, red brick-and-concrete constructions, where you stepped up to the front porch directly from the footpath. No front garden, and nothing at all forgiving about it. It was hard to imagine anyone making music inside these walls.

The woman I'd spoken to on the phone yesterday said she wasn't sure if she could help, but her mother did keep records.

'Mum was meticulous,' she said. 'She had a few fine students, and I do clearly remember Abigail Hampton up at the manor being one of them. We heard so much about her under our roof, you see.'

'Really?' Her words shocked me. But when she finished, saying, 'There'll be something here so you'd be welcome to come over and peruse what I can dig up,' a wave of anxiety came over me. Suddenly, I felt sick in the stomach because this search for my grandmother was becoming too real.

I rang the bell and saw a curtain move before the door opened. Daisy was Ida Edward's daughter. She had a fresh face for a woman who must have been well into her later years. Soft custard-coloured curls that framed her flawless peaches-and-cream complexion made her appear younger, though.

'Do come in out of this weather.' She smiled welcomingly. 'After you rang, I thought, what a strange coincidence this is. I've just come down, barely a week ago, to sell off the house. I live in Ireland, you see,' she said over her shoulder as she walked ahead. Her solid shoes, polar vest and unfashionably long woollen skirt made me think Daisy might be a school music teacher, like her mother before her. Stacks of boxes piled up in columns lined the entire length of the passage, making it difficult to pass.

'Come through,' she said, 'sorry about the mess. I've laid out most of what I think might interest you; it's not much. Dad passed away last year, Mum's been gone for a while, so as I'm never coming back here to live … Anyway, what I mean is I'm sorting through things, so your timing couldn't be better. How did you know where to find me?'

'Oh,' I said, 'it was just one of those things. Your mother's name came up in a conversation I was having at the local B & B where I'm staying.' I turned sideways to follow Daisy, squeezing past more boxes. 'George and Edith were quite adamant about Abigail having engaged private tutors from the village, and they mentioned a few names.'

'That'd be right. If they're local, they probably knew about my mother.' She stopped and shrugged her shoulders. 'I left home a long time ago.'

'I think they did, yes,' I said, talking to her back as Daisy set off again. 'I tried some of their other suggestions, too, but they didn't work out. I was about to give up, when a Cheryl Busby remembered that your mother not only taught at the manor, but that Abigail had been a special student of hers.'

'A stroke of luck, then,' she said. 'Yes, my mother, Ida, was an outstanding musician. She studied music and theory at a time when not many women did. She taught your grandmother music harmony and theory, I believe.'

I wanted to pinch myself. Was this really happening? Hearing Daisy talk about Abigail as a girl was like a dream.

'Our mum was always holding out Abigail Hampton's results to my brother and me.' Daisy grimaced. 'Don't know really what she made of Charlie and me. I did nursing, and my brother became a gardener. No aptitude for music, either of us.' She chortled. 'Not what our mother was hoping for, I think.' She waved her arm above her head.

'Useful, though,' I said softly, not expecting Daisy to hear.

'You could say,' she responded brightly (nothing wrong with her hearing), like she didn't give two hoots what her mother had wanted for her brother and her.

'But you said you didn't know you were related to the Hamptons until recently, is that right?' she asked, sounding like a quiz-show host asking a question to which he (quiz-show hosts are mostly male) already knew the answer.

'Yes.' I was trying not to stare at the surroundings, green-and-black-papered walls and dark mahogany furniture. No lightness here; Ida Edward's household had been a serious one.

'What an incredible story,' she turned to me, her eyes wide with wonder, 'but nothing would surprise me when it comes to families.'

'Once I found out that my grandmother was who she was,' I explained, 'and I there was no record of her in Melbourne, I just had to try to discover where she lived and what happened to her.'

'Understand. It's quite extraordinary. Anything in particular you're looking for?'

'No, I'm just trying to form a picture of her as a young woman, and from there, I hope it will help me figure out her story.'

'Of course. No records in Melbourne, you said, such a shame. I'd feel exactly the same.' Daisy's eyes were soft with empathy.

'You knew her, then?'

'I have a few memories, but I wasn't old enough to know her really well. Alright, there it is.' She pointed to a cluttered dining table strewn with papers and three mismatched dining chairs. 'It's just those little ones there, with the vase on top. I'll leave you to look while I put the kettle on. How do you take your tea?'

Half an hour later, Daisy and I were sitting at the table still chatting. 'You can take it,' she said.

I looked down at the tiny battered black-and-white photo I was holding in my hand. The little girl, ten years old at most, pictured standing in the garden at Hebden, her long skirt, wide-brimmed hat, dark socks and lace-up shoes a mirror of what the round-faced woman next to her was wearing. Their hands were linked, and they had irrepressible grins on their faces. The picture of Abbey with her music teacher, Ida Edwards, was so lovely it took my breath away. My throat tightened with emotion at the sight of them standing on the front step of the manor, presumably after a music lesson, so happy, like they hadn't a care in the world. Abbey's older face was hard to conjure up, in light of this.

'Yes, but I can only tell you what I remember,' Daisy said, responding to my questions. 'I think Mum met Lady Rose at some local fair and that's how it came about. The two of them hit it off right away,' she said. 'The countess played rather well herself, I believe, so they had plenty to talk about.'

'I can just imagine.' I was loving every word I was hearing.

'Apparently, Lady Rose told my mum, you take care of the theory, and I'll look after the practical playing side. And that's what happened, for a while, anyway.'

'Hearing you say this is giving me goosebumps,' I said, which made Daisy pause and stare at me for a second.

'My mother was awfully proud to be one of the special tutors for the manor. I suppose you can accuse me of singing her praises, but my mother was ahead of her time, too. Not that you'd think it.' Her eyes roamed the room. 'Dad was in the stone trade … it's slow work,' she said in her father's defence. 'But just the same, it was always going to take more than Mum's talent for the piano to take it any further. It wasn't the time,' she said, without a trace of bitterness, 'but my mother loved teaching too, so for Abigail and others, that was their good luck.'

'I'm sorry I missed meeting your mother.'

Daisy appeared not to hear my remark, with her mind still busily delving back. 'I'm quite certain Mum believed that the only reason Lady Rose ever sent your grandmother to the London School of Music later, was down to her influence. Mum knew that Abigail would study at Mathilde Vern's music school. And who was she, you ask? Well, she was a protégé of Clara Schumann, no less. I remember Mum told me that once Abbey found out about Mathilde's college, it was all she wanted, and that she probably drove her parents crazy until they let her go.'

'Your mother thought she would react that way?'

'Oh yes, as much as Mum loved the practical joking side of Abbey, she always considered her determined and wilful. Qualities you need, she said. That's why she believed her star student would do what she herself hadn't been able to achieve. You know, beauty, talent, tenacity *and* the means. I think she truly believed that Abigail was the one student who could carry on and make a career for herself.' She gestured dismissively to the headline of a faded newspaper clip lying on the table in front of us. 'And she wasn't the only one. Have a look at that.'

I leaned forward. '*Finishing of a Lady*,' the headline read. I skimmed the article that contained a brief description of my grandmother, but no photo. '*As Abigail Hampton heads to London for further study, the bright young star of the piano said ahead of her departure, "It's my dream to play the piano in concert halls."*'

'You know, for women back then, they were mostly from the upper crust, those who could afford to study,' said Daisy, 'but here's the funny part. Learning to play the piano for them wasn't primarily about the music, but making themselves more attractive, and more marriageable. Imagine that.' She snorted derisively. 'When times get tough, you can tinkle out a tune for your husband.'

I laughed. This softly spoken nurse was not afraid to speak her mind.

'In my line of work, that kind of nonsense is hard to take,' Daisy continued, her cheeks flushing pink. 'Studying music for Mum meant more than that. For her, it was all to do with the music itself, and the higher power of it. I can't be certain, but I'd say that approach must have rubbed off on your grandmother.'

She looked at me to see if I understood.

'I don't play myself,' I volunteered, 'but I know the effect of listening to music, profoundly.'

We sat for a bit, sipping our tea in silence, with only the quiet chinking of our teacups to fill the air. I was hoping Daisy might say more and maybe elaborate why, in her view, this hadn't happened for Abigail. Instead, she smiled brightly at me and said, 'So, what happened do you think? Clearly, Abigail did not die giving birth if you're here.'

'I'm trying to find out,' I said. 'I don't have the answer yet, but I hope to.'

'I can tell you that my mother never believed that story about your grandmother, not for a second,' she said emphatically. 'She believed Abbey would have contacted her if she'd been in any sort of trouble. And, as I'm sure you can imagine, it was very sad for my mother, too, never knowing what actually happened.'

'It would have been,' I said, thinking how I would feel if any of my friends vanished without a trace. How painful it would be to have to listen to all the different theories without ever finding the truth.

'Mind you, Mum must have known more than she let on about what went on up at the manor. Not that she ever said. My mother was many things, but a gossip wasn't one of them.' She stirred her tea unnecessarily.

'Did Abigail have lessons with your mother over a long period of time?'

'Oh yes, she started when Abbey was just seven or eight and continued well into her teens. Mind you, her contact did drift a little after Abigail started going up to London.' She placed her cup down carefully. 'But like I said, she didn't buy it for one minute, that story. After Abigail disappeared, the Hamptons vanished from our lives completely, too. Such a pity, a miserable end to my mother's dream that Abigail would be the one to break through.'

'Your mother wouldn't be the only teacher to have suffered from a student who failed to deliver on their promise,' I said. But hearing Daisy use that word, 'disappeared', shocked me because hearing it spoken out loud confirmed what I already thought. That my grandmother had staged her own disappearance. Now that I knew that she'd had to leave behind dear friends like Ida, who'd loved and cared for her, the story wasn't getting any better.

I held back from telling Daisy about Abigail claiming 'orphan' status in Australia. No point to be served, when she had been so kind. I was touched when she offered me the charming vase Abbey had gifted to her mother, a delicate piece depicting a pastoral scene similar to the setting in the black-and-white photo. Abigail must have been as sweet as she looked to offer this lovely gift to her teacher.

'Thank you, Daisy, but I couldn't. This belongs to your mother and you.'

She patted my arm, her eyes moist with tears. 'Good luck, then,' she said, as I embraced her. 'I hope you find what you're looking for.'

So, Abbey had been a spirited young woman.

'She looked as if butter wouldn't melt in her mouth, but she was feisty and never afraid to speak her mind,' Daisy had said.

The picture she'd painted of Abigail was of a bright young woman capable of anything, the world firmly at her feet.

I would never forget her parting words. 'Not lacking in opportunity was your grandmother. My mother was right, I think. It must have been something awful that happened, for her to give all that up.'

Those words made me shudder. I was grateful to Daisy for sharing her childhood memories about a formative time in Abigail's life. But while her descriptions answered some of my questions, they also posed painful new ones.

Thinking about the dock where the ships left for Australia and Abbey boarding alone, leaving beloved friends as well as family, made my stomach churn. Why did she do that?

It was hard to feel over the moon about what I was finding. My grandmother's actions appeared even harder to fathom in light of this new knowledge about her. On my way back, I stopped at a little pastry shop in the main street of Gravesend, to pick up a teacake for George and Edith.

I had seriously doubted that their 'local knowledge' would amount to anything. But after making endless calls to people they insisted had worked at Hebden, I'd been about to give up when one of their contacts remembered Ida's name. Now, I had important information and a whole new slant on my grandmother, news to pass on to Edith and George, and (what was wrong with me?) I had a sudden urge to share this with James, too.

His persistence and not leaving any stone unturned, was exactly how he had found me. Now I was doing the same to find Abbey. But no, I wouldn't call him, I decided firmly.

Maddison

Cobham, two days later

The piano-viewing day finally dawned. None of the cars parked in the driveway were James's MG. I was a little surprised that I'd heard nothing from him since our rainy interlude on the street, but I wasn't going to allow him to distract me from my purpose. I was here to see first-hand the piano that had brought me to England.

When I pulled up outside a two-storey red brick gable covered in ivy, John Nettlewood's family home was much as I expected it would be; black slate roof, white windows, classic, conservative and quiet; quintessential English country style, circled by a significant garden. Nothing truly stand-out, but pleasing to the eye and not ostentatious. Driving through some of the old streets on my way here, parts of this area looked as if time might have stood still. Although the rows of beautifully preserved historic buildings lent a quaint charm to the area, and while John's house probably wasn't as old as some, it would have been standing for at least one hundred years. The external impression was that things were done properly here, if a little slowly.

John's forebears, from what I'd gleaned through the archive, had been tangled up in my grandmother's life in different ways. I was keen to fully explore the extent of this entanglement. To me, there seemed to be more to this than John Nettlewood solving his problem of finding a female descendant to ship off an old piano. Actually, I still had not understood why the piano should be so important for him. For Rose perhaps, but to her lawyer so many years later? There had to be more to it. Right from the beginning, I'd sensed he was holding something back, and since accessing Rose's diaries and stumbling across Abigail's hidden letter, I was sure of it.

Emboldened by knowledge that Gerard was alive and that I even had his phone number secretly stashed in my bag, I was full of determined purpose. Today would be interesting. This was going to be my sincerity test for John. I needed to judge what his family connection to my grandmother was, and maybe even figure out what was going on between James and Crystal. James had gone out of his way for me. My fragile intuition kept telling me that I could trust him. But could I? Perhaps by the end of today, everything might be clearer. I took a deep breath and approached their front entrance.

The bell had barely sounded when the door, painted in black gloss, swung open. A casually dressed John in open-necked shirt and golf shoes stood ready to greet me.

'You found us, then?' he said warmly, but the words had barely passed his lips when an attractive woman in her late fifties, heels and swept-up hair materialised at his side. He said, 'Maddison, meet my wife, Janet … Janet, this is Maddison.'

She fixed a bright smile on me and extended her hand. 'A pleasure to meet you, Maddison, after all this time. Do come in.'

The atmosphere was spikey. I felt awkward as we moved through the foyer, me following Janet, leaving John to hang my coat. The solicitor's wife led us into a large sitting room that was empty. No James or anyone else. Wall-to-wall floral paper was the main feature, except for two large and ornate gold-framed mirrors. Not what I was expecting at all. On either side of the room, large comfortable sofas covered in embossed fabric sat next to two occasional antique chairs positioned to face the centrepiece of the room, the piano. And what a centrepiece it was. I had never seen one so beautiful. John joined his wife, and together they watched my reaction.

'Oh, it's lovely,' I said, reaching out to touch the instrument. 'May I?'

'Of course, it's yours,' said Janet evenly.

The temperature dropped several degrees. I was wondering how to deal with this unwelcoming vibration, laced it seemed, with palpable annoyance at my presence. What would the protocol be? Not to respond in kind if I wanted to get to the end of this intrigue. That much I was certain of. But I was spared having to decide on which intonation of voice to use, when a group of young women led by a perfect-looking blonde, their daughter, I surmised, came bursting into the room.

'Maddison, hello, I'm Crystal,' she cried, grabbing my hand in both of hers. Her greeting was the polar opposite of her mother's. 'It's so lovely to meet you, James has told me all about you.'

'Unfortunately, James won't be joining us today, Maddison,' John added quickly, as if he'd read my mind, or perhaps he was trying to cover for his wife's frigid body language.

Crystal's smile revealed ultra-white teeth like a row of perfect snow-capped mountains. And the faint orange hue of her skin colour was a dead giveaway that she'd spent a fair amount of time in a tanning salon. Tight-fitting winter-white knits clung to her like a second skin, and flattering tight slacks showcased a perfectly proportioned body. John's daughter was a beauty, and probably ten years younger than me.

'This is Millie, Harriet and Freddie,' she cried, pointing to each friend, who I noticed were all standing back and giving me the once-over. 'I told them about you being Lady Rose Hampton's long-lost great-granddaughter and all ...'

I wasn't sure how to react to this introduction, so I just smiled in their general direction and said, 'Hello.'

'I'm here to play for you,' Crystal announced, glancing back to her friends, 'but we all wanted to see what a real romance writer looks like.'

The girls laughed. Her tone was playful, and her expression appeared genuine, so I took her comments at face value.

'And?' I questioned boldly, wishing I'd worn something more glamorous. 'I pass muster, hopefully?'

'You look fine to us,' said Freddie, the tallest in the group.

'Whew, that's a relief.' I fanned my face, exaggeratedly.

'Actually, I was hoping I might get a few tips from you,' the tall redhead said tentatively. 'If you don't mind. I have a couple of abandoned manuscripts in my cupboard at university.'

Millie chimed in with, 'She wants to be a romance writer, don't you, Fred?' which turned Freddie's face pink. 'We've been giving her heaps about it, then Crystal told us about you, so …'

'No problem. I'm happy to chat. I'm going to be around for a while yet.'

Freddie was clearly embarrassed.

'Call me, I'm staying in Gravesend, John has the number.'

Freddie nodded her head, but kept her eyes averted. 'Thanks, I will.'

'You're not returning to Australia this week, then?' Janet finally joined the conversation.

'No. I've started working on a new story. So, I think I'll just stay put for a while.' I smiled at Freddie. 'It must be something in the water around here. It's been a great spot for writers for hundreds of years. I'm enjoying myself terrifically, too.'

'Of course,' John murmured, and exchanged a look with this wife, who smiled stiffly.

'You must have found the Leather Bottle Inn?' Crystal enthused. 'We love that pub, Freddie especially. She wants a lock of her hair to live on after her death. Just like Charles Dickens.'

'Stop it, Crystal,' Freddie snapped.

'Well, it's true.'

Freddie's face was like thunder.

'That's a good dream to have,' I said. *That's where James mentioned he was staying. Has he been meeting Crystal there?*

'Yes, it is. Only joking, come on, Fred.' Crystal grabbed her friend's arm, and when Freddie's face cracked a grin, the previous mood returned.

I could see why James would be interested in her, of course. Crystal was smart and beautiful. Heavens, even her own parents seemed to be hypnotised by her charms. The way their eyes lingered on her, watching her every move, as if they'd never seen her before.

Crystal turned to me. 'Would you like me to play something for you? Daddy told me you don't play, so I thought you might like to hear the sound of the instrument.'

'Please, everyone, sit down now,' Janet interrupted, sounding a lot like my neighbour Ruth, whose instructions always produced a similar result.

'I would love to hear you play, Crystal,' I said, and plonked myself down on the nearest sofa, while John and Janet found 'their' seats, which not surprisingly, were two single antique armchairs positioned squarely facing the piano. Freddie and the girls squashed up together on the other sofa.

'I hope you like Chopin.' Crystal wriggled her bottom into position on the stool.

I heard one of the girls whisper they wished Crystal would play something else, 'like a good Elton John tune' and I saw the others nudge her to be quiet. It wasn't until that moment, observing how familiar this scene looked, and Crystal's demeanour towards the instrument, that it struck me: she might be unhappy about losing her piano.

The room fell silent as she started to play. Her fingers moved easily across the keyboard, generating a cascade of melody to flow forth like a babbling brook, soothing and beautiful. Crystal sat tall with only a slight furrow on her brow to suggest she was concentrating.

A complete picture of winsomeness, she played on until the piece ended, and the room exploded into wild applause. Her girlfriends whistled enthusiastically. Her mother, clapping madly, jumped up.

'Darling, that was marvellous.'

Her father, whose smile stretched from one ear to the other, looked positively delirious.

Crystal bowed graciously to the room, then turned to me. 'It's all yours now, Maddison,' she spoke softly, reaching out her hand to pat the lid of the piano. 'This lovely instrument has lived in this room for a long time. I'm going to miss it, and I can tell you that I wasn't prepared to give it up easily. But now that we've met, it's fine. I hope you're going to love it as much as I have.'

I could only stammer, 'Thank you,' by way of response.

With that she burst into tears. 'Sorry, sorry, I am pleased, really I am.' She looked as if she was going to say more, but her mother rushed to her side, produced a handkerchief and announced, 'It's time for tea. You girls come and help me. We'll leave John and Maddison to finish their business.'

Crystal gave me a strange backward glance as she was led away, her mother and her hub of girlfriends all showering her with compliments.

John crossed the room towards me. 'Is it to your satisfaction, Maddison?'

'The piano is beautiful, I'm honoured,' I said, finding my tongue at last. 'But I'm feeling a little guilty to be taking it from Crystal. She plays so wonderfully, and as you know I hardly play at all.'

'Please, you have no cause to worry about that. My mistake. I should have told her a long time ago the piano was only on loan until we found you. She thinks that piano has been her lucky charm, that's all. But I have a surprise in store for my daughter. One that she will be very pleased with. She plays quite well, don't you think? But not in a league with your grandmother, from what I've heard.'

'Oh, she really does. I have only a distant memory of Abigail, but her mother mentions how talented she was in her diaries ...'

'Ah, yes of course,' his eyes turned away, 'but if I might confide in you for just a moment.' He lowered his voice.

Finally, I thought, *he's going to tell me what happened.*

'I have one of those white baby grand pianos arriving the same day this,' he gestured to the antique piano now looking forlorn in the middle of the sitting room, 'moves out.'

'What a lovely surprise,' I murmured, shaking my head at my own misplaced expectation. Of course he was going to be talking about his daughter.

I could just imagine Crystal, seated at her white baby grand, shimmering gown, looking for all the world like a real-life princess.

'Good. Well, if you are satisfied, I shall just get on with arranging the shipping.' The sound of his voice thankfully interrupted the vision that had appeared in my mind of James gazing at Crystal adoringly as he presented her with a red rose.

'Yes please.' I nodded. It was hard to believe that this instrument would soon be heading for my mountain home; a precious link to my family that I knew I would treasure and even learn to play one day.

'Very well, consider it done.' He smiled. 'Any questions?'

I hesitated. This was not a perfect time, but then I didn't know when that would ever be. With arrangements for the piano all agreed upon, I wasn't even sure if I would ever meet John again after today.

'I'm not sure how to ask.'

'Just come right on out and say it,' he said brightly.

'As you know, I've been down in the local archive, reading the Hampton family history.'

His eyes sharpened. 'Yes.'

Here's test one for you, John Nettlewood. 'My grandmother's brother, Gerard. I can't seem to find when he died.'

'Dead? Gerard? No, I just …' he stammered, and I noticed colour rise in his cheeks. My question had clearly caught him off guard.

'Gerard is still alive, yes, but I'm afraid his lordship is rather elderly … He lives in the Bahamas you know.'

Good answer, you're telling the truth so far. I smiled. 'But I'm wondering, if he is still alive, why is it that you've never thought of mentioning him to me. Is there any reason for that?'

'The reason I've never mentioned the earl to you?' he repeated, looking alarmed. 'I'm not sure, Maddison. Perhaps because our dealings were only about Lady Rose's last will and testament and her piano.' It was a lame response; I could see that he knew it. His head inclined and he leaned forward as if to anticipate what I would ask him next.

'My other question is about Rose's diaries,' I said.

This time he was quick to respond. 'I'm not sure I could give you any assistance there, Maddison, you are in the right place down at the archive.'

'Yes, but I think one of Rose's diaries is missing.'

'I wouldn't know anything about that,' he said abruptly. 'It was all a long time ago.'

'I'm wondering what might have happened to it.'

'Any number of explanations for a missing diary, I would think, wouldn't you?' he said, lifting his eyebrows. 'Rose could have burned it, or maybe it's still locked up in the school somewhere. Maybe she just never wrote a last one? Have you thought of that?'

His answer was sending clanging alarm bells in my head, given I'd not mentioned anything to him about it being the last one that was missing. 'Maybe, but I don't think that's correct, John. You see, the last diary the archive has runs out at a particularly difficult time for Abigail. The "missing" diary would pick up where the previous one left off, to finish the story, if you see what I mean.'

'No, I don't, not really.'

'Perhaps if I explain, then,' I said.

'Very well.'

'You see, the archivist in Strood told me that as legal representatives to the Hamptons' estate, either your father or you would have handled every part of the Hampton-family material before it was officially given over to them.'

'Yes, probably that is so, but I fail to see the relevance.'

'I thought you might have come across it, or you might even have it stored somewhere without being aware of it?'

'Me? No, no.' He shook his head vigorously.

'Is it possible that you might have a diary, or a few stray letters somewhere in your own archive of Hebden Estate files?'

John was staring at me, his expression a mixture of anxiety and disbelief. 'What is it that you are searching for?'

His manner and the terror in his eyes suddenly brought a clarity to what I'd read so far. Somehow, I knew exactly what I needed to ask.

'It's a bit sensitive, John, and please, I don't want to appear ungrateful for all your efforts.'

'Go on,' he said.

'It seems rather strange to me, but from my reading of the diaries so far, it appears that your grandfather, Llewellyn, was somehow involved in Abigail's disappearance. And someone, I'm guessing your grandfather again, wrote to Rose about it. It's not clear what happened, or what their relationship was, but I think it's the crux of my grandmother's story.'

The panic on the lawyer's face was palpable. But at the same time, I could swear I felt Abbey kiss the top of my head, the way she had at the piano when I was little.

John

Cobham, same evening

John sat with his fingers spread across his temple. During the fateful morning tea, he had never intended to tell Maddison about Gerard's offer, but somehow it had just slipped from his mouth. In a bid to deflect her persistent questioning, he'd been driven to employ desperate measures.

'I'm not sure I can give you any more facts on that topic,' he'd said. 'However, I can tell you that when I informed the earl of your existence, he suggested right away that you might like to spend a night or two at his gatehouse home. Unfortunately, his health won't allow him to join you at the moment.'

The bewildered expression on her face was not what he'd expected. 'You mean the gatehouse here, at Hebden? Is that where he lives?' she'd asked incredulously.

'Yes, although he's not in residence often anymore. The sale of the manor didn't include the gatehouse, yet it did make provision for the school to look after the property in his absence,' he had patiently explained.

Noisy chatter and laughter with Janet and the girls re-emerging from the kitchen holding up plates of his favourite sponge cakes had afforded John the time he needed to gather his wits and formulate a strategy.

'We'll speak of this again later, Maddison,' he'd whispered. 'I'll be in touch.'

John had seen the haunted look in her eyes, and recognised what it must mean for her to have found herself part of a bigger story here. She seemed quite a solitary character, and not just because of her occupation. John sensed that her life had not been easy. Much to his surprise, she still hadn't raised one question about any further inheritance, or even hinted at it. Perhaps it was true. She had come here simply to find her grandmother's story, which as a writer of fiction, she would be thrilled by. That was, if she were ever to know what the full story was, and if he had anything to do with it (no matter how much sympathy he might feel for her situation), was *never* going to happen.

His biggest mistake had been his own error of judgement. Why had he thought she would just come, claim the piano and leave?

Whatever happened from here, John was comforted by the knowledge that he had done all in his power to keep the unwelcome truth about their family from his wife, his daughter and the world at large.

He was close to holding it all together. Only one unfinished task remained. Get rid of Maddison and send her packing back to Australia.

It was late now, and hearing the familiar pitter-patter of his wife's footsteps heading off towards the kitchen, John slipped into his study and retrieved the letter from Gerard he'd put aside earlier. His eyes flicked down, but as he began perusing the words before him, his face turned ashen. John could barely believe what he was reading.

I've decided that when I come over, John, we're going to throw a party, like in the old days. We must show Maddison how it's done. Invite all your young ones. It's celebration time!

The euphoric tone of the earl's instruction turned John to stone. A party? Gerard and Maddison together? John rose to his feet slowly, poured himself a stiff drink and collapsed into his wingchair. He gulped back a large slug of his favourite single-malt whisky, then another. The burn of the golden liquid as it slid down his throat, a sensation John usually relished, along with the heat of its warm afterglow, this time served only to intensify his terror. Was he presiding over a ship that was doomed? Was he going to sink along with it?

Maddison

Gravesend

The Earl of Hebden offering me the use of his home was quite unbelievable. Remembering our conversation about society connections before I left home, I wanted to text Amy and Beth, to tease them. The mere thought that I might be staying in an earl's home would give them a laugh. It wasn't royalty, but it was closer than I ever expected to be. I couldn't of course tell anyone, not yet. Not till I could answer the barrage of emails from Australia about what was going on. Which I couldn't, until I knew myself.

Still, his offer had raised the issue that I'd been wrestling with. If Lord Hampton was aware of my existence, what was the problem with me calling him? He had to be with it enough to suggest I stay in his house. My worries about having to explain who I was just vaporised. Why shouldn't I speak to him? He was my grandmother's brother, after all, my very own great-uncle. I should thank him for his kind offer. Then I could just play it by ear on all my other questions.

I decided to wait until midnight and then try my luck calling him. At least I wasn't worried about killing him with shock anymore. As I waited, I was as jumpy as a kitten. Organising my room, packing and repacking my clothes on shelves and in drawers, writing postcards. I even jotted down a few things I might say. I had never spoken to a lord of the realm before. The interminably long minutes ticked by, taking forever.

By ten-thirty pm, I was pacing around the room. Maybe I could call earlier? I decided to text James. He'd asked what I planned to do with Gerard's number. Now I could tell him that I planned to ring the earl this very evening. *What would his reaction be?* I wondered as I texted him. The truth was I did want to talk to James. Even if I was no closer to knowing if he and Crystal were an item, although I'd noticed that Crystal had mentioned him only once, and in passing, at the tea party. After that the name James Carlyle had completely disappeared from the conversation. Was that a good thing? *Probably*, I thought, and impulsively hit 'send'.

Nothing happened, despite my willing him to respond. As midnight finally approached, my phone lay silent and blank on the bedside table. James obviously had better things to do than answer me, and of course my brain reverted to my picture of James as the Rosenkavalier presenting Crystal with his rose. I helped the clock tick down to the right time to call my great-uncle by wriggling my fingers and fidgeting. What a strange moment. I thought about my mother, about Abigail and Rose, too. I thought about their bravery; Marianne, a single mother doing whatever she could to support us, Abbey leaving her home and family, forging a new life in Australia, and Rose sailing to England, from country piano teacher to Lady Hampton. Would they want me to call? Of course they would. Gerard was my only living relative. That thought spurred me on. I picked up my phone, put the number in and hit the green button.

It rang about seven times before someone picked up. A woman's voice. 'Good evening.' I detected a faint accent, French maybe.

With my heart thumping out of my chest, I said, 'Yes, good evening, my name is Maddison Browne, and I'd like to speak to Lord Gerard Hampton, please.'

'I'm afraid he's not here. Will you leave a message?'

'I could call again tomorrow if that's more suitable.'

'No, no, Lord Hampton will not be here tomorrow, either. He is on his way to England. I'm not sure how long he is away. I could get a message to 'im if it's something urgent.'

'Thank you, but that won't be necessary.'

'May I tell 'im who called?'

'That won't be necessary, thanks all the same. I'm ringing from England, so I'll try to meet up with him here.'

After a polite, 'Very well,' the phone clicked in my ear.

On his way to England. Did that mean he was coming to his home in Cobham? John had made no mention yesterday about my great-uncle travelling. Quite the opposite, in fact. He said Gerard had offered me his home because he couldn't come. Something wasn't right. If the earl was on his way here, then I was going to meet him, even if I had to force John Nettlewood to organise a meeting for me.

Maddison

Next morning, seven am

I was sipping tea at my computer, when my phone buzzed.

'How did you go? Did you ring the Bahamas?' It was James.

'You're up early,' I said, trying to ignore the little flutter in my chest at the sound of his voice.

'So are you.'

'I have to be to figure out what's going on around here.'

'Has something happened?'

'I was going to ask you the same thing.'

'Not sure what you mean.' He sounded puzzled.

'John told me that the earl wasn't well enough to travel, but when I rang his home last night, they said he was on his way here.'

'That's strange. When did John tell you that?'

'Saturday at the piano party.'

'How was that?'

'Crystal played the piano for us,' I said, 'she was wonderful.'

'And the piano received your seal of approval?'

'Yes, of course it did. I was expecting you to be there. She must have been disappointed that you couldn't make it.'

'Maddison, Crystal is a sweet girl, but she and I ... it's not what you think.'

'Now there's a line I've heard before.' Although it was true, I wasn't completely convinced this was true of him.

'Not from me you haven't,' he said firmly. 'Listen, the forecast says better weather tomorrow. What about that walk along the coast line I mentioned? You can ask me anything you like about Crystal, the Hamptons and the Nettlewoods. What do you say?'

I hesitated briefly. I should refuse, but I didn't want to. Besides, this was an opportunity to find out more.

'Come on, grab your walking boots. I'll pick you up, say ten-thirty am?'

'Okay,' I said, thinking, *This time, you won't get away without telling me everything you know.* 'I'll be waiting out front.'

The morning was chilly, with the same tease of spring in the air. No rain, a brisk wind and a wintery sun showing its face intermittently through grey clouds. It was just like a day at home on my mountain. The instant I saw his rattling old car turn into the street, annoyingly, I felt my pulse quicken. *Please let him be one of the good guys*, I pleaded silently.

'It's a perfect day for it,' he called out, glancing up at the sky.

'You braved the MG again?'

'Yes, what an adventurer I am. I may never be able to drive a warm, comfortable car ever again.' He laughed, and my serious face folded a little as I got into the passenger seat.

'You must have shares in this car, or does your friend use a lot of buses,' I said as we drove off.

He laughed again. 'Aaron is actually in Denmark on a six-month contract.'

'That's lucky.'

'Yes, he's a good mate. And he owes me a few favours, which means I get to use his car while he's away,' he said quickly. 'So ... the earl is on his way, you said?'

'Yes, I rang last night and the housekeeper said he was en route to England.'

'That's good news, isn't it?'

'I think so.' I told him what John had said about Gerard not travelling.

'Sounds like he changed his mind, then. He might already be here.'

James parked the car near the water. 'Not much help, am I? So much for my career as a new Sherlock Holmes.' Gathering up the small backpack from behind his seat, he held it aloft and pronounced, 'But I have coffee.'

He made me smile again in spite of the confusion I was feeling about everything.

'Would you like me to make some enquiries? It's not like he'll be moving fast at his age.'

'Thanks, but I'll speak to John myself if I don't hear soon.'

'Okay, then, keep me posted.'

I examined him; he wasn't talking like someone intimately acquainted with John or Crystal's social calendar.

'This could be a little ambitious for me,' I said, reading the sign aloud, 'the Saxon Shore Way, starting point for a hundred and forty kilometres of coastal pathways,' as I sat down on the bench.

'We don't have to do it all at once,' said James, who'd perched next to me, and handed me a takeaway cup. 'One bite at a time works, I find.'

I laughed, and so did he.

'Okay, full disclosure?' he asked, studying my face.

'This'll be good,' I said jokingly, but holding my breath for what was to come – I so didn't want him to be involved with anyone.

'Okay,' he said, 'here we go. Crystal was staying in university digs up the road from Aaron and me.' His eyes widened slightly to check I was listening, which of course I was. I was all ears. 'She and Aaron hooked up at a party, and for a time, it seemed like they were equally smitten.'

'Alright so far,' I said, taking a sip, before adding, 'not bad coffee for this part of the world.'

'Anyway, and this is the awful bit. I really don't like talking about this, but you need to hear it. Aaron got this terrific offer from a company in Denmark and decided his career would be enhanced if he took it. Well, Crystal went completely nuts. Aaron said part of the reason he wanted to go was to break off with her. She was too clingy and moody. He thought she might have even been on medication. Beautiful but unstable, he said, and he didn't want to spend his life dealing with that.'

My thought immediately was for poor fragile Crystal. Someone she adored dumped her because of her great need to be loved. Surprisingly, I found myself taking up her cause, condemning this Aaron character as superficial and not having cared enough about her, when I heard James clearing his throat. 'Hello,' he said, 'shall I go on?'

'Sorry, yes of course, please.'

The frown on his face deepened as he started to speak again. 'One particularly horrible night after Aaron had gone to Copenhagen, Crystal appeared on my doorstep. She was a mess, threatening to kill herself. I got her into the house and talked to her. Talked her out of what she was threatening to do. It really was a terrible thing to see her like that. Finally, when she'd calmed down a little, I got her parents' number and called her mother. That was the first time I met Janet. She must have broken all speed limits to get to her daughter that night and she asked me never to tell John what had happened.'

I was listening hard.

'And now for the really unfortunate part. Crystal reappeared a few weeks later, only this time she'd transferred her obsession with Aaron onto me. I didn't know what to do; I was afraid for her and what she might do if I didn't play along.'

James looked pale as he twisted the empty coffee container round and round in his hands. 'It became very tricky especially when I drove Crystal home for the first time. It was no big deal for me, I was hiking in the area anyway, but she introduced me to her father as a special "friend", which I never was. Well, in her mind maybe, but not in reality. John seemed like a nice bloke. And then I put my foot in it by asking him about the piano. I felt I had to redress the damage somehow, and incredibly, the easiest way to help him turned out to be my offer to assist with his search for Lady Rose's heir. It didn't seem that hard to me. And you know the next bit: I found you.'

I stifled a nervous laugh at the implausibility of what he was telling me. 'I believe you, but thousands wouldn't,' I said.

'It sounds crazy, but it's true,' he said, 'every word. And there's one more thing. I'm certain that Janet has never told John about Crystal's actions after Aaron left. So there you have it, another fine situation I got myself into.'

'I had no idea.'

'How could you. As a story, it's a mood changer.' He took aim and binned his cardboard cup with deadly accuracy. 'Except for the part about finding you.'

I chose to ignore his last comment, not wanting to be sidetracked. 'Most people would have just called Crystal's family and left her to them,' I said, delving back into the story.

'Yes, I guess probably they would have, but my family's a bit like … If you can help someone, you just do it. My mother is always taking on "black sheep" students at the conservatorium. My father, too, he volunteers for sea rescue.' He laughed and turned to me. 'I must have caught it.'

'So, Janet just kept quiet about the emergency visit?' I asked.

'She did,' he said.

'Does your friend Aaron know how hard it's been for you?'

'It doesn't matter. He's doing well up there. He's not looking to come back to London anytime soon.'

'What's Crystal's situation now?' I asked tentatively, still trying to weigh up if James might have had some other reason for staying involved with Crystal's family way beyond the cause of good Samaritan. 'In the end, I suppose it can't hurt being friendly with a lawyer who is from a well-connected family,' I said, prodding him unnecessarily.

'She's doing okay, I think,' he said, answering my first question. 'And yes, I won't deny that it helps to know people, but it wasn't about that for me. It was a situation I found myself in, and sure if John wants to give me a reference for a position, that's okay, although I think my firm in Brisbane would have a little more weight.' He looked fierce for a moment, so I stayed quiet.

'Crystal is better now from all appearances, so hopefully, I'm off the hook.' An expression of relief passed over his face.

I let the mood settle for a moment before I said, 'I don't know what to say except, it's amazing that you had time to find me in the midst of all that, and your studies.'

'Ask a busy man.' He grimaced. 'But I can't take all the credit for finding you. I did recruit a few university mates to help.'

'You must have good mates,' I said, aware that I was the one now trying to lighten the mood.

'You'd be amazed what long-term students will do for free beer. But trust me, it was no pushover to snuffle you out.' He looked directly at me. 'But what is it they say about grey clouds and silver linings?'

I was weighing up just how unlikely it was that we should ever have met, when he said, 'When I packed up and left Brisbane, a friend suggested I was leaving because I knew I wasn't going to find what I was looking for there.'

'And was he right about that?'

'He was, yes. My mother was horrified, of course. She thought I was being irresponsible letting the great job I had go, and a few other things, too. But sometimes I think events just put you in the right place at the right time. How about you?'

'I know what you mean,' I waved my hand, 'the past few weeks, with family revelations and everything else, it has changed a few things for me.'

He gave me a questioning look.

'I certainly didn't expect to be hanging around in Kent. And the sequence of how things happened to bring me here I find weird, it's hard to explain.'

'Important things are like that,' he said.

I'd only known James for a few weeks, but it felt now as if I'd known him longer.

Gazing out over the water, a giant container ship was passing along the estuary. Fresh air was clearing my head. 'Come on, James, let's walk,' I said, throwing back the last dregs of my coffee.

'Okay.' He jumped up and put out his hand and pulled me to my feet.

We set off eastward from Gravesend at the same time a huge container ship was being escorted into the estuary by a sturdy little tug boat. I thought of Sydney Harbour. I could never go to the water's edge there without becoming utterly mesmerised by the constant flow of container and cruise ships being towed in and out of the harbour. This was different, but breathing in fresh salty air, the effect was the same. With gusts of chilly wind blowing hair around my face, my energy was rising.

We walked briskly for quite a way following a few twists and turns, past a sailing club and further inland past a derelict industrial estate until the path ended abruptly and we were suddenly looking down on a grassy embankment.

'Looks like a nice spot to take a breather.' He shrugged off his pack and dropped it to the ground.

Gazing out at the stretch of water, I was thinking how Abigail and her mother had sailed along it. How conquering Roman invaders and marauding Saxons had landed on it. But foremost on my mind was his arm next to mine, and the feeling of his warmth standing so close to me.

He kneeled down to open his pack and I watched him reach in and pull out a synthetic sheet to spread on the ground.

'You could walk the Nullarbor with that stash of supplies.'

'You can laugh,' he said, cheerily ignoring my teasing, 'but I'm an experienced hiker, remember?'

I sank to the ground and wrapped my arms around my knees, taking in the panorama across the river and the fortress on the other side. It was perfect, perched on an embankment overlooking the water, watching birds diving and coasting on the swirling air currents I settled in.

'You're nothing like I thought you were when we first met, you know that?' I said.

He looked surprised. 'Is that a good thing?'

'I never pictured you as the outdoorsy type at all.'

'Pin stripes are good cover, right?'

'Something like that.' I laughed, realising that was exactly what I meant.

'I'm full of surprises, but I could say the same about you,' he countered, sitting down next to me. 'You're not who I imagined either. And you're certainly not who John thought you might be after meeting you.'

'I think it's your turn to explain now.'

'It was nothing really, I think he was joking.'

'I doubt that,' I said. 'John Nettlewood doesn't strike me as a man with much humour.'

He hesitated, scrutinising my face for a minute. 'Okay,' he conceded, 'in the interests of "the whole truth and nothing but" … John was a little terrified you were going to be one of those nightmare estate cases. You know, or probably you don't. Some people can become hard to deal with once they're involved in an estate matter, especially something huge like Hebden.'

'What do you mean?' My carefree mood turned to something else.

'Remember John had the piano in his own house when you met, so I think he was worried about that, and concerned too that you might start asking in-depth questions about other things.'

'Like what?'

'Things like how selling Hebden Estate was handled, how the funds were distributed, that sort of thing.'

'What? He thought I was going to ask for money?' My cheeks flamed.

'It wasn't unreasonable that he should think that. Virtually anyone else would have. Try to understand, Maddison, that in our business people say these things, then act differently.'

James was speaking gently, being completely honest, and so I felt my anger dissipate a little. 'Why did he ask me to come in the first place, then, if he thought I was going to be trouble?'

'John strikes me as a person who feels his responsibilities more intensely than most,' said James. 'He was doing what he thought needed to be done to carry out the final wishes of a very important client.'

'What did you think would happen?' I asked.

'Me? Honestly, I thought you might ask a question or two. No problem with that. As far as my expectations were concerned, I can say I had none, and I was pleased that you proved John wrong about the estate. Not that he seemed relieved in any way, did he?'

'No, he certainly did not,' I said. 'Quite the opposite, actually.'

'Yes, quite the opposite …' James echoed my words.

Gulls cried loudly above as silence descended between us.

I was wondering if he was as acutely aware of my presence as I was of his.

'Did your interview go well?' I asked suddenly, intentionally changing the subject.

'Well enough,' he responded easily. 'I'm going to Zurich tomorrow with a team of theirs for some kind of test. I'll know how well it goes if they make me an offer. If I don't stuff it up, they just might.'

'Oh, well done, I'm sure it'll go well,' I said, aware of how shocked I was to hear that he was going away. I was thinking he'd stay in England, and I'd be back in Australia. All my worrying about whether I was completely over my past and if I was ready to be caught up in something new, terrified of rejection, had all been for nothing. He had been making other plans all along. I felt let down and more than a bit foolish. *That will teach you*, I said to myself. *Making up stories without knowing the facts.*

'I'll be working in London, and you'll be writing up a storm in the family's gatehouse,' James said, his thoughts almost a mirror of my own.

'I don't think so,' I said.

'Why not? You're the last surviving Hampton, after all.'

'You're sending me up now.' I was worried my face might have changed colour again.

'No, I'm not, it's true. As of now, you *are* the last surviving Hampton child,' James repeated, his eyes brimming with mischief.

'Maybe,' I said, 'but I'm a woman, remember, so what does it matter?'

'You being a woman certainly hasn't gone unnoticed,' said James with a wry grin. 'All I'm saying is, maybe it's the right time to see if a great-niece can take the title? Maddison Browne, the Countess of Hebden. That has a ring to it, don't you think?'

'Now you're being plain silly, James,' I said dismissively.

'It's not as crazy as you think, just a few small changes to the law and it could happen.' He paused. 'Probably not in your lifetime, but it could, otherwise the title is going to die out.'

'How bizarre is the world?' I shook my head in disbelief.

'Yes, I know, but that *is* a fact. One small change to the law would mean one huge change for womankind.'

'But as you said, not in my lifetime.'

'Probably not,' he said.

I took my time opening the water bottle before taking a sip. 'I haven't told you about a letter I found in Rose's diary yet, have I?'

He shook his head slightly.

'From Abigail to her mother. I took a photo.' I retrieved the letter on my phone and handed it to him.

I watched his eyes moving back and forth as he read it.

'What do you make of it?'

'Something serious happened,' he said, looking at me. 'Did they ever meet again after this?'

'Not that I've found yet. Unfortunately, the final diary is missing from the archive. If I can find it, I hope it will explain everything, a finale to the story.'

He shrugged. 'You're a better sleuth than I'll ever be.'

The clarity in his eyes when he looked at me told me he genuinely didn't know anything more about any missing diaries.

The sun was peeking through the clouds as we sat on the grass. It was beautiful, but I was wondering why I should have felt the need to test James, when really I'd already known the answer. Was I ever going to lose that fear that people were lying to me?

I turned to speak and found him leaning forward. 'Would you mind if I did this?' he said softly.

His face was very close to mine. I murmured something, I don't remember exactly. Next thing, his lips brushed against mine once, then twice, and then met for good. His mouth was soft and warm, and the smell of his skin up close made my heart beat hard.

High-pitched squeals and the sound of laughter cut through the air as a group of children chasing a furry terrier appeared over the hill, tearing their way down the embankment towards us. Jolted by the unexpected company, James and I pulled back. And from how startled we must have looked, one of the grown-ups following behind the children waved his arm and called out, 'Ooi, don't mind us, keep at it, makes the view even better.'

As the children ran off, James, with his body close enough for me to feel his warmth, whispered, 'I've been wanting to do that since the first time I saw you. Have I done the wrong thing?'

My heart was still banging furiously as I admitted to myself, *And I have wanted you to.* Instead, I drew back, and with his kiss still burning on my lips said, 'You haven't,' then mumbled stupidly, 'but I have to get back ...'

My toes were not even inside the door when I heard Edith's voice call out. I had the impression that they might have been lying in wait for me.

Declining a cup of tea, I excused myself and ran straight upstairs as a little voice in my ear whispered, *You didn't pick it last time, either.*

My hand started to tremble as I fitted the key into the lock. James didn't seem untrustworthy. Not at all. Actually, he was lovely and we'd just spent a wonderful few hours together. *Stop overthinking*, I told myself. *It was just one kiss.* But it was too late, my terrors were off and running.

Two seconds later, I was at my laptop typing furiously, pouring onto the page all the questions I had about him.

Who would help Crystal's father for so long without any payment?

Was he running away from someone, another woman, or something in Brisbane? At thirty-plus years of age, most lawyers I'd met were already married with kids and partners in law firms.

What was he really doing here?

Where was he living?

Who was he living with?

What were the 'other things' he'd left in Brisbane?

What was his story, really?

Apart from ruling out any possibility that he had murdered a wife and children back home, I couldn't answer one other question about him. He knew a lot about me, but I knew virtually nothing about him. I didn't even know his mother's name. *For goodness sake, what does that matter? You even knew the name of your ex's dog from when he was five years old. And that helped did it?*

No amount of knowing particular facts overrode the important question of trust. The suspension of disbelief when you leap into the unknown, that blissful state when you believe every word your beloved tells you. I'd been in that place, and it would take more than one kiss to overcome my terror of how that ended.

Then I remembered his smile as he drove off, and it made me feel warm inside. What I could say for sure was that I liked him, a lot.

I deleted all the questions I'd typed into my laptop. *What kind of romantic are you?* I asked myself, as another little voice in my ear chipped in. *You know that writing romance is a whole different thing to being caught up in one.*

Yes, thank you very much, I do.

Fatigue kicked in after all the walking and the sea air, so I determined to allow the rest of the day to take care of itself, and this thing with James would have to take care of itself, too. Right now, there were too many secrets and too many people to think about – Abbey, Rose, James, Gerard, not to mention the secretive John Nettlewood.

Too many mysteries for one evening. So, rather than trying to solve everything at once, I let my mind wander back to the moment James had kissed me. The thrill of his body next to mine made me realise just how much I'd missed that feeling.

Back to work with music playing, the hours passed. My main character was falling in love but struggling with outside conflict. I had three plot arrows, all pointing to a different ending. I was unsure how the situation was going to end. *If I just work through all the motivations*, I thought, *the rightness of one would show itself soon enough.* A quick change of action could drastically alter the ending with a surprise twist. I wrote on, allowing the story and the characters to carry me through the night.

John

Cobham, two days later

'Morning, John.'

John almost fell from his chair and only just managed to hold on to the phone.

'Gerard!' Here was the last person he had expected to hear from.

The shock of discovering that the earl was already in London staying at his club, 'recovering from the flight and catching up with a few people', was too much. For an instant, the full brunt of resignation pulled at John's shoulders. In the blink of an eye, any possible chance of controlling what happened from here had slipped through his grasp like sand through an hourglass.

Gerard's phone call while Maddison was still here wrecked any vestige of hope he'd been clinging to, to salvage the situation. She had steadfastly resisted any encouragement from him to hasten the date of her departure. 'Thank you, John,' she'd said the last time he raised it, 'but I'm comfortable here for a while longer if it's all the same to you.'

'Yes of course, as you wish,' he'd been forced to reply, relieved that she couldn't see him, or she might have read his face. Motivation was easier to mask on the phone.

Unless he could come up with some new strategy, the party his wife and daughter were flat out organising would not only be a greeting to Maddison, but a farewell to the respect he and his law firm held in the community. And worse, he would be a complete disappointment to his wife and daughter.

Janet and Crystal had been more than delighted with Gerard's suggestion that they take the running for his party.

'Is there a budget?' was Crystal's first question.

'Only the best,' Gerard's instructions had been to John. 'Dig out the heavy silver and let us drink from my finest crystal. Tell your ladies that cost is not an issue. Please understand, John. This is probably the last great Hebden celebration.'

'Not as such, Crystal,' John hedged. 'Gerard said he wants "the best", but we can't be spending all his money.'

'If the best is what he wants, then that's what he will get,' said Janet, barely able to contain her delight. 'Crystal and I will prepare his lordship a dinner party he will never forget, won't we, darling?'

'Oh, I've always wanted to design my own grand affair, but what if we don't agree on what to do, Mummy?'

'We will, darling, we always do,' said Janet, already on the move. 'John, do you have the keys to the gatehouse?'

'And we will need your credit card, Daddy,' added Crystal.

'Come on, we have work to do,' Janet said, bustling to gather her daughter, her bag and her car keys.

John couldn't remember the last time he'd seen his wife so excited.

'You'll find details for Gerard's caterers of choice on the sideboard,' he called after them.

And that was almost the last he'd seen of them for three days. Early mornings, late nights, phone calls at all hours, Janet had taken to the task of party organiser with gusto. Crystal had even moved back into her old room to give herself over to it completely. John daren't complain. This was his family doing one last service for the Hamptons. He wouldn't begrudge Janet and Crystal. The joy on their faces as they dashed around organising a grand white-tie dinner for Gerard was plain to see, but to his own pessimistic turn of mind, it was more a preparation for his own 'Last Supper'.

Later that day, standing by the window in his office that overlooked the street, his heart shrouded in dread, John checked his watch. He hadn't found a way to prevent this meeting taking place. Overcast sky, and wind with sufficient muscle to lift discarded food wrappers off the street to whirl them high in the sky like mini-roller-coasters, seemed to be a symbol of what was about to happen. He had given his staff an afternoon off to secure complete privacy. The conversations taking place here today were for no ears other than the earl's and his own.

John's secretary had given him an odd look when he informed her that the office would be closed for a half-day.

'Is everything alright?' she asked. 'Anything I can do to assist?'

Annie had been with his firm for many years. She probably thought of herself as family because of all she knew about their daily lives. But even with someone trusted like her, John couldn't allow for the possibility of a leak from a line overheard or misunderstood. He had no idea what would happen when Gerard and Maddison finally met face to face. But every bone in his body told him that he was navigating troubled waters.

His eyes fell to the framed family portrait that had sat in prime position on his desk for decades. John was fond of this photo. It filled his heart with pride seeing his grandparents, Llewellyn and Bettina, founders of the firm, sitting proudly with their son, David. They would be horrified that the glue of silence that had bonded them all for so many years, may be about to come unstuck.

Well, not on my watch. Not if I can help it, John thought, drawing himself to his full height. He was going to protect his family if it were the last thing he ever did.

Glancing down once more to the street below, John spotted a black limousine edging slowly towards his office. It wasn't uncommon to see flashy imported cars cruising the streets these days, but John was in no doubt that Gerard had arrived.

From his office vantage point, he observed passers-by on the footpath turn and stare, curious to identify the occupants as the car slowed. Amongst locals, there was still an expectation that it could be one of the royal family riding in a vehicle like that. John stared too, strangely removed, as if he were watching a movie unfold.

For a moment, he thought it might actually be a film as a uniformed driver stepped from the driver's side, opened the passenger door and stood to attention waiting for his passenger to alight.

First the cane, a wooden walking stick, popped through the open door, followed by two feet wearing shoes too light in colour for this time of year. Finally, the earl himself, attired in coat, hat, with a bright orange scarf slung around his neck, emerged. His first action was to glance up, and sighting John at the window, he raised his cane in salute. John waved back, and took the stairs down to meet him. Gerard looked as bouncy as ever.

'John, haven't you installed a lift in these premises yet? Don't you rake in enough fees to pay for one? You must keep up with the times, surely?'

'Gerard, what a pleasure it is to see you. Let me take your arm.'

'I hope you're feeling strong, sometimes I need a forklift to get me up the stairs. But luckily today, I am feeling pretty good. I can't tell you how pleased I am to be here. And you? How arc you?'

'I am well, thank you.'

'You look a little drawn if you don't mind me saying so. You need to get some sunshine. You and Janet should come over to the Bahamas and visit me. You are welcome any time, you know that.'

John muttered something about being too busy and 'one of these days'.

'Tell me, then, how are your womenfolk getting along? I simply can't wait to see what they've done with the gatehouse.'

'From what I can gather, it's going well. And they seem to be having fun doing it.'

'It's just as well I have a strong heart with all this excitement. Is she lovely, John?'

'Who Maddison? Yes, she is lovely.'

'But does she look like my Abigail?' Gerard persisted.

'She has a family face. But as for the rest, you'll have to decide for yourself,' said John, leaning forward to open the door at the top of the stairs.

'After all these years, and me still being here, it's a miracle, I'd say, wouldn't you? A granddaughter of Abigail's simply appearing like this. About as improbable as landing on the moon seemed to me in my youth,' said Gerard, tugging at his scarf to loosen it. 'Where is everyone?' he asked, looking around at the empty desks.

'Half-day holiday,' John said briskly, and took Gerard's coat, guiding him towards the most comfortable chair. 'It was a very fortunate set of circumstances that led us to finding Maddison, you know.'

'Yes, I know that Crystal's boyfriend gave you a bit of a hand.'

John felt his jaw loosen. Had he misheard?

'Lost for words, John?' Gerard laughed, his eyes twinkling with amusement. 'Aren't you going to ask how it is that I know such things?'

'I don't believe I've made mention of how we conducted the search or with whom?' John replied, trying not to sound too sharp.

239

Gerard laughed at the lawyer's obvious confusion. 'My dear John, what can I say? You know even an old toff like me can be on social media. Your beautiful daughter, Crystal and I have been internet friends for some time now. She keeps me up with all the local shenanigans.'

'Oh,' John grunted, momentarily lost for a more appropriate response. 'And what shenanigans are they?' he said at last.

'Oh, nothing serious,' he said, 'but it has worked rather well recently, when she had a few questions for me about the party. About what I would like and so forth. But then, I had a few questions for her about other matters.'

John felt hot blood rushing to his cheeks. What else had Crystal told the earl? He was seriously annoyed. Why had his daughter not mentioned this to him? He wanted to ask 'what other things', but held back, not wishing to appear as out of depth as he felt.

Unperturbed, Gerard continued chatting, seemingly oblivious to the tumultuous effect his words were having.

'She has a new boyfriend, I hear,' he said cheerily.

'And what else has my daughter been keeping you abreast of, Gerard?'

'Nothing really. Just lately about this new chap of hers. I told her I know his family. Not a bad bunch. If it works out it could be a good match, John. I told her she should invite him to the party.'

'Gerard,' said John firmly, 'I appreciate your input, but I hope this won't get awkward. You see, I have already invited Crystal's ex-boyfriend, the one we were talking about earlier, a young Australian fellow called James Carlyle. He was the one who helped with our search to find Maddison.'

'Oh, never mind that. Nothing like a bit of rivalry in the love stakes, I've always found.' Gerard chortled dismissively, waving his arm in the air. 'Now, shall we get down to business. You and I, John, we have a lot to talk about.'

Maddison

Cobham, same day

My tummy was fluttering with anticipation as I drove towards the offices of Nettlewood and Son. John's call asking if I was free today had come with little warning. I knew my great-uncle would most likely have arrived in England by now, but as I'd heard nothing, I'd decided to give it another twenty-four hours before confronting the lawyer. I was in my room, comfortable in tracksuit and socks, reading through my work from the night before, when his call came.

'Good morning, Maddison,' he said politely. 'I'm sorry to disturb you, but contrary to our earlier conversation, the Earl of Hebden has arrived in London, unexpectedly. He is anticipated in Cobham this very afternoon.'

'I see,' I said, and quickly decided not to mention that I knew anything about the earl.

He continued, 'Your great-uncle has also expressed a keen desire to meet with you. I wonder if you would be available to come to my offices today?'

'Today?'

'Yes,' he said. His voice certainly wasn't communicating any sense of joy or wonderment at this surprising development.

It was short notice by anyone's standards, but to meet my only surviving relative anything was doable.

'I'd be delighted to,' I said quickly, not trying to hide the excitement I felt.

After we agreed on a time, I'd rushed around getting ready, packing up my computer and trying to think straight, all the while scolding his secretive ways. *Surely, he must have known before this*, I thought. *Why leave it to the last minute to call?* My intuition was on fire; I was thrilled, and curious. This was it. Today I would find the final part of the Abigail puzzle.

My great-uncle was from another time and world. His young years spent at Hebden Manor would have been lived like the characters from the historic TV dramas I loved to watch. But there was a large disconnect between his world and mine, especially as I had only scant memories of my grandmother. Yet, here I was about to meet her brother. What would he be like? How should I address him? I was wavering between flurries of pleasure and apprehension.

My thoughts roamed freely as I negotiated the narrow winding streets leading to John's office. From the first moment the letter about the piano had arrived in my letter box, with its obvious and undeniable connection to my 'orphan' piano-playing grandmother, my own life had taken on as much uncertainty and surprise as any of my fictional characters. With forces careering me towards places and people previously unknown, I was feeling like a tumbleweed in a storm, was constantly being lifted up, buffeted around and flipped over. But now, I was close to the most important discovery of my life.

Common sense said that I should use my time to think about meeting Gerard, not entertaining thoughts of James. But I couldn't help it. When he'd confirmed he was now making plans to stay in London, I'd felt a sharp stab of disappointment. Maybe I had allowed myself to think other things from the way he spoke about missing home. It wasn't pleasing that my first summation of him being a 'big pond' type had been proven right. We talked so easily and I'd never met a man with so much understanding. His reaction when I told him how alone I felt after my mother died when I was eighteen, and he'd put his hand on mine, almost melted my heart away. Understanding always made me teary. If Bethany or Lucinda had said those words I could have held back, but for some reason James's reaction had brought tears to my eyes. But I'd be going home soon, and his calling was here. London was a long way from my mountain. Or, for that matter, his home in Brisbane. It was my never-ending story in love and romance. Something always went wrong. This time at least it was over before it really got started.

Up ahead, I could just see the Fox and Hound pub on the next corner. My heart was thrumming as I turned right. Not far to go now.

I looked up at the window of John's office and took a deep breath. Here was a moment I never dreamed could happen in a million years.

Climbing the stairs, I realised that in my own imaginings, I actually had created some picture of Gerard of how he, as an earl, might be. But at the same time, with every step, I was preparing myself for disappointment. *Don't worry if he is not too friendly. If all he can do is fill in the rest of Abbey's story, let that be enough.*

I rang the bell. John opened the door and greeted me.

'Maddison, do come in.' His smile looked tentative. 'Gerard is waiting for you.'

I smiled, and looking past him saw someone who was nothing like the picture I'd created in my head. First impression, he was old, but didn't appear to have lived as many years as I knew he had. An orange scarf casually slung around his neck gave him a youthful look and the rich suntan lifted years from his face. Immaculately groomed, grey hair, and taller than I expected, there was something about his bearing that made me think of an old Hollywood star. But I could see the deep resemblance to my grandmother, instantly.

I stepped slowly into the room and hesitated, sensing some undercurrent of tension beyond my own apprehension. John took my coat, and I waved across to my grandmother's brother, the Earl of Hebden. Probably not the most appropriate greeting, but I was feeling uncomfortable and searching for the right words to use. This sudden loss of confidence was unexpected. *You are an experienced, successful woman*, I told myself. *What is the matter with you? Surely you are not scared to meet a relative?* But my feet felt as if they had been nailed to the floor. Then, when I thought the situation was going to end in disaster, the whole scene opened up.

Nothing could have prepared me for the warmth of Gerard's greeting. The earl was on his feet, arms open, bright blue eyes glistening as he stood waiting for me to approach. Up close his age was more evident. Deep lines from years of living cut into smooth skin of what must have been a fine complexion. The weight of cheek skin dragged the bottom rim of his eyes downwards, which gave them a slightly sad look. But the vigour in his voice was of a man much younger.

'Maddison, at last, let me look at you,' he said, his hands briefly holding me at arm's length. 'How beautiful you are.' He turned briefly to the lawyer. 'You were right, John.' Then to me, 'I might be a foolish old man,' he brushed his hand across his eyes, 'but I can't tell you how delighted I am to meet you. Come, let me feel my own flesh and blood,' he said, and hugged me briefly.

'We haven't a second to lose, you and I.' He was holding my arm firmly. 'But first, let us make a toast for this occasion. I don't suppose you've some champagne hidden away in that fridge of yours, have you, John? I need some bubbly urgently to steady my nerves with all of this.' He waved his arm in the air.

I shot a glance at John, whose close-lipped smile was hardly reassuring.

Again, I was unsure how to proceed. How should I address the earl? I'd meant to look it up after the phone call, but ran out of time. I turned to John for help, but he had pre-empted the request for champagne and was already wrestling with a bottle, trying to open it.

Gerard scrutinised my face for a second, then as if realising my predicament, he laughed and said, 'Oh, dear girl, you must call me Gem. I'm your Uncle Gem.'

I jumped when the cork popped loudly. 'Okay, Uncle Gem,' I said, smiling at him. 'I'll get used to it.'

'And so will I, my dear, so will I,' he said, patting my arm again.

John appeared not to be listening. His focus was on pouring streams of bubbles, fizzing and crackling, into delicate champagne flutes.

'I call on you now, John,' said Gem, 'given we are indebted to you for this joyous occasion, to say a few words.'

John, who was already on his feet and not looking at all joyous, said solemnly, 'Yes, yes, of course.' He looked first at me, then to the earl and said, 'Here's to the family gathering that almost never was.'

Only the shortest while ago, I had been at home in Melbourne. Now my grandmother's brother, the Earl of Hebden, was receiving me as a member of the Hampton family. Excitement rippled through me from the tips of my fingers right down to my toes.

'I'll second that,' said Gem. 'And I propose another toast to you, John, as the one responsible for finding Maddison, thank you!'

I raised my glass, and for the hundredth time wondered how it was that I found myself here.

My great-uncle was warm and made me feel welcome. I wouldn't say he wore his heart on his sleeve, but he was clearly someone affected by emotion. It was his ease of communication, and a sense of unreality about the whole situation, I thought, that unleashed my tongue.

Minutes later, with John sitting by listening attentively, Gem and I were chatting easily. I'd paraphrased our life in Australia, about my mother and my uncle.

'Uncle Gerry?' Gem's eyebrows shot up.

'Yes, he was Gerard, too. Abigail must have named him after you.'

He coughed and lowered his head without saying a word.

I carried on, telling him how the family tree had 'spawned' an actor, and a government bureaucrat-slash-beach bum. Once I mentioned Abigail's piano playing, and her work to raise funds for orphan children, he choked up suddenly, and said, 'Oh, darling girl, this is too much. All these years of not knowing what happened to my dear Abbey,' he said, 'and here you are to tell us.'

As Gem's breathing became laboured, John picked up the champagne and took the opportunity to refill his glass. Gem took a minute to gather himself then asked me, 'Tell me, what did you think of the old manor house? It must have been a shock for you.'

'Yes, it was the first time I saw it,' I said. 'It was late one afternoon on a foggy wet day. I thought it was out of this world,' I added, trying to describe my reaction.

'Out of this world.' His face opened up again with a smile. 'Yes,' he said, that's exactly how it was and how it still is. I don't think there's a prettier ballroom in the whole of England.'

'I'm sure,' I murmured.

'You've seen it?' His eyebrows lifted. Age had not dulled my great-uncle's perceptions.

I certainly wasn't going to tell him how I'd been stalking around the adjoining woodlands and been intercepted by security and sent on my way.

'Well, I've seen it from the road and surrounds,' I said.

'You mean John hasn't shown you around yet?' he asked askance, as his eyes turned directly to his lawyer.

'Not yet, no,' I said hurriedly, not wishing to make anything of it.

'I see.' Uncle Gem switched his thoughtful gaze from me back to John. 'In that case, I'll show you around myself,' he said seriously. 'I'm not in England often, and who knows, this may be my last hurrah, but whenever I am in residence, I virtually have the run of the place. We can do it after the party I have decided to throw to welcome you to the family'.

John's face gave nothing away. 'There you are, Maddison, who better than the earl himself to offer you a guided tour of Hebden Manor?' He spoke smoothly, gesturing his open palm towards Gerard.

'Now, before I leave you to take my rest, tell me, Maddison, how have you been spending your time?'

'Me? How have I been spending my time?' I repeated rather foolishly. *Here was my chance*, I thought, drawing a deep breath.

'Well, mostly I've been down in Strood at the archive searching the Hebden papers and reading your mother's diaries,' I said, not daring to look in John's direction.

'And is that interesting for a young woman like you?' Gem asked sceptically.

'It is, yes. You see, while receiving your mother's piano is a great honour, what really brought me to England, Uncle Gem, was your sister, Abigail.' I turned my eyes to John to include him in what I was about to say. 'Until the letter from John's firm showed up in Melbourne to inform me otherwise, I grew up believing that my grandmother was an orphan, with no family at all. Now I know that was not true. I'm trying to piece together why she left her family and England for Australia. And why she never returned.'

'I too was shocked to discover that I had a great-niece, Maddison, make no mistake about that,' Gem said quickly. 'I, for one, never knew that my sister went to Australia. I'd have been happier to know that she had. I've always thought that my sister died in childbirth on the Continent. That's what I was told. You know, when you're away in boarding school … you just accept things. But reflecting on the situation now, it does sound a bit thin, doesn't it?'

I noticed that John had left his glass untouched after the toast. And he wasn't saying a word.

'What have you found in these searches, Maddison? Do you have anything to report?' Gem persisted. 'Have you found what caused her to leave us?'

'I haven't found the actual reason yet,' I said. 'I was hoping that you might be able to help …'

'Alas, my dear,' he said, 'I am as intrigued as you must be to have come all this way. Unfortunately, I know nothing that might help. You know I would if I could.'

'Yes, thank you. I think if only I could find another of your mother's diaries, I'm pretty sure it would reveal the truth of what happened. But …' I glanced sidelong at John.

'But what? Go on,' said Gem.

'It appears to be missing.'

'Where is it, my dear?' Gem pressed.

'Well, that's just it, Uncle Gem, I don't know where the final volume is.'

'Are we sure there was another?' Gem's eyes flicked between John and me.

'Not one hundred per cent,' I said, 'but it would appear from the way the diaries are written that there is another.'

'Really? Well, what can we do about that?' Gem appeared genuinely concerned.

I could feel adrenaline rising up my arms and into my throat. *Stay calm*, I counselled. *Don't lose it now.* I began slowly, 'The archive people said that John's firm were the last people to handle the documents from Hebden before it was all committed to them. But John is adamant that he has no knowledge of any missing diary. So, I have one question for him.'

'Yes, my dear and what is that?' said Gem with a perplexed frown. John's face was a mask.

'It is my strong belief that there's one person in the room who knows about this diary. And my question is,' I turned, 'where is it, John?' I said in my strongest voice.

John blinked, then bored his eyes straight into mine. I'd shocked him with the directness of my question. So I held his stare, determined that I wasn't going to be the first one to look away.

Gem interrupted the silence. 'Ah, my dear Maddison, I was transported back to my youth,' he said. 'You are exactly like my sister, Abigail. We all learned very quickly not to get in her way.'

When John still didn't answer, Gem took a stronger stance. 'Is Maddison right, John? Have you kept any Hebden papers here for privacy or security reasons ... like this diary?' And what could it possibly contain that you should feel the need to hide it?'

John averted his eyes, picked up his stem and swirled the contents around and downed the last drops, like a shot of spirits.

'The question isn't difficult,' said Gem impatiently. 'A simple yes or no is all that's required, John. Do you have this diary or not?'

I was holding my breath.

John placed his glass down. 'Is this an official request, Gerard?' he asked. 'Because unless it is, I will not respond just because Maddison has it in her mind that she'd like to see it.'

'So, you do have it!' Gem exclaimed. 'And yes, you should regard any of my questions as official.'

My heart began to beat harder.

'Very well,' said John, his face pinched like someone in excruciating pain. 'As legal counsel for Hebden, you leave me no option but to respond with the truth.'

'You are exasperating me now, John,' harrumphed Uncle Gem. 'Will you just get on with it.' Then he turned to me. 'And what is so important about this diary for you, Maddison?'

I wasn't flying blind anymore. If ever I was going to find out what happened to my grandmother, it was now. I might end up with egg all over my face, I might even lose my great-uncle after having just found him, but I took another deep breath and told him.

'I believe the final diary holds the critical clue to what drove my grandmother away from here. I need to know the answer, for myself, for my mother, my other Uncle Gerard and for Abigail herself. She kept the secret, whatever it was, for her whole life. I think that you, John, know what it is, and I think that for some reason you've been hiding the truth. Not just from me, but from Uncle Gem, too.'

John Nettlewood could not mask his fury. If looks could kill, I was dead on the floor.

I heard the threat in Gem's voice. 'You will hand this diary over right now, John.'

'Gerard, I beg you,' John pleaded.

Gem raised his hand like a traffic warden to stop further discussion. 'Maddison is Abigail's granddaughter. The shape of her face alone brings to mind my dear sister.' Gem's eyes misted over for the second time. 'What a day this has been.'

I couldn't help feeling exhilarated by the accuracy of my intuition. The diary had been in John's possession all along. But I too was choked by Gem's reaction, hearing him say that my face resembled Abigail's, which was what my mother used to say.

'I'm not asking you, John,' said Gem.

'Gerard, this is for your eyes only.' John's shoulders slumped a little.

'I've never read my mother's diary,' Gem responded heatedly, 'and I don't intend to start now. If Maddison believes this will enlighten us as to what drove my sister away, I here and now commission her to read it and tell me what, if anything, I need to know. There will be no further discussion.' Gem looked right at me. 'Are we agreed?'

Would it contain the final piece of information to finish the story? I couldn't be certain. But I nodded my assent.

What struck me most was that John simply opened his top drawer and lifted out a small diary exactly like the ones I'd been reading in the archive. *Was there no limit to this man's intrigue?*

Handing me the diary with the utmost reluctance, John's face shifted from grey to pink.

The cover of the diary, smooth with age, was like the others, and the feel of it in my hand made me shiver. I could have improvised an ending for Abbey from what I knew already, but I didn't want to do that. I couldn't rest until I found out what actually happened to her. The truth lay in my hand. I was absolutely certain of it.

'Surely, knowing the reason Abigail left is more important than whatever you are worried about,' Gem addressed John, who was standing behind his desk, eyes downcast, his shoulders dropped low like someone defeated in battle.

I had no clue what would happen from here on, but I'd never had someone take my side like this before. And although I was trepidatious regarding what I was about to discover, I knew Abbey would be smiling if she heard her brother's strength.

The atmosphere in the room was icy. John looked positively unwell, his face pinched and drawn. I felt like throwing up.

Only Gem, euphoric at the turn of events, said, 'You know, Maddison, my experience of people who write diaries is that it can be a lot of old fiddlesticks.' His eyes flicked over to John, whose gaze remained steadfastly averted. 'But if you find anything about Abbey, you promise you will fill me in?'

'Yes, I will,' I said.

John was doing his best to ignore Gem and me, gathering documents on his desk and setting them down again in small piles.

'Oh, and on a happier note, Maddison, before I get on my way, I thought you'd have jumped at the chance to stay at my place.' He leaned forward to leverage himself to his feet. 'Don't all romance writers love historic houses with mysterious letters hidden under the floor, ghosts roaming about, that sort of thing? Not that we have any of those, but you know what I mean.'

'Thank you, I …'

'Of course, it could be just what Barbara told me long ago, I suppose. But then I have no ability to understand romance.' He chuckled quietly to himself. 'I did think you might like to stay in a centuries-old gatehouse, given that you and she are … how shall I put it, on the same professional path.'

'Barbara?'

'Cartland, my dear, Dame Barbara. I knew her well. Only other romance writer I've ever met. Some thought she was all pancake makeup and pink tulle outfits, but I found her to have an iron constitution and a steely determination regarding her career. She was always great fun at a party, too, of course. Gone now sadly. Like all my friends.'

Discovering that my great-uncle had known Barbara Cartland socially, one of the most prolific and popular romance writers of the last century, caused my insides to vibrate. My mind rushed to the sisters at home. Joan loved Cartland books, pure romance, she said, suited her to a tee. Tons of fantasy and no sex.

'Next thing you'll be saying that you knew Agatha Christie, too, Uncle Gem.'

'Alas, that is one pleasure denied.' He smiled. 'Now tell me, Maddison, where are you staying?'

I glanced at John, who was still busily sorting paperwork. 'I'm at a nice little B & B called the Cosy Cottage.'

'I'm afraid I've never heard of it,' he said, a frown etched on his forehead. 'Is it nice, or are they nice people at least?'

'Yes, they are thank you, very nice.'

'Oh, dear girl, you must come and stay with me for the party. Do you hear? And I won't take no for an answer.' He reached out and squeezed my hand. 'Please tell me you will.' His blue eyes looked straight into mine. 'It's not the size of the manor house, but it is spacious enough for a decent crowd, I promise.'

'Thank you,' I said, 'I would love that.'

'Excellent.' He beamed at me. 'We'll be in touch. John can give you the details.' Gem appeared not to be suffering from any residue from their antagonistic exchange at all. In fact, he seemed almost chipper. I was still on edge, and so was John Nettlewood.

Without hesitating, John stepped forward and took the older man's arm. 'I'll see Gerard down the stairs, Maddison, if you wouldn't mind waiting for a moment?'

From the doorway Gem turned back to me. 'Not long ago, I could have leapt down these stairs two at a time, you know. Pity you had to meet me like this,' he said with a sad smile.

Completely out of my depth about how to react to varying emotions that were whirling around inside, I waved farewell and stood listening to the sounds of his departure. Why had John asked me to stay on? Was there more?

No sooner had the door below banged shut, than John reappeared, slightly out of breath.

'There you have it, Maddison, you've finally met the earl,' he said crisply. He walked straight to his desk and said, 'Please understand that when you asked me about the diary last Saturday, I refused because I saw no reason to expose its contents to you. As you've just heard, Gerard had no knowledge of what really happened to his sister.' He spoke quickly in a cool tone. 'It is my view that Gerard will live to regret this decision. Forcing my hand simply to satisfy some curiosity you have about a grandmother you barely knew ...'

'I believe the earl was interested on his own account,' I replied smoothly.

'Perhaps. But it would have slipped by without mention had you not come along raising the past. You don't know what you've started.' He began gathering what looked like old letters from his drawer, and sealed them into a plastic slip.

What are you hiding? Where is all this antagonism coming from, and why?

'The earl has instructed me to show you what I have, so I must,' he said dispassionately as he handed the plastic cover to me. 'This provides the rest of the answers you are looking for. Once you have those explanations, Maddison, it is my fervent hope that you will let this matter rest where it has been safely hidden, with my firm, for almost three generations.'

His words stung my ears. 'You mean you've had certain information without telling anyone, even the earl?' I could hear my tone was accusatory, but I didn't care. Imagine keeping secrets from Gem about his own family, with no thought whatsoever for his suffering about his sister.

'It's not as simple as that, Maddison,' John said brusquely. 'I expect that Gerard will come to rue this day. But, until you have the full picture, I can say no more. Once you've read the diary and the letters, perhaps you may understand the decisions I've been forced to make.'

I stared at him, thinking how deceitful he had been, and I reminded myself to always trust my first impressions of people.

His last words to me before I left his office, however, did make a new impression. 'Maddison please, I implore you to keep the contents of this material confidential, given the important issues that would have to be addressed, should, heaven forbid, the contents of the diary ever become public.'

I made a rapid departure, thinking, *What important issues, what was more important than my poor grandmother?* and got back to my lodgings in record time. Only when I was safely in my room, my heart thudding, did I dare open the 'missing' diary. Praying that this slender volume would deliver the full story, I read the opening lines, and immediately my breathing slowed, becoming shallower with every intake.

This diary is an end. Once a joy for me, it pains me greatly now to write. I can no longer bear to articulate the tragic events that have befallen us over recent times. If anyone should be looking for this truth when I am no longer here, a time when I will not have to suffer judgement in people's eyes, then I have written this for you.

I pulled back in recognition. Rose had bequeathed her piano to me, and now, I was the one about to discover her darkest family secret. This entry felt so personal, it might have been written for me alone.

I began purposefully, taking in every word, mapping the story as I went. My reactions were becoming more emotional with every twist in the tale as the story drew to its inevitable conclusion, and the truth of what happened to Abigail became unbearably clear.

Rose

Hebden Manor, 1936

The next morning, I set off before William had even seen the light of day. A simple request that I be driven, and for a car to wait outside for the duration of my appointment, was all it took. My heart was jumping with anxiety as I left the house and slid in behind the waiting driver. With dew glinting on the lawn and shafts of early sun dancing through the trees, the car was rolling along the avenue past my beloved Pleasure Garden, I was through the gates and away.

Soon after, I descended from the car directly outside my destination. A gratuity to the driver meant I'd no need to explain my reasons to be driven to the village. It was simple enough, completely credible, given the man I was seeing was none other than legal counsel for the Hebden Estate and the entire Hampton family.

My legs trembled as my foot landed on the first step, but carefully following signs to the newly opened offices of Llewellyn Nettlewood Solicitors, I slowly made my way, breathing hard and reminding myself to remain calm. But his figure, waiting for me, larger than life, at the top of the stairs, unleashed a reaction in me that spiralled into uncontrollable fury.

'How is it that you of all people bring me here to discuss the whereabouts of my daughter?' I demanded, all fear gone, as my foot hit the last step to the landing.

'My Lady,' Llewellyn said, moving forward, his arm outstretched.

I made no attempt to shake his hand, and in a voice devoid of courtesy, I said sharply, 'Don't My Lady me, where is our daughter, and what part have you had to play in her disappearance?'

'Please come in. Thank you for coming,' he said hastily and closed the door.

I took the chair offered and stared into piercing blue eyes. The very eyes that had almost persuaded me to betray my dearest husband. Nausea like a whirlpool circled the insides of my stomach, before spilling out into every crevice of my being. I pinched my palms.

'First of all, I must beg your forgiveness, yours and Will's,' he said.

'I can't speak for my husband,' I said coldly, 'and for myself that is not something I can guarantee until I hear what you have to say.'

'Rose,' he implored.

'If you know where our daughter is, then you must tell me this instant,' I said.

His sigh of resignation told me he understood that I was not going to alter my attitude until I heard what he had to say. 'Very well,' he said,' I'll explain as best I can … But first, I need you to know, Rose, how fond I am of your daughter.' He leaned forward and spoke in a quiet, urgent voice.

I did not want to hear him speaking of his affection for our daughter. I felt my eyes narrow as I said, 'Answer my question.'

'This outcome was not something I ever envisaged,' he said hesitantly. 'I do most sincerely regret what on my part was an impulsive act. I allowed myself to …' he paused, 'such indulgence I can only attribute to the time, the influence of dancing, the mood of the evening, and the intoxicating company of your beautiful and highly attractive daughter … It's no excuse, I know,' he added. 'It is nevertheless a reflection of the facts … though shameful they may be.'

'Where is Abigail?' I growled at him.

'She is safe and staying with friends of mine in London for the time being,' he replied.

'We've been crazy with worry. Why has she not contacted us?' I heard the desperation in my voice.

'Because,' he said, 'I think she fears you will not be pleased.'

'Well,' I huffed, 'she's right about that.'

'Look, I think it would be best if I just come right out and say it,' Llewellyn said with a haunted look. 'The critical point here is that Abbey is expecting a child.'

His words hung suspended in the air.

'What?' I resisted the urge to flee from this loathsome revelation. Staring at him, I prayed my worst fears would not be realised when I asked, 'And who is the father of this child?'

'Rose, I think you already know the answer to that question,' he replied, 'but I will say it aloud if you wish ...' He paused. 'I am the father of Abbey's baby.'

Did he just smile even slightly? I sat completely still, stony-faced, as if someone had bludgeoned me to silence. My mind was spinning out of control. I couldn't move, I was trying desperately to weigh up what I should do. Our beautiful Abigail during her time in London had dallied with this insincere, smooth-talking man, who was not of her own generation, and he had led her to this? I fought to retain my composure by sitting taller and clasping my hands on my lap.

Llewellyn moved uncomfortably in his chair, waiting for me to react. 'Lady Rose?'

'You were presumptuous enough to approach me, brazenly,' I began quietly, 'without the slightest provocation to suggest that I, behind my husband's gaze, should embark on some illicit liaison with you.' My eyes turned on him, and my voice grew stronger. 'Now, you tell me you have violated our daughter, a young woman barely starting out in life, just because you could? And without any precaution? What kind of man are you?' He squirmed beneath my icy stare. 'You are disgusting,' I hissed. 'I should call the constabulary.'

'Please, please, don't do that.' Llewellyn jumped to his feet. 'If you will permit me to speak.' He leaned across his desk to face me. 'I know you have every right not to listen, but I have a way to solve this tricky situation that might best serve all the interested parties.'

'Interested party, is that what you think I am? On top of everything else you refer to me,' my voice lifted another notch, 'Abigail's mother, as an "interested" party? And you dare describe my daughter as being in a "tricky" situation? Is there no limit to your insolence?'

'Please, unworthy as I am, I beg you to listen.' Llewellyn was patting the air with both hands to calm the atmosphere.

Feeling only profound relief that I had, in the end, come alone without Fletcher, or anyone else who might overhear this conversation, I stared at the hateful man before me as the reality of his words sank in. How would we survive? Abigail was ruined, Hebden slurred, William's reputation, mine too as her mother, all compromised with scandal. Is this what I've been striving for all this time? Would I have to hear again how unsuitable a match I was for a titled Englishman? That it was my wild Australian character that had infiltrated the English aristocracy in such an undesirable fashion? With no possibility of Abigail marrying into a wealthy family that could perhaps even shoulder some of the weight necessary to keep Hebden going? What would we do? What could this despicable man possibly say to rectify a situation that appeared to me completely unsalvageable?

'Very well,' I said, in a voice devoid of emotion. 'What have you to say?'

'Lady Rose, I must confess, while it is true I was infatuated with your daughter, smitten some would say, so much that for some time

I lost all reason, I assure you that my sense of reality returned with a hearty jolt when I learned Abigail was with child. It was not something either of us planned.'

My steely gaze on his face, I motioned for him to continue.

'Bettina, my wife, and I ...'

'I am not interested in you or your wife. Where is my daughter staying?'

'I'm afraid on that score, I swore a vow of silence to Abigail for now. And yes, I understand why you would not be interested in my situation. But perhaps if you hear me out, you will see that my reason is heading towards the best solution for what has become a most difficult situation. And one unfortunately that concerns you, as much as it does me.'

I pursed my lips to silence myself.

'Is it necessary for me to go on,' he said, scrutinising my reaction. 'Do I need to outline what a disaster it would be should any of this become public knowledge? Not just for myself, or you and William. But surely for Abigail, too?'

Are you insinuating that you know my daughter better than I? I thought, but held myself in. 'What are you proposing?'

I saw a strange look pass over his face. *At least he has the grace to cast his eyes down*, I thought, *if only for an instant.*

His voice lifted as he started to speak. 'You see, Bettina and I had been planning for some time to leave London and move to Cobham. I intended to resign from Parliament even, settle down here in the village, you know, to concentrate on matters local, on a permanent basis.'

'And now?'

'What I am saying,' he said, 'is that could still happen, if "matters" were to be handled in a particular way.'

'Get on with what you mean before I lose my patience altogether,' I said hotly, feeling highly agitated again.

'Alright, My Lady. Here is my suggestion for a solution that best serves the interests of all concerned.' He paused, stared directly into my eyes, and in a brisk, business-like tone continued to outline his plan. 'Firstly, the Hamptons announce that Abigail has gone abroad for a time. Perhaps, because she is to be married or for some other highly plausible reason. That would be up to you to decide on what to say. She could have the baby there, and the child could by private agreement be "adopted", unofficially, and in secret by myself and Bettina.'

My head started to pound as I listened to his words, as thoughts of what it would mean circled in my head. *Take away my daughter's child? Is this what I must do for our lives to continue, to avoid a disastrous scandal?*

'What you propose is that I must lie to everyone including my own husband?' I said, my voice lifeless and dull as if it belonged to somebody else.

'Not exactly,' Llewellyn replied. 'It might take some organisation, but what if William were to be told simply that Abigail is expecting a child. The father could be described as "unknown". Wouldn't that be best? She was going away to have a child that would be adopted out? In this way, Abigail's actual situation need not interrupt my professional arrangement with the earl at all. And may I suggest that you consider your husband's overall wellbeing. Do you see what I'm getting at, Rose?'

Oh, I saw it clearly. I sat still, aware of my breathing becoming shallow. I wanted to pummel him and yell at him, but could not even find strength enough to lift one arm. I was frozen as if a paralysis had overtaken my entire body. Llewellyn talked on, persuading me of the merits of his plan, his words slithering over me, slowly sinking into my brain. My throat was locked.

'My wife would welcome the child, since despite time passing, we have had none of our own,' he said. Then, as if sensing victory was close, he added, 'This would mean that after a respectable period of time, Abigail could announce that the potential groom was unsuitable and she would be free to return to live her own life, without so much as a whiff of scandal even. Dare I suggest that this little tragedy might make her more marriageable. Some kindly wealthy Baron perhaps, who could assist with your expenses?' he said, shoving the knife in.

It was hearing those words that snapped me out of my deadened state. I leapt involuntarily to my feet, and slapped him hard across his cheek. 'How dare you say such a thing to me.' My hands, arms and legs were all shaking.

He dropped his eyes.

The shame of what would happen were I not to agree with his plan was more than I could bear. That in my reign as lady of the manor such a scandal should befall the Hampton family was my worst nightmare.

My mind began processing the ramifications of his proposal. If the child were a boy, this situation would be tantamount to giving away a potential heir. But what was worse? I felt my insides start to tremble.

'Can I offer you a beverage, Lady Rose?' I heard him say.

I didn't respond, but just sat shaking my head.

Llewellyn's confidence that he could persuade Abigail to have the child without mentioning 'our' arrangement made me feel sick to my core. How could I act this way against my own daughter? The answer was all too clear. For befuddled as I was, I found myself entrapped by his reasoning and his 'greater good' arguments.

The more Llewellyn talked, the more I panicked, wanting only an invisible solution. His persuasive tone purred on until I was convinced that his plan was for the best. William need never know, and 'saving' Abigail's reputation meant that she would be free to make a life for herself afterwards, I repeated to myself.

At last, after more toing and froing, and against all of my better judgement, I capitulated. But even as I heard the word 'yes' escape my lips, a premonition so dark passed over me that for an instant, I feared I may have actually blacked out.

'It's for the best,' he said, 'you'll see.'

All that remained from there was for the two of us, together, the perpetrator and I, to decide on which way the situation would be handled. I struck an agreement with the man who had almost led me astray, and then had fathered a child with my own daughter. My heart pounded so violently when I shook his hand, I thought it might burst wide open and bleed on the floor right there. This was my darkest hour.

'I must impress upon you once more, Rose,' he said, 'this must be kept completely between us.' His hand was on my back, guiding me as he accompanied me to the door. 'It is the right thing,' he repeated.

I saw victory in his eyes, and in that moment, overwhelmed with frustration and fear for what I had just agreed to, I hated him with every fibre of my being.

By the time I got back to the manor, the household was bustling around preparing for lunch. Glancing at the ordinary everyday scene before me, weighed down by the huge rock of anxiety wedged in the pit of my stomach, the reality of my actions settled. What had I done? Agreed that my own daughter be sent away to have her child, oblivious of the arrangement her mother had made with her seducer? And once the child was here, the baby would be quietly handed to the father and his wife to raise as their own? William's business could carry on and Llewellyn would continue to be his trusted adviser. The only question I dared not ask myself was how would Abigail react when she found out?

All I knew for certain was that I would never willingly speak to Llewellyn Nettlewood again in my life, and I hoped that somehow I would be able to keep Abbey safe until she recovered from this horrendous ordeal.

William was sitting by the window in the library reading the paper when I came in. He looked up, and his smile melted my heart.

'Where have you been, darling? We've had tea without you.'

Maddison

Gravesend

I was spellbound. The reality of my grandmother's situation written by her mother's hand had me by the throat. Caught up in the behaviours of all the characters, I wanted to throw my hands in the air, yell at Llewellyn and warn Abbey, tell her to 'watch out'. But all I could do was devour Rose's words like someone deprived of sustenance. I read on.

Never in my wildest dreams did I imagine Abigail would want to keep the child. When I told her about my agreement with Llewellyn for the 'unofficial adoption', she howled like a wounded beast. Her child with the man she loved, being raised by another woman, she would have none of it. But by then, the baby was gone. Then immediately afterwards, so was Abigail.

I wrote to Llewellyn and told him the great cost of our actions. How forcing Abigail to give up her baby had caused her to run away from us. Depriving William and me not only of our daughter, but of a grandson, too. Will had believed that Abigail would return to us. But I knew that she would not. It broke his heart when I told him that she had died in childbirth. It broke mine to have to tell him that lie. And it breaks mine every day not knowing if she is safe, or where she is, our beautiful daughter gone, forever.

Sometime ago, I was in the village and I saw a woman tending to her young child. You can guess it was Bettina with baby David. She was caring so lovingly to his needs that it tore my heart in half. She saw me, and came over to put the boy in my arms, my own grandson, a stranger to me. She told me she was so grateful and cried. I embraced her. For the life of me, I don't know why I did that. I suppose it was relief that at least our grandchild was being raised in a loving home.

I don't wish Llewellyn harm anymore, my grandson needs a father, and now with William gone my life is over. If I could reverse my actions I would. I am sorry, so sorry for everything. Abigail told me that I had no right to treat her that way, to take away her baby, and she was correct. I had followed my love to marry William despite everyone's disapproval, so why couldn't she have the life she chose for herself, too? I am ashamed to say that I told her this could not be the way for her, given she had chosen to fall in love with a married man. It was such a bitter row. Never in my worst nightmare did I think she would take herself away from us, or that we would never hear from her again. How I kept the truth from William over those years I have no idea. It pains me to reflect how my actions, undertaken entirely for the better good of the family and its history, inflicted so much grief onto my loved ones and upon me.

My cheeks burned hot as if I'd been slapped. Rose's confession was brutal. I'd been thinking that the truth, when I found it, would not be easy. This was much worse.

My grandmother ran away because she was heartbroken. Abigail never forgave her lover, her mother or her father, despite William, as far as I could tell, having had nothing to do with the decision to take away her child.

Now at last I knew, beyond doubt, the reason Abigail took that dangerous sea journey to Australia. Why she had taken on the cause of abandoned children. Not that her son had been abandoned exactly, but my grandmother must have felt that she was. Sacrificed for the wellbeing of everyone else, to maintain the status quo, the continuation of the estate and her mother's pride. It explained why she chose never to share her story with her Australian-born family. She would have known that her absence had been covered up, and to reopen that chapter of her life with its tightly held secrets was more than she had been able to manage. For her, once her feet stepped onto that boat, there had been no going back. I thought of the serious expression she wore in nearly every photo I had, and felt an irrepressible urge to hug her, to say I understood. If Abigail was standing in front of me now I would throw my arms around her and thank her for her spirit, her courage, her heart, and for being my grandmother.

'Some might say you were foolish in love,' I murmured, 'which is another of your traits I share.'

Feeling tense with anxiety as the new revelations sank into my brain, I thought about Rose. The daughter of an Australian law man, who in her efforts to uphold ancient British lore and not wishing to be seen as a foreigner breaking traditions, had taken her duty to such a painful extreme, the consequences were more far reaching than she could ever have imagined. In her desire to be worthy of her role as the lady of the manor, Rose Rooney broke many hearts; her husband's, my grandmother's, and eventually her own.

I saved the letter John Nettlewood had squirrelled away in the plastic sleeve until last. The script, visible through the transparent cover, was written on thick paper and had a different style. This was a flowing, flamboyant font, with long tails and high tops. At a glance, I saw the correspondent was Llewellyn Nettlewood. This must have been hidden by his grandson, John, for decades. What would he have to say for himself, I wondered, extracting the letter from its cover.

My dearest Rose,

Abigail gone! Your news has left me bereft of words to express my sorrow. And I can think of no other action than to raise our son, David, in the best way I know how. Bettina as you know is deeply grateful. She has never been happier. While for my part, I must express my gratitude to her for staying with me. I can tell you honestly that David has a loving and devoted mother. In answer to your question, unfortunately, after we struck our agreement, Abigail never spoke to me again. I despair to say I have no clue where she might be.

I too am sorry for my past behaviour, and while I would never wish not to have loved Abigail, please know that I never wished to harm her. Nor you or Will, who was kinder to me than my own father. Who among us can explain all of their actions? Who can truly understand what it is that attracts one of us to another? Heaven help me, I can only say that I loved your daughter with all of my heart, and I wonder why I was not able to keep that love contained within the confines of what society expects of us.

Dearest Rose, my regret runs deep. Please, if there is ever any matter that I can assist you with, now that you must shoulder even more responsibility running the estate, please know that I am your humble servant, day or night. And I will remain so whilst there is breath in my body. The pledge I made to you, so painfully forged, shall be unbroken.

I threw the letter down in disgust. All I could think as I followed Llewellyn's letter of apology, was how Abigail's heart would have been broken all over again had she ever read it. Llewellyn, the great love of her life, hadn't really loved her at all.

Maddison

Gravesend

It took me all night to put everything into context, and the next morning I was still agonising over the revelations contained in Rose's final diary. What if Abigail had realised that Llewellyn didn't love her enough and that he was a philanderer who'd taken advantage of her? What a double heartbreak that would have been for her. I was almost glad that I wouldn't ever know the answer to that question.

Buying myself some extra time to process the ramifications of the situation as I now understood it, I let a day pass before contacting Gem.

About an hour after I left a message, my phone rang. When I picked up, a voice I didn't recognise said, 'Maddison Browne? My name is Joel, butler to the Earl of Hebden. Could you please, if you are able, present yourself at the gatehouse at eleven am this morning? You will need to ring the doorbell nearest the carpark and wait until you are attended. Can you do this?'

I said I could and heard the phone click in my ear.

'What you're telling me, my dear, is that John is not just trusted by our family. He *is* family?'

'Yes,' I said.

Sitting in Gem's opulent study, watching the shock of the extraordinary facts I'd found in Rose's last diary transform his face, I did panic for a second. I'd had time to calm myself since reading the letters, but the last bit of terrible truth was hard to take. I worried that it might be too much for Gem.

Fortunately, I found Uncle Gem was made of sterner stuff. 'John is my illegitimate great-nephew,' he repeated, keeping his eyes fixed on me. 'I'll be dashed.' He paused, processing it further. 'It does sort of make sense,' he added softly, as if talking to himself, 'if you think about it. And you, dear Maddison, how perplexing this must be for you.'

'Yes, last month I had no family, now I have a great-uncle, a first cousin and his family.'

The fact that I was also related to the Nettlewoods was a scenario so bizarre it was laughable. *Heavens, what next?* I desperately wanted to tell my mother. *Keep at it, we'll find ourselves in line for the throne.* My life was seriously starting to resemble fiction. I recalled Lucinda's words before coming here: 'It might change your life forever, Maddi.' She had no idea how right her words had turned out to be.

'I don't know how I'm going to deal with John from now on,' I said. 'I understand that he is my cousin, but he kept this from everyone. He has never even told you about your own sister. Who has the right to do that?' I asked.

'For whatever reason, he obviously felt that he alone must keep that secret,' said Gem, surprisingly circumspect. 'It couldn't have been easy. I've kept a few secrets in my life, too, let me say.' His eyes glistened intensely. 'I have first-hand experience of how it feels to masquerade in order to maintain society's expectations.' Then without waiting for any response from me, he added, 'But you find in life, Maddison, that you *can* trust people. Some people like John *are* trustworthy. In the end, they are who they say they are.'

James flashed into my mind. Because I'd been bruised so badly by one man, I found it difficult to trust another. But Gem had a different take. He saw John's actions, keeping these devastating family secrets out of sight, as proof of his honesty and his goodness. That he'd carried generations of secrets, under duress, fibbing along the way, Gem saw as a demonstration of John's trustworthy character. It sounded odd and slightly back to front to me, but I took the point. He'd held the line and kept his word.

As if reading my mind, he added, 'Not many people can be so steadfast in today's world, isn't that right, my dear? How easy it would have been for him to break that solemn bond. But he didn't.'

I sensed Gem's eyes on me, so I said, 'It seems odd now, but John in his first letter described me as belonging to the "broken arm" of the Hampton family.'

'Yes, that sounds right,' he said, staring at me.

'But now I see that he belongs to another "broken arm" himself.'

'Don't think too harshly of your cousin, Maddison, he was just trying to do the right thing,' Gem said gently.

I nodded, unconvinced. *In his own secretive way.*

Gem seemed remarkably to be taking all the new information about who was related to whom in his stride, which I found somewhat surprising, until his next words offered clear indication of why he wasn't worried. At all.

'This all raises an interesting point for me, though,' he said pensively. 'I thought that you were my last remaining close relative. Now I can see that this latest revelation may be good news for the title. I don't know. I'll have to look into it.' He leaned forward and said conspiratorially, 'As much as I would like you to have the title, Maddison dearest, it can never be because you're a woman.'

'So I am,' I said with an irony completely lost on him.

'This may not be a stumbling block ad infinitum,' he continued earnestly, 'but, Maddison unfortunately, it is even in this day and age.' He sat back and fell silent, staring at some invisible object on his desk.

It wasn't as if I had come here trying to infiltrate English aristocracy. But just the same, hearing Gem and James too say the words aloud, how women were not eligible to participate in the title game, worthy or otherwise, whereas even an illegitimate man was better than a legitimate woman, made me hope that it wouldn't be too long before that changed. And not to benefit myself (I liked my freedom), but as a reflection of the world we lived in.

Gem spoke suddenly. 'What we need is some solid outside legal advice on how to proceed. Would your young man be willing to help?'

'James, you mean?'

'Yes, what do you think?'

'I'm sure he could,' I said. 'But my young man, as you put it, is just a colleague.'

'Ah yes, a colleague. Do you have a number for him?'

'Only a private one. He's in Zurich at the moment.'

'If you think he won't mind answering one or two of my questions, could you let me have it?'

I didn't think James would mind me giving his number to the earl. I imagined his smile as he recounted the story to his family back in Brisbane and their disbelieving faces thinking he'd made it all up. Giving legal advice to an earl, the son of a boat fixer, you've got to be kidding.

'You might consider looking through the final diary yourself, Uncle Gem,' I ventured, jotting down James's phone number. 'Reading your mother's own words on how it all happened.'

'Oh, I can imagine perfectly well what happened, my dear.' Gem's mood had transitioned from far away and thoughtful, to a return of his more spirited self. 'I may read it one day, but right now, as a result of this extraordinary twist in our family's affairs,' he turned his wrist from side to side to demonstrate, 'I have pressing things to attend to. Shall we have tea?'

I declined. I needed to get back. I'd made up my mind about the right ending to my story and couldn't wait to return to work. There was seriously no better feeling (when words were flowing), when it was just me, a blank page and a computer.

Gem escorted me to the door, and seemed pleased to talk about the forthcoming party and how delighted he was that Janet and Crystal were organising the whole affair. 'I'm afraid my party days are over,' he said, 'except for this last one. I'm most grateful to them for taking it on.'

I couldn't read his mood, but I sensed that it had altered again. My own feeling about this place was shifting too. I suddenly felt a huge wish to be back on my mountain, looking up at clear blue skies and cherishing my liberty, away from centuries of stultifying family secrets.

Studying the imposing backdrop of Hebden Manor as I drove away, the sight of it caused me to shudder involuntarily. It was truly daunting to think that this building, sprawling like a giant bird of prey, wings stretched out, turrets swirling, untamed, after being repurposed as a girl's boarding college, had once been Abigail's home.

Trying to walk in my grandmother's shoes for a minute, I wondered if I would have had her courage to leave. Or would I have stayed and tried to live on my own terms despite my personal anguish? I hoped I would have been as brave as she had been.

What was clear from her letter to Rose was that her anger was overwhelming. I thought I understood the reasons, but I also deeply wondered what she must have found within herself to create a second life in a far-off land, raise a family (even if my mother called her a 'cold fish'), with the shadow of Hebden and everything it meant hanging over her.

The memory of sitting on her knee at the piano came back to me, her softness, her kiss on my head. That wasn't a woman with hatred in her heart. Somehow Abbey had found a way to forgive. It was a strange thing to feel proud of someone you'd barely met. But I was. I felt only awe for her, that she was my grandmother, and that she'd decided to forge her own destiny.

Rather than live with the unbearable anguish created by her situation, she'd picked up her broken heart and left behind her lover, her son, her mother, father, a brother, friends, a possible career and immeasurable comfort and security. She'd set off to make a new life with the only thing she knew how to do. Play the piano. At least nobody could take that away from her. A picture of her playing passionately flashed before me. Then, Daisy's words about 'the higher power of music' came to mind and what playing music had meant to her mother. That must be what had given Abigail the strength and fortitude to start afresh and carry on, too.

My grandmother and her mother, Rose, were similar in some ways. Both had been headstrong, complicated, larger-than-life women like great characters of fiction. A rush of emotion flooded through me as I reflected on the lives of my own flesh and blood; regret, joy, inspiration, sadness and love.

The night I first saw Hebden I'd made a pledge to find Abigail's story. Now I'd done it. And far from thinking poorly of her, which I think I'd been half expecting, I now understood some of how she lived her young life, and what happened for her to become my grandmother.

I felt a watery smile tugging at my mouth. Abigail had kept her secret for her whole life, in exactly the same way her grandson, John Nettlewood, had kept his. Steadfast and unwavering. *What a tangled web we weave.*

Part Three

Maddison

Two days later

My biggest regret was that I would never be able to share any of this with my mother. I could just picture Marianne deciding which role she would play in the miniseries. I imagined her pulling a face, standing tall and drawing herself up to her most regal stance, saying, 'I'd make a great countess.'

The irony of it was that she'd lived more like a hippy than a titled Englishwoman, so she probably wouldn't even have been offered such a role, although it was actually her own heritage. Marianne and her brother, Gerry, had certainly not lived their lives bound by the social traditions of ancient England. In Australia, they'd been freed from that. And Abigail, after her experiences, must have agreed with that. Thoughts of my grandmother and how she'd raised her children were churning around in my head as I drove through the gates into the grounds of Hebden.

Gem's gatehouse was a sizeable building, and in my part of the world it would be described as a mansion. I veered off onto the short service road and followed signs to the pebbled carpark. My guess was that this sandstone-coloured building with slate roof, two-storey turret and plenty of windows, had never been used for its original purpose. A gatehouse, at the time it had been built, would have been the first line of defence against marauding attackers. But this building was located too far from the manor for that, and was too handsome to have served as a fortress. I wondered suddenly if this was where Abigail had met secretly with Llewellyn? But before I could follow that line of thinking, I saw Gem's butler, Joel, hurrying across the carpark and waving in my direction. His sleeves were rolled up in the manner of one who was busy. I clambered quickly out of the car to meet him.

'Do you have a bag?' He glanced down at my empty hands. 'I believe the earl is expecting you to stay.'

'No, not today.'

He hustled me into the residence.

'Maddison, there you are,' Gem stood and pressed my hand to his lips. He'd been waiting for me in his study and appeared a little preoccupied when his butler showed me in. 'How are you, my dear? Thank you for coming, I have a little something to discuss with you.'

I sat opposite, admiring the warm décor of my great-uncle's personal space.

Carefully scrutinising my face, he said, 'We have here what I would call a "situation", and I need you to be a part of the solution.'

I had no idea what he was talking about. 'If I can,' I said, with what I hoped looked like a casual shrug.

'No doubt you can, my dear, let me explain.'

His face was so serious, my heartbeat kicked up.

'I am an old man. You will have worked out that with no children of my own, as the Earl of Hebden, I have responsibilities towards the future.'

'Yes.' *I suppose so.*

'I have spoken to that young man of yours. And he's got me the advice I required and rather promptly too, I might add.'

I let it pass. No point restating again that James was not 'my young man'.

'James has informed me, contrary to what I'd always thought about "illegitimate" heirs to titles such as Hebden, that they *can* in fact be eligible to take the job. With one proviso and this is the stumbling block.'

I sat unusually still, listening, without trying to anticipate what he might say.

"According to the law, in cases like this, any claim to a hereditary title by a person needs to be made public. This means the birth parents and their particular "family" situation must be named publicly, spelling out the direct claim of their offspring. This should take place at the time of the announcement. Are you following this Maddison?"

'Are you saying that you wish John to take on your title?'

'Quite right, my dear. But yesterday when I went to his office armed with my proposal, informing him that as my sister's grandson I was anointing him to take on the Hebden title...'

'What happened?' .....

'To my absolute astonishment, he turned me, and it, down.'

'You mean he said no to becoming the earl?'

'He did. I was so dumbfounded,' said Gem, 'that for a moment I was unable to utter a single word. Who would do such a thing? And could you guess the reason he gave?'

I shook my head.

'He said he did not wish to become the earl if it meant disturbing the past.'

'Which part of the past was that?' I asked, thinking John Nettlewood was someone who never stopped surprising me.

'He doesn't wish to have the reputations of Rose, Abigail, David, Bettina, Llewellyn, and even my father, William, sullied and portrayed as having been loose with the truth. He demands that their reputations be allowed to remain intact.'

'Perhaps he also doesn't wish to be seen as "illegitimate" himself,' I offered, recalling how John alluded to 'serious issues' that would require redressing, should it become public that he was Abigail Hampton and Llewellyn Nettlewood's illegitimate grandson.

'Yes, yes, but in any case, he won't listen to me. I thought that if you were to come with me, together we might have more success persuading him.'

'Me? I wouldn't imagine that …'

'Please, would you join me for a meeting at the school library, shortly? I've reserved a room for us. It would feel like my darling sister were here. And, Maddison, if she were here, this would be her business, so I need you to stand in her place. You'd enjoy seeing inside the manor, wouldn't you?'

I wavered, thinking about everything my grandmother had gone through for me to be here. I had come to find her, but I'd never envisaged becoming embroiled in a matter as ancient as the continuance of hereditary titles. This was a tussle between the earl and his illegitimate nephew. Yet at the same time, in the back of my mind, my grandmother's voice was asking me to do what Gem had requested. And yes, of course I'd love to see inside the manor.

Gem leaned forward and gripped me by the wrist. 'It would mean the world to me. Don't you see, Maddison, we can't allow hundreds of years of family history to disappear without a fight. Isn't the Hebden name and reputation the only reason for all these years of secrecy and heartbreak? Isn't that what it's really been about?' Gem beseeched, gazing into my eyes. 'I was resigned to certain outcomes before you came along. Now … well I simply must get this to happen, so please help me.'

The next thing I knew, I was following Gem, who had waved his way into reception at the grand manor and been handed a key. My head was on a swivel trying to take in what would have been the main entrance to Hebden Manor. Black-and-white terrazzo, high ceilings, gold-coloured walls and a sweeping staircase rising up to the heavens. It was breathtaking. Then before I knew it, we were in a modern lift being carried directly to the next floor, and Gem, with renewed vigour, was setting forth like a hunter on safari, stick raised, pointing out directions as we passed closed doors. I heard muffled sounds that I presumed were lessons in progress. Until finally, at the end of a long, wide corridor, he stopped outside an unmarked door and jiggled a key that turned the lock.

The door swung open to reveal a magnificent room. So, this was Hebden Manor. Abigail could have walked here in her bare feet, on this worn-looking red carpet, and who knew what else. A stolen kiss with her seducer, perhaps? Wooden bookcases packed with hundreds of ancient tomes cloistered behind glass doors gave the room an overwhelming mood of strength and warmth. A wall of French doors opening onto an outdoor terrace filled the room with light. An eye-catching statue of a woman, some sort of goddess probably, lunging out above a massive marble fireplace mantle, her strong arm strikingly forged into space as if she were in flight, would not have been out of place in any art gallery. Although I suspected fires were rarely lit in that grate these days. This was no place for students, as far as I could tell.

Gem, who read my face, said, 'This was my father's study.'

'It's beautiful,' I breathed, soaking in as much of the surroundings as I could, committing it to memory. Yes, my grandmother would have spent plenty of time here.

'Yes, it is,' he added. 'Now the headmistress of the school uses it as her own private space to contemplate the universe.'

There was a light tap on the door, and John entered the room. I saw his face register surprise. 'Maddison …'

Quick as a flash, Gem said, 'I insisted.'

John looked at me. 'I presume, Maddison, that you have ...'

'Read the diary and letters? Yes, I have.'

'So, now you know my grandfather and —'

'Yes, she knows the truth,' Gem interrupted impatiently. 'That your grandfather was a charming rogue, and that for all of these years, you, as the truly honourable man you are, have been fulfilling his oath to my mother.'

John merely raised his eyebrows at this onslaught.

Gem continued. 'But why are we all standing here like this? Please, can we just sit down as the family we are.'

Moving across to the antique velvet setting, I glanced at John's profile and thought how the strain of dealing with this was bringing the lines on his face to the surface.

We all sat, and John, who chose to ignore Gem, directed his attention towards me. 'So, now you know the whole story. Nothing to be proud of. Abigail was barely a woman when her affair with my grandfather began,' he said flatly. 'And my father, David, was raised as Llewellyn and Bettina's natural son.'

I nodded. 'Which makes us first cousins,' I said. 'Who was it that said real life is stranger than fiction?' I laughed self-consciously. 'But as you might imagine, knowing that I'm descended from such feisty women has been quite a pleasing discovery for me.'

'No imagining, they were feisty,' Gem muttered, making his presence felt again. 'Now, can we please move on to the business at hand? The resolution of our family predicament.'

'I was of the view that it was already finalised,' John replied, glancing at me.

'My dear nephew, the time has come to talk,' Gem said firmly. 'Maddison, could you please tell your cousin that as the law will not yet permit the title to pass to you, that he *must*, as my blood nephew, take the title of Earl of Hebden when I am no longer here.'

'Gerard knows very well what my position is,' John responded again directly to me, 'but he refuses to listen.'

'You don't wish to become the earl?' I asked him.

'That's right, I do not,' he said.

'What rot is this?' Gem burst forth heatedly. 'You have been custodian of the family secrets your whole life, John. And although your connection may not be entirely legitimate, you are prepared, you are politically able, you are perfectly poised, you have Janet and Crystal, you are the whole package.' Then, in a softer tone, he added, 'I need you to reconsider.'

Gem looked imploringly at me.

'John,' I said, trying to remain calm and not ruffle his feathers any more than they already were, 'to me, as a newcomer to all this, it would appear to be not only an incredible honour, but the natural line of the law. Abigail was your biological grandmother.'

'Yes, that is true, my grandmother by birth. But my actual grandmother was Bettina, whom I was extremely fond of, and whom even now I do not wish to harm, not even her memory.' He sighed. 'I've explained this already. My grandfather made a promise to Lady Rose that no one would ever know the truth.'

A knot of emotion gripped my throat. Poor Abigail.

'Well that's done for now, John, isn't it?' said Gem. 'The game is up, I'd say, wouldn't you?'

From the set of his mouth and the expression on his face, John was never going to agree to Gem's plan for succession. His face was drawn when he replied, 'I am the third generation of Nettlewoods to have kept this promise, Gerard, and I am not going to be the one to disregard all of their collective suffering. Which seems to me to have been quite significant.' His eyes roamed between Gem and me.

'We have only to air the truth, John, is that too much to ask?' Gerard intoned. 'If we don't do this, the whole thing, the title, the name, the family, are gone forever. No more history, no more Earl of Hebden. What do you think of that outcome?' He was glaring at John, who steadfastly said nothing.

I turned to John. 'I'd like to say just one thing before we leave.'

'Go ahead,' he said.

'For one minute, I'd like you to consider Abigail. She sailed off yes, but she never came back to make trouble. Never tried to contact David, no matter how that must have hurt every day of her life.'

From the way John's eyes were blinking rapidly, he mightn't have ever considered the question of Abigail's silence before.

'If she'd had her way,' I continued, my emotions well and truly stirred, 'your father would have been the heir, so the title would have come to you anyway. Why is no one asking what she would want? You are her grandchild. I put it to you that she maintained her silence for the Hampton family, and for you, too. Think about what she gave up,' I said. 'Would she have done that if she thought it was all for nothing? No, because she too wished to see the Hebden title carry on,' I said emphatically.

At that moment the school bell, deafeningly loud, drilled through the walls like a buzz saw. Lunchtime. The silence in William's old study was quickly replaced by the sound of running footsteps and schoolgirl voices squealing in the corridor.

'We are wasting our time here,' said Gem gruffly, grabbing for his stick and flapping his arms as he struggled to his feet.

Without hesitation, John jumped to his aid.

'I think we have come to the end of the road with this, John, don't you?' said Gem, upright once more.

'I do,' John responded grimly.

'Very well, Maddison, you and I have just enough time to visit the ballroom. If you wish to join us, John, you are most welcome.'

'I'll keep moving if it's all the same to you, Gerard. I am sorry …'

'It's a bit late for sorry now!' said Gem, releasing himself and starting for the door. 'After you've announced the end of hundreds of years of history, there's nothing more to say. Come on, Maddison.'

John opened the door and we were suddenly caught up in a stream of high-spirited schoolgirls rushing past, paying no heed to us at all.

Outside the entrance to Hebden Girls, I pulled up the collar of my coat and said to Gem, 'I don't know if it made any difference.'

'Perhaps not, but you were terrific, my dear. John and I were getting bogged down in Rose and Llewellyn's agreement, but my dear sister kept the secret, too, you are so right about that.' He patted my arm, which he seemed to be doing much of the time lately.

'I don't think he's going to change his mind, but …' I paused as the thought of another, different way the situation could be handled flashed into my mind. One that I hoped my grandmother would agree with. 'Gem, did James say that John had to make his status within the Hampton family public himself, or was it just that it had to be made public?' I asked.

Gem had taken a few steps ahead of me, but he stopped. 'What did you say?'

'Does John have to make it public himself, or can it be made public by anyone?'

'And who would that be?' he asked.

'Say … someone like you?' I was in boots and all making this suggestion, but it had occurred to me many times that the longevity of institutions like the aristocracy had served society in the past, and would continue to way into the future, even when the gender shake-up happened, as it surely must one day.

Gem paused, grabbed me and kissed both my cheeks. 'Maddison,' he said, speaking close to my face, 'thank God for you and for thinking outside the square.'

'It's not graceful,' I said, 'but strong needs require strong means.' I could hardly believe what I was saying. And although there might be a smattering of convict-colony mentality about my suggestion, it wasn't unlawful.

'I think, my dear, that John's going to have to learn what I was taught,' Gem said. 'That a hereditary title comes with noblesse oblige, a duty of birth. I have mine and now John must face up to his.'

His body infused with renewed purpose, Gem marched off towards the car, holding his stick in the air like that band leader in *The Music Man*. 'That's it, my dear, noblesse oblige. Come, we have a plan to hatch.'

Maddison

Gravesend

Lost in thought all the way on the drive home, my heart lurched when I saw his car pull up behind me.

I jumped out. 'James, I thought you were in Zurich.'

'Got back early this morning. Don't you answer your phone anymore?'

'What do you mean?'

'I've been ringing you for days.'

I remembered turning off my phone to avoid any interruptions with Gem. I reached into my bag. I'd forgotten to turn it on again.

'I thought you might have gone back.' His head was partially through the window, his elbow resting on the door. 'I was about to head off when I sighted your car going in another direction.'

'I've been up at the manor.'

He climbed out. 'I've got an appointment with Gerard tomorrow, but I came early to see if I could persuade you to have dinner with me.'

Aware of the ridiculously pleased feelings whirling inside me as I looked at him, I said casually, 'Hope you didn't mind me giving Gem your number.'

'On the contrary, I was delighted to help. It'll be interesting to see what happens.'

'From what I gather, you've fired him up so much he's set to take on the world.' I stepped closer, wrapping my arms around my chest against the cold.

'Is that right?' He laughed. 'Well, maybe I deserve a reward. Feel like a bite to eat?'

He drove to the Leather Bottle Inn and we made our way inside.

'So, you've got to the end of it, then.'

'Yes, I have, and it's not a pleasant story,' I said, hanging my coat on top of the piled-up rack in reception. I explained what happened to Abigail's child. 'And it was organised behind poor Abbey's back. All for reputation.'

'No wonder she couldn't take it.'

'Yes, and no wonder John kept it a secret. It would have been good to have known before this,' I said, reminded of my mother and my uncle, and how their lives may have been different if they'd known.

'I'm sure for your mother and your uncle, too,' said James, reading my mind again.

'Exactly,' I said.

I heard someone call out, 'Hey, James, where're the rest of your mates?'

'Not about today,' he responded with a wave.

As we made our way inside, James ushered me forward and pointed up to the wall of framed images of Charles Dickens.

I glanced briefly at the sketches, and at the author's old briefcase and memorabilia, lying on the stand below.

'Personally, I find this lock of his hair a bit gruesome,' I whispered to James. 'But at least now I can say that I've seen it.' I wrinkled my nose to hide a shiver. Understanding why Freddie would want any of her lovely strands preserved in this way, was beyond me.

'You and your mates seem to be well known around these parts,' I commented as we made our way through to the dining area.

'What can I say? We can be a pretty lively bunch after a day of hiking, and this is one of our favourite haunts.'

Walking into the main room, the atmosphere enveloped us like a warm embrace. Locals sitting by a friendly log fire happily eating and drinking, accompanied by their hounds snoozing under the tables. It was a scene barely changed from how it might have looked one hundred years earlier.

'This is gorgeous,' I said, picking the chair closest to the fire. Heat from the crackling wood in the grate immediately warmed my legs. 'It feels like a time warp.'

'Nothing beats the English pub in my book,' said James.

He seemed relaxed. And as reflections of firelight flicked over his face, I was struck by how James looked every bit my sort of romantic lead.

'So, what's this about Gerard being fired up?'

I told him about the confrontation between Gem and John, and John's refusal to take on the Hebden title. 'They were arguing like ten of the best about it. Gem insisted I go along as Abbey's representative, so I was caught in the middle of it.'

'And here was I imagining the upper classes sailed through life with no issues.' He smiled at me, his eyes filled with warmth. 'How did it end up? Was there any resolution?'

'Yes and no.'

'What does that mean?'

My earlier feeling of being slightly awed at finding myself a member of this Hampton family had been replaced by wondering if the bold plan Gem and I had hatched would actually work.

It was a little strange to find myself here, standing in for my 'orphan' grandmother, but by the time I finished outlining the details of my suggestion that Gem had embraced as the only solution, James was shaking his head in amusement.

'It's a pretty outrageous plan, isn't it? John won't be pleased.'

'No, he won't, but as Gem said, he'll just have to get used to it.' I began to laugh quietly. 'What a pair of troublemakers we are.'

'Speak for yourself,' said James with mock sincerity. 'I merely offer professional advice to the letter of the law. You on the other hand,' he pointed playfully at me, 'have changed the parameters for many things since setting foot on English soil.'

'And without even trying.' I laughed out loud now. 'What if I really set my mind to it?'

'It's going to be an interesting party, isn't it?' said James.

'I think it's fair to say, it's going to be a *very* interesting party,' I said. 'Legal opinion, though, could it come back to bite Gem?'

'I think if you read Gerard's entry in *Who's Who*, you'll see he has always been a sharp political operator. He would understand the political issues, but I can't see any legal issues from what you've told me.'

'It's going to be frantic tomorrow making sure everything is in place.'

'And then? What are your plans after that?'

I took a sip of warm ale from the mug that just appeared on the table. 'Well, I made a pledge to my grandmother that I would stay until I found what happened to her. And I'm pleased to say that's a promise fulfilled.'

'So, coming over here was worth it.'

'Oh, yes.' I smiled at him. 'More than I could have imagined. Finding her story has helped explain some things in my own life, if that makes sense. And I've had inspiration for a new story, too. In fact, I'm going to move up to the gatehouse with Gem to finish it.'

'Ah, the big house beckons,' he said knowingly. 'And here was I thinking that inspiration would strike by bringing you to this place.'

'A fine thought, James,' I grinned, 'but thankfully, I'm already underway.'

'I'm glad to hear you're staying on anyway,' he said, catching my eye.

'For a while at least,' I said, a bit too quickly. *The chemistry between us hasn't gone away yet*, I thought, as I met his gaze.

'A while is good,' he replied. 'Do you remember when we first met in London you mentioned your unusual family back home?'

'Did I? Ha, they're a piece of cake compared to this.'

'Probably, but I've been curious ever since.' His eyes, blue as an Australian sky, staring right into mine were making my pulse quicken.

'Oh no you don't, James Carlyle.' I shook my head. 'This time, it's my turn to cross-examine you. You know all about me, while I, on the other hand, know virtually nothing about you. Not even your mother's name.'

'Straight to the tough questions, then.' He laughed. 'Louise, my mother's name is Louise.'

'And your father?'

'He's James, too, but most people call him Jim. My sister is Zoe. Is this helping? And by the way, I don't know very much about you at all.'

'Confirm this for me, please. You don't have a wife and three children waiting for you back in Brisbane, do you?'

He laughed again, and raised both hands in the air. 'Not that I remember, no. Although, I've had a few girlfriends.'

I looked questioningly at him.

'One in particular before I came over here …' he hesitated. 'It didn't work out. Sale of a jointly owned property, settlement expected any day.'

'Well, that's me lost for words,' I said.

'I came here because I hadn't found the right situation,' he said, 'and not only in my professional circumstance.'

'I know that feeling,' I replied. 'So, you've never really been attached to Crystal at any time, but someone back in Brisbane?'

'I *was* attached,' he said firmly, 'it's over now. And right, never with Crystal. But you mentioned there was someone special waiting for you.'

'Did I? Done and dusted that one, too.' Our eyes met knowingly.

What is it, I wondered, *when both parties are telling white lies about past romances?* He'd never mentioned that relationship in Brisbane. It must have been serious if they'd owned a house together. But was that different to other untruths? Yes, I decided, it was. A little playful fabrication to spice up interest wasn't going behind backs and cheating. It was perfectly fitted to the rules of the game.

He picked up his glass. 'Well, here's to the change that your coming here has made in both of our lives.' I clinked my mug against his. He leaned forward. 'You're right about one thing, I do know a bit about the Hamptons here in England, but it was your side of it, the offspring down under that I was wondering about.'

'I wouldn't even know where to start.'

'Start wherever you like,' he encouraged.

'It could take a while …'

'I'm not going anywhere …'

'I'm not sure.'

'Please.'

'Alright,' I grinned, 'just because you asked so nicely.'

I was making myself vulnerable by telling him more, but it didn't matter. I'd passed the point of no return. 'My mother, Marianne, was an actor, I told you that. I'm her only child. Our life was crazy and unpredictable. Back then, you know, it wasn't an easy choice of career, not for a single mother anyway.'

James muttered soberly, 'I'm sure, probably the same today.'

'Yes, but I never realised until later how much she compromised her own ambition to make sure we had food on the table and all the rest. It makes me feel bad to think about it.'

'How is that?' James asked.

'Well, she took a regular job as a magician's assistant, for instance. And although Grigor the Great had a big following, lying in the magic box to be sawn in half wasn't acting in any meaningful way for her. Up to ten shows a week in the busy times. It meant Marianne had to fit any other roles she wanted to do around that.'

'Not so different for all mothers, is it?' said James. 'Juggling timetables?'

'I guess not, it's just that while other kids' mothers were picking them up from school for milk and biscuits, my mother was likely jumping around a shopping centre in an Easter bunny costume to make ends meet. We shifted house a lot, too.'

He stared at me with a curious expression on his face. 'Was that hard?'

'The hardest thing for me was her striking exit from life. A freak accident that killed my mother outright. In the wee hours of the morning, only a block from where we were living. She was on her way home from a theatre job, a small character role she was playing. She loved that sort of thing, Shakespeare especially, said it made her feel like the real deal, you know a real actor. Anyway, she must have told the taxi to drop her off on the nearest corner so she could walk the last stretch on foot. That's where she was struck by a service vehicle.'

'Maddison, I'm sorry, you don't have to talk about this if you don't want to.' James reached across and touched my hand.

'It's alright, sometimes I like talking about her. I was eighteen years old. At the time, it felt weirdly typical of her. Marianne had never wanted to be "usual", and in the manner of her dying, she certainly achieved that.'

We sat silently for a minute or two, watching the fire.

'I think it's been important for me to find out about Abigail because of that,' I said, 'because of my early life, and not knowing much about my relatives.'

'What about your father, where was he in all this?'

'Not sure even who he was. Never really mattered actually.'

'So, no men around at all?'

'Well, the actors in the shared houses, and mum's brother.'

'What was he like?'

'Uncle Gerry? He was nice, played it straight for a while. Held down an admin job in the public service until his marriage broke up.'

James raised his eyebrows.

'I'll tell you about that one day. Interestingly, now that I have my grandmother's story, I understand more, why both of her two children lived outside "the norm". No obvious blue blood visible in the lives they led.'

'Why don't you tell me now?'

'Because it's a bit of a story.'

'A story that helps me know more about you, please.'

'Just the short version, then, and only because you've insisted. Stop me any time.' I laughed, but James did not.

Was sharing upbringing an important component to two people becoming friends, I wondered? Yes and no. Yes, because that sort of information exchange created a foundation of knowledge from which to explore similarities, or differences, or hone possible interests in common, shared experiences or even intense dislikes. No, because it made no difference, as far as I could tell, to whether a person was attractive to you. Or more particularly, if you could trust them.

I launched off. 'Uncle Gerry was (I thought then) the last of my direct family. His wife ran off with a new man to Queensland and was last heard of living on the canals of Surfer's Paradise.'

James's face registered surprise.

'Anyway, what he did next was most astonishing.'

'Go on.'

'Uncle Gerry ditched his boring government job in Canberra and went bush. He ended up in the top end. Became quite obsessed with the beach, apparently, and the accompanying loose lifestyle that goes with it. I don't know for certain what the circumstances of his death were, but I flew up for his funeral, as the only remaining representative of his family (his ex was nowhere to be seen), and found that my uncle had been teaching tourists to surf. Where he'd learned to do that himself, I don't know.' I looked at James. 'What would Rose Hampton make of that, her grandson surfing?'

'She would have been amazed, I think. Did he have any kids?'

'He and his wife, Cilla, had one, a girl called Wendy. She died very young from some rare complication related to whooping cough.'

I noticed in my line of vision, an older man approaching with two plates. I paused. The cottage pie smelled delicious. 'Too sad?' I asked, suddenly feeling hungry.

'It is sad, but please, I want to hear the end.'

'Are you sure? It's not very romantic.'

'I'm sure.'

'Okay, you asked for it. Uncle Gerry's funeral wasn't held in a church or even on the actual beach as you might expect, given his late-onset passion for the sea, but rather it was staged on a partially covered outdoor stage that reminded me of a doughnut stand at an agricultural show.'

'So far so good,' said James, smiling.

'And even that isn't the worst of it. The saddest part was that when I arrived in that hot and steamy place, I found barely a soul present to remember his life.'

'These things happen,' James said quietly.

'Yes, but I'm still shocked that his last breath came in a place that was so foreign to his earlier life. To end in a place where nobody knows who you are, where you came from, or what you did before.'

James sobered a little. 'People make choices in their lives, Maddi, we all do. Sometimes for love, and sometimes, like Abigail, for other reasons. Sounds to me like your uncle was living a life he enjoyed. He might not have done anything differently, even if he had known of his connection back to the Hamptons.'

'So, that's the part of the Hampton family's "broken line" you didn't find, Mr Detective. But that's enough about them. How about you? Tell me about Zurich.'

'Not a lot to tell, it was an assignment to test the waters. It seemed to go well.'

'Will you take it if they make an offer?' I asked, thinking, *Of course he will.*

'They already have, and I've said yes.'

His words felt like a body blow. 'Congratulations,' I managed to say without, I hoped, sounding too shocked. 'Why didn't you mention it sooner? We must toast your success.'

After clinking mugs, the mood between us became more subdued. As we finished our meal, I noticed how much time had passed. Empty plates. The fire was low, and we were almost the last people in the room.

I was back in the real world. 'When do you start?'

'Pretty much right away. What about you? You said you'd stay for a while. Any thoughts on how long that might be?'

'Depends on how long it'll take me to finish this book. Once I do that, I'll plan my return date.'

'But you could stay, couldn't you?' He reached out and took my hand in his.

'I suppose I could, it is wonderful here, but my home is there.'

His eyes locked deeply into mine. 'This might sound stupid or premature, maybe both, but every part of me is telling me that you are the person I've always been waiting for. Please, Maddison, let's give this a chance. It's worth it.'

My heart was screaming to say yes, to see if this attraction was real, but my brain overruled it. Too risky. But was it really? I was writing again, and loving it. If the same thing happened, another disappointing real-life romance, where would I be?

'No matter how wonderful I'm feeling at the moment, James, or how I feel about you, this can't go anywhere because we're on different paths.'

'That's funny, I've just read your second book, where there's almost the same situation in play and your characters manage to work it out.'

He had me laughing once more. 'That's fiction. Being a character in one of my books is a bit different to real life. I had a boyfriend once who thought he saw himself in every word I wrote.'

'And was he?'

'Parts of him, I guess, but let me say it didn't end well.'

'That's him and not me. I've got no objection to being your dashing leading man.' James grinned mischievously. 'Sweeping the winsome Isabella off her feet, making a life together ...' he said, making exaggerated reference to characters in one of my books.

'But,' I said, joining the game, 'Hans had to give up everything to be with the girl he loved. I can't see you doing that.'

His face changed. 'But it's not about Hans and Isabella, this is about you and me, real flesh-and-blood people.' He leaned in and lowered his voice. 'If you can work it out in your stories, why can't we work it out in real life? I just know I haven't met anyone like you before in my life, Maddison.'

'James ...'

'I daydream about you, you know that? I think I fell in love with you the first time I saw you.'

My pulse was going berserk. Was I in the middle of my own book? I couldn't have written a more romantic scene. His blue eyes, Dickens, an old English pub, and the leading man I'd always dreamed of sitting before me telling me he loved me. I felt lightheaded as I looked at him across the table, with my nerve endings all tingling.

Feeling his touch, a shock of pleasure ricocheted up my arm. I looked at him and thought, *If there were no table between us, we would be kissing.* We sat gazing at each other, until movement in the room brought me back.

'Maddison ...'

'Yes ...'

We stood almost simultaneously to leave, and as I felt his arm around me and his lips brush the side of my neck, the room, the people, and my last resolve melted away.

What did it matter if it wasn't forever?

Maddison

The day of the party

I'd floated through the following two days in a frenzy of activity. That buoyant bubble-of-love feeling had unleashed volumes of new energy, and the inertia of my previous life seemed a long-forgotten nightmare. I was well and truly back writing with the same frenzy of my earlier books. Untroubled by doubts of whether I could finish the story, sure of my characters, and sure of the lines, and this morning reading through, I thought this story just could be my best work so far.

After that very special night at the Leather Bottle Inn, James and I had exchanged some lovely messages and I couldn't wait to see him again. Interspersed with that, I'd done everything I could think of to ensure Gem's and my plan was going to work. Publicists were on hold and ready to go, and from what I could tell, the scene was set for a momentous day. I desperately wanted to tell someone, but I had to wait. *Time enough to tell, when it's done*, I counselled myself when the urge to tell became strong.

I'd decided also just to leave a note for Edith and George to tell them I'd be back in a few days. It was easier that way without expanding on it. Not yet.

Gem had offered to share with me everything he could remember about Abigail and their early life at Hebden. Walking together exploring the estate gardens would be the best way to prompt his memory, he said, and I couldn't think of anything more perfect. Twenty-two hectares of mysterious garden, meandering serpentine pathways vanishing into the distance, listening to stories about 'our' family. He said he wanted to hear all about his Australian relatives, too. I had to admit sometimes I panicked that this was all part of some crazy dream and that any moment I would wake up back in my old life, stuck on what to write, eating too much junk food, and miserable.

The front doors of the gatehouse were wide open when I arrived. A sea of helpers making last-minute preparations meant I had to spend a few seconds looking for a familiar face.

'Maddison, do you like what we've done?' Crystal cried out, rushing towards me from the far side of the large room. Even in workday casuals, she could have just stepped out of a magazine; tight jeans, oversized shirt, hair dragged coquettishly into a ponytail. I wondered how to greet her. *Does she know that we are related?* I'd wait for her reaction, I decided.

'Hello, Crystal, you've done a great job,' I said, glancing around admiringly.

'Do you really think so?' she flashed her perfect teeth and placed her hand on my arm. 'How's it all going with you?'

'Surprisingly well,' I said with a smile.

From her response, it was obvious that she didn't know we were cousins. John could tell them in his own time, I supposed, and let it go. She was going to find out soon enough, anyhow.

'Mummy and I have had the best time doing this for Gerard,' Crystal enthused. 'Of course, we couldn't have done it all without dear Joel.' She tapped the butler as he rushed past to attend the door.

'The blue room is ready and waiting, Maddison,' he called over his shoulder. 'I'll be right back.'

'Will James be coming along tonight?' Crystal asked casually, like she didn't care if he came or not.

'Yes, he will,' I responded, as pictures from the wonderful night we'd spent together flashed back into my mind. *His tender kisses, the heat of his body, waking up together and it all feeling absolutely perfect.* 'The earl gave him a personal invitation,' I added, feeling my heart beat harder at the thought of seeing him soon.

'Oh good,' she said, 'I haven't seen him in ages. He's just the loveliest man, isn't he?'

Janet appeared at that moment, gliding through from one room to another, but catching sight of Crystal and me, she changed course.

'Maddison, what do you think?' She gestured around the room. Her manner was friendlier than our last encounter, when she'd given me the distinct impression that she would be glad to see the back of me.

Up close, tired lines had crept in around her eyes, and with no lipstick and her hair out of place, she hardly seemed daunting at all. Obviously, it took some effort to create her usual perfect presentation. It was clear to me that John's wife had given her all in organising this party for Gerard.

'Janet, I was just congratulating Crystal, what an undertaking.'

She leaned in and whispered, 'It was rather, but don't tell Gerard. We wanted to do something really special for him, because you never know … when it will be his last. He wanted something grand like in the old days, when his mother was alive,' she said. 'Well, we couldn't dial up all the famous people Rose would have been able to, of course, but Crystal and I are pleased with what we've done. And so is he, which is the main thing.' Janet gave me an odd look, and just for a moment she seemed to want to say something, then changed her mind. 'Now, if you two will excuse me, I must dash as I have a hair appointment. Are you sure we are ready, Crystal?' she said to her daughter.

'Yes, Mummy we are. Please, just go.' Crystal sounded like an exasperated teenager, but her mother appeared not to notice.

Okay, I thought, watching Janet departing, *your secrets are safe with me, and mine is safe with you. For now. And as for you*, I told myself, *you have become a fully fledged member of this family. Abigail would be proud of you.*

A text from James confirmed he was on his way, which made me feel edgy with anticipation. I wasn't sure how the evening was going to pan out. Whether the scheme Gem and I had concocted would take off, or backfire on us completely.

I also wasn't sure how things would work out with James. All I knew was I couldn't wait to see him.

Maddison

The gatehouse finale

My room was huge, 'The best in the house,' said Joel, showing me upstairs to what he described as 'Barbara's room'. I smiled to myself. Would my old neighbour Joan believe that I'd slept in the same bed as Barbara Cartland? Not unless I took a photo.

I hung my dress in the enormous wardrobe, folded my things away in one of the drawers, then drifted across to the large picture window, where glimpses of Hebden were visible through the trees. It was so like a scene from Disneyland, I wouldn't have been at all surprised to see Tinkerbell with her magic wand flying around those red turrets, rising sharply through the canopy.

I was reminded of Gem escorting me into the ballroom he'd been so proud to show me. A piece of renaissance Italy in the south of England, complete with its own Botticelli-inspired ceiling. Goddesses in flowing gowns, with long yellow tresses flying across delicate blue skies, lyres and harps in hand, were breathtaking.

'The hall these days is used for school pantomimes and official functions,' Gem had explained. 'They bring a few chairs in and it doubles as a school theatre and assembly hall. But when I was growing up,' his eyes were far away with memory, 'this is where we partied. Abbey and my mother played here for our guests. Not too many famous faces of screen and stage missed dancing on these floors, Maddison my dear,' he added, 'someone for every taste.'

More than once I'd had to pinch myself as I listened to him talk about their life, the Hamptons of Cobham.

Now, waiting here in my room, I sensed that this was the calm before a storm, that prescient time when latent electricity hangs ominously in the air awaiting the first clap of thunder. I smiled to myself. When Gem stood up to make his speech tonight, it would be just like a bolt of lightning hitting the room.

Flickering candlelight cast a romantic mood over the room, and with soft music playing, a delicious promise of food in the air, the gatehouse was humming with excitement, and so was I. If everything fell into place the way it should, this was going to be a night no one would easily forget.

I'd retouched my makeup and given myself a last-minute once-over, quietly rejoicing that I'd taken the time to pick up a dressy black-and-burgundy number while I was in London. I liked the crooked hem and how it worked with high evening ankle boots. *See, even my shopping habits have improved, Amy*, I thought. The last time I'd seen my friends, they'd been giving me heaps about how I would never attract company if I persisted with only wearing lumpy walking boots and a mountain coat. *No complaints tonight, girls, I hope.* I wanted to look my best.

The first familiar face I saw was Janet. She was talking animatedly to an older man. From the sash slung over his shoulder, he was probably the local mayor. Only a few hours earlier she'd seemed to need a good night's sleep. Now, here she was transformed, a glamorous hostess with high hair, a glittering dress, and Uncle Gem standing dutifully by her side. I was in awe of her change.

My eyes skimmed the room. James couldn't be far away. When I spotted him, he was coming through the door looking positively dashing in a formal tie. My heart jumped and banged even harder when I realised he'd entered with Crystal and her entourage of friends from the tea party.

He saw me instantly and broke away to head in my direction.

'Maddison,' Crystal called to me, flashing her brilliant smile. 'Look who I found in the carpark.'

I waved a greeting.

By Crystal's side was a man, thickset like a rugby player, and quite a few years older than her. He turned his head to see whom she was talking to.

Freddie started pushing her way through the crowd towards me, too, and she was quicker than James. 'Maddison, I'm so glad you're here,' she said, her soft mouth trembling. 'I'm sorry I haven't been in touch yet. But I will, I promise.'

'Hi, Freddie, any time, as long as I'm here.'

'I keep forgetting that you live so far away.'

'Yes, Australia does feel like another planet.' I laughed. Not even a spark of comprehension from her. She looked lovely in a powder-blue dress, but humour was lost on Freddie.

Her eyes darted about the room. 'The earl throws a jolly good bash, wouldn't you say?' she whispered, as if she were confiding a big fat secret to me.

'Yes.' And before I could say more, she was gone, drink in hand, searching for other fish to fry.

James was still negotiating his way to me. He was being stopped at every turn. For someone who didn't live around these parts, he certainly seemed to know a lot of people at this gathering.

I noticed John being received by the butler. Around him, there was a circle of faces I didn't recognise, but from the exaggerated mannerisms and self-important airs, they were most likely local politicians. My cousin, John, walked with the ease of someone accustomed to formal situations. From a distance, with his longish hair and upright stance, he looked more like an aging rock star at a music-awards night, than the local solicitor. He saw me across the room and nodded formally. Actually, the whole Nettlewood group looked like they were at an A-list opening night.

At last James was by my side. 'Maddison, you look beautiful,' he said, and kissed me lightly on the mouth.

'You look pretty good yourself,' I responded, my pulse kicking up at the feel of him so close.

When his fingers intertwined with mine it felt like the most natural thing on earth.

Suddenly Crystal appeared, dragging her new beau towards us. 'James, I hear from Daddy that congratulations are in order.'

James shot me a confused glance.

'Oh, have I put my foot in it?' She said like a cat that had just swallowed the cream. Her eyes flicked between James and me.

'Perhaps, but only if I know what I'm being congratulated for.' James turned to me.

'A job with one of the Magic Circle firms, James,' Crystal gushed. 'Special Counsel, that's quite a coup. One step away from partner, first go. Everyone is so impressed.' She batted her eyes and laid her hand on his arm, which made me suddenly feel not so warmly towards my new second cousin.

I must have looked nonplussed as Crystal's beau interjected. '*Magic Circle* means one of the top-five international law firms. It's an awfully big deal for anyone who gets a job offer with them. Particularly a senior role like that.' His smile was more like a grimace.

'Thank you, everyone,' said James, his eyes coming back to me.

'This is Jonathan, by the way,' Crystal cut in, 'the Honourable Jonathan Mayhew-Evans, to be precise.' And to her partner she said, 'Meet James and Maddison, the ones I was telling you about.'

Crystal's companion offered a quick nod to me, and another 'well done, old boy' to James, then nudged Crystal along to join the next group.

'Here we are, this is your party and I want to be next to you when the fireworks start.' James squeezed my hand.

At that point, James grabbed two glasses of champagne from a passing waiter and handed one to me, touching his glass to mine. 'To happy endings.'

I toasted him without any idea how this romance could achieve that, with James flying high in London and my life back in Australia. I decided to leave those thoughts alone for a few hours and just enjoy the 'fireworks' and James's company.

The sound of happy conversation, laughter and champagne corks popping continued, until at last Gem's butler called the room to attention.

'Ladies and gentlemen, please take your seats, and tonight may I ask you in the spirit of "informality", to please find your own place cards. If you could all make your way to the table.'

'I hope we're sitting together,' I said. 'If Janet's in charge of arrangements, she might seat you next to Crystal,' I teased James.

'Are you kidding? If Crystal has her way, we'll be as far away from her and Tommy the tank engine as possible. Wait here.'

I watched James push his way through, casually checking for names. I saw him bump into John and the two of them shook hands, no doubt John congratulating him on his new job.

I could see Crystal through the crowd hanging off every word Jonathan uttered. His age and size made him look an unlikely match for someone of her fragile beauty, and James's description did fit, he looked quite a bit like a tank engine.

I would be sitting with Gem on one side, James revealed on his return, and he on the other. The evening was starting to feel much better again.

The guests all seated, Gem slipped in beside me, leaned across and almost shook James's hand off. 'Absolutely delighted you were able to join us tonight for the fun and games,' he said, his cheeks spiked with pink.

'The pleasure is all mine, sir, I wouldn't have missed it.'

Gem's eyes flicked between James and me. 'And are you ready, Maddison?'

I flashed my best confident smile and nodded.

'Splendid, then let's get on with it, shall we?'

While plates were cleared away and drinks replenished, the butler pinged his glass with a spoon and Gem got to his feet, which caused a hush to fall over the room. Gem cleared his throat.

'Official guests, family and friends, I would like to welcome you all to the gatehouse tonight. There are several matters I have to share with you this evening, but first, the reason I decided to throw this party.' The way his eyes roamed around the room, drawing the crowd in, I saw how a younger Gerard Hampton would have commanded the House of Lords.

He was keyed up, and my heart was banging madly.

James squeezed my hand. 'Are you alright?'

I smiled at him sideways and bobbed my head.

'Just when you think life can no longer throw you any surprises, I have discovered after all these years, and I mean a lot of years …' He paused dramatically for the laughter to ripple around the room. 'That I am an uncle.'

'Is it a love child, Gem?' yelled a voice from the end of the table.

'In a way, yes she is. Only it's not what you are thinking.' Gem stole a glance at me, and as if on cue, my face flushed.

'Some of you who've known this family for a time will remember our terrible tragedy. In the nineteen thirties when my sister, Abigail, and her baby died in the throes of childbirth. At least that is what I was told after she disappeared without a trace. I had misgivings at the time. But I believed my parents as I'm sure many of you did. However, now it has come to light that this story was false.'

The room was humming. A camera light flashed. Gem paused then picked up where he'd left off.

'The discovery that my sister did not die, that she sailed to Australia where she began a new life for herself, is both sad and joyful. Sad, for the reasons she left us, joyful because she lived a good and happy life and her granddaughter, Maddison Browne, who is with us now, can tell the story. But I'll leave it to her to say how this all came about. Maddison?' Gem reached down to draw me to my feet.

There was a faint ripple of applause as I stood up. Gem wrapped his arm around my shoulders, we grinned as if it were some comedy photoshoot, and a camera flashed again.

'Some of you may be aware already, but as her proud uncle, for those who don't know, Maddison is a romance writer of some reputation. And she confessed to me this afternoon that what she has discovered over the past few weeks, finding out about her English family, has been stranger than any fiction but equally as exciting.'

'Let her say a few words, Gerard.'

Gem pressed his hand on my back and sat down.

I glanced around. 'This all began about ten weeks ago. A legal letter arrived at my home in Melbourne, explaining to me that I'd inherited my great-grandmother's piano. Now you need to remember that until that point, I didn't know who my grandmother was, let alone my great-grandmother. I'd never had any inkling of my family link to Hebden. So, as you can imagine, I was curious.'

I could feel people listening.

'The letter was from the Hampton family's trusted solicitor, John Nettlewood.'

I saw heads lean forward to locate where John was sitting.

'When Lady Rose willed her precious instrument to the last female member of her family, it might have seemed an easy enough task. But it took years of searching until eventually John,' I gestured to him, 'finally tracked me down. "The broken arm" of the Hampton family is how he described us in his letter.' I looked down at my cousin, who appeared relaxed and even had a smile on his face. *Don't get too relaxed*, I thought.

'It is true that I came here not knowing what to expect. I never knew a lot about my grandmother. She died before I was old enough to remember her well, but I know that she had never spoken about her family in any way. So, without doubt, these past few weeks have been the most exciting time of my life, and finding my English family has changed it in so many ways. So, my heartfelt thanks to everyone who made it possible,' I said, and sat down.

Another voice called out, 'Aren't you going to tell us more about what happened?'

Gem was on his feet. 'Patience, please, it's a long story. We will be serving coffee and cognac in the drawing room shortly. After that, dancing. But please bear with me while I take care of this most important piece of business.'

The room went quiet again.

I looked past Gem to John. He saw me and raised his eyes questioningly. I shrugged. What Uncle Gem had just described as the 'business' end of the evening, appeared to have John worried.

Gem launched into the final stage of his campaign. 'This is a great day for the Hampton family because Maddison's arrival has solved what has always been a painful family mystery. At the same time, it has also brought into focus another matter of grave importance. Some of you may have been wondering what would happen to the Hebden title when I finally enter the other realm. I am pleased to say you need worry no more.'

Gem's guests were in the palm of his hand, as he showed the same ability only the best of storytellers possessed. Glancing down to the other end of the table, I saw that Crystal was listening intently. To my left, John's face had drained of all colour and he sat like a man awaiting execution. His wife was agitated, eyes flicking from Gem to her husband over and over. The rest were all waiting to hear the end of the story.

'You see, another "broken arm" of the Hampton family has been uncovered in all of this,' Gem said, warming up to the climax. 'My sister's baby did not die either. He, and it was a he, was brought up in a loving family, who incredibly lived not far from this very gatehouse.' He stopped to look around. 'My sister's son has passed away, but her grandson is a fine man whom I have known and trusted most of my life. Yet, until recently, I was completely unaware of our blood connection. I had no idea that he was, in fact, my nephew.'

The room exploded with questions, flying left, right and centre.

'Who is it?'

'How could he now?'

'That's impossible.'

Gem clicked his fingers as if he were keeping time to his favourite tune. The butler was there in an instant and produced an iPad for Gem to read from. 'Thank you, Joel.' Gem produced his glasses and propped them onto the end of his nose.

'Ladies and gentlemen, if I may read to you a headline from the website of today's edition of the *Sun*,' he paused dramatically, '*Heirs and Affairs.*'

Gem loved teasing his audience. *You are such a ham*, I thought affectionately. *You and my mother would have made an incredible double act.*

Clearing his throat for the umpteenth time, and with obvious enjoyment, he read aloud, '*In an exclusive interview today, Lord Hebden reveals a surprising twist to the succession of his family's title. For the full story see our Sunday edition.*' Gem pulled off his glasses, adding, 'And by the way, this exclusive *Sunday Sun* was penned by my great-niece, Maddison.' He turned to me and blew a kiss. 'Thank you, Maddison, for everything.'

Someone squealed, 'Oh good, she'll have all the ins and outs,' which was followed by peals of laughter.

John's face had frozen. I tried to catch his eye, thinking a smile of encouragement might help, but he steadfastly maintained a straight-ahead look.

The room became deathly silent again. Until someone called out, 'Get on with it, Gerard. Just tell us who it is.'

Gem, ignoring all encouragement to spill the beans early, faced the room. 'As most of you will know, I like a hot climate and living in shorts these days. I do bring myself back to the Lords often enough to do the right thing. Now, I am relieved to say that the House and your representation will remain in capable hands. Let me finish by saying that out of an incredible sense of loyalty and a promise made many years ago, not by him, but in fact by his grandfather to my mother, the heir apparent demanded that I not make this announcement. But his promise of secrecy was to my family, and tonight I release him formally from that oath. I hope that he will not think too badly of me, but in doing this, the greater good is served.'

There was murmuring around the room, but Gem stayed firmly on track.

'For now, as the earl, I will do as an earl must.' He turned to me, and I saw a mixture of joy and relief in his eyes.

'With no heir of my own to carry the title, the individual I am about to name is the rightful and legal heir to the title Earl of Hebden. It falls to my nephew to take on the responsibility of this honoured duty. I ask you to be upstanding and to raise your glasses.' He waited for everyone in the room to do so before he turned to an ashen-faced John and raised his own glass to him. 'To my nephew, John Nettlewood.'

The room turned to uproar, with guests clapping and cheering. The high-pitched squeal emanating from Crystal at the end of the table was pure hysteria. She was clapping her hands like one of those electrified children's toys, while her new beau, with a grimace solidified on his face, attempted to calm her.

The man in question, however, rather than standing tall, was dealing with a minor emergency tending to his wife, who appeared to have fainted. The shock that she was about to become Lady Janet had been too much. John, with the help of two other women, was leaning forward and guiding his wife's head between her knees, his own face having changed colour from grey to scarlet.

James was trying not to laugh. 'Now that does seem to have put a proverbial cat among the pigeons.'

I looked into his eyes, and responding to the emotion of the moment, planted a kiss squarely on his lips. 'One of the things I love about you, James Carlyle, is that you're a master of understatement.'

Gem was tapping his glass again. 'Quiet please, I would like to add something, if you will.'

He glanced down to John, who was still focused on his wife.

'While we wait a few seconds for Janet to rejoin us, I'd like to mention the many ties the people of Cobham share with Australia. My mother, Lady Rose Hampton, who dedicated her life to the wellbeing of our part of the world, was born in Australia. My sister, Abigail, in her hour of need, fled there and ultimately lived her life out in that part of the world. My great-niece was born in Melbourne, and the person who my nephew, John, recruited to search for female descendants, is also an Australian from Brisbane. Happily, he has come along to celebrate with us tonight, too. James Carlyle, thank you, I am eternally grateful.'

James gave a quick, embarrassed wave.

Janet was sitting upright once more, slightly dazed but smiling tremulously. By her side, a female friend had sat in her husband's place and was holding her hand. Crystal too had appeared to sit by her mother's side, while John stood next to Uncle Gem, where Gem's hand signals had summoned him.

He was smiling tentatively now, his colour normalised. The emergency with his wife had allowed him sufficient time to gather himself. My cousin appeared calm, resigned almost, as if there was nothing he could do to change the situation. He might as well enjoy the new life that Gem had just unleashed upon him.

He glanced down to acknowledge me, then made a speech about responsibility, traditions, social 'glue' and the importance of it, which won him plenty of warm applause. He finished by raising his own glass directly to the earl, saying firmly, 'Noblesse oblige,' at which point

Uncle Gem stood, raised his own glass formally and answered with the same words.

By now, tears of pride were running down my cheeks, matching those staining my old uncle's face.

'Alright, everyone,' Gem called out exuberantly, offering us another glimpse of his younger spirited self, 'coffee in the drawing room, dancing everywhere else. We are here to celebrate. Please enjoy yourselves and don't forget Maddison's full story will be in tomorrow's Sunday edition of the *Sun*.'

My world had been turned upside down since the first moment I set foot here. Looking at my great-uncle circulating the room, his face beaming, one arm around John's shoulders, it was plain to see that his world had been turned over, too. Discovering that he was not the last of the Hamptons, and that the Hebden title was going to be in safe hands after all, meant the world to him. And I thought he was as pleased to know me, as I was to be fully acquainted with all of my extended family.

Loud music came blasting through invisible speakers, and flashlights popped to capture the moment as guests changed into party mode.

'I wouldn't be surprised if these photos make it into tomorrow's paper,' James whispered in my ear.

'I'm pretty sure they will, with the hot PR team my publisher put behind it.'

As John, with Janet draped on his arm, approached, I got to my feet to greet them.

'Congratulations.' I opened my arms to kiss her cheeks, and caught a grateful nod from my cousin. I still found it most strange that he had never discussed the possibility of not taking the title with his wife and family. I was just as bad now. I had well and truly joined the ranks of the Hampton family, keeping secrets until they were forced to be revealed.

James joined in, shaking John's hand. 'Should I go back to addressing you as sir?' he asked with a cheeky grin, which caused them both to laugh.

'James,' Janet gushed, 'how lovely to see you again. My you look so dashing in a white tie.'

'Lady Janet.' James clicked his heels and bowed slightly, which made her squeal with delight.

'We miss you,' she said, clasping his hand in hers. 'How clever you were to find Maddison.'

'Yes, in so many ways, Lady Janet.'

John raised his eyebrows towards me. 'Not what you expected at the start?'

'Not for any of us. But it's not so bad, right?'

His eyes shone brightly. 'Thank you, Maddison, for your part in this.'

I almost fainted when he stepped forward and embraced me. 'I didn't make it easy for you. And for that, I am sorry. We'll talk when this all dies down. But I hope you understand now the reasons for my behaviour.'

'Yes,' I said. 'I do, and now I also know that nobody keeps a secret like a Hampton.'

'Include yourself in that description, Maddison,' he said, smiling warmly at me. 'What now for you?'

'Oh, Gem has invited me to stay a while here with him, which I've decided to do,' I said. 'That way I can have a good look around the manor, hear his stories and I'd love to hear some of yours, too. We have a few lifetimes to catch up on.'

'Very good,' he said. 'Yes, that'll be my great pleasure.'

'And you must come to us for a quiet dinner, next week,' said Janet, having recovered herself entirely.

'Enjoy the rest of your evening,' John said, already sounding like the earl. He touched his wife gently on the arm, moving her on to receive the long line of guests waiting to offer their congratulations.

I looked around for Crystal, who appeared to have vaporised. No sign of Freddie or Harriet, either.

'I think I need some air, how about you?' I said to James.

I felt his arm wrap around my back. 'I thought you'd never ask. You can catch my dance moves later.'

Maddison

Mt Macedon, five months later

The piano party was in full swing.

Beth's husband, Jack, called out, 'So, Maddi, the piano seems to have arrived intact. What are you going to do with it now?'

'She's going to learn to play it, of course,' chimed Amy.

'I'm not sure about that,' I defended laughingly. 'But it will be living with me for the rest of time, I know that.' I looked across at Rose's beautiful grand piano. It was so far away from Hebden Manor, but it looked perfectly at home nestled under the front window of my sitting room.

The picture before me, warm fire burning, a cold spring day, Amy, Beth, and Lucinda and their respective husbands all present, Ruth dashing about supervising children, Joan busy as a bee in the kitchen … it looked as if not much had changed except everything had. It wasn't a lavish celebration, but it was relaxed and friendly.

'How does it feel to be home?' Lucinda asked, warming her back in front of the fire. 'We thought you'd forgotten us and might not be coming back.'

'As if.' I smiled, aware of the deep contentment I felt to finally know about my forebears and where they'd come from. That I'd managed to play a small role in righting the realm, and seen my cousin, John, ordained as the next earl had been an unexpected twist in all of this. I was pleased that the Hebden title would live on, but having found answers to other important questions about my grandmother and her mother, Rose, meant so much more to me. There were no words to describe how I felt about that. Solving the mystery of my people, the women of my mother's family, and being able to discover what generations of them had done before me, how they'd boldly challenged traditions, each in their own way, felt like my heritage. It had filled an empty part of me. And although Abbey's journey had been tough and tragic, she'd found a way to live on her own terms. She was with me in my life now, and I would draw on her strength, determination and her capacity for love, forever. My heart would never stop aching for what happened to Abigail, even as I felt grateful for the risk she undertook by crossing to the other side of the world on her own.

It no longer seemed to matter to me that I would never know whether or not my own mother had loved my unknown father. But, given what I knew now about Abigail and Rose, I liked to imagine that she had. What I knew for certain was that Marianne had loved her life as an actor, and she'd loved me completely. That was more than enough for me.

'It feels good,' I added, trying to ignore the ache I felt because James was missing. Five weeks had passed since I'd said an emotional goodbye to him. He'd said so confidently that either I would come over to promote my latest book, which was about to hit the bookshops, or I would spend Christmas in Cobham. There'd been no extended silence factored in, at all. We had discussed and discussed it, and I thought he'd accepted that I didn't want to move to England. That even with family there, relocating my life and career was a step I wasn't ready to make. Not yet anyway. I wouldn't rule it out forever, it was just something I couldn't do now. Although James tried hard to convince me, emailing photos of cosy cottages with open fires, and little notes about how much he missed me, I thought he'd accepted it. But what I feared might happen in a long-distance romance seemed to be actually happening. His messages had petered out, and more than two weeks had passed with no word from him, not even a response to my texts.

I heard Lucinda saying, 'I don't know if I would have come back from the Bahamas to all this cold.'

I joined in the spirit of the party, but I was sad that James and I had obviously just met at the wrong time for both of us. And even more surprising was that he hadn't even wished me luck for the piano party. He would have known that I was waiting to hear from him. 'Well, the Bahamas was rather lovely,' I said, 'but I was really there to accompany Uncle Gem and help him pack up. He's relocated back to England.'

'Gosh it sounds weird hearing you talk about uncles and cousins,' said Amy.

'I know.' I smiled. 'But I have got quite used to it myself.'

'And are they all really nice, Maddi?'

'Yes,' I said, 'they are. It's only a short time that I've known them, but I couldn't have wished for nicer.'

Gem was truly that, and I loved him. He was kind and funny and he had shared so many memories of his sister and his mother that I actually felt now that I knew them.

Since the gatehouse announcement, John and Janet had been nothing but warm and hospitable. Janet hadn't been able to wipe the smile from her face. It was as if her life had suddenly become what she'd always thought it should be. Lady of the manor sat well with her. She'd been accepting invitations left, right and centre to chair local charities.

John's only concession to his future role was to inject new blood into his legal practice to free up time for other activities. He told me very earnestly before I left that he would be down to visit soon, that he'd always wanted to see Australia. And I believed him. They would show up, and I would help them make the most of it.

Crystal, too, whenever she was in Cobham, had taken to dropping into the gatehouse to say hello. She was certainly the one who'd inherited Abigail's talent for piano playing. I had a strong feeling that she and I could be firm friends further down the track. And even the stockbroker wasn't such a bad bloke. He'd bought Crystal a ring almost immediately after the party, and just before I left to come home, they'd set their wedding date and sent a formal request for my attendance.

'Must be a bit weird, though with all those lords and ladies in your family tree,' Amy teased. 'Are you sure we don't have to call you Lady Maddi!'

'Fat chance!' the rest chorused in unison.

'Well, you'd better get used to using titles when the Nettlewoods arrive for a visit,' I returned, which quietened the topic a little.

'What do we call an earl?'

'Your Lordship.'

'Oh my God, Your Lordship,' said Jack, laughing out loud. 'My mother calls my father "Your Lordship" when they're having an argument.'

'And it's what I call you sometimes,' added Beth.

'So, no holiday in the sun at all?' Lucinda asked, getting back to the Bahamas.

'Not really. My uncle did show me around all his favourite bars and restaurants, that was nice. And there were a few wonderful days when James flew over, too, but he couldn't stay because he had to get back to work.'

'Honestly, Maddison you are so unusual. I wouldn't have been able to stay away from those beautiful beaches, coconut cocktails and gorgeous bodies.'

'It was lovely.' I shrugged.

They wouldn't understand even if I explained how I'd spent any spare time finishing my latest book over there, locked in a room with a huge overhead fan and a balcony that overlooked the garden and a swimming pool. For those hours, my bodice-ripper, *Rose's Folly*, had commanded my full attention. The story involved a steamy love affair between an English aristocrat and a lowly music teacher, who despite their love, found they had many bridges to cross to find true happiness. The words had flowed easily from the start, and when I showed it to Gem, who'd read it, a first for him, he said, 'My mother would love it and so do I. Especially the part where Rose's bad decision, her "folly", is finally resolved. Adjusting to a few changes is all it would have taken my mother to have had a different outcome, too,' he added sadly. 'Fiction is better than real life in that way, isn't it?'

'Yes, I suppose it is,' I said, thinking about Gem's words, and how an author could reshape a situation, redo a character's reaction, remodel a point of the story and even alter the eventual outcome to the lives of their characters in the briefest of time. Whereas real people had to deal straight up with what happened to them, without being able to try one situation first to see if it worked before trying another. That ability to immediately fashion the world to your own perspective was a beloved freedom that belonged only to a writer.

'What about this James, Maddi, or should we call him Prince Charming?' Lucinda asked in a loud voice that broke my reverie. 'Or even more to the point, when are *we* going to meet him?'

'Not sure,' I said, hedging.

My heart was suddenly heavy. James and I had spent so much wonderful time together. He'd seemed to know who I was, the real me. He'd shared every step of my amazing journey of discovery with my family. He loved music. We'd walked and walked. We'd been to London to hear Lisitsa play Rachmaninov live, and what a special night that was. He'd joked about being fodder for my leading men. He was a dream. On weekdays, I'd stayed at the gatehouse with Gem, and on the weekends

James had either come to Cobham or I'd gone to London. Now almost two weeks had passed without a sound from him. I think a part of me might have even resigned myself to the fact that he would meet someone else, someone who would love his London life, who would do what he wanted when he wanted. I just hadn't thought it would be this soon.

Ruth, hearing 'Prince Charming' mentioned as she entered the room, piped up, 'Is that your Prince Charming that Amy is talking about, Maddison?'

'Yes,' I said, feeling sick to my toes. 'One day you'll meet him,' I said, and felt like I should cross my fingers.

'We're so pleased for you, we can't wait to meet him in person,' she said, before she darted off in pursuit of the children.

At one point, Amy took me aside to tell me her news. She was expecting another child. 'A little surprise,' she said. I hugged her and told her I was happy for her. Even if she didn't look so happy herself. 'It'll be alright when I get used to it,' she said, 'it's only that I was getting some order back. Never mind.'

With the piano in my line of vision and my friends around, I was cradling a glass of wine and thinking of everything that had happened, when Beth sidled up. 'Still no word?' she said.

I started, assuming she meant James. *Had she read my mind?* But then quickly I realised that she meant Katya.

'Not yet,' I said, 'but you never know. So many unexpected things have happened to me recently, I can't help but think she will just appear one of these days.'

Almost the minute my feet touched back on the ground in Melbourne I'd followed up on Beth's investigation about Katya. She'd found the actual accommodation, a hostel located in Fitzroy where Katya had been known to stay. After waiting for a few weeks with no sightings, I'd arranged for a robust upright piano to be installed in a room for whenever and if ever she returned. While I had to consider that I might never find out who Katya really was, supervisors at the accommodation house had promised to call me the instant she showed up. I was hopeful that once word got out that there was a piano there, it might not be too long before she reappeared.

For me, Rose's piano was a symbol of positive change in my own life. Since discovering my long-lost family, I felt more complete and I was working easily again. And although it looked as if love had passed me by once more, I hoped that my donation of Katya's piano (as I thought of it) might have a positive impact on someone else's life. I only had to remember Crystal, and how playing Rose's piano had helped her mental state, to believe that this was possible.

The afternoon passed happily, and after Joan, Ruth and I served lunch, everyone gathered around to contribute playing a little something on the piano. Beth's boys, so sweet, played chopsticks as a duet, and I even embarrassed myself by trying to finger my way through 'Fur Elise', the only thing I could remember.

'Put it this way, Maddison,' said Amy, 'as the great-granddaughter of a music teacher and granddaughter of a prodigy, it can only get better with your own piano to practise on.'

We all laughed, and as dusk fell and shadows disappeared, so did my guests. I waved everyone off, standing out in the chilly night air, feeling happy that it had gone well, but glad it was over.

My eyes fell to a treasure the old archivist from Brighton had delivered in my absence, a newspaper article about my grandmother she'd found in a local newspaper from 1968. There was no photo of Abigail, but a lovely shot of three smiling children present at the fundraiser where Abbey must have been giving a concert.

'*Mrs Browne is her real name*,' said one of the little girls, '*but we call her the "Piano Woman"*.'

I'd framed it and placed it on top of her piano, where it belonged. The piano saga had come full circle. And so had I.

Still, the huge knot at the base of my stomach refused to budge. I was missing James desperately. I didn't want to ruin what had been a lovely afternoon, but as I washed the last few dishes and tidied up the kitchen, I knew in my bones that I had seriously made the wrong decision by not staying in London with him.

I should have been more flexible. A younger version of me would have just done it and lived with the consequences. Love didn't come along every day, and nobody knew that better than I did.

Just call him, I told myself, searching frantically for where I'd last put my phone. *Find him and tell him you made a mistake, that you love him, that you will go wherever you have to go, to be with him.*

Maybe it was already too late to salvage what we had, but I had to speak to him. James had believed we could work it out. I'd been the one bound up, carrying too much baggage from the past.

I had the number on my screen and was preparing my speech to him, how nothing was worth it without him, when I heard the crunching sound of a car slowly pulling into my stone driveway. Thinking it was probably one of the girls who had left something behind, I peered through the front window. But instead of one of the kids racing in to pick up a toy they'd forgotten, I saw a taxi with its boot up. I waited, certain that the driver must have the wrong address. Then a figure emerged and stepped into the lights from the car, a bag in each hand.

My pulse started to pound. I rushed to open the front door, and peering into glaring headlights croaked, 'James?'

'Yes, it's me. Who else would be this late to the party?'

He grinned, dumped his bags on the ground and took me in his arms.

'It wasn't worth it, Maddi,' he whispered in my ear, 'not without you.'

Acknowledgments

I am enormously grateful to everyone who helped bring this publication to life.

To Gregory, who is my first reader always and who believes in my writing. No love big enough.

To editor Alexandra Nahlous, a huge thank you for your sharp eye, inciteful comments, and genuine kindness.

To Louise Morris, I owe special thanks for warmth and hospitality, and the trouble you went to, allowing me access to private Clarke family documents in search of material for one of my characters. The outcome turned out differently from the original purpose, but your great-grandmother Lady Janet Clarke's handmaiden and music teacher, Florence Morphy, was the inspiration for my Rose Hampton character. Although Rose is not based on Florence directly, or her actual life, she was a spark for this character. Also, the historic newspapers in your family archive from around the time of the Great Exhibition were extremely helpful.

To the wonderful author Anna Romer, for offering encouragement, and sending lists of helpful things to read whenever I was in a spot of trouble. And for reading my manuscript at the same time you were working on your own latest book, I can't thank you enough. Truly a friend.

To author Chandani Lokuge, your close reading of this story was invaluable, and I can only offer you my deepest thanks.

To friends who offered encouragement and feedback, my love and blessings!

And special thanks to the completely wild woman I encountered once in the city, who really lit the flame for this story.

And my deepest thanks of all go to you the reader and booklovers everywhere. Please, if you enjoyed 'The Piano Woman' or if you have read my DS Bec Harpin crime series (Making Up Amanda and One Night), it would be wonderful if you could reach out and leave feedback on Amazon, Goodreads or whatever platform helped you to find 'The Piano Woman'.

I would also love to hear from you so please feel free to get in touch via my website or socials. It means the world to me to know that my stories connect with you. If you visit my website you'll also find a link to sign up for my newsletter and I will send you a free DS Bec Harpin short story set in the aftermath of the dramatic ending of 'Making Up Amanda'.

www.rozzibazzani.com

Made in United States
Cleveland, OH
14 January 2026

31301992R00187